hushed

JOEL PATCHEN

A Novel

To all those who have been
forgotten,
abused, and *ignored.*

hushed

© 2014 Joel Patchen

Published by Anna's Choice, LLC
Colorado Springs, Colorado
www.annaschoice.org

Cover and Interior Design: Granite Creative, inc.

ISBN 978-0-9818870-6-7

warning

The following novel contains adult themes and profanity. Please read with the understanding that the author's intent is not to be vulgar, but to accurately portray the subject matter as it is occurring in our culture today.

Anyone who is under the age of seventeen, has experienced trauma in the areas of sexual violence or abortion, or is offended by the use of such content may want to consider proceeding with one of the author's other works, such as *Letters to My Dad: Diary of a Preborn Daughter*.

contents

chapter 1

An Ideal Beginning

The lake's beauty surrounded by the colors of fall was matched only by the loveliness of Jenny Foster. Perched on a rock, wearing cutoff jeans and a yellow blouse, Jenny was the ultimate foreground attention-getter against an extraordinary backdrop of fall hues...a true work of art. Looking out over the glistening lake, Jenny breathed in the fresh smell of pine and remembered walking with her father along the far shore. She missed him. There was so much they didn't get to do, but she was grateful for the time they had together. Perhaps more than anything else, she missed their walks. The day was perfect, easily the best of the season. A gentle breeze blew across the lake as Jenny soaked in the glorious view and smiled. Any eye would have been drawn to the slender beauty against the rich autumn foliage, but the only eyes available to behold the sight were those of Tom Rose.

"Isn't it beautiful, Tom?"

"I can think of something more beautiful."

"Stop it, I'm serious," Jenny said coyly. "I just love the fall. Look at these colors. The weather is perfect, and nothing is more glorious than the fading of life at the end of its season."

Reflecting, Tom said, "There is something dynamic about the fall."

"I've been coming to this lake forever, even from childhood. I can remember my dad bringing me here when I was in first grade to skip rocks and hike through these woods. It's probably my favorite place in the world."

"I know; that's why I brought you here," said Tom. "Let's walk around the lake to the feeder stream, and then, if we feel like it, to the falls."

Taking his hand and gazing into Tom's brown eyes, Jenny accepted, "Sounds good to me, handsome. Let's go."

The sun was high as they began their walk. Hand in hand, the energy from their togetherness was as strong as the energy of the wilderness about them. Their strides were neither hurried nor slow, but, rather, smooth and purposeful. They hadn't a care in the world, and why should they? They had each other. The pretense and performance of early courtship had matured into familiarity and trust. These were happy days, the best of their lives. Stopping halfway around the lake, Tom paused and pulled his girl toward the water.

"Jenny, try this one—it's smooth and angled, perfect for a launch."

"It does look pretty good. Up for a little competition, Tom?"

"Sure, but you know I'll win!"

"Doubt that," retorted Jenny playfully. Caressing the stone between her thumb and forefinger, Jenny paused to feel the weight and form of the rock. She had been tossing stones all her life, and she knew the key to skipping was selection, balance, wrist action, and body position. Tom stood in admiration as Jenny assumed an athletic stance and cocked her arm. With a fluid and controlled motion, she threw the rock. Like a bird in flight, the stone flew with such elegant power that Tom realized instantly he was overmatched.

"Whoa, you're not messing around, little lady!" Tom said, smiling. "That stone must have skipped seven or eight times."

"Try nine!"

"All right, step back, and let a man go to work."

Tom hiked up his belt, steadied his feet, and let out a primal grunt as he hurled his stone of choice, sidearm, toward the undisturbed water. Before Tom's dark stone had touched down, Jenny playfully mocked, "Just a bit outside." Splash! The whirling object hit the water like a bomb, producing a touchdown so unique (possibly a cosmic first) that it created a ripple wave the precise image of a mushroom cloud and a jet skier with a penchant for spray. Undeterred, like the phoenix rising from the ashes, Tom's stone had one more lift in its belly before sinking out of sight.

"Nice work, Tom, real manly."

"Double or nothing?" asked Tom.

"We didn't even establish what we're playing for," said Jenny. "Dinner at Earl's?"

"You're on."

Tom knew he didn't have a prayer, but any opportunity to watch Jenny in action was worth the expense. She was just so beautiful, and Tom believed she'd be his forever. After a few more shaky tosses and some good ribbing, Tom charged Jenny, lifting her high over his shoulder. Feigning irritation, he growled out, "No one mocks me and gets away with it!" This, of course, was just what Tom wanted—Jenny's body next to his. Carrying Jenny, who was kicking and screaming in flirtatious laughter, he proceeded toward the feeder stream at the far end of the lake.

The dryness of late had made the trail that skirted the lake slick and unforgiving. Slipping on some loose gravel, Tom fought to maintain control. Stumbling awkwardly, he was barely able to secure Jenny before the two fell to the ground, emitting embarrassed laughter. Rolling into a tangled embrace, Jenny's cheek brushed Tom's, and before a moment passed, their lips found each other's for playful, wet kisses.

Exuberant, Tom said, "It's your fault we're in this mess."

"You're the clumsy one," Jenny retorted.

"Hardly." Pausing, Tom looked deeply into Jenny's eyes. "Seriously, Jen, you make me happy."

"Kiss me, handsome."

Losing themselves in the moment, they delighted in the pleasure and closeness of budding love. But after several more kisses, Jenny composed herself and reminded Tom that they'd better get moving if they were going to make it to the falls. Straightening up and dusting themselves off, they took a few sips from their water bottles and pressed forward. In the flow of the afternoon, they talked about school, Tom's final year of residency, and Jenny's soon-to-be nursing career. They were excited about their futures in medicine and their future together. The emerging 90s looked promising indeed.

The trail winding up the hill to the falls was narrow and full of awkward stones and roots. Aspens, shrubs, and pines lined the path, while dirt crunched under their feet as they hiked over the beautiful, beckoning terrain. The heat was beginning to fade in the shade of the trail, but their rapid ascent kept them warm and intent. Shadow and light played hide-and-seek, while the two lovers journeyed up the mountain.

Crossing the upper stream, the two stopped briefly

to splash each other and play among the jutting rocks and shallow current. During a moment of rest, Tom bemoaned not having his fishing rod as he beheld the clear water and enticing pools. Wishing to stop Tom from his all-too-familiar trout stories, Jenny reminded him that the last time out he'd gotten skunked and, worst of all, that he'd accidentally slammed his fly rod in the car door.

"Thanks for the cheery memory, Jen," Tom said, laughing.

"Just trying to help," said Jenny.

Splashing Jenny one last time, Tom hopped deftly from one large rock to another and exited the stream. Followed by his girl, he moved swiftly up the trail approaching the last obstacle before the meadow at the base of the falls. His heart was full of joy and eagerness as he ascended the trail. Tom couldn't get his mind off what lay ahead. Hearing Jenny call out, "Wait up!" pulled him back to the present. Lost in his musings, Tom was getting ahead of himself. Slowing down, he turned to look for Jenny. As she came into view, Tom drank in her beauty. She was lean and fluid—breathtaking as the sun illuminated her cascading hair and wet blouse that clung to her elegantly feminine form. But she was more than a beauty to Tom. Jenny was his best friend, the keeper of his secrets, and the woman with whom he wanted to spend the rest of his life. He couldn't have chosen a better girl, a better day, or a better moment to implement his plan. Reaching for her hand, the two resumed their journey.

When they arrived at the modest rock wall that rose at the end of the trail, Tom gave Jenny a boost and helped her navigate the rocky crevice that was part of a larger rock face impeding their progress to the falls. Climbing carefully but together, they ascended the familiar and emerged on top of the plateau. The high mountain meadow was modest and serene, full of dancing wildflowers, swaying grass, and a soft mist floating through the air.

Looking at the falls in the distance, Jenny remarked, "It's always worth the hike and the climb to get to this spot."

"It's awesome, isn't it?"

"Listen to the falls; they have such a gentle, hushed tone this time of year."

"We couldn't start off the week any better," said Tom. "Aren't you glad you played hooky today?"

"Clearly a better choice than sitting through Nurse Quimby's lecture on nurse etiquette and practice," agreed Jenny.

"I've got a surprise for you, Jen."

"What is it?"

Taking a silk blindfold out of his daypack, Tom instructed Jenny to turn around and not peek.

"Kinky."

"No, it's not like that! I want to show you something at just the right time," said Tom. "Follow me, Miss Foster." Taking Jenny's hand, as if for the first time, Tom led his hopeful bride-to-be to the far edge of the meadow near a small crop of trees. The sun, now much lower in the sky, washed the meadow in the glow of late afternoon. Positioning her in the ideal spot, Tom looked around to make sure everything was as he had arranged it and perfectly in place.

"How much longer? The suspense is killing me!"

"Patience, Jen," Tom said sternly but playfully.

It was all there: the cooler, the table with two chairs, his grandmother's silk tablecloth and her wedding candlesticks, matches, the ice bucket, the battery-operated CD player, the roses (not a petal had been lost), the portable camping stove, the take-out from Earl's, which Earl himself had helped Tom prepare so it would stay fresh, and their favorite sparkling wine, asti spumante. The weather had been nothing short of perfection the whole day, from the time he hiked in with his surprise in the early morning hours, to the time he met Jenny at the lake just after lunch, to this very moment, which he'd planned in his mind over and over since the beginning of their courtship.

After some quick arranging and a few last-minute touches, Tom delicately removed the blindfold. Jenny's eyes opened wide in wonder at what Tom had prepared for her. Overcome by her love's efforts and the simple beauty of his presentation, Jenny's eyes filled with tears. "Oh, Tom, it's beautiful!"

"I hoped you'd like it," Tom said with a smile. "May I show you to your seat, Miss Foster?"

Gathering herself, Jenny said, "Why certainly, sir."

Placing his arm around the small of her back, Tom escorted Jenny to the table, pulled out her chair, and guided her gently to her place setting. Jenny smiled as she took in the dinnerware. The bright orange camping plates certainly enhanced the ambiance. Moving the boombox into position, Tom selected his favorite homemade disc and pressed play. The evening stillness soon gave way to instrumental jazz. Jenny smiled again, for it was a song she knew well. As Tom served the meal, Jenny noticed his grandmother's candles. Was this more than a roman-tic dinner? Could this be the night her handsome prince proposed? She hoped so. Looking at Tom, she couldn't believe how lucky she was. This good man, intelligent and strong, about to become a licensed OB/GYN, was in love with her. She was the apple of his eye, and nothing could be finer.

"A bet's a bet," said Tom. "The lady played for Earl's, and Earl's she shall have."

Seeing her favorite dish from Earl's, chicken parmigiana, arranged on her plate, Jenny exclaimed, "No way! How did you know I'd pick Earl's?"

"You don't think I pay attention to the little things, but I do. I know Earl's is your favorite. Besides, just to cover my bases, I picked up the tiramisu from Tuscany House."

"This is awesome, Tom. How long have you been planning this?"

"Since this morning, about six o'clock."

"You devil!"

"Let's eat, I'm starving." Tom lit the candles, sliced the bread, poured some sparkling wine, sat down, and smiled at Jenny with a satisfaction she had never seen. This was his day, his moment, and he knew it.

Dinner went off without a hitch as the two young lovers relaxed in the meadow. Tom was witty, engaging, and insightful, while Jenny was lovely and in all other respects his equal. The dusk of the approaching evening and the setting sun made a delicious backdrop for Tom's plans. In the fading light, he cleared the plates and pulled out the tiramisu. Handing the dessert box to Jenny, Tom looked his best friend in the eye and said, "I hope you enjoy the dessert, Jen. It was pricey!" Taking the box, Jenny slowly opened the lid and gasped at the fulfillment of her dreams. Inside was a gorgeous one-carat diamond solitaire, perfectly set in a platinum band. As if the ring weren't enough, Tom had placed the Tuscany tiramisu off to the left in the divided container, just so Jenny wouldn't feel cheated.

Taking a knee next to the table and gazing into Jenny's remarkable eyes, Tom spoke low and clear: "Jennifer Marie Foster, will you marry me and make me the happiest man alive?"

"Yes, Tom. Yes, I will!"

It was a beautiful day to be alive, to be filled with dreams for the future and the promise of youth.

chapter 2

The Wicked Lie in Wait

The basement on Ash Street was less than two blocks from Eastbrook Academy. It was old and musty, with very little character. A single recessed window on the south side of the main room was all that kept the lower level from being devoid of natural light. Two naked incandescent bulbs were the only lights afforded the place. One hung in the kitchen and the other in the main room. The basement apartment was dingy and dark. A small table and a solitary chair were pushed up against the north wall of the kitchen. The linoleum was scratched and old, faded and stained. The bathroom was rusted and in desperate need of caulking. Curiously, though, the apartment was clean. Nothing was out of place or unkempt, and there was very little dirt or dust to be found. In the corner of the basement, just off a narrow hallway, was a small bedroom containing a squeaky twin bed and an old desk.

A rather large man in his late thirties was tossing and moaning on the bed. His name, as far as anyone knew, was H.T., for everybody called him that, or Mr. H. H.T. was the sort of person everybody on campus knew, yet nobody knew. He worked as a grounds person, or a janitor, or a handyman, or something, but he was always around. When he wasn't working, he was walking and taking pictures. He loved photography. H.T. was odd, alone, and as far as anybody could tell, harmless. He often had night sweats and terrors. When they came, it was unclear whether he was actively being tormented or remembering being tormented, but H.T. must have suffered in silence for many years. Who had time to notice him? In the busy world of med school and bills and activities and everything, no one paid attention to a man like H.T. Honestly, who had paid attention to H.T. at any point in his life? H.T., however, was paying attention—and the pain came in waves.

Waking from his sleep with a jolt, H.T. stared nervously into the darkness until his eyes could focus on the room. He was sweaty and perplexed. Reaching for his flashlight, H.T. scanned the room until he felt reassured. Making his way to the desk, he switched on a reading lamp and sat down. Disconnected thoughts ran through his brain as he blinked and rubbed his eyes. For a little while he sobbed quietly; then, angrily, he yanked open a desk drawer and pulled out his whiskey and a shot glass.

In the dim light of the room on the old desk lay pictures of Jenny Foster. One was of her and Tom walking hand in hand at Franklin Park, another of her sitting in a lounge chair at Lakeland community pool, and still another of her standing in front of Albert Hall with her textbooks. There were pictures of other girls, too, but Jenny was by far the center of attention. As H.T. stared with contempt at her pictures, he knew he wanted to do it soon...as soon as possible.

✶✶✶✶✶✶

For months, H.T. had been watching Jenny and waiting, but on this October night, he was ready. Dressed in black with his face covered, H.T. waited outside Jenny's house in the shadows by the trash. It was a modest house on the edge of a poorly lit street ten miles from the Academy campus and a mile away from the foothills. Jenny had lived there all her life, through her father's death five years earlier and her mother's illness, which now required in-home nursing care. Typically, the nurse went home around suppertime, but tonight was special; Jenny had arranged to be out with her friends.

As the beams from the headlights bounced off the garage, Jenny exited the car full of laughing girls. "See you Monday, Mrs. Rose," said Gwen.

"You're a lucky lady, hot stuff," echoed another friend from inside the car.

"He's just so dreamy, I'm gonna die!" screamed a voice.

Jenny, leaning through the passenger window, said, "You guys are crazy. I can't wait for the bachelorette party. If tonight's movie experience is any indication, I'm going to need to take out more insurance."

"You know that, baby," someone shouted.

"Congratulations, Jenny, you deserve it!" said Gwen.

"Thanks, girls, I'll see you all on Monday," Jenny responded as she slowly backed toward the porch. "Drive safe, you guys."

"We'll wait till you get in," said Gwen.

"Bye," Jenny said.

"Bye. Congratulations, girl."

As Jenny opened the front door, Gwen waved and pulled slowly down the driveway into the street. Once inside, Jenny was greeted by the nurse and given a full report on her mother's day. She was pleased with what she heard, especially with the news that her mother was more coherent than usual and feeling less pain. After watching the nurse depart from the front-room window, Jenny ascended the stairs intent on tending to any of her mother's remaining needs. Reaching the master bedroom, she edged the door open slightly and peeked in. Seeing that her mother was asleep and everything was in place, Jenny relaxed and went downstairs.

H.T. waited patiently in the dark, something he prided himself on, like a lion in cover. Calm and calculating, he waited. Routine, familiar, H.T. was used to waiting.

Trying to unwind, Jenny poured herself a glass of water and turned on the TV. Thirty minutes later she noticed it was eleven o'clock, and she still hadn't taken out the trash, a ritual she performed every Friday night. Gathering up several bags, Jenny stepped outside.

chapter 3

The Woods

For the past six years, H.T. had been preparing an underground room in the woods to execute his crimes. Almost every weekend he would load up his backpack and disappear into the woods for long hikes, photography, and camping. When the weather was too cold, too hot, or impassable, he refrained, but unless he felt he was being watched, he came. It was a remote spot that required stamina, fitness, and determination to reach. Long hours had been spent in its preparation, seclusion, and sound proofing. He'd thought of everything, even a way to get in an anesthetized person weighing between 110 and 150 pounds. H.T. knew the route and the terrain so well he could navigate it blindly.

Jenny, in her small moments of faded consciousness, smelled the woods and heard the ground crunch beneath her attacker's boots. Her mind was scrambled. Nothing seemed real. She didn't feel terror or panic, only cloudiness and a throbbing pain in the back of her head. Feeling herself being lowered down, all was hard and cold.

Waking groggily, Jenny found herself naked and tied to a chair. H.T. stood over her, wearing a mask that covered all but his tortured eyes.

"Please, you're hurting me."

Hitting her, H.T. shouted, "Shut up!"

"Please," Jenny pleaded.

"I know, I know," H.T. said, calmly. And then in an unearthly tone, "My mother used to hurt me, too, but I'm not a little boy anymore."

In terror Jenny screamed, "Help me!"

Striking Jenny with great force, H.T. put his finger to his mouth and uttered a sadistic, "Shh."

Tasting blood, Jenny began to lose consciousness and pass out. There in the dark woods, H.T. did what no human should: *violate another human being, a fellow child of God!* He hurt Jenny in all aspects of her person without regard, compassion, or humanity. What he did was pure, unrestrained evil, and the pathology for his actions no longer mattered.

Sometime later, Jenny's abuser came back for more. "Let me go, please…let me go," begged Jenny. "My mother needs me, my mother needs me." Enraged at the mention of a mother, H.T. threw Jenny against the earthen wall of his secret torture chamber. Gasping for breath as immense pain radiated through her body, Jenny stared with wide-eyed terror at this hulk of a man who showed no pity or remorse. Broken, humiliated, and bleeding, she could look no longer. Closing her eyes tightly she curled into a protective ball desperate for a momentary reprieve, but none would be afforded her. Reaching down and pulling aggressively on Jenny's hair to expose her neck, H.T. put his sharp knife against her throat.

"Don't kill me, don't kill me, please. I'll do what you want," assured Jenny.

"I know you will," H.T. uttered with a sadistic confidence.

Dragging Jenny, he proceeded with the wicked intentions of his heart.

chapter 4

Aftermath

Tom sat with his eyes fixed to the floor holding Jenny's hand. He'd looked at her a thousand times, and many times this morning, but he just couldn't look at her anymore. Her swollen face and bruised body enraged him. Who could be so heartless? He wanted to kill the monster responsible for this brutal, damaging act. He wanted to kill—period—as the pain raged inside, but Jenny's abuser was beyond his reach, unknown. Tom felt his inadequacy deep in his soul. He was helpless—a victim, like Jenny—violated, unable to rescue or fight back. The past week of fear, doubt, and hell had been the longest of his life. Sitting by Jenny's side at St. Mary's Hospital, he was undone and overcome. He was in shock, in mourning, and in relief all at the same time. Overwhelmed, Tom's pent-up stress and tension released like a flood. Straining to hold back his anger and tears, Tom fled the room.

Before the days he'd thought he might never see her again, the two had gone to Franklin Park for a picnic. Tom still remembered her scent, her hair, her welcoming smile. As always, Jenny was lovely in her long dress. Walking along the pond, they laughed and talked and schemed—planning their wedding day and beyond. There was talk of future children, her mother, his residency, and the honeymoon. A trip to France was in the works since Jenny had never been outside the United

States—a beautiful, glorious, sexy two weeks in France—
the Louvre, the Eiffel Tower, Nice, and its beautiful
beaches and surroundings. Perhaps a visit to Normandy
would be included because Tom was a history buff. Her
eyes, her smile, her lips… Tom just couldn't believe this
was happening. How? Why?

"Excuse me, sir. Captain Denton would like a word
with you."

"I'll be there in just a moment." Re-entering the
room, Tom Squeezed Jenny's hand and whispered, "I'll be
back as soon as I can, sweetheart."

The police had been in regular contact with Tom
over the past week, ever since he got a call from Jenny's
frightened and disoriented mother early Saturday morning. Discovering that Jenny was gone panicked Tom, and
he immediately phoned the police. The whole community of Eastbrook was terrified and on alert. Search parties
had been organized, Jenny's friends and fellow students
worked around the clock, evidence was gathered (though
there was precious little), posters were hung, calls were
made, news reports were issued, and funds were raised, all
in an effort to locate Jenny.

"How you holding up, Tom?"

"Not very good, Captain. It's just so difficult seeing
her like this."

"It's impossible to deal with something like this, let
alone advise you in this, but she needs you, Tom, now
more than ever."

"I know, Captain, I'm trying to remain strong."

"I'm sorry to have to ask you this, Tom, but we got
a lead on that strange imprint we found in the mud by
Jenny's house. It appears it's from a medical boot cover.
Did Jenny have access to covers made of polypropylene
and coated with polyethylene? Did you or anyone else
she knew?"

"We use covers like that at General, and I think they use something similar at the Academy, but you can get those at any medical-supply company," responded Tom.

"Do you know who keeps track of the stock of boot covers at school?" asked Captain Denton.

"I don't. Probably Dr. Johnson or someone from his department."

"Did Jenny have any strained relationships at the Academy, any conflicts with staff, students— enemies?"

"Not that I recall, everybody liked her."

"Thanks, Tom. I'll keep you posted."

"Captain Denton, did you get any more leads from the truck stop off the interstate?"

"Unfortunately, no. All we have is Jenny's blood and the testimony of the driver who found her in the bathroom."

"No other truckers saw anything?" probed Tom.

"The driver who found Jenny was the only one there at four a.m., and, as far as we know, maybe the only one all night. But we're still gathering evidence, and I haven't had the opportunity to speak directly with officer Tyndale who's been patrolling that section of the interstate the last couple of nights. Maybe he saw something unusual that can give us a lead."

"Captain?"

"Yes, Tom?"

"Find this monster!"

"We will."

Tom slowly walked away from the captain and returned to Jenny's side. He didn't know what to do, and there was nothing he could do. Afternoon turned into evening, which turned into morning. As light broke through the hospital window, Tom got an even clearer look at Jenny. She'd been through hell. Tom closed his eyes for a long moment, kissed Jenny lightly on the forehead, and despondently walked out of the room. He felt abandoned and alone. Slowly making his way through the hall, into the stairwell, and out to his car, Tom began to burn. His mind was frantic and wild—haunted by images as he drove silently home—visions of Jenny beautiful and bruised, a menacing-looking man, and his own weakness. Pulling up to his apartment, Tom walked up the steps, closed the door, and proceeded to destroy everything in his path. Screaming and tearing and pounding. Lying in the destruction, he wept.

A week later, Jenny was communicating for the first time. The stress and abuse she had endured had left her in a state of shock. Life was returning to her eyes, but her effervescence, hopes, and liberty were dampened and far from what they once were. She would never be the same. In her moments of clarity she wondered if Tom still loved her, if she had a future—any future.

Entering Jenny's room with flowers and a smile, Tom said, "Hey, beautiful, how are you feeling?"

Jenny wept.

"I'm here, Jenny," Tom said softly. "Hey, hey, I've been here every day. I'm not going anywhere; we're going to get through this together!"

Choking back her tears, Jenny muffled, "Thank you, Tom, thank you." Collecting herself, she asked, "How is my mother?"

"She's good, sweetheart. I've checked in on her and the nurse every evening. She knows you're safe, but I haven't told her anything else."

"Good, you shouldn't; she can't take it right now."

"I thought I'd lost you."

"Me, too."

Embracing, the two wept.

chapter 5

A Regrettable Choice

After a long and difficult month of physical healing, Jenny was released from the hospital. Her ribs were feeling better, and her skin was healing, but the pain she felt went very deep. Since when has what's visible ever told the whole story? Despite some lingering bruising under her eyes and a scar on her thigh, Jenny was still beautiful. But the damage to her heart and mind were the real scars. The difference in her now, besides the obvious, was that her inner beauty was suppressed, locked away, and hidden. She spent long periods of the day weeping or staring into space, and her nights no longer contained peace. She wasn't ready to take care of her mother—she needed someone to take care of *her*. Tom, recognizing her need, decided to drop out of his last year of residency at Eastbrook General and take care of Jenny and her mother. Faithfully, Tom endured. He served as both security and support. His heart broke every time he looked at Jenny. The devastation of human brutality was evident and overwhelming, but Tom believed someday her joy would return and she would live again. Perhaps not like she once did, but still beautiful, richer maybe. He had to believe it. Without it, hope was gone.

Jenny was lost in a fog most days. In the wake of her attack, Jenny hadn't been paying attention to her body. Frankly, she wasn't paying attention to much of anything, even Tom. Late in her second month after returning home, Jenny realized she'd missed her period. Could it be the lingering physical effects? Was her system locked up because of the stress? While everybody else in Eastbrook was celebrating the New Year, Jenny was beginning to think the unthinkable had happened to her.

On a Tuesday morning when Tom was out shopping, Jenny started up the car and went out—something she hadn't done since before her abduction. She was nervous and timid, but she had to know the truth. Her eyes scanned everything, the garage, the driveway, the neighborhood, the cross streets, the windows, the alleys, the parking lot (especially, the parking lot), and the aisles at the pharmacy. Every man she passed seemed suspicious, and every unseen area a threat. Making her way to the pregnancy tests, Jenny found a moment of focus. She grabbed a name brand she used to recommend to other worried girls during a past summer internship, an internship she was hoping would look good on her nursing résumé, and proceeded to the check-out. Thoughts jumbled in her mind: Not like this, not now. How? What would Tom say? What will others think? How dirty. How despicable. Why? Why? Breaking free, she gathered her courage, quickly paid for the test, and walked out the door. Jenny was halfway to her car before she realized she'd forgotten to survey the lot for safety, and panic set in. Sprinting to her car, she hopped in and sped furiously toward home.

Exhausted from what used to be a simple trip to the store, Jenny sat down on the sofa and stared at the test. She couldn't move, breathe, or think. Nothing seemed real, but her unfolding nightmare continued. What would she do? What would she say? How could she endure? She had never felt more alone or frightened. If only she had stronger faith, greater moral courage, or sterility. After more agony, Jenny rose, went into the bathroom, and shut the door. Peeling back the wrapper and coaxing her frozen body to do what's supposed to come naturally, Jenny completed the test. Afraid to look, she just sat there in the stillness. Working up the courage for the twentieth time, she peeked: *positive*. Jenny slid off the toilet with a groan too deep for words.

Twenty minutes later, still lying on the floor, Jenny heard Tom's voice, "Jenny… Marie… I'm back." Laying down some groceries, Tom called, "Jenny, where are you?" Uneasy and disturbed, he yelled, "Jenny, answer me right now! You're scaring me!"

"I'm here, Tom," Jenny's voice, barely audible, leaked from the bathroom.

"You scared me to death. What's wrong?"

"I'm pregnant."

"Oh, God!"

Before Tom could think, he asked, "How?"

Jenny's response was quick and bitter, "You know how!"

"That's not what I meant," Tom retreated as he reached down and held Jenny. "I'm sorry, sweetheart. I'm sorry, so sorry."

Jenny cried, and then sobbed, and then wailed. After what seemed like endless weeping and embracing, Tom carried Jenny's limp body upstairs and placed her in bed. He was overwrought and numb. He couldn't really cope, but he knew enough to know that they needed to find out how far along Jenny was.

The next morning, Tom took Jenny to a friend's office and examined her. Jenny wouldn't let anybody else near her but Tom. After an emotionally difficult exam, Tom confirmed that Jenny was around 12 weeks pregnant. As the bewildered couple rode home, neither said a word; they both knew the reality of the situation, and they both knew they had a choice.

A week passed without much discussion, and then Tom said, "I know a doctor from my residency that performs abortions, and she's really good."

"Do we have to talk about this?"

"Unfortunately, yes. Each day you get further along, it only gets worse, more complicated, and more dangerous."

"Seriously, Tom, you want to kill a child?"

"You don't?" blurted Tom. "Think of what that animal did to you!"

Staring right through Tom, Jenny exited the room. She felt betrayed, conflicted, and violated. Realizing his insensitivity, Tom swore and kicked a hole in the cabinet door below the sink. Frustrated and angry, he left the house and walked down the street.

Another week passed and then another, and with each passing hour the stress and distance between Tom and Jenny grew. When they went for their morning walk, the wordless void grew with all they didn't say, and the tension mounted. Tom was afraid. Jenny was afraid. Neither knew for sure what to do, and neither wanted the baby. Still, they were both medical students, and they knew what was inside Jenny's body. Fearing she'd lose Tom and the now fading dreams of her heart, Jenny cracked.

"Let's do it, Tom. Let's get an abortion."

"Is that what you want?"

"I guess, but I don't want to do it here."

"Not in Eastbrook?" clarified Tom.

Jenny looked at Tom with longing and torture, "Not in the state, Tom. I don't want to have it here where we live, where we are going to start over, to have a family."

"Whatever you want, sweetheart," reassured Tom. "I'll ask around and make the arrangements."

"Thanks, handsome…. It'll be all right, won't it?"

"Yes, sweetheart, it will," said Tom.

The next day, Tom called a friend in the medical field and got the name of an abortionist in a neighboring state. It had been a long time since Tom's friend had worked with Dr. Henderson, but he assured Tom that Sheila had a successful abortion practice, specializing in first- and second-trimester abortions, and that she was conscientious and smart. Tom, knowing time was of the essence, scheduled the abortion for the upcoming Saturday. Feeling relieved and longing for closure, Tom comforted himself with the idea that Jenny only had a few more days to suffer. During the interim, Tom planned the trip, booked a hotel, and made all the necessary arrangements to keep Jenny comfortable. Anything he could do to take her mind off this difficult time, he did. Tom also made sure Marie had 24-hour nursing care for the next week. He wanted Jenny to relax, and he knew that involved making sure her mother was safe and cared for. Tom decided they would leave on Thursday and make the six-hour drive in a leisurely eight or nine hours. He planned for a pleasant lunch near the state line at a familiar café. Sparing no expense on the hotel, Tom thought it would be a good idea to stay at least three nights, Thursday through Saturday, with an optional fourth night if they needed or wanted it. As serious and difficult as things were, Tom hoped it would be good—perhaps even a rebirth.

The plans were made, the trip was set, and the time was upon them to leave. Standing by his car, Tom asked, "Jenny, are you ready?"

"Brrr, let's go," said Jenny, rubbing her arms.

As Tom backed the car down the driveway, Jenny's mother waved goodbye from her wheelchair. The air was cool and brisk on this bright, late-January day. Tom was pleased with the weather. He considered it a good omen that there wasn't any snow in the forecast for the weekend and that the roads were clear and dry.

Jenny was thankful for the heater and happy to be on her way as she looked back at her mother. She didn't know how she'd feel today, but to her surprise she felt relieved, relieved to have made a decision, relieved to still be together with Tom, relieved to be at the end of her nightmare.

"Did you tell your mother?"

"No, I couldn't. I just told her we were going away for the weekend to relax."

"It's probably best," Tom said.

"Yeah, probably."

Driving through the countryside was familiar and refreshing. They'd been together on the road many times, and Jenny always found it to be a comfort. Reflecting on some of their past conversations in the car, Jenny rediscovered joy as she remembered the time Tom had passionately argued for the intrinsic value of a Cheeto. She remembered the times they flirted, laughed, and spoke of deeper things. She remembered driving with Tom late one night not long after her father died in a hunting accident, and how he comforted her. Jenny remembered why she loved Tom. As the fields and trees and hills rolled by, she began to hope. In the stillness, she looked at Tom and fell in love all over again.

Taking his hand, she said, "Tom, I love you."

Tom sighed and smiled, "I know, me, too." His mind had been flooded with memories, as well, and dreams of their future. "I thought we'd stop at Café Bon Appétit for lunch."

"Oh, Tom, that would be lovely," Jenny said in the same tone she once had before the attack. "I think this is going to be for the best. I feel different today."

"Me, too, sweetheart. Me, too."

Despite the circumstances and the dread of the days to come, Jenny and Tom had a delightful drive, lunch, and evening. It was as if, even for a moment, they stepped back in time and recaptured the magic of the past.

But like many euphoric times, reality hits in the morning. And both faced the looming appointments of the next couple of days. Friday's appointment seemed to ease Jenny's tension some as the procedure to dilate her cervix was less painful and briefer than she had anticipated. The staff at the Women's Clinic had been gentle and caring, and Jenny was relieved that none of their efforts had triggered a flashback. Having already experienced some intense flashbacks during less intrusive events, Jenny had been dreading this moment more than anything. Passing one of her greatest fears, she was encouraged. Jenny was sure now she could do this. She felt relieved knowing that tomorrow's procedure would be conducted under anesthesia. It would be over soon, she thought. She just wanted to forget the whole thing. Despite some mild discomfort, Tom and Jenny managed to enjoy the rest of their day together. The time away from home seemed to help them reconnect. Facing this crisis had helped them discover each other again. Both Tom and Jenny were secretly hoping that tomorrow would close this chapter of grief and open a brighter path to recovery, a reemergence of the life they once knew.

Rising early Saturday morning, Tom and Jenny went for coffee, sat mostly in silence, and took a tension-filled walk around the hotel grounds. Returning to their room, they gathered their essential things, brushed their teeth, and had a final glass of water. As directed, Jenny had fasted from around midnight to make sure she avoided any complications from the anesthesia she was about to receive. Tom, looking at Jenny with a half-smile, clasped her hand and guided her toward the clinic.

It was a busy day at the Women's Clinic, as all Saturdays are, and Dr. Sheila Henderson had eighteen abortions scheduled, three in the second trimester, including Jenny's at around sixteen weeks. Arriving at the clinic at 9:30, Sheila was still a little fuzzy after a night of revelry and drink. Sheila's job and her lifestyle were catching up to her, and she was far from the promising young doctor she used to be. Tired, fuzzy, and disengaged, she began her day with some uneventful vacuum-aspiration abortions. All was going routinely as her mind slowly began to clear. Sheila was completing a second-trimester dilation and evacuation abortion (D&E), when Tom and Jenny arrived at the clinic.

Tom pulled into the clinic parking lot past the lone picketer who held a sign that read, "God loves you and your baby." Sure he does, Tom thought to himself. Jenny just closed her eyes and steeled her courage. Walking briskly into the clinic, the two disappeared behind the door. Jenny sat down in the lobby, while Tom checked in and filled out some last-minute paperwork. Jenny tried to be calm, but she wasn't. Even yesterday's better-than-expected visit didn't bring her relief. Nothing she read or focused on helped alleviate her tension. She was about to enter the unknown, and it scared her. She told herself she'd been through worse, and, in her case, perhaps she had.

"Jenny Foster," called the nurse, "It's your time."

Tom gave Jenny a hug, kissed her on the forehead, and said, "I'm right outside. I'll be waiting right here for you when it's over."

"I love you."

"I love you, Jenny."

Jenny turned and walked with the nurse through the door to the procedure rooms. Entering a small room with little décor or warmth, the nurse gave Jenny instructions and told her to press the com button when she was ready. Jenny nervously prepared and pressed the com. A few minutes later, Dr. Sheila and Dr. Brad walked into the room.

After glancing at her instruments for a moment, Dr. Sheila looked up and said, "Welcome back, Miss Foster. In case you don't remember me, I'm Dr. Henderson, and I'll be taking care of you today. Do you have any questions?" After a moment of uncomfortable silence, Sheila said, "You seem nervous."

"Yes."

"Well, don't be, I've done thousands of these procedures, and you're going to be just fine. I'm going to have Brad here, our anesthesiologist, administer the anesthesia, and when I come back, we'll get started, okay?"

"Okay," Jenny said anxiously.

Seeing Jenny's trepidation, Sheila took Jenny's hand and said, "Relax, sweetheart. Everything is going to be just fine."

As the anesthesia began to take hold, Jenny faintly heard Dr. Sheila's muffled voice from the hallway, "Damn, I need some coffee to shake the cobwebs…" Fading, Jenny closed her eyes.

Returning to the room, Sheila checked Jenny's vitals and glanced at her patient's chart. Moving into position, she didn't even notice the rough scar on Jenny's thigh. The hysterical girl in room two and the one with severe cramps in recovery had made her already-busy day a nightmare. She knew she shouldn't have stayed out so late with her friends, but they wanted to throw off restraint and cheer her up after Ted dumped her. She didn't remember much from the day before, but she did remember Jenny. Even the pretty ones don't often find their prince, she thought. Men! Who can live with them? Despite being interrupted during the procedure, Sheila worked quickly. She willed herself into overdrive, feeling the pressure of her commitments, and performed Jenny's abortion with haste. Satisfied she'd removed the last piece of fetal skull, she wrapped up the procedure and took a final quick look at Jenny. Calling for Nurse Sue, Sheila said, "Sue, would you take Miss Foster to the recovery room and prep clients twelve and thirteen for me? I'm in the weeds."

"Yes, doctor."

Almost an hour later, a recovery nurse, who had been in and out, mostly out, noticed that Jenny had profuse bleeding pooling around her legs, way more than the normal amount. Calling for the doctor, she checked Jenny's blood pressure and breathing. Arriving ten minutes later, Sheila and Sue entered the recovery room. Immediately, Sheila feared the worst and rushed to Jenny's side. Checking her vitals, her color, and her cervix, Sheila feverishly went to work trying to diagnose the source of her bleeding. Groggy, Jenny began to come out of the anesthesia and moan. Moment by moment her pain increased due to her new injuries, Sheila's rapid probing, and the declining sedation. Scared, Jenny pleaded and moaned. Lapsing in consciousness, she felt the hot breath of a monster as the lights began to blur. What was happening to her? Where was she? Would anyone ever find her? Oh, God… Cursing under her breath, Sheila was now sure she'd screwed up. She had lacerated Jenny's cervix and possibly perforated her uterus during the procedure. How did this happen? Perhaps it was her tumultuous life of late and its distraction, perhaps it was the lingering effects of her alcohol consumption, or perhaps it was the nature of the procedure itself. She didn't know.

Returning to focus, Sheila shouted, "She needs a hospital! Sue, grab sixty units of Ringer's Lactate, laminaria, and a curette. Donna, get your car ready. She needs to go now!"

"Doctor, don't you want to call an ambulance?" pleaded Donna

"Hell, no! It's bad for business. Just get things ready to go. She'll be all right. Valley is only five minutes away."

Sitting in the waiting room, Tom began to notice something was wrong. The receptionist had disappeared some time ago and had never returned. Peering through the patient access door, Tom could see a few nurses dart back and forth. Beginning to feel awful in the pit of his stomach, he leaned over the reception counter and yelled, "What's going on back there?" When no one responded, he rang the bell on the counter furiously. Over the chime of the bell, he heard someone shout, "Oxytocin, damn it!" Frantically, Tom burst through the door and ran down the hallway, clumsily knocking over a nurse as he turned the corner. Gathering himself, he pressed forward to what appeared to be the recovery room. Flinging open the door, he discovered the doctor bent over Jenny as blood dripped from her table. Seeing the pooled blood on the floor, Tom knew this was serious.

"What the hell is going on here?" blurted Tom.

"I'm trying to save her life!" Sheila shouted.

"What have you done? What have you done?" exploded Tom.

Hurriedly, Tom pushed past Sheila and grabbed Jenny up in his arms. Terror gripped him as Jenny's eyes rolled back and fluttered. Rushing her out of the clinic, he briskly laid Jenny in the back seat, sprinted around to the driver's side, and stepped hard on the gas. A minute from the clinic, Tom realized his mistake. He didn't know where he was going. Panicked, he slammed on his brakes and pulled over. Think, Tom, think! Luckily, he remembered that before they'd left for the trip, he'd marked all the nearby hospitals on his map of the city. Frantically, Tom assessed his location, oriented his bearings, flipped a u-turn, and rushed to Valley Hospital.

"Hold on, Jenny, hold on! I'm right here; it's going to be okay. Please, God, let it be okay…"

chapter 6

Lost

The date was February sixth, and the ground was cold and hard. It had snowed the night before, and a fresh inch of white powder covered the dormant grass. All the trees were bare, and if it weren't for the evergreens, everything would have looked dead. Tom stood by the casket, staring into the open hole in the earth. As the pastor said, "Ashes to ashes, and dust to dust," all Tom could taste were ashes. Like embers burning inside him, Tom was filled with regret, longing, self-hatred, rage, and contempt. Nothing would bring Jenny back, and perhaps nothing would bring Tom back either. Much had been lost in the fall and winter of 1990.

Marie was inconsolable at first, feeling the acute loss of a daughter, and then, as she deepened in her depression and illness, she became numb. On her good days she was bitter, and on her bad days she was oblivious and confused. Tom begged Marie for forgiveness when she recognized him and tried to tend to her when she did not. In the end, the pain was more than he could bear. After a year of attempted reconciliation and penance, Tom left Jenny's home for good.

During that same year, Tom tried to revoke Dr. Henderson's license and seek a just verdict from the American legal system. But that would prove more difficult than he thought. The process was long, ugly, and tedious.

With the waiver Jenny had signed, the small-print list of possible complications she'd been given, Henderson's liability remained unsubstantiated. Tom's alleged assault on Dr. Henderson, and his impulsive removal of Jenny from the attending physician's care, degenerated the case into a classic conflict of testimonies, with Tom holding the inferior position. Dr. Henderson's questionable sobriety and her inept procedural actions could never be proven. Nothing was conclusive. Exasperated, Tom snapped—distraught over the whole affair.

For the next two years Tom rebelled against everything and everyone in his past. His fragile faith, weakened tremendously when his seemingly devout Catholic father left the family for another woman in his teen years, was completely dumped after Jenny's death. Never having experienced a deep faith, Tom was now sure Christianity was a fraud—and if it wasn't, well, God was a monster! He hated a God that would allow such a tragedy—to abandon someone as precious as Jenny to such wickedness was unforgivable. Wandering through the country looking for escape, pity, pleasure, comfort, and whatever work he could find, Tom changed. Joy and peace eluded him, and none of the things he pursued truly satisfied. Still, he kept searching and trying to forget. He would dream of Jenny during the day and weep for her at night. There was nowhere to hide, no safe harbor from grief and pain. No one really avoids pain or consequences in life, but sometimes their reality is far more palpable, and for Tom that reality was the void Jenny left and a rock in his throat. Trying even harder to forget, Tom lost himself in his many adventures and dalliances. He spent a week in a Kansas jail for drunk and disorderly. Contracted herpes from a girl he met outside Reno. For two months, he worked in a fast-food restaurant in Flagstaff. Tom slept in a bus station in L.A. and a public park in San Diego.

He was beaten up and robbed while hitchhiking near San Francisco. Tom was fired from a bank in Albuquerque after he lifted ten dollars from the till, had a warrant issued in Texas for unpaid parking tickets, and maxed out his last credit card at a strip club in Buffalo.

Landing in New York City, Tom thought he'd finally found a new place to call home. He liked the city, the anonymity, and the twenty-four-hour action. Eventually, Tom settled into a routine that pleased him and even began to experience some good times and carefree moments. One night, heading home from a Manhattan restaurant where he worked as a waiter, Tom met a girl who reminded him of Jenny. She was tall and pretty with a liveliness in her eyes. He liked her instantly. She smiled easily, and he sensed she laughed often.

"You want to grab a bite to eat?" asked Tom.

"Sure, handsome," said Jamie.

No one but Jenny had ever called him "handsome," but somehow when Jamie used the term of endearment it carried that same weight and charm. Surprisingly, he liked it.

"How about a little joint I know near Times Square? They have good food and a late bell," suggested Tom.

"Sounds fun. I could use a drink."

"Me, too," Tom said.

Tom was infatuated with Jamie from the start. She was carefree and fun and straight to the point. Walking and flirting from Third Avenue to Fifth, the two caught the subway to Times Square. Arriving at the Square, they walked three blocks north to the bar. It was a quaint little place with three floors and a front patio. Music was resonating from the basement, and people were seated, standing, and crawling all over its appointments. Eleven p.m. in "the city that never sleeps" was nothing special, but it was New York, and there was still plenty of action. Tom and Jamie grabbed a couple of drinks, ordered some cheese fries with ranch, and navigated their way to the front patio. The air was pleasant for an April evening as the lights from the Square buzzed and flickered in the distance.

"So, tell me about yourself, Jamie."

"Oh, I'm just a small-town girl with big-city dreams," Jamie said flippantly. "Seriously, there's not much to tell."

"I doubt that," Tom replied.

"Well, let's just say I've got a few too many head shots lying around my apartment. I came here for Broadway, but Broadway hasn't come for me."

"I don't know what your talent's like, but I know you're pretty enough."

"Not everybody shares your opinion, but thank you. I was naive about the competition and the intangibles when I first arrived."

"What do you mean by 'intangibles'?"

"In this town, a performer needs the look, the skills, the will, the contacts, a flexible morality, and the right timing, or you might as well settle in for a life of obscurity!"

"Yeah, I bet that's true."

Noticing for the first time Tom's accent, Jamie asked, "Are you from the Midwest?"

"There about," said Tom.

"Me, too. A little different pace here in the city, isn't there?" replied Jamie. Tom nodded. "So, what about you, Tom? What's your story?"

"Not much to tell."

"Hardly," Jamie said.

"Well, let's just say, I don't tell it."

"Why a waiter?"

hushed

"Simple—free food, good tips, no hassles, and an open bar after closing."

"You like to dance?" asked Jamie.

"I'm not much of a dancer, but I'll tag along if you want to go."

"I know a fun place a couple of blocks over, and they mix the perfect Crown and Coke."

"Times a wastin' then. Let's go."

Teasing as they went, Tom and Jamie made their way to the dance club. Arriving at around midnight, the place was jumping with activity, youth, and sexual energy. The men and women at the club were there to meet and be met, and everybody who wasn't presently dancing had a drink in their hand. Conversations were loud, and the music even louder. Tom ordered two Crown and Cokes and wrangled up a small table in the corner with a decent view of the dance floor.

"Whaddya say, handsome? Wanna dance?"

"Not just yet. You go ahead. I'll watch," encouraged Tom.

Picking a spot near the edge of the dance floor where Tom could see her, Jamie began to dance. Tom instantly liked what he saw. Jamie was elegant and graceful, with a good feel for the music. Her sense of rhythm was mesmerizing. As the beat pulsed, she became more provocative and sensual. Tom had always noticed and admired beauty, but these days he put very little, if any, restraint on his carnality. Joining Jamie once or twice, Tom mainly just drank and watched her move.

Getting up to relieve himself, he noticed an old billiard table in the back corner of the club. Coming back from the restroom, he investigated further. It hadn't been played in a while, and nobody in the place had come to play pool or noticed it. Finding a warped cue, a broken rack, and about ten of the fifteen balls, Tom improvised a setup and began to shoot. Losing himself in a rhythm, Tom didn't notice Jamie noticing him.

"Steady hands," said Jamie. "You're pretty good at this, especially for a man who's a little frosty!"

"I've always been good with my hands."

"Sounds fun," Jamie said invitingly.

Without looking up or thinking, Tom said, "I used to be a doctor."

"I knew you had a past—waiter, my foot." "Did I say doctor? I meant I was studying to be one."

"What kind?"

"Don't laugh—an OB/GYN."

"Have a thing for the ladies, do you?"

"I suppose," said Tom.

"Well, doctor, it's getting pretty late. You wanna go back to my place and examine me?"

Tom laughed and said, "Sure. I am good with my hands."

Leaving the club, the two walked across the street, down the steps, and into the subway. Boarding, they settled into each other's arms and rode to the Bronx. Journeying down the dark tunnels and into the night, Tom was a long way from home, from Jenny, and from who he could have been.

chapter 7

The Gift

In the heavy distance, Tom heard the phone ring. It sounded like it was in the bottom of a trash can stuffed with pillows. Lifting his head and rubbing his eyes, he noticed the thick red hair of the girl he'd ended the evening with the night before. She was full-figured, fair-skinned, and made a snorting sound when she laughed. Tom didn't remember where he'd met her or what he'd liked about her. All he knew was that he wished the phone would stop ringing. Crawling out of bed, Tom made his way to the incessant phone and answered.

"Hello."

"Tommy, is that you?" said the voice on the other end. "I've been trying to track you down for months."

"Max? Maxy?" said Tom.

"Yeah, it's me. The last good number I had for you was in New York. What are you doing in Las Vegas?"

"Things didn't work out in New York. I needed a fresh start."

"In Vegas?"

"Don't start. It's warm, and the girls are pretty."

"Okay, little brother," Max said understandingly. "I want to ask you a favor."

"What is it, Max?"

"I want you to come back home."

"I'm not ready," Tom said wearily. "Besides, these hands are about to get hot! I can't let Binion's keep all my money."

"No, I don't mean for good, just a vacation."

"Vacation?" said Tom. "You need a fishing buddy or something?"

"Sandy's pregnant, and I want you to be here for the birth of your nephew, my firstborn son!"

Tom paused, "Wow, congratulations, Max. When did this happen?"

"About five months ago. I've been trying to reach you since June. You're a hard man to find, Tom Rose."

"I wouldn't miss it for the world, Max. When is she due?"

"Believe it or not, she's due on Christmas, December 25th."

"Crazy eights," Tom said, referencing a game the brothers played often in their youth and an expression they still used. "I guess I'll be home for Christmas."

"I'll pay for your flight back. Just let me know the dates you want, okay? Oh, and Tom, try to keep this number until after your nephew is born, would ya? I don't need any more headaches trying to locate you," Max implored. "Besides, I wasted all my bribe money finding you this time."

"Whatever!" retorted Tom. "I'll do some checking on airlines and call you in a week or so."

"Sounds good, little brother."

"Hey, Max."

"Yeah."

"Congratulations, man, you deserve it."

Hanging up the phone, Tom's mind flooded with memories. Until recently, the two brothers had always been close. With only two years to separate them, they had done everything together. When they were younger, it was wrestling, races, jungle gyms, epic Monopoly games, cards, imaginary fights with bad guys, *Star Wars*, and baseball. And later it was hearts, skiing, fishing in the mountains, double dates, high school dances, and football. They were best friends and brothers in arms, and even when they fought, they respected one another. Life was good back then.

Staring out the dust-covered window, Tom reflected back to the time Max had saved his life. When Tom was twelve, their dad had taken the boys out for spring fishing on the big river. The current was swift and high, and the boys had been warned not to go out too far in the water. However, like all boys, the warning had gone unheeded. Tom, wearing some oversized hand-me-down waders, ventured out beyond the safety of the bank on a bridge of boulders to free his line from the riverbed. Pulling hard in several directions to loosen the line, Tom peered over the boulder, hoping to get a better look at the source of the snag, and slipped on some tight green moss. Splashing hard in the water, Tom was sucked under the deep hole and disappeared. Popping up a few seconds later downstream, he found himself pinned between a log and a rock. As his waders rapidly filled with ice-cold water, Tom became disoriented. He couldn't move, but before he could panic or scream, Max was on top of the large rock cutting the straps from his waders, kicking the log loose, and pulling a dazed, cold, and wet Tom from the clutches of death. Breathless and scared, the two brothers lay there exhausted. Staring at the blue as the endorphins released, they began to laugh. It was one of the scariest and best memories of his life, and as long as he lived, he would never forget. Drifting again to that day and the chastening he received from his father, Tom saw himself standing sheepishly by the river. After his dad cooled off

The Gift

and he warmed up, the three spent the remainder of the day fishing and enjoying one of their best outings. On the ride home, they laughed and glamorized the rescue and just how close Tom came to experiencing his final fishing trip.

Before another memory could surface, Tom's guest had awakened. Standing behind him and rubbing his shoulders, she asked, "Want some coffee? I need something to knock back the cocktails."

"Sure. Let's go catch some breakfast. There's a great little place near Sam's Town."

"I want to grab a quick shower first."

"Okay. I'll join you," Tom offered.

After breakfast and a somewhat awkward departure, Tom returned again to thoughts of his brother and home. Max had tried to be there for him in the months following Jenny's attack and death; but in his grief, Tom had pushed everyone away, something he now regretted. Tom knew Sandy from before he started college, but it had been years since he'd seen her. He'd missed their wedding, and he wondered just how angry she'd be. Tom wasn't surprised they were starting a family, but he was bitter about it. He was bitter about so many things. Why was his brother so lucky to be starting a life when his had been torn apart? Why was he mad? What was he doing in Vegas? Nothing made sense, but out of respect for his brother, Tom knew he had to go.

✶✶✶✶✶✶

Four months later, Tom walked off the plane in Eastbrook, down the concourse, and into the baggage claim where Max stood with a familiar grin.

"How was the flight, little bro?"

"A bit bumpy, but I rode her all the way in!"

"I see Vegas isn't rubbing off on you," Max rejoined. "It's good to see you, man."

"Good to see you, Maxy."

"Thanks for coming."

"So how's the proud papa to be? Excited?"

"Definitely, and nervous, too. It's a big responsibility to think about being a father."

"That's why you don't think about it, old man."

"Old man? We'll see who's old tonight at the pong table!"

"Oh, yes, we will!" said Tom.

Waking up on the morning of the 23rd, Tom couldn't believe the snow. He hadn't seen a storm like this in Eastbrook since he was eleven years old, and that storm had shut down the city for three days. It was snowing before they'd turned in for the night, but it had all the appearance of a welcome Christmas snow, accumulating six to eight inches of fresh powder. Somehow in the night, the weather pattern had changed, and the wind and the precipitation had created drifts three and four feet high all over the city. Everything was shut down and blocked off. Eastbrook stood still, and all operations ceased. Standing by the front window with his coffee in hand, Tom watched the wind drive the snow into a furious dance. Intermittently, Tom would lose site of the houses across the street in a white blur. This was a killer storm in its ferocity, speed, and surprise. Tom gloried in it. His mind harkened back to earlier times—times with family, friends, and Jenny. Recalling snow caves, sledding, snowmen, warm fires, cocoa, and snowball fights. For a time, he remembered what it was like to be a child—free, uncomplicated, and full of joy. Daring to hope, Tom thought maybe this Christmas would be different. Maybe this year it would be good and blessed.

Walking up behind him, Max said, "Some storm. Can you believe this? Reminds me of the blizzard of '73."

"I was just thinking about that."

"Remember that awesome snow cave we tunneled out over the three-day school closure?"

"Yeah, I remember Dad showing us how to use candles to glaze the inside walls of the cave," said Tom.

"That cave didn't collapse for a month!"

"Good times for sure," remarked Tom. "There was still snow in some spots of the yard two months later."

"Too bad my son isn't old enough yet to appreciate it," said Max.

"We better hope it lets up soon or we're going to have a devil of a time getting to the hospital in a couple of days."

"Yeah, I better check the weather and start digging out—better safe than sorry."

"You got an extra shovel and some boots?" asked Tom.

"Sure do."

"I'll help."

As Tom and Max began the long slow dig out of the garage, Sandy rose from an uncomfortable night's sleep. Walking down the stairs, she felt a mild pain in her back and legs, but assumed it was from her hot, uncomfortable night in bed. Moving into the kitchen to whip up some eggs, Sandy began to feel better, but still a little off. Looking out the window cracking eggs, she couldn't get over the volume of snow that had fallen in the night. It looked bitter cold, but she, too, was captivated by its beauty. Losing herself in the moment, she accidentally knocked the carton of eggs off the counter and onto the floor. Frustrated and muttering under her breath, she began to pick up the cracked shells and mop up the runny yolks. Bending over a second time, Sandy felt a sharp pain followed by a muscle spasm in her lower back. Breathing in deeply through her teeth, she reached for her back, and gently stretched her torso. Through her pain, she noticed a warm sensation running down her leg. Feeling the wet of her pajamas, Sandy hobbled painfully over to the garage and yelled, "Max! Max! Get in here! My water broke!" Panicked, Max ran to Sandy, followed by Tom.

"I'm here, baby." Max said breathlessly.

Assessing the situation, Tom took charge immediately. "Help me get her to the sofa, Max." Tom and Max grabbed Sandy's arms and guided her to the sofa.

"Max, call 911 and have them send an ambulance," Tom said assertively.

Seeing that Sandy was worried, Tom looked her in the eyes and said, "How do you feel, Sandy?"

"I'm scared."

"It's okay to be scared, but you're going to be fine. Max is calling the hospital, and I'm going to check and see where we're at, if that's okay with you?"

Returning from the kitchen, Max stared at Sandy's wet pajamas in a bewildered state.

"Max, I need to examine Sandy, and I'm going to need a few things. Do you still have that medical emergency kit I prepared for you while I was in med school?"

"Yeah."

"Where is it?

"Um, um, I think it's in the master bedroom closet."

"Okay. I'm going to go look," said Tom. "Stay here with Sandy, be calm, and help her relax and breathe."

Tom moved quickly upstairs, located the medical kit, turned on the hot water, grabbed a fresh clean bed sheet and towels, and washed his arms and hands with the liquid antibacterial soap he'd retrieved from the emergency kit. Arriving downstairs, Tom could see that Sandy was having contractions. He knew what that meant, and he sensed delivery might take place there on the sofa.

"Tom, she's in labor," said Max.

"I see that, Max. Go get me the space heater, and shut the door to the garage."

"I'm sorry about this Sandy, but I'm going to have to remove your pajamas and assess your condition."

"Please!" Sandy shouted as she felt another contraction coming on.

Putting on a pair of surgical gloves from the medical kit, Tom cut off Sandy's pajamas and reached inside. To his complete surprise, part of the baby's cord was already in her vagina. Tom felt the cord, checked for dilation, and pushed his fingers up to his nephew's head. Luckily, the head was down in the proper birthing position. Harkening back to his years of training and study, Tom knew his nephew needed to be born quickly, and he didn't have the proper equipment, anesthesia, or instruments to perform an emergency C-section. He also knew the ambulance wouldn't arrive in time with the current weather conditions. Sandy let out another scream of pain and fear as Tom calmly told her to breathe. Tom knew if the baby progressed any further, his head could severely compress the umbilical cord against Sandy's cervix and cut off his oxygen supply. At that point, his nephew would only have a few minutes before brain damage or stillbirth became a reality. Calming himself, Tom reviewed the facts and his options. On the positive side, Sandy was fairly well dilated, and his nephew was luckily not breech or transverse. On the flip side, emergency abdominal surgery would be difficult if not impossible. Making his decision, Tom decided to attempt cord replacement, a technique he'd picked up during his residency, followed by a natural speedy delivery.

"Sandy, I need you to move into a different body position while I help guide the baby into the proper position for delivery."

Crying in pain, Sandy asked, "Are you kidding me? What's wrong?"

Seeing the concentrated look on Tom's face and his wife's distress, Max said, "Level with me, Tom. What's the matter?"

"Max, Sandy, you have to trust me. Everything is going to be all right. Sandy, I need you to roll off the couch and place your arms and face flat on the floor with your butt in the air. Max, I need you to go get a basin of warm water, a quart of drinking water, and some small clean washcloths."

"Oh my God, Tom. Is the baby okay?" pleaded Sandy.

"He's fine, and he's going to be fine. You just need to do as I say."

While Max ran to get the items Tom requested, Tom gently guided Sandy into the knee-chest position, propped her head sideways on a pillow, and returned to the task at hand. Locating the cord and his nephew's head, he applied gentle but steady pressure to the presenting baby, while monitoring the cord for pulsation. After moistening the exposed umbilical cord with a warm washcloth, managing a few more contractions, and several minutes of tense focus, Tom felt the window of opportunity was now. Slipping the umbilical cord gently past the presenting head, he worked methodically. With several deft movements, Tom accomplished his task. Feeling confident that he'd succeeded, he instructed Max to help him roll Sandy over and lift her onto the clean sheet. Looking into Sandy's exhausted and fearful eyes, Tom encouraged her and Max, "You guys did great. You're doing great. The baby's okay. It's going to be fine, but now you've got to push."

"Push, baby, push!" encouraged Max.

The rest of the labor was a blur. Sandy screamed and pushed, Max sweated through his encouragement, and Tom skillfully managed the group. Each member of the team became lost in the miracle and the mission. No energies were spared, no prayers went unanswered, and no gratitude was left unexpressed as little Jonathan came forth from the womb. Tom, wasting no time to celebrate, attended immediately to both mother and child. Satisfied, he breathed a sigh of relief and accomplishment. Walking into the kitchen to clean up, Tom knew he'd been fortunate, but his decision had paid off as there was no apparent harm to mother or child. With tears in his eyes, Max knelt by the sofa and gazed at his courageous wife and his newborn son. He was overjoyed and relieved. Clean and wrapped in soft towels, little Jonathan Rose lay beside the space heater and his exhausted mother. This would certainly be a Christmas to remember.

More than an hour later when the doorbell rang, Tom walked to the front door with a smile of accomplishment on his face. Greeting the paramedics, Tom said with a grin, "It's about time you fellas got here!"

chapter 8

They That Sow in Tears Shall Reap in Joy

Psalm 126:5

The voice of nature whistled through open windows as the blinds tapped against the window frames. Going toe-to-toe with the breeze, a tiny oscillating fan hummed in the distance. It was the first hot night of the summer, and Rachelle, asleep barely an hour, tossed and turned during an unpleasant dream. She muttered and groaned, twisting the sheets in her hands. Sweating yet cold, she unconsciously heard the cry of little Jaleesa. Please, she thought, let me be, let me be. But the cry intensified. Waking in the dark to the sound of the wind, drained and disoriented, Rachelle reached for the bedside table and clicked on a tiny lamp. Gathering her bearings, slipping on her house shoes, and tightening her robe, she walked across the hall and into the baby's room.

"Hush, baby. Shh. Mama's here. Mama's here," whispered Rachelle as she cradled little Jaleesa in her arms.

Gently rocking her daughter, Rachelle began to sing:

"Sweet, sweet, little baby girl.
Don't be afraid of this great big world.
I have you and you have me.
Together we make a family.
Sleep now, Jaleesa, sleep for me.

Trust me, baby, great things we'll see.
Forever I'll hold you in my arms.
Captivated by you and your many charms.
Sleep, baby, sleep, you're safe with me.
Sleep, baby, sleep, upon my knee...."

Falling asleep to the motion and the smooth sound of Rachelle's beautiful voice, Jaleesa couldn't have been more pleased. Rachelle, on the other hand, was tired. It was so hard to be a mother, she thought—to meet the needs of another at the expense of oneself. Satisfied with her comforts, Rachelle gently returned Jaleesa to her crib. She was beautiful, though, this little girl. Covering her daughter with a soft pink blanket, she gingerly backed out of the room and into the hall. Walking into the bathroom, Rachelle turned on some water, splashed her face, loosened a paper cup, and drank several rounds to quench her thirst. Semi-refreshed, she returned to her bed, tired and sore. Maybe now she would sleep better, she thought. She could only hope.

Around six a.m., God's radiant sunshine fell mercilessly upon Rachelle's eyes. Pulling a pillow over her head, she squinted and tried to return to sleep. She had been in and out of bed all night with Jaleesa, and this last hour of her much-needed sleep was now rudely interrupted by the coming of the dawn. Lying there pretending things would get better, Rachelle became angry. She began to bounce her leg as the frustration mounted, and then she smelled it. Her mother was cooking fresh bacon and, hopefully, her perfectly prepared omelets. A favorite of Rachelle's, the eggs were always fluffy without being dry, the vegetables were fresh, the meats cured, and the temperature perfect for consumption. Despite her difficulties during the night, the smell of her mother's cooking somehow made things better and more bearable. Rising, Rachelle turned on the water and looked out the window. The lilacs, roses, and tulips were all in bloom, and the grass was beginning to green nicely. The ocean in the distance was rose colored and majestic. Beautiful and beckoning, nature reminded Rachelle of a Psalm she had memorized: "Weeping may last for the night, but a shout of joy comes in the morning." Walking to the shower, she picked up her shampoo, opened the door, and stepped under the soothing spray. There under the massage of the water she washed away the fatigue and the baby blues of the night before.

Leaving the warmth of the shower behind, Rachelle quickly dressed in comfy clothes and picked up her Bible. After a short devotion, she walked downstairs and into the kitchen.

"Omelets, Mama?"

"Yes, baby, I know you had a rough night with my granddaughter."

"It's killing me. Three months ago she was sleeping through the night, and now it's back to every two hours or so."

"This will pass, Rachelle. I had the same struggles with you and your brother. Little J.J. is probably just hitting another growth spurt," Aaliyah insisted.

"Thanks for making breakfast, Mama. I really appreciate it. You and Dad have been so good to me."

"It's my pleasure, baby, we're so proud of you."

Entering the kitchen from his morning walk, Lucas Jacobs strolled in through the garage. He was a tall man, about 6'3", well-built, and handsome. He was in good shape for a man in his early forties, and his presence always filled a room. Lucas was the definition of energy, athleticism, and strength.

"I smell bacon and onions. It must be omelet

time!" Lucas said. "How are my three beautiful girls this morning?"

"One of us is old, the other is tired, and…"

Interrupting, Rachelle said, "And one of us is a little stinker!"

"Jaleesa didn't sleep again? I'm sorry, Ray-Ray. Tonight I'll keep the monitor and give you a baby break, how's that?"

"Like you'll wake up, you sleep through everything. Besides I seem to remember taking more shifts years ago when it was li'l Ray-Ray!" chided Aaliyah.

"And to think I was just about to say a beautiful woman such as yourself couldn't possibly be old…but maybe you are!" retorted Lucas.

"Thanks, Dad, but I'll manage."

"Seriously, Rachelle, I'll look in on Jaleesa tonight. You need your rest. Where's my little grandbaby anyway?"

"Upstairs making up for all the sleep she didn't get last night," Rachelle said enviously.

"Omelets are ready," said Aaliyah.

"Let's eat!"

"Amen," echoed Rachelle.

"Lucas baby, would you say grace?" asked Aaliyah.

"Be glad to," said Lucas. "Father God, we're grateful for all Your blessings and Your mighty provision. Bless our home, our children, and this food we are about to eat. Give us strength and courage, Lord, as we serve You today and always. Amen."

"Amen," said Aaliyah and Rachelle in concert.

Getting up from the table after a relaxed and delicious breakfast, Rachelle went upstairs to wake Jaleesa, feed her, and give her a bath. It was baby dedication Sunday, and Rachelle wanted her little girl to look and feel her best. Jaleesa laughed and cooed under the running water and the released warmth of the sponge. Captivated by the joy and innocence of her little girl, Rachelle temporarily forgot about her struggles and her recent past. Gazing at her one-year-old daughter made Rachelle glow and beam. She couldn't get over the inexplicable love she had for this little girl. Smiling and praising, Rachelle carried her toweled, tickled, and diapered bundle into the bedroom.

Laid out on the bed were two yellow dresses Lucas had managed to find a month earlier for his daughter and her little J.J. They were a perfect match in color and material, both flowing, light, sleeveless summer dresses. Their match was all the more remarkable given that one fit a tall eighteen-year-old girl and the other a newly walking one-year-old. Jaleesa was adorable in her tiny white buckle shoes, dainty dress, and beautiful black pigtails secured with yellow ribbons. Her mother was no less than radiant. It was no accident that Rachelle had been Homecoming Queen and voted most likely to succeed by the class of '94. She was graceful, athletic, and feminine in every respect. Rachelle was the whole package—intelligent, hard-working, responsible, and genuinely caring. It was no surprise to anyone who knew her that she had earned academic scholarships to several colleges and graduated valedictorian at age seventeen. After washing her face and completing the final touches on her hair, Rachelle whisked up little Jaleesa in her arms and walked downstairs.

The ride to Havers Town Chapel was pleasant and quiet as the Jacobs family rode in silence to the morning worship service. Rachelle loved praise music, and as the car rode along, she listened to her Discman play a compilation of songs one of her close friends had recently given her. Looking over at Jaleesa, as the sun danced on her pretty dress and her perfect complexion, she was proud to be her mother. Even though little Jaleesa was never part of her plans, she couldn't imagine the world without her. She believed God had a plan for this bright new life, and that in the midst of their struggles He would see them through.

The morning's sermon was appropriate for dedication Sunday as the meat of the message came from the text of Luke 18. Rachelle listened with a tear in her eye as the pastor read, "*Permit the children to come to Me, and do not hinder them, for the kingdom of God belongs to such as these.*" It was a fine message about the worth of every individual and the things one can learn from children. Connecting most with the pastor's comments about the trusting nature of children and how willing they are to believe in their parents' teachings, Rachelle reflected on little Jaleesa and how unquestioning she was. Jaleesa accepted things as they were and loved her Mommy with all her heart. She brought a joy and innocence to each day, especially now that she was beginning to talk and express herself.

The dedications following the sermon were short and simple, and everyone clapped and cheered after each child's dedication verse was read. With Lucas, Aaliyah, the elders, and the other parents standing by, the pastor prepared to read Psalm 131 over Jaleesa.

"Father, we dedicate little Jaleesa Jacobs to You this morning, and we pray for her protection, salvation, and Your abiding grace over her. May You bless her always and speak over her the words of this beautiful little Psalm: "*O Lord, my heart is not lifted up; my eyes are not raised too high; I do not occupy myself with things too great and too marvelous for me. But I have calmed and quieted my soul, like a weaned child with its mother; like a weaned child is my soul within me. O Israel, hope in the Lord from this time forth and forevermore.*"

Rachelle, feeling a twinge of upset in her stomach,

left the service promptly after the dedication. Handing little Jaleesa to her dad, she excused herself to the restroom. Feeling a sudden rush of dizziness and a dull pain in her bowels, she moistened a few paper towels and entered the stall at the far end of the room. Wiping her forehead and trying to relax, Rachelle heard two women enter the bathroom.

"Can you believe how hot it's been the last two days?"

"If it doesn't let up soon, I'm going to have to hand water to keep the yard from burning up."

"You might even be fooled into thinking that's why the elders are dressing so casually, but I know better."

"This never would have stood back in the day."

"Isn't that the truth!"

"Did you see Rachelle Jacobs and the other single moms up front today?"

"I know. How far have things fallen?"

"Even the good girls can't keep their pants on these days!"

"How embarrassing for Lucas and Aaliyah. They must be so disappointed."

"No doubt. The morality of the young isn't what it used to be. Well, I better get going—it's off to lunch with Harold and the kids."

"That sounds nice. Are you going to..." faded the voices as they left the washroom.

Feeling even worse, Rachelle began to cry. Tears streamed down her cheeks as her nose began to run. Why had this happened to her? Why was she so unlucky? What was wrong with her? Pent up stress and heartache flowed from deep within her soul. Tears and more tears. Why, why, why...?

chapter 9

Rose & Taugney

It was a perfect spring morning as Tom drove down the beautiful budding streets of Eastbrook. The air was losing its chill as the sun warmed his skin. With the top down, the air smelled of renewal—crisp, light, and pure. Like the recently turned century, Tom had also turned a corner. He gloried in the day. Joy and dreams could once again be found in Tom's heart. The future looked promising, and he was glad. Early morning rays flickered through the trees, creating a pattern of light and shadow that made the pavement whirl. Turning up the radio, Tom nodded to the music as the miles passed. With the wind ruffling through his hair, he broke out in a smile. Tom was happy again, truly happy.

Stopping to get his favorite cup of coffee from Ted's, Tom felt his euphoria and the renewed joy that bubbled in his heart. Reflecting back, he couldn't believe he'd arrived at this point. It had taken ten long years to realize this dream of working in his own medical practice. After losing Jenny, everything fell apart, and Tom believed he would never return to medicine. But with the birth of his nephew, Tom had rediscovered himself. That single event brought him back from the dead. He realized he could still be of service. He could still use his gifts to help people. And, he could still enjoy living. Re-entering his residency and the classroom was difficult at first, but with some counseling and the help of old friends and professors, Tom made it through and progressed rapidly. School and medicine had never been hard for Tom. He possessed a great auditory memory, a love of reading, steady hands, and a sharp intellect. Even after his initial bumps and a seven-year absence, Tom thrived—successfully completing his updated accreditation and everything that stood in his path. Scoring ridiculously high on his final board exams, Tom began to practice immediately under the tutelage of Maggie Adams. A choice he made eagerly. Tom could have practiced anywhere, but he wanted to study under the best abortion doctor in the city so his skills would be complete and refined.

Tom worked tirelessly at Planned Parenthood, taking advantage of every opportunity that came his way. Impressing Maggie and all his colleagues, Tom quickly made a name for himself through his exemplary service. One such colleague was Jim Taugney. Jim was a former dean of the College of Obstetrics and Gynecology at Eastbrook Academy. He'd offered Tom a place in the world as a fellow partner in a new private downtown clinic. Taugney, with his years of experience and distinguished medical career, even offered Tom the opportunity to have his name appear first on the bill. This was done, in part, because of Tom's immense skill, but also because of Taugney's wisdom. He knew Tom was a rising star—a workaholic who brought a sizeable financial commitment to the practice and an incredible upside to profitability once the silver-headed Taugney decided to retire, something Jim hoped was only five years away. Dreams of fishing and boating through endless days of bliss already paraded through his mind. For his part, Tom was excited to work with a local legend, and the prospect of being the sole owner of the practice in less than a decade was more than compelling. With a recent family inheritance, frugal saving during his first years of practice at Planned Parenthood, and a small loan, Tom had obtained the finances necessary to join Taugney in the venture.

Pulling into the parking lot, Tom observed with pride the sign on the building facade that bore his name, *Rose & Taugney*. Walking toward the door he paused once more to take in the charming single-story office building. The beige brick building was set behind about thirty parking spaces, situated on a corner lot. Mature trees dotted the grassy parking, and the mulch beds were full of green as the spring flowers began to awaken from their winter sleep. The tall, glass entrance doors beamed in the sun along with the three windows visible from the street. Overall, the building was clean and inviting. 1206 Thirteenth Street was the ideal location as far as Tom was concerned. It was in the center of town not far from several lower-income neighborhoods, but still close to Jefferson Park, quaint shops, and Ted's Black Gold Coffee Hut. Tom believed this facility would afford him the opportunity to help the less fortunate and those in need, while allowing him to readily enjoy the pleasures of his success and hard work.

Opening the front door, he took in the still-new lobby. It was comfortable and modest, complete with a large fish tank, magazine rack, soothing nature photographs, and a television suspended from the ceiling. The chairs, a comfortable, inviting light brown, lined the waiting room in a U shape, with the receptionist station conveniently facing the open U at the south end of the room. All in all, the room was professional, unassuming, and typical.

"Morning, Dr. Rose."

"Morning, Sally. How are you today?"

"Good, thank you," responded the young brunette from behind the counter.

"Could you set out the tea and water?" asked Tom. "I have patients arriving at 8:30."

"Right away, Dr. Rose."

"Thanks, Sally."

Exiting through the patient door, Tom walked back to his office. Sitting down and sipping his coffee, he reviewed his medical charts concerning the women he would soon see. It was going to be another busy Friday with ten procedures scheduled before lunch. If a few walk-ins showed up, it could get overwhelming, he thought. Thursdays, Fridays, and Saturdays were the busiest for the staff at Rose & Taugney. In addition to their ongoing physicals, breast exams, birth-control counseling, STD tests, annual exams, obstetrics, adoption referral, and the like, these were their abortion days. Depending on the demand, Tom and Jim would perform anywhere from ten to forty-five abortions per day between the two of them. Saturdays were always the busiest, but Fridays ran a close second.

After Jonathan was born, Tom knew he wanted to practice medicine again. The sheer joy of being needed and helping others was the ultimate high, especially when difficulties arose and he was there to make a difference. Tom had always wanted to lead a life of significance, and the rush of delivering Jonathan safely turned his life around—helping his brother, sister-in-law, and nephew when they needed him the most. At first Tom wasn't completely sure he wanted to face doing abortions after what happened to Jenny, but the regret of losing her and the obvious need for safe abortions compelled him to make them an integral part of his practice. Tom reasoned that no one who found themselves in a difficult circumstance like Jenny's should have to suffer from a doctor's incompetence and malpractice. He vowed that the girls under his care wouldn't suffer such cruelty and negligence.

Spending the first two years after his residency at Planned Parenthood learning the trade, Tom felt well-prepared to offer first- and second-trimester abortions to his patients. In stark contrast to Jenny's experience, Tom would make abortions safe, and he would be there for the women he treated. Picking up his last two files, Tom looked up as Gwynn entered the office.

"Tom, Morgan and Gail have arrived and are ready to begin their procedures."

"Thanks, Gwynn. Can you prep rooms one and two, and make sure recovery has everything we will need?"

"Already on my way," said Gwynn.

"Thanks. I'll be ready in ten," Tom said as Gwynn exited his office.

The lobby was slowly filling up as nervous women, girls, men, and boys entered the clinic and sat or stood in various places. Some tried to read, others paced, one couple sat holding each other, a few stood outside and smoked. Still others watched the fish or just sat and stared into space. Calling Morgan from the patient-access door, Sally waited as Morgan hugged her boyfriend and walked slowly to the door.

"How are you this morning?" asked Sally as she escorted Morgan toward room one.

Forcing a smile to cover her lie, Morgan looked at Sally and said, "Fine."

Handing Morgan a surgery gown, Sally said, "Gwynn will be in shortly after you undress to answer any questions you have and complete your paperwork. If you'd like, you can place your clothes in the tub to your left."

Tying her gown tight, Morgan waited nervously on the examination table for Gwynn. She couldn't believe she was here. Only eighteen, she'd been so careful with

Shawn. They had always used condoms, and recently she'd started the pill. She felt her parents would kill her if they found out. Good Christians don't have sex outside of marriage, let alone with a boy from a secular family whom her parents didn't particularly like. She felt desperate and alone. Last night was awful. Her cramps had been severe as the laminaria worked to dilate her cervix. Worse by far were the lies she told to her parents about the reason for her pain, and, in spite of it, having to get to school early for a key English exam. Her best friend covered for her and drove her to the school parking lot where she met Shawn and then drove to the clinic. She just wanted today to be over and her life to get back to normal.

"How are you feeling, Morgan?" asked Gwynn as she entered the room.

"Crampy and nervous," responded Morgan.

"I'm sorry about the cramps, but what you're feeling is normal and may continue for a couple of days, but after that you'll be back to yourself again as if nothing ever happened," reassured Gwynn.

"I just want this to be over with," said Morgan.

"I know, I know, and it will be soon. I need to have you read a little info, ask a few questions, and have you sign at the bottom, okay?"

"Okay."

"Obviously, you've experienced some cramping with the laminaria. Any other problems last night?

"No."

"Good," said Gwynn. "Nothing heavy to eat or drink since midnight?"

"I had a small glass of water this morning before I came."

"That's okay, but nothing else, right?

"Nothing."

"And you abstained from sexual intercourse, using a tampon, or taking a bath?"

"Yes."

"All right, Morgan, I'm going to give you a couple of minutes to review the medical disclosure and consent forms, and then I'll be back to get you when you're ready," informed Gwynn.

Reading the complications that could result from abortion made Morgan nervous and confused. Some of the terms she encountered were completely foreign to her, but she trusted Nurse Gwynn and Dr. Rose to take care of her. She trusted them to have her best interests at heart, so she signed the paper. Taking her place on the table, Morgan noticed some metal instruments on a tray. This sucks, she thought. Trying not to think about it, she focused on a cheerful poster stuck to the ceiling. She desperately tried to think of better days.

Entering the room with Gwynn, Dr. Rose took Morgan's hand and smiled at her. Unlike many abortionists, Tom insisted he have contact with his patients from beginning to end.

"Hi, Morgan. Gwynn told me you're feeling some painful cramps?" Morgan nodded. "When we administer the local anesthesia, that will help, and following the procedure I'll write you a prescription that will help manage your pain, okay?" Tom comforted.

"Okay."

"I know you're nervous, but Gwynn and I are going to take good care of you. Try to relax. Gwynn is going to confirm gestation, while I conduct an examination and get you prepped for the procedure," said Tom.

As Morgan lay there with her feet in the air, she did her best to detach her mind from her body. She heard Gwynn say that all the instruments had been thoroughly sterilized and confirm that after viewing the ultrasound the embryo was ten weeks gestation. Morgan felt uncomfortable about being exposed as Tom worked. But for the most part, he worked gently as he removed the laminaria, positioned the speculum, and applied the vaginal antisepsis. Soon things began to numb and she knew they were about to begin. An eerie silence descended on Morgan before the doctor inserted the cannula and started the suction machine. As the tube reached its target, Morgan experienced a sharp cramp and some uncomfortable sensations. It was at this moment that she thought about her baby for the first time. What was she doing? Why was she here? It was too late, too late, she thought. Please forgive me, please! Suddenly a new wave of pain hit, and Morgan grunted with tears in her eyes.

"Oh, my God! Oh, my God!" Morgan cried.

Gwynn, looking her squarely in the eyes, said, "Morgan, honey, it's okay, it's okay. We've got you. It will pass. Breathe and relax. Breathe and relax."

From that moment forward, Morgan resigned herself to the choice and went dead inside. Tom, having observed the majority of the amniotic fluid, placenta, and fetal parts pass through the tube, informed Morgan that the worst was over. As he removed the cannula, he told her not to be alarmed by the loud sucking noise she was about to hear. Morgan did not respond, but Gwynn assured him that she was fine and her vitals were good. Throughout the remainder of the procedure, Morgan lay in silence while Tom curetted the walls of her uterus. After one final pass with the cannula, Gwynn exited the room while Tom removed his equipment and took one last look at his handiwork. Walking around to Morgan, Tom lowered his mask, took her hand, and said, "It's over, Morgan. You did great. Everything is going to be fine. When Gwynn returns, she'll take you to recovery, and I'll be by shortly to check on you." Morgan looked up at Dr. Rose and nodded.

This was the part of the job that Gwynn dreaded, but she knew it was necessary and important to ensure the health of their patients. It was her job to arrange and account for all the parts of the embryo or fetus—placental parts, fluid, and tissue. To be sure everything was tiny and torn up. But she could often recognize parts of arms, intestines, legs, hands, feet, and heads, especially with the second-trimester fetuses. Gwynn didn't think she'd ever get used to it, but she did it routinely. Entering the room, Tom checked the small clump of tissue as well.

"Nice job in there, Gwynn," said Tom. "Can you give me a hand with Gail before you move Morgan to recovery? And make sure you check her vitals one more time before you move her?"

"I always do."

"Thanks, Gwynn. I'll see you in two."

Tom dumped the bloody tissue into a medical waste bag and dropped it in the trash on his way to room two where Gail, seated in her gown, waited anxiously.

"Morning, Counselor," Tom said with a smile as he walked in the room. "How's the new job treating you?"

"Busy and tense, but the job would be great if it weren't for this little hiccup. This really couldn't have happened at a worst time," said Gail.

"Well, we're going to take care of it and get you back on your feet in no time," assured Tom. "How's your dad these days?

"He's good," Gail said nervously. "You won't say anything about this to him or anyone, will you, Tom?"

"Not a peep. This is completely professional. Everything that transpires here is a hundred percent confidential."

Interrupted by Gwynn's arrival, Tom said, "Go ahead and lie back, Gail, and we'll confirm gestation and get started."

Leaving room two after her latest assist, Gwynn crossed the hall and entered room one where she found Morgan weeping. This was not the first woman she'd seen distraught and emotionally drained from an abortion experience. Holding out some tissue, she comforted Morgan, encouraging her to let it out and release her pain. After sitting in silence with Morgan for a few moments, Gwynn informed her that all her vital signs were strong and that after a short time of rest, she'd be off with her boyfriend and a brighter tomorrow.

Upon reaching the recovery room, Morgan joined two other women who were resting and awaiting release after their morning abortions by Dr. Taugney. The room was a silent fellowship of grief and pain. No one smiled or engaged with anything. The three just stared blankly and soaked in their despondency, while Gwynn continued to check in and do her best to comfort and mother. All the patients, in their own way, felt as if they'd gnawed their foot off to escape a trap, and now, wounded and bleeding, they weren't quite sure they'd made the right choice.

Having completed Gail's procedure, Tom made his way to recovery. Approaching Morgan's side and reviewing her chart, he said, "Morgan, the procedure went great, your vitals are strong, and your bleeding is very slight. I'm going to have Gwynn give you some pain medicine along with a refill script and schedule a follow-up appointment for you to come see me in the next couple of days. I'm very proud of you; you did very well. If you need anything, anything at all, just call us here or use the 24-hour hotline. Do you have any questions or concerns I can address?"

"No," Morgan said.

Shaking her hand, Tom smiled and said, "Take care. You did great."

Sliding off the table, Morgan gathered her clothes and dressed in silence. The worn fabric no longer felt familiar, but foreign and coarse. Having dressed, her body moved independent of her mind toward the exit. Continuing on autopilot, Morgan entered the lobby to the relieved smile of her boyfriend. Putting his arm around Morgan, Shawn gave her a half-hug and led her out of the clinic. The brightness of the sun failed to register as they made their way across the blacktop. Helping her gently into the car, Shawn noticed Morgan wasn't the same person who'd gone into the clinic an hour earlier. Something had changed—but he couldn't finger it. Shrugging it off, he figured it was the medicine she'd taken or the lingering pain from the procedure. Driving away in the silence, Morgan wilted.

chapter 10

A Painful Reminder

Crawling to the highway, Belia Lopez pulled her battered body across the pavement. Using what little strength she had left, she rolled over and stared at the night sky through swollen eyes. Believing this was the last thing she'd ever see, Belia gazed with purpose. Resigned, she thought to herself, at least I get to stare at something radiant and pure before I leave this world. Her eyes had seen much lately that was ugly and devoid of goodness. There in the dark, bleeding and broken, she heard the faint sound of gripping rubber and the growl of an engine. Painfully closing her eyes, she waited for the impact.

This night a quarter moon struggled to dominate the sky as Bill drove, making the canopy of silver dots even more apparent. With the music playing, the window cracked, and Bill caught up in the beauty of the night sky, a fallen tree flashed in the far edge of his periphery. Pumping the brakes furiously and swerving to miss the timber, he fought with the rig, the road, the shoulder, and all the obstacles of panic before he brought the truck to a stop. Breathless and shaken, Bill tried to regroup as a massive surge of adrenalin dumped in his system. Chastising himself for his lack of focus, Bill realized his good fortune and breathed deeply. Slowly gathering himself, he steered the rig across the eastbound lane and back on course. Pulling off to the side and mostly out of the lane, he took a moment to calm down and thank God. Feeling better after his moment of reflection, Bill grabbed his flashlight and stepped outside. Nervously awake, he walked through the dark to remove the debris. After walking maybe forty yards, Bill noticed it was not a tree after all, but a young woman. Sprinting the final thirty, he reached Belia in utter delirium!

"Holy Mother of.., can you hear me? Please, God, tell me this isn't happening. Ma'am! Ma'am!" Bill shouted.

Frozen and briefly unable to speak, Belia finally responded, "Yes."

"Oh, thank God. Thank you, Jesus!" exclaimed Bill.

Looking at Belia's body for the first time without the damper of shock, Bill realized her injuries did not come from his truck. He had played no part in her condition. Grateful, he began to calm down. But then panic arose as he contemplated the state of her condition and how this had happened. Was her attacker still in the area? Could he be next? Hurriedly, he scanned the roadside, hills, trees, and underbrush with his flashlight. Pull it together, William, he thought. This woman needs your help and you've got to get her off the road. Bill knew he needed to move the young woman quickly; even this late at night another vehicle was bound to come along. Without hesitating any longer, he gathered Belia into his arms and briskly but securely carried her back to his truck. In the light of the cab, he could see the amazing cruelty with which this woman had been subjected. She'd been tortured, and the sight of her condition made him feel queasy and faint. Reaching back behind the seat, he grabbed a blanket and gently covered the young woman. Who could do such a thing? What could he do? What if she dies in his cab? What if the police think he did it? Whispering a brief prayer under his breath, Bill refocused and began to think. She needs a hospital. I'm closer to

Eastbrook than Fort Reese. The police need to be notified. Grabbing his CB radio, he tuned to channel nine.

"Emergency 911, can anyone hear me? Over. Emergency 911? Over."

"Officer Tyndale reporting. Over."

"Officer, I have a woman in need of immediate medical attention. Over."

"To whom am I speaking?"

"This is Bill Arnold of Uptown Produce."

"What's your position? Over."

"Mile marker twenty-six, Highway 122. Over."

Realizing he was twelve miles out, Officer Tyndale turned on his lights and raced toward marker twenty-six. Instructing Bill to head toward Eastbrook, Tyndale radioed dispatch to send an ambulance to the junction of Highways 122 and I-67. Passing Bill from the westbound lane a few minutes later, Officer Tyndale flipped a U-turn, prompting the two vehicles to slow to a stop. Looking at Belia, Tyndale instantly knew what had happened. Sadly, he'd seen this before. Loading Belia into his patrol car, he took Bill's information quickly and sped off toward the junction.

✱✱✱✱✱✱✱

Sitting on his couch after two long deliveries at General, Tom switched on the news in time to hear a report about a young woman found on Route 122 who'd been badly beaten and sexually assaulted. Flooded with emotion, Tom couldn't take his eyes off the screen. The serial rapist, known as the Beauty Queen Butcher, who'd tormented Eastbrook and the surrounding towns and cities was back. There hadn't been an attack since '95 when they found the Vietnamese girl, Kieu Lang, dead in an outhouse by Miner's Gulch Trail. Kieu had been abducted late one night behind her father's restaurant. In the wake of a six-year hiatus, most people hoped the monster had fled, died, or developed a twinge of conscience after Lang's death. Lang was the BQB's only victim to die from the force of his brutal assault. Tom sat in painful disbelief. He was furious with the state and local police. Why couldn't they catch this monster? Anger and despair pulsed inside of him. He could see Jenny's face, bruised and beaming, like two sides of a coin. Tom struggled to breathe as sweat began to bead.

Squinting hard and rubbing his brow, he saw Jenny as clear as day. She was in her red bikini, reclining on a lounge chair at Lakeland pool. The vision was so real he could see and feel her breathe. Little water beads were glistening on her taut figure. Watching the scene unfold, Tom saw Jenny reading without a care in the world as he approached. He could feel afresh his mischievousness as he dumped an entire bucket of water over her, destroying her paperback and her serenity. Jumping to action with wild abandon, Jenny let out after Tom in a playful, yet ferocious, manner. Hollering and laughing, Tom fled with fearful joy. Melting in the vivid memory of the two at play, Tom was happy. Enraptured, he began to smile. It was so real, so rich, so alive! Tom could feel her skin, hear her laugh, and watch her run. Nothing was more beautiful than Jenny in her carefree days. Tom gazed upon her beauty as he indulged the trance. He longed for the days of summer, the days of youth. Suddenly, as quickly as she had come, Jenny disappeared, and the vision frayed. Feeling the weight of his loss, Tom struggled to maintain his vision, but all was gone. Angry and alone, he stared blankly as the news played in the background. He missed Jenny—he missed her so much. If only he'd insisted she'd stayed in Eastbrook and gone to his friend. Why him? Why Jenny? He'd give anything to have her back. Anything!

chapter 11

History Repeats

"Look at him run, Max, he's such an awesome little man," said Tom.

"Isn't he," echoed Max.

"Hey, Jon-Jon, let's go play on the slides!" encouraged Tom.

"Yeah, the slides, the slides!" said Jonathan, bouncing up and down.

It was a bright Sunday morning in early September. The trees were still green, but you could feel the yellow coming. The sun was warm, even though the heat had left. All around was beautiful and calm, except for the laughter of children. Sandy was smiling as she sat under the pavilion bouncing little Katie on her knee. Max, reclining on a bench, reveled in the sight of his brother and his firstborn at play. The two were great together as they chased and played over, under, around, and through the playground. Ever since the Christmas birth, the two had shared a close bond.

"Uncle Tommy, throw me up un down, up un down!" pleaded Jonathan.

"Up and down?" teased Tom.

"Yeah, yeah, yeah, up un down, up un down!"

"Oh, I don't know, Uncle Tom's back is a little sore."

"No, it isn't. You strong," reminded Jonathan. "Up un down, up un down!"

"Okay, but if I drop you, it's your fault," Tom scolded playfully.

Grabbing Jonathan under the arms and bending his legs, Tom thrust his nephew high into the air. Jonathan giggled and screamed with a broad grin as his hair lifted in the breeze. After several tosses and catches, both boys were laughing and smiling at one another. Nothing was better than family, Max thought as he beheld Sandy, Katie, Tom, and Jonathan. This is what life is all about.

"Again, again, again!" shouted Jonathan.

"It's time for your pops to have a turn, Jon-Jon. I'm wore out," said Tom breathlessly.

"No, you not," said Jonathan.

"Yes, I am," retorted Tom. "Maxy, get your butt over here. Your kid wants a toss."

"You're doing just fine, bro, I don't see why I need to step in."

"Lazy bum!"

"Again, again, up un down, Uncle Tommy."

"Last time, Jon-Jon."

Tom loved it. Living alone, he delighted in his time spent with his nephew and niece. It was fun to shower them with gifts and give their parents a welcome break every now and then. Katie was so cute and soft, but he especially loved Jonathan. He loved his smile, his laugh, his enthusiasm for life, and his courage. The little boy wasn't afraid of anything. Tom knew he would go far, and he couldn't have been more proud of little Jon-Jon. Winded and laughing, Tom gently returned Jonathan to the grass. Just as his feet reached securely, Max came out of nowhere and pasted Tom to the ground. As the two brothers wrestled and heckled on the ground, little Jon-Jon dove on top. "Arghh!" he shouted. The three of them fell in a heap of sweat and laughter.

"This was fun, Max. We'll have to do it again some-time. I've got to get going to an appointment."

"On a Sunday?"

"Yeah, it's a sensitive case," said Tom.

"You work too hard, little brother!"

"I know."

"Thanks again for coming," said Max.

"It was fun." Turning back toward Sandy, Tom shouted, "See ya around, Sandy."

"See ya around, Tom," Sandy called back.

Noticing Katie, Tom decided to run over and give his niece a kiss. "I almost forgot about li'l Katie." Kissing his niece, Tom looked at Sandy and said, "You look great, Sandy."

"Thanks, Tom," Sandy said appreciatively.

"I'll stop by next week. I gotta go. I'll see you guys then."

Starting up his engine, Tom merged with traffic and headed toward the clinic. He was meeting Mr. Lopez concerning an urgent matter, and he wanted to get there early to brighten up the place and ready the hospitality comforts. Tom wasn't exactly sure what the case involved, but he knew it was something difficult. Private consultations during off-days always were. In Tom's short career, he had already dealt with a few cases of fetal abnormality and one case of date rape. Arriving at the clinic, Tom spotted Tammy's car in the parking lot as he rounded the corner. What else would he expect from Tammy? She was always punctual and professional. When he stepped inside, Tom observed that Tammy was on top of everything. She had meticulously prepared the conference room and the refreshments.

"The appointment's at two, right?" asked Tom.

"That's correct," said Tammy.

"I'm going to hit my office and finish up a few things before they get here, if you don't mind," said Tom. "Looks like you've got everything well in hand."

"Sure, go ahead," assured Tammy.

Tammy was an indispensable resource for Tom and Jim. She had worked as an abortion counselor and scheduler for fifteen years prior to joining the staff at Rose & Taugney. Tammy worked five days a week talking to women by phone or in person prior to and sometimes after their abortion procedure. She knew how to skillfully guide women through their abortion decision and help them navigate the complex emotions that went into making the choice for abortion. Her expertise and ability always comforted Tom and made it easier to do these tough consultations. Tammy was now in her fifties, but she had been there in the early days of the fight for reproductive freedom. She'd seen it all, and she had the battle scars to prove it. As a true believer in the cause, she carried out her job with the utmost fervor and zeal. Having had two abortions herself, Tammy could relate to what these women were going through. She'd been there.

At 2:05 p.m., the doorbell rang and Tammy unlocked the front door to let Mr. Lopez into the clinic. He was a medium-sized man with a stern exterior, but today he walked with a discernible heaviness—lethargy accompanied his slight limp. Mr. Lopez was a powerful man who demanded respect, and one had only to look at his hands, rough and cracked from a lifetime of hard work, to perceive it. Entering the conference room, he sat down and waited for Dr. Rose. Tammy poured him a glass of water as she asked if he wanted anything else. Declining, he slowly sipped his water.

"Mr. Lopez, I'm Dr. Rose," greeted Tom as he extended his hand. "I'm sorry we have to meet like this."

"Me, too," replied Mr. Lopez.

Taking a seat, Tom asked, "What can we do for you today, sir?"

Swallowing hard, Mr. Lopez, without looking up, said, "My daughter was raped three months ago by the BQB, and now she's pregnant."

Tom moved uncomfortably in his chair.

"I hear you have some experience with this animal, Dr. Rose," continued Mr. Lopez.

Collecting himself, Tom responded, "Not with him, I can assure you, but with one of his victims."

"I want to schedule an abortion as soon as possible."

"I'm so sorry, Mr. Lopez. My heart goes out to you and your family."

"Thank you."

"Does your daughter feel the same way about this?" inquired Tom.

"Belia doesn't know what she wants. I'm doing what's best for her," Mr. Lopez replied.

"We can appreciate that Mr. Lopez, but it's her decision. We'll have to hear it from her," interjected Tammy.

"I concur, Mr. Lopez. Without Belia's consent, we can't move forward, I'm afraid," said Tom.

"If she provides her consent at the time of the appointment, is that all right?" asked Mr. Lopez.

"Yes, that would work," said Tammy.

"When can we schedule?"

"How far along is she?" asked Tom.

"A little over three months," responded Mr. Lopez.

"Because of the nature of your case and the special needs of Belia, if she agrees to termination of the pregnancy, I recommend we do the procedure next week on Sunday during non-business hours."

"Get things ready. I'll bring her," asserted Mr. Lopez.

"If we don't hear from you beforehand, we will need to see Belia after the close of business on Saturday, say 5:30, for preparation," said Tom.

"Thank you. She'll be there," Mr. Lopez confirmed.

With all the courage he could muster, Tom said, "Again, sir, I'm deeply saddened by what happened to Belia. Please pass my sympathies along to her and your entire family."

"Thank you, Dr. Rose."

Tammy escorted Mr. Lopez to the door and smiled a sympathetic smile as he put on his jacket. "I'm terribly sorry this happened, Mr. Lopez," said Tammy. "We'll take good care of her. Dr. Rose and Dr. Taugney are excellent at their jobs."

"They came highly recommended," said Mr. Lopez.

"You won't regret it, Mr. Lopez," assured Tammy. "Sir, if I may, how old is Belia?"

"She's twenty-one."

Watching Mr. Lopez leave, Tammy locked the door and returned to the conference room. Tom had disappeared. Not having any outlet, she decided to busy herself with tidying the conference room. Cleaning up, she noticed the bathroom light was on and the sink was running. "Tom? Tom, are you okay?"

"I'm fine. I just need to go home and rest."

Coming out of the bathroom, looking white as a ghost, Tom fainted and fell past Tammy's late-catching arms. After propping Tom's head on a pillow and placing a wet towel over his forehead, Tammy called Dr. Taugney. Arriving forty minutes later, Taugney found Tom lying on the sofa next to a trash can.

"Tom, are you all right?"

"Yeah, my nerves just got the best of me," replied Tom. "Did Tammy give you the news?"

"She filled me in. It's awful. I don't know why they can't catch that SOB. Plain police incompetence that's what it is!"

"I need you on this one, Jim. She needs general anesthesia after what she's been through, and I need every available resource in the room."

"I'll be there, Tom," assured Taugney. "Let's get you home, shall we?"

The following weekend was one of the hardest of Tom's life. When he met Belia for the first time, it was déjà vu. The young woman was healing, but the trauma she'd been through was evident, especially the scar upon her neck. She rarely spoke, and when she did it was soft and barely audible. Totally detached from all that was happening around her, Belia moved through the motions like a ghost. The lethargy in her movements suggested a woman who was still in great pain. Tom was gentle and caring in every phase of his duties, showing great patience and compassion. Excusing himself for the second time, he left Belia in Taugney's capable hands. Entering the restroom, Tom turned on the water and cried. It was impossible to bear and rougher than he thought it would be, but for Jenny, he would do it.

chapter 12

Born for Such a Time as This

Hearing the shrill alarm, Christopher reached over and hit the snooze button for a ten-minute reprieve before facing the day. Desperate as he was, no sleep would return. Feeling stiffness in his neck, he made his way to his floor mat and dumbbells. Massaging his neck to work out the kinks, Christopher realized yesterday's paint fight, which seemed like the right call at the time, had now come at a price. Still, he had dominated Kirk and Amy! Despite the extra two hours it took to clean up the mess and cover up the splatter, the looks on their faces had been well worth it when he turned the tables on their little prank. Christopher loved working with people. In many ways he was still a child at heart. Never wanting to fully grow up, he had always delighted in free-spirited adventure and the carefree joy of spontaneity—perhaps even more so now having come full circle through trag-edy. Now he had purpose, and yesterday's paint war in the newly refurbished food pantry at the church was only a small part of it. He liked helping others and shepherding youth. It was his way of giving back and partnering with God after being angry and absent in his college years. He'd experienced God's work, and he knew he wanted to be a part of it, helping other young people process and manage the complexities of life.

This was his third year on staff at FSO, the uniquely named Christian church For Sinner's Only, and each year he'd become better and more comfortable leading the church's adolescent youth. But today was a big new step. Today, was the launch of another outreach the Lord had placed on his heart: clinic prayer and rescue at the front doors of the city's abortion centers. Two years ago, he'd attended a pro-life conference, and what he learned deeply stirred his heart. Setting off on a path of research and prayer, Christopher resolved to become involved. The value of each and every life wasn't lost on him, and now he was ready to put his feet to action. Pausing before he walked out the door, he put his fingers to his lips and kissed them before placing them on a picture of his sister. Without any further hesitation, he left.

Christopher fished his cell phone out of his pocket and pushed the power button: 8:43 a.m. Friday, March 21, 2003. "It's a quarter till nine, Leon," informed Christopher.

"Thanks, I'll stay till 9:30, but then I've got to split for work," Leon replied.

"However long you can stay is fine, I'm just glad you're here," said Christopher.

"Not the best turnout for our first run, is it?"

"No, but it's not about the numbers, it's about the heart. Jonathan knew that when he challenged the Philistines. He said that nothing could keep the Lord from saving, whether he used many or few."

"I'd prefer the many," said Leon.

"Me, too," replied Christopher.

"I'm a little surprised, though. After the meeting at church and the announcement in the bulletin, I thought there'd be more than five."

"Look at Amy. Do you think she's intimidated?" asked Christopher.

"No. Amy was born to pray," Leon said with conviction.

The rain fell gently against Amy Dover's face as she knelt on the sidewalk at the far end of the parking lot in front of Rose & Taugney. Her lips moved with fluidity like a ballerina in the midst of an enchanted twirl. Gently swaying in the Spirit, Amy held her hands high. Rain mingled with her tears as she poured out her soul for the living and the dying. Nothing was more hauntingly beautiful than the simple honesty of her prayers. She knew the Lord was mighty to save and that only He could do this work. So it was to Him, and Him only, that she appealed. To see her passion was to be inspired.

Wherever two or more are gathered in Jesus' name, the Scriptures say, and today there were five— Christopher Thompson, Amy Dover, Jael Jackson, Leon Mackey, and Cindy Taylor. These few had come to pray, to counsel, and to rescue the weak from the powerful, the blind from the darkness, and the hurting from despair. Cindy held up a sign at the driveway entrance that read, "I Regret My Abortion." Leon placed signs along the curb facing oncoming traffic depicting smiling babies of various races with captions that read: "Choose Life, Your Mom Did," "Abortion Stops a Beating Heart," and "Life, What a Beautiful Choice." Jael stood on the opposite side of the drive from Cindy, holding several brochures containing information about fetal development, risk factors for abortion, symptoms of post-abortion syndrome, the nearby alternative pregnancy resource center, and adoption literature. Christopher stood in the drizzle holding a ragged Bible that was torn and marked.

The rain had been falling gently since 8:15 on this cold and blustery day. Undeterred, Christopher and his friends prayed and waited for people to arrive. Taugney's car was already in the lot when Dr. Rose pulled in for work a little before nine. Passing five new faces, Tom let out a sigh and a few choice words as he pulled into his spot. Stepping out of the car with umbrella in hand, Tom stared at the group.

"We're praying for you, Dr. Rose," said Jael in a loud voice.

"Don't do this, doctor. Don't take any lives today," joined Cindy.

"You know they're babies, Tom," said Leon.

Turning and walking away, Tom heard Christopher say, "You won't help any women today, Dr. Rose. Nobody wins with abortion!"

Without turning back, Tom shouted, "Why don't you people shut up and go home!"

Christopher returned, "We'll never leave, Tom, but you will. By the grace of God, you will!"

Slamming the front door to the clinic as he walked in, Tom spewed, "Ah, hell—the crazies have found us. It's Planned Parenthood all over again. I knew it was only a matter of time. How long have they been here, Sally?"

"Since about 8:30," Sally replied.

"This is the last thing I need—kooks on the sidewalk."

"Maybe it will be short-lived, and they'll get tired and go away," offered Sally.

"No. Once they come, they don't leave. The faces may change and the numbers, but somebody always comes," lamented Tom. "Call Maggie Adams at Planned Parenthood and ask her for recommendations on a good security guard. We need a presence out front to calm the girls and keep the peace."

"Yes, Doctor."

"Luckily, it's not that busy of a day," said Tom. "I'll be in my office. Let me know when the first patients arrive."

Walking down the sidewalk in the rain, a young couple snuggled close. Huddling arm-in-arm under their umbrella, they slowly approached the driveway to the clinic. Jael could see the heaviness of their predicament etched on their faces as they drew close. Holding out her hand, she said, "Can I give you some literature about your options? Can I help you in any way?"

Without looking up, the young man replied, "No, thank you," and briskly ushered his girlfriend past Jael.

"You don't have to make this choice. Plenty of people want to help, even adopt," Jael pleaded as they disappeared inside the clinic.

Moments later, a mother and her daughter drove quickly past Jael and Cindy, parked, and rushed from their car to the clinic. Leon yelled out to them that help was available. But, they, too, disappeared into the clinic. Ten minutes later, two more cars arrived—one with teenage girls and the other with a man in his thirties and a young girl of nineteen or so. With each new arrival, each couple, each girl, Amy continued to pray and weep. A wiry-looking man in his late thirties or early forties, stepped out of his car and escorted his sixteen-year-old daughter into the clinic. When he came out of the clinic fifteen minutes later to have a cigarette, Leon called out to him, "Sir, don't leave your daughter and your grandbaby in there. It's your job to protect them. Only you can shield them, love them, and show them the right path. Fight for them. Fight for them, Dad!" Turning to go back inside, he heard Christopher reading from Psalm 142:

"When my spirit grows faint within me, it is you who know my way. In the path where I walk men have hidden a snare for me. Look to my right and see; no one is concerned for me. I have no refuge; no one cares for my life. I cry to you, O Lord; I say, 'You are my refuge, my portion in the land of the living.' Listen to my cry, for I am in desperate need; rescue

me from those who pursue me, for they are too strong for me."

Furious, the man screamed at Christopher, "Screw you, you judgmental hypocrite!"

Calmly, Christopher replied, "I'm sorry I've offended you, sir, but perhaps the truth of God is stirring in you? Is there any way we can help you see the truth today? Can I help you rescue your daughter from this terrible choice?"

Laughing, the man put out his cigarette, and said, "Help me? Help me? You and your fairy tales can't help me!"

Hopeful, Christopher said, "Yes, I believe God can."

"Bull!" said the man as he disappeared inside the clinic.

Hours later, Leon had gone. The rain had stopped, and several of the women had exited defiant, sullen, or in pain. No one took the literature. Amy had remained on her knees for over an hour, but now she was up walking from one side of the clinic to the other as she prayed. Some of the signs had blown over, and all the rescuers were cold and weary. The morning had been rough, and the people rougher. Drained, Christopher called together the remaining group: "That's it for today, guys. Let's close in prayer and come back next week." Bowing their heads as they prayed, the tiny group held hands and closed their eyes. Finishing with heavy hearts, they embraced one another and left.

Driving home, Christopher grappled with the day and the struggle: why so few from the church had come; the angry clients he'd encountered at the clinic; the efforts of those brave intercessors who'd come to the sidewalk, and how they could be improved; the call he felt to pro-life work—was it real?

Thirty minutes later, he arrived home despondent

and weary. Walking up the steps to his house, he turned the key and stepped inside. It was empty and quiet, unlike his heart. Facing the stairs, Christopher ascended with fatigue, entered his bathroom, and turned on the shower. Slowly undressing, he waited for the steam to rise. Standing there under the warmth, he continued to think about all the babies that had died that morning and all the women and men who, whether they knew it or not, had just rejected one of God's greatest gifts to them. Sorrow rose in his soul like a mountain, and he began to weep. "Oh, Jesus, forgive us, forgive us, we know not what we do." Weary and heartbroken, Christopher slid down the wall of the shower and ended up sitting on the cold, wet floor, weeping as the water showered down on him. All was brokenness as the water ran cold.

Exiting the shower, tired and disillusioned, Christopher shaved, dressed, and went back downstairs. Slicing some fruit for lunch, he could feel a spirit of oppression cover him like a wet, wool blanket. Trying to distract his mind from a million thoughts that raced through his head, Christopher decided to get his mail. Leaving his house, the cold stung his face with renewed brutality. He longed for peace as he entered the elements, but it eluded him. *God, I need to hear from You. Give me a sign, something to help me know I'm on the right path. Help me, Lord. Help me,* he prayed. Returning to the house, Christopher shuffled through the bills, the junk, the solicitations, and then he saw it—a letter from Mom:

Dear Chris,

I felt the Lord wanted me to write you this letter, and I hope it finds you well. I've never told you what I'm about to share with you, and I beg you'll forgive

hushed

the delay. There never seemed to be a need or a
time to communicate this to you, and so I did not. In
light of your heart's passion for the preborn and their
parents, now is the time. I'm so proud of you and the
man you've become. I love you very much, but I didn't
initially. In 1974, I was foolish, selfish, and sexually
active. Pleasure, pride, and fun ruled my days as a
young college student, and I thought I would live forever. Then one day I got pregnant by a man I barely
knew. Wanting nothing to do with me or the baby, he
left, and I decided without hesitation to abort. It was
an age of feminism and a woman's right to choose. I'd
like to say I agonized over the decision, but I did not.
I went to a local clinic, confirmed the pregnancy, and
scheduled the abortion. Driving myself to the clinic
that morning, I had no worries, no fears. I thought it
would be a harmless procedure like going to the dentist,
and then I could return to my carefree life. I gave
very little, if any, thought to you. And for that, my son,
I am deeply ashamed! Arriving at the clinic, I saw a
small group of people standing in front of the Women's
Center. They were carrying signs and talking to people. As I got out of my car, I dropped my keys, and
an older gentleman named Gerald picked them up
and handed them to me. With a look of compassion in
his eyes, he said, "Ma'am, you dropped your keys. Can
I assist you in any other way today?" "Thank you,"
I said, "but no, I have an appointment with the doctor."
"What for?" he asked. To this day I don't know why
I told him, but I said, "to have an abortion," which, of
course, he already knew. Looking me in the eye with
all seriousness, he said, "Ma'am, have you ever lost a
child?" Taken aback, I said, "No, I'm too young." With
a tear in his eye, he said, "I have, and it's the worst
thing that can ever happen in your life" (a truth I

didn't fully appreciate until we lost your sister to a drunk driver on the night of the prom). He went on to say, "You're about to experience that today if you have this abortion. Let me help you make a better choice and live without regret." Dumbfounded and moved by his compassion, I agreed to have a coffee with him and talk about it. Christopher, that man saved your life! You're alive today because of him. He didn't just help me that day. He helped me find work, return to school, and provided us with $200 a month until your fifth birthday, when I assured him his generous support was no longer needed. I want to encourage you, Son, to follow God's leading and keep on doing what you're doing. God has a plan for each and every life, and yours is no exception. I believe you were born for such a time as this!

Your loving and grateful Mother

    Astonished, Christopher put down the letter and sat in the swell of emotion. Life never ceased to amaze or challenge, he thought. Marveling at God's interventions in his life, he felt an even deeper connection to those he was trying to save, but this new revelation also carried fresh pain. Growing up without his biological father had left a mark, a feeling of abandonment. But hearing of his mother's initial reaction brought home the reality that he, too, was unwanted. In the growing stillness of the moment, Christopher heard a Voice say, "I've always wanted you! And this is the path I've chosen for you, walk it out—First Corinthians 1:26." Grabbing his Bible, Christopher opened up to the verse, and read a passage he had all but forgotten: *Brothers, think of what you were when you were called. Not many of you were wise by human*

hushed

standards; not many were influential; not many were of noble birth. But God chose the foolish things of the world to shame the wise; God chose the weak things of the world to shame the strong. He chose the lowly things of this world and the despised things—and the things that are not—to nullify the things that are, so that no one may boast before him.

chapter 13

Soren Ulf

Soren Ulf sat behind his desk and rubbed his eyes. He hadn't slept well the night before, and he was feeling more irritable than usual. It was ten o'clock at night, and he knew he still had a long night ahead of him. Trying to take his mind off of his irritations, he pulled out his digital camera and scrolled through his latest pictures. Scanning the various photos of female genitalia, he paused on a particular shot. He loved the clarity and symmetry of this photo and all the things it conjured in his mind. Lost in his meditations, he forgot about everything except his current fantasy.

Interrupted by the screams of a woman, Soren slammed down his camera and called for Nurse V. Having finished an earlier round of sedation, Nurse V. had walked outside to smoke and never returned. Soren, upon entering the hallway, noticed he was alone and began to swear. Frustrated and hot, he ascended the staircase to the procedure room. Passing through the doorway, he fixed his eyes on Latasha. Moaning and writhing on a recliner, Latasha screamed out in pain as she experienced the ebb and flow of labor. Walking briskly over to her, the fifty-six-year-old slapped her hard on the thigh and forcefully said, "Shut up. You'll wake the other clients." Latasha was surrounded by six other girls, all on their own recliners. The girls were naked from the waist down and noticeably pregnant. Some were bleeding, some looked dead, all had IVs in their hands, and all were there for late-term abortions ranging from twenty-three to thirty-five weeks gestation. Soren was one of the few late-term abortionists in the region, and, as such, his business was usually busy and lucrative. Upping Latasha's dose of Demerol, Ulf glanced around the room at his other girls. He had a Hispanic, three blacks, an Asian, and an Indian immigrant to round out the field. It was quite a mixed bag, and that pleased him. Leaving the room, he slammed the door and went back to his office.

Knocking on his office door a half hour later, Nurse V. reported, "Dr. Ulf, two of the women have passed and are ready for termination."

"Where the hell were you?" Ulf inquired angrily.

"I was outside taking a break. It's the first I've had all night, and you know we're short-staffed," responded Nurse V. defiantly.

"Fine, I'll be up in a minute," said Ulf.

Getting up from his chair, Soren stood in front of the mirror and slicked his silvery black hair, dabbed at the coffee stain on his shirt, and zipped his fly. He was a pitiful-looking man, short and squatty with vacant eyes. For over two decades he'd owned and operated Reproductive Freedom, a clinic that drew little public attention. The facility was unkempt and unsafe, and everybody that worked there knew it. But nobody cared because the money was good, education wasn't required, and, in general, they were treating and weeding out the dregs of society. Soren carried on his mission in broad daylight with very little interference. He hadn't seen a regulator in over a decade. The last time they'd visited, he'd promised to clean up the place, properly sterilize his instruments, buy a working defibrillator, and hire another licensed doctor to cover for his long absences from the clinic. Of course, none of these things had been done, and no one had been sent to do a follow-up report. Dr. Ulf was thus left to his own devices—free to practice in any way that pleased him. Soren was determined to control the population and weed out from among society the undesirables and the disabled. Dr. Ulf hated all stock that was non-white, especially blacks.

Latasha's baby girl wriggled on the floor, twitching and struggling to breathe as Dr. Ulf approached. Seeing that Latasha was completely knocked out, he took the tiny baby in his arms, cut the umbilical cord, and promptly shoved his large scissors into the back of her neck. This resulted in a pathetic shriek and a violent reflex before Latasha's little girl went limp.

Looking over at Nurse V. as she gazed at the room's lone television, Ulf yelled, "Quit slacking and come get this dead fetus, while I take care of the next one."

Aiming the remote at the television, Nurse V. retorted, "Geez, Soren, that was the good part."

"You're such a smart ass," exclaimed Ulf. "Hurry up. Bag this fetus, take it downstairs, and put it in the freezer with the others. Also, could you grab me a jar for this next specimen?"

"I'm on it, Doc."

chapter 14

Born of the Spirit

"Do you believe Jesus Christ died for your sins on the cross? Do you believe He rose again and is the true Light of the World? If you do, I want you to come forward this morning and give Him your life," Pastor Jim implored as his words echoed through the modest church on the edge of town. Jaleesa, sitting next to her mother at the end of the pew, had absorbed every word of the morning message—a beautiful presentation of grace blending chapters eight and nine of the Gospel of John. The love of Jesus and His power to redeem anyone greatly appealed to Jaleesa. Pastor Jim spoke with eloquence about the woman caught in adultery and the man born blind—two distinct people, one avenue of grace. Jaleesa knew her mother, Papa, and Gammy loved her, but she'd come to understand that Jesus loved her even more. She loved Jesus' heart, and she believed He was the Light of the World! Rising, she left her mother and her grandparents and walked down the center aisle toward the pulpit. Pastor Jim shed a tear as he witnessed Rachelle's daughter approach. He had prayed many times for this child and her mother. Others from the crowd slowly joined Jaleesa in the confession of faith. In all, fifteen people gave their lives to Christ and joined the family of God. When it was Jaleesa's time to confess, Pastor Jim said, "Jaleesa, do you believe that Jesus is the Christ, the Son of the living God?"

"Yes!" Jaleesa affirmed.

"Do you believe He died for your sins and rose on the third day?" asked Pastor Jim.

"Yes!" said Jaleesa emphatically.

"God bless you in that confession of faith, child," congratulated Pastor Jim.

Several in the congregation cheered, and Rachelle beamed as little Jaleesa entered the Kingdom of Heaven. While the new believers returned to their seats and the congregation stood, the piano began to intone *The Old Rugged Cross*. Moved by the Spirit, the crowd sang out the hymn with the fervor of the redeemed:

"On a hill far away stood an old rugged cross; the emblem of suffering and shame. And I love that old rugged cross where the dearest and best, for a world of lost sinners was slain. So I'll cherish the old rugged cross, till my trophies at last I lay down; I will cling to the old rugged cross, and exchange it someday for a crown."

One voice of praise, however, stood out from the rest. Among his many talents, Lucas possessed a powerful voice. Booming and smooth, it must have reached the heights of heaven, as it could be heard clearly above the throng. His voice gave you goose bumps and made you believe God did indeed exist, for how else could you explain so marvelous an instrument? Whether it came from the ancient cultures, or from the legacy of a suffering people, or the benevolence of God, one could not tell. But when it sounded, it made you recognize the gift and the Giver:

"Oh, that old rugged cross, so despised by the world, has a wondrous attraction for me; for the dear Lamb of God, left His glory above, to bear it to dark Calvary. So I'll cherish the old rugged cross, till my trophies at last I lay down; I will cling to the old rugged cross, and exchange it someday for a crown."

Walking out of the service, Rachelle and Jaleesa stopped to talk with Pastor Jim. "I'm so proud of you and your decision for Christ, Jaleesa," said Pastor Jim. "Congratulations, Rachelle, you've raised a fine daughter."

"Well thanks, but I've had a lot of help," said Rachelle.

Slipping beside the group, Christopher interjected, "I'm so proud of you both. That was awesome!"

"Thanks, Christopher. We love you guys," Rachelle said.

"And we love you," echoed Christopher. Turning to Jaleesa, he said, "There's something powerful about coming to Christ as a child, especially at the age of eight. I'm going to tell Miss Johnson that someone is paying attention to her lessons."

"I sure have, Pastor Chris," Jaleesa said enthusiastically.

"Amen, J.J. Give me five."

The group laughed and hugged as they said their goodbyes and exited the service. Waiting by the car, Lucas and Aaliyah were glowing with pride. They, too, had prayed for their daughter and her little Jaleesa, perhaps more than anyone else, and they wanted to celebrate.

"Lunch is on us," said Lucas. "What do you say, J.J., you want to go to Tuscany House or Casa de Salsa?"

"Let's go to Salsa, Papa. I love their chips," said Jaleesa without hesitation.

"Salsa it is."

Driving through the streets of Eastbrook in the fall was truly beautiful. The city streets were lined with reds, golds, greens, and purples that flickered and glinted in the afternoon sun. Snow-capped mountains rose in the distance like giant castles with fur coats made of bristlecone, aspen, and spruce. Depending on where you were in the city, the shops had that uniquely quaint small-town feel, and everything was neat and tidy. Eastbrook College and the Academy lent their energy, dreams, and enthusiasm to the location, making the city a rich tapestry of young and old, the not yet and the not anymore, the rising and the risen. The restaurants were good, the sports bars were full, and the people were out everywhere—running, walking, playing, shopping, filling parks, going to the movies, driving in and out of the mountains, fishing, splashing in the river that meandered through town. You name it; people were doing it in this burgeoning, wide-awake city.

Returning home after a hearty meal and a pleasant celebration, Lucas and Jaleesa sat down to watch that day's smorgasbord of football. At halftime, Lucas rallied the troops, and the whole family began to clean up and clear out the office for Sasha, the new houseguest. Sasha needed a place to stay and some help with her finances while she completed her pregnancy. Christopher had introduced Lucas, Aaliyah, and Rachelle to Sasha a week earlier after encouraging her to make a decision for life at the clinic and keep her baby. Knowing what it was like to be alone, afraid, young, and pregnant, Rachelle and her family graciously offered to provide the shelter and resources Sasha needed until she was established. Regardless of what Sasha chose, single parenthood or adoption, the Jacobs' were glad to help and felt blessed by God to be able to do so. They were no strangers to hard decisions. They had been through much when Rachelle got pregnant, and again when they decided to move the eleven hundred miles to Eastbrook three years ago, but God had always proven faithful, something they felt confident he would do again as they prepared to add Sasha to their family.

"I got the desk in place upstairs; now all I need is the

computer," said Lucas.

"Ray-Ray, grab the printer, and I'll get the monitor and the keyboard," said Aaliyah.

"I'll get the cords," chimed Jaleesa.

"I see how it works; leave the heavy piece for the old man," teased Lucas.

Walking up the stairs, the four laughed and teased. The house was that perfect temperature between summer and late fall that makes everything pleasant and refreshing. With an eye for arrangement and decoration, Aaliyah had transformed her living room into something inviting and manageable. Possessing an interior decorator's skill and a can-do attitude, she worked Lucas's office, her dining set, the piano, and a bookshelf and chair into a harmonious collaborative whole. As Rachelle and Jaleesa busied themselves with computer placement and set-up, Lucas and Aaliyah entered the garage to get the full-size mattress and box spring. Carefully navigating the stairwell and door jambs, the two managed to get the bed downstairs with only a slight rub on one of the rounded corners.

Putting together the metal frame, Aaliyah said, "I told you this bed would come in handy when we moved."

"That you did," said Lucas. "You want some water, love?"

"Sure. That'd be nice."

Returning with two tall glasses of ice water, Lucas observed that his bride in her thrift was ready to put the mattress and box springs on the frame.

"Let me help you with that," offered Lucas.

"I'll take this corner, you take that," instructed Aaliyah.

"I can't believe we've held on to this old thing all these years. You remember when this used to be our only bed? I hated this thing; it was never long enough, and we always rolled together."

"Was that so bad?" Aaliyah said flirtatiously.

"Well, come to think of it, no," Lucas said with a smile.

Walking back upstairs, the couple held hands as they remembered with fondness the days of their youth. Discovering Jaleesa had found his secret stash of chocolate in the desk drawer, Lucas shouted, "J.J., you put down Papa's candy or I'll get you." Jaleesa screamed with delight and began to run. Catching his granddaughter on the stairs with a quick burst and a roar, Lucas lightly tickled the little girl and deftly lifted the bag of chocolate. She was bright as a light, and he couldn't imagine life without her. Loving every minute of it, Lucas turned to scold his daughter, "Lordy, Rachelle, you've got to keep a better handle on this here little one. She just about ate all my coping candy!"

"You know she's just looking out for your health, Daddy."

"Papa, give me some candy," pleaded Jaleesa.

"Oh, no, J.J., I reckon you've had enough," Lucas said sternly.

"Papa, please, please,"

"Nope, I've made up my mind."

"Papa."

"Read my lips." Exaggerating, Lucas mouthed in silence the word, "No."

"Papa…"

"What?" Lucas said, a little agitated.

"Will you join the pastor in baptizing me?"

Smiling with a tear in his eye, Lucas gathered up little Jaleesa in his arms and said, "Of course, baby doll, of course."

chapter 15

Disappointment and Hope

Kneeling, Christopher began to pray, "Lord Jesus, Forgive me for my sins, and lead me in the path of righteousness. Temper the words I speak today and fill me with Your Holy Spirit. Give me the grace to forgive others, care for the least of these, and love in the midst of atrocity. Instruct my tongue and my mind to bring forth a message of life, redemption, hope, and love. Anoint Your Word and use it powerfully today! Please change hearts and minds regarding abortion. Even now, Lord, keep those who are considering abortion from choosing it. Forgive us all for this sin of abortion that permeates our nation. We are all guilty of allowing innocent blood to be shed in our land. Forgive our leaders and our presidents for tolerating or encouraging abortion. Bring more people into the pro-life movement from the church, from the government, and from society. Forgive those in the church and our leaders who remain on the sidelines or encourage abortion. Forgive the body of Christ for engaging in abortion and allowing this atrocity to continue through apathy and ignorance. Lord, You are mighty to save, and only You can truly rescue and deliver those caught in the schemes of the Devil. Come, Lord Jesus, and rescue! Rescue Your precious children today at the clinic. Father, protect those who pray and counsel and those inside the clinic from harm or injury. Give

us the victory, Jesus, and guide all our efforts. Amen."
Rising, Christopher put on his shoes, grabbed his keys,
and walked out the door.

Driving toward the clinic, Christopher reflected
over the past year with mixed emotions. Much had happened, but very little had changed to his satisfaction.
Jael Jackson went back to work when her husband was
laid off and could now only counsel once a month. Leon
Mackey was promoted at work and moved to a neighboring state. Tom Rose and Jim Taugney had a driveway
put in behind the building, which afforded them quick
access to the clinic and precious little exposure or contact with those on the sidewalk. Christopher knew for
a fact that three women had left the clinic after choosing to let their babies live—Sasha being the latest. But
countless others had gone ahead with their abortions.
New faces would come occasionally to pray and disappear as quickly as they had come. Some had stayed, but
it was primarily the same core group of people who had
remained steadfast. Jay Sullivan, a retired police officer,
was hired by the clinic to provide security. A measure
designed to reassure clients, patients, and employees that they were safe. A move that was typical, but
unnecessary, Christopher thought. After all, the prayer
and counseling effort in front of Rose & Taugney was
peaceful, harmless, and controlled. As he turned onto
the freeway, he contemplated with pain the overwhelming rejection of babies in the womb and the lack of
human decency he'd experienced. Countless angry men,
abandoned women, broken women, callous women,
teenagers, imposing parents, rich people, poor people,
suspected forced abortions—it was more than he cared
to remember, but remember he did. Nevertheless, the
moral rightness of his cause, God's call, and his faithful
friends carried him forward. He knew he could count on

hushed

Amy Dover to remain faithful in prayer, Cindy Taylor to continue counseling—trying to keep others from making the same tragic choice she had made—and others in the movement like Father Ramsey and his dedicated parishioners for their support and encouragement.

Father Rick Ramsey, a Catholic priest who for the last twenty years had observed Mass and conducted a silent prayer vigil in front of the local Planned Parenthood, often provided Christopher with helpful insight and guidance. Guidance Christopher sorely needed. Trying to recruit pastors and youth leaders to come to the sidewalk had proved most difficult for Christopher. It seemed everywhere he turned the clergy were too busy, uninterested, or refused to get involved in so political an issue. It frustrated Christopher that his peers, fellow men of the faith, couldn't see or admit that abortion was beyond politics. Even Jim, Christopher's own senior pastor, seemed reluctant at times to get involved, fearing tax exemption interference, pressure from the board, or member displeasure. Christopher couldn't see how any pastor or believer could side with political interests over people. Millions were dying, and the indignation, alarm, and urgency of God's people in no way fit the circumstances of our national crisis.

Some pastors even felt that politics were the only hope for a solution. But Christopher didn't agree. After three decades of political apathy, ineptitude, and complicity, he doubted there was enough courage and conviction in Washington to see the job through. Too many politicians had flip-flopped for power and sold out their own people and the truth. Liberals had happily adopted the abortion agenda and its mantra of choice in the wake of denying the very value they purported to cherish to millions of innocent little boys and girls. And many conservatives had simply tickled the ears of their constituents

98

with rhetoric and speeches, failing miserably to protect the preborn. Both sides were too busy bickering, pursuing power, and lining their pockets to care about America's future and her most vulnerable and innocent children. No, thought Christopher, abortion won't be solved by our petty politicians but by the people. Only an informed and outraged citizenry could bring America back to its senses and greatness. When his temper flashed, as it often did during that first year, Christopher benefited from the calm, experienced hand of Father Ramsey. On more than one occasion, he realized that passion wasn't often the better part of wisdom. Christopher had learned a lot from Rick about patience and perseverance during his initial year of clinic rescue.

One Saturday morning when Christopher was down and discouraged, Father Ramsey encouraged him to not get too high or too low. He said, "The pro-life struggle is not a sprint, it's a marathon. You've got to pace yourself, get plenty of rest, and keep your mind sharp. This is an effort worthy of our very best. We cannot lose heart, and we cannot give in. We must in all things love and forgive like Jesus." Christopher took his advice, adjusted his perspective, recalibrated his expectations, and began to prepare for the long haul.

As a result of Christopher's presence every other Saturday at Father Ramsey's gathering in front of Planned Parenthood, the largest abortion provider in Eastbrook, several Catholic men and women decided to join Christopher in the sidewalk counseling and prayer effort at Rose & Taugney. Many Catholics were beginning to support both Christopher's efforts on Fridays and Father Ramsey's on Saturdays. Christopher welcomed the diversity, encouragement, and increased prayer presence these additional people brought to the sidewalk.

Arriving at the clinic, Christopher immediately

noticed a large truck that was parked on Thirteenth Avenue with a giant picture of an aborted baby mounted in the pickup bed. He also noted a modest group of Catholic intercessors were standing across the street far away from the clinic and their normal place of prayer. Parking his car, he approached the clinic coming up Almond Street. Nearing the driveway, Christopher encountered the reason for their distance. A man he had never seen before stood on the sidewalk intermittently yelling, "Repent for the Kingdom of Heaven is at hand" and "All baby killers go to hell!" He was dressed in a Catholic Bishop's costume carrying an inflatable blow-up doll—an obvious parody of those defrocked priests in the Catholic Church that had molested young boys. His presence was virulent, controversial, and offensive. Amy Dover paid him no attention and remained steadfast in prayer. For everyone else, the man was an uncomfortable presence and an obvious distraction. Situating himself on the sidewalk near the front door to the clinic, Christopher began to read his Bible and pray.

Noticing Christopher had a Bible, the man approached and said, "Nice to see a fellow Protestant out here, where do you attend worship?"

"I prefer the term Christian or Jesus follower, but I suppose you could classify me as a Protestant," replied Christopher.

"My name is Art," said the man.

"Hi, Art. I'm Christopher."

"Where did you say you worshiped?"

"I didn't. I attend For Sinners Only, and you?"

"Pine Creek," said Art. "That's a funny name for a church. Catchy, I suppose. Interesting hook, too, as long as you don't stay that way."

"We do try to walk in obedience, but I don't think

any of us can claim to be sinless," Christopher remarked. "What are you trying to do here, Art?"

"Save babies and witness to the Catholics about their faulty doctrine."

"And how are you doing that?" asked Christopher.

"Through my pictures and visual aids, I stand as a reminder of the truth!"

"What truth?" Christopher inquired.

"The truth that the Catholic Church is not infallible, that the priests aren't God, and that abortion kills babies," said Art.

"Abortion does kill babies, but I don't think there's any church that's infallible, Protestant or Catholic. A casual observation will prove that, and I've met a few priests, and I don't believe any of them think they're God."

"Are you going to defend those idolaters?" accused Art.

"No, it's not my responsibility to defend them. I'm sure they can defend themselves if they want to, but I don't think your methods are very effective, Art. I think this is the wrong place to address your concerns with the Catholic Church. Surely, if you want to engage the Catholic community, there are far better venues than this. I'm here to offer assistance to women and men who find themselves dealing with an unexpected pregnancy and save lives, not settle theological divides or doctrinal differences."

"That Bible you're holding says, 'What agreement has the temple of God with idols? For we are the temple of the living God.' We can't have fellowship with them," stated Art.

"We're all called to love and help our neighbor, and

that's all we're doing here," responded Christopher. "The Catholics and I don't agree on everything, but we do agree on many things, including the intrinsic value of every human life. Abortion is fundamentally a human rights issue, and I would join anyone who is fighting for the rights of the preborn and trying to encourage their parents to make a better choice. Recognizing the dignity of life and its need for protection is not exclusive to any group."

"Sounds to me like you're a sellout."

"I don't see it like that, but I do hope you'll rethink your approach. Often, parents bring their children with them when they pray, and I don't think your doll is appropriate for them or anybody else. Furthermore, if I showed up here and saw a person mocking one of our fallen Protestant ministers, it wouldn't endear me to that person or make me want to listen to anything they had to say. I would also challenge you to look closer at the approach of Christ when confronting sin or ministering to people. Jesus did not come mocking; he came shocking with his love."

"I suppose you're against the pictures, too," said Art.

"No, I'm not actually. They depict the horrible truth of abortion, and I've seen them used effectively, but they also prevent a dialogue with some people. They're just not my preference," said Christopher. "If you'll excuse me, Art, I'd like to return to my prayers. Please consider what I said about your approach."

Walking back to his truck, Art stood and pondered. He seemed perplexed by Christopher's demeanor. It wasn't very often that Art met someone he couldn't dominate, exasperate, or bully. Feeling frustrated and uncomfortable following the exchange, he removed his costume, deflated the doll, and sat in his cab. After watching Christopher and Amy pray while Cindy handed a few clients fetal development brochures, Art drove off and passed out of sight. Slowly, but surely, the Catholics came across the street and formed a prayer chain that moved back and forth along the sidewalk in quiet intercession.

A collective breath went up from the counselors as the mid-morning sun began to warm the parking lot. Returning to the day's true mission, the counselors and intercessors readied themselves for another important day. As client after client poured in, the atmosphere was even colder than usual. Several cars passed on Thirteenth honking their horns repeatedly with their outstretched middle fingers held high in the air. Most of the men and women seeking abortion quickly passed the counselors and disappeared. Those who did take their time entering the clinic mostly responded to the offers of help with profanity and anger. This was shaping up to be another rough Friday, and Christopher began to feel fatigued. Looking at his cell phone, he realized he'd been on the sidewalk for over two hours. Beginning to feel relief that he'd finished his morning time commitment, Christopher contemplated leaving the dreadful, depressing clinic. Looking at his Bible once more, he noticed two highlighted verses in Ecclesiastes that read, "*Whoever watches the wind will not plant; whoever looks at the clouds will not reap. As you do not know the path of the wind, or how the body is formed in a mother's womb, so you cannot understand the work of God, the Maker of all things.*" Feeling the rebuke, he regained his courage, uttered a prayer, and continued to press forward.

An hour later, as Christopher was searching for a particular Scripture that eluded him, a car pulled to the curb and rolled down their passenger window. Hearing the wheels pop on the pavement, he turned around and noticed the driver motion for him to come over. Leaning his head through the window, Christopher said, "Can I help you, ma'am?"

"I was driving by, and I felt the need to come and thank you for what you are doing. A little less than a year ago, I came here for an abortion, and two of the nicest ladies gave me some literature and offered to help me with my pregnancy. I thanked them and went inside, but after looking at the materials, I came back outside and left. A couple of days later, I contacted the local pregnancy resource center using the number they provided me with, and after receiving their assistance chose to continue my pregnancy."

"God bless you, ma'am. That is such an encouragement to me."

"Would you like to see my baby?"

"I'd be honored," said Christopher.

Rolling down her back window, the woman said, "Take a look."

Christopher peered around the rear-facing car seat and beheld a beautiful baby girl. Her skin glowed with the perfection of newness, and her eyes were bright and clear. Her lips glistened in the sun, and Christopher thought for a moment he'd seen her smile. Caught up in the euphoria, he yelled to the others still on the sidewalk, "Guys, come over here and look at this beautiful baby God rescued." Realizing he'd forgotten to ask for permission, he said, "Sorry, ma'am, is it okay if my friends have a look?"

"Certainly, I'm in no hurry," said the woman.

Cindy and several others piled around the car, gazing in wonder at what God had done. Each person enjoyed the moment—gawking and playing with the little bundle. Smiles spread like wildfire among the counselors and intercessors as each felt their disillusionment and fatigue abate. It was the highlight of the year, and everybody present knew it. As the crowd gathered, Christopher sat on a rock by the curb watching with particular delight. In the fervor of the moment, he lifted his eyes to heaven and offered a prayer of thanksgiving.

chapter 16

Trepidation

Perspiring under the oppression of the July sun and soaking up whatever heat the blacktop hadn't swallowed, Jay was miserable. It must be getting close to triple digits, he thought. He felt himself become weary as he stared at the approaching clients and prayer chain that moved forward and back like a conveyer belt. When he accepted the job as security for Rose and Taugney, he assumed it would be an easy assignment, but he never factored in the boredom or the mental strain of seeing the two sides of the conflict up close and personal. He told himself that it was early and that he could adjust and endure, but he already didn't like his job. Several feet to his left, Amy stood praying in a strange tongue as the occasional tear rolled across her pleading face. Breaking into English, she cried, "Father forgive us, we know not what we do! Forgive Tom Rose and Jim Taugney and those who work for them as they guide their clients in the destruction of Your children. Lord, speak to the hearts of the moms and dads about the precious life they have been entrusted." Returning to her tongue and then silence, Amy continued to pray. Across the lot, in unison, the Catholics were saying the Rosary. Cindy tried to hand a nervous young couple a brochure as Jay motioned them to his side, quickly ushering them inside the clinic.

Returning to his post, Jay discovered that Christopher had arrived. Standing near the driveway, Christopher began to read from Scripture: "*Woe to him who quarrels with his Maker, to him who is but a potsherd among the potsherds on the ground. Does the clay say to the potter, 'What are you making?' Does your work say, 'He has no hands?' Woe to him who says to his father, 'What have you begotten?' or to his mother, 'What have you brought to birth?' This is what the Lord says—the Holy One of Israel, and its Maker: Concerning things to come, do you question me about my children, or give me orders about the work of my hands? It is I who made the earth and created mankind upon it.*" Trying to ignore the words, Jay fumbled with his hat and glasses—but to no avail. The words were clear and cutting, and no amount of distraction could remove the sovereignty of God or the power of His words. As Christopher continued to read his Bible, Jay attempted to halt the words. "Morning, Chris, I thought you might not show up today as late as it's getting."

"Morning, Jay," greeted Christopher. "Pretty hot today, isn't it?"

"You can say that again. I can think of a lot of places I'd rather be," said Jay.

"There are a lot better places to be," responded Christopher.

"Well, I got to be here, but you don't. Why do you come here? Why do you guys want to meddle in other people's choices?"

"It's precisely because of choice that I'm here, Jay. I choose to come and speak for those who are given no choice," rebutted Christopher.

"Come on, Chris, you know a man's got no right to tell a woman what she can and can't do with her body."

"That might be true if it were only her body, Jay. But

that's the problem—there's always more than one body involved in a pregnancy. The developing baby has its own genetic code, gender, blood type, circulatory system, and organs. To be fair, Jay, three bodies are involved in a pregnancy: the father's, the mother's, and the newly created baby's."

"We're not talking about fully developed babies. These embryos aren't even viable," challenged Jay.

"Nothing is viable if you remove it from its natural environment and protection. If I take a fish out of water, it dies. If people leave a newborn baby girl alone and exposed to the elements, she, too, will eventually die. I guarantee all of these babies are viable if we'll just leave them in the womb where they belong!"

Looking out his office window, Tom shook his head and prepared for a mildly busy Thursday. He was weary from work and this new prayer presence out front. Hearing a knock on the door, he stepped back from the window and said, "Come in."

"Tom, Laura and Hansa are prepped and ready," said Gwynn.

"Come look at these fools," invited Tom.

"Won't they see us?" asked Gwynn.

"Not with the new tempered bulletproof glass we had installed after the death threats," Tom said confidently. "I'm glad I'm not Jay, having to deal with those nut jobs every day!"

"No kidding. At least he found himself some shade," said Gwynn.

"I doubt it's helping; it's brutally hot."

"For sure!"

"Double check recovery for me, will you, Gwynn? I'm going to peek at the girls' files, and I'll be right out," instructed Tom.

Leaving the office briskly, Gwynn knocked into Sally who was passing by with her arms full of the morning mail. In the collision, envelopes spilled everywhere and expletives flew as Tom rushed to the scene. Recoiling, Gwynn said, "Oh, my God, Sally. Are you okay? I'm so sorry."

Looking up from the floor, Sally spouted, "Geez, Gwynn. Blow the whistle next time you're coming!"

The girls looked at each other for a moment and then burst into laughter. Tom reached down and helped Sally to her feet, while Gwynn began gathering the mail. Making sure Sally was okay, Tom noticed an envelope that had made its way into his office and retrieved it. Handing it to Sally, the three of them began to scan the floor for more items. With the mail gathered and corralled, they had one last chuckle and parted ways.

Sally entered the reception area and set the jumbled stack of mail on the counter. Rubbing her shoulder, she felt a strange sensitivity and began to feel some stiffness in her neck. Stretching, she gazed out on the lobby of waiting women and a few men. She'd never really noticed before, but none of the people were smiling. They all seemed apprehensive, conflicted, or numb. Are we really helping people here? As quickly as the thought came, she suppressed it and returned to her tasks at hand. Reaching for her coffee cup, Sally noticed it was empty. Begrudgingly, she departed for the break room.

Tom and Gwynn were in the middle of Hansa's procedure to terminate her nine-week-old fetus. Normally, Hansa had the most striking brown eyes. Eyes that drew you in and let you know there was an intelligent, strong, beautiful woman behind the veil. Today they held forth only fear and shame. Hansa did not utter a word or make a sound during the abortion, but you could see it all in her deep brown eyes. Finishing the procedure, Tom congratulated Hansa on what a great job she did and how proud he was of her. She did not respond. As Gwynn escorted Hansa to the recovery room, a tear spread out over her cheek—a tear she didn't bother to wipe.

Gwynn, exiting recovery, noticed Sally leaving the break room. "Sally, would you inform Sabrina that we're ready to see her now?"

"Will do," said Sally.

"How's your neck?" asked Gwynn.

"I'll be fine."

"You are fine, girl!" teased Gwynn.

"I'm an amazing woman, no?" Sally self-deprecated.

Returning to her desk with a smile on her face, Sally set down her coffee and leaned over the counter. Peering into the lobby, she announced to Sabrina that they were ready for her. She was surprised upon opening the door to see just how small, short, and tiny Sabrina was. Looking at her closely, as if for the first time, she could see she was a girl of no more than fourteen. Concerned, Sally asked the young girl if she was with someone, and she pointed to a gruff-looking man in the corner. His eyes were shielded from view by his baseball cap, but he looked menacing and fierce.

"Okay, sweetie, let's head on back," Sally said, trying to sound undisturbed. Waiting until they were out of sight and the door was fully closed, Sally asked, "Sabrina, is this abortion something you want?"

The young girl didn't make eye contact and failed to respond. Finding Gwynn in room two, Sally instructed Sabrina to sit on the table. Gaining Gwynn's attention, Sally asked her to step out into the hallway.

"Gwynn, look how young she is. I'm not so sure she wants to be here or that everything is on the up-and-up."

"I've learned it's better not to ask. It's none of our business anyway," said Gwynn without emotion. "Go on back to your desk. I'll handle it from here."

Disturbed, Sally slowly walked back to the front desk, pausing once to look over her shoulder at the closed door of room two. The girl was so young, but what could she do? Her job was simple and straightforward. She was paid to look good, be friendly, encourage clients, file paperwork, make coffee, clean the lobby, call the women back when scheduled, and tend to the mail. The mail! She'd completely forgotten about it. She needed to get things squared away for the evening deposit, especially since tomorrow was payday. Hurrying to her desk, Sally gathered up the scrambled envelopes and began to sort them. They looked like a deck of freshly shuffled cards that had been attacked by a child. Falling from the pile, Sally noticed an envelope that looked like a medical supply reimbursement check lying face down at her feet. Turning it over, she saw the word "urgent" stamped on the front and in the clear window the typed names Rose & Taugney, 1206 13th St., Eastbrook. Opening wide a pair of scissors and using a single blade, Sally slit open the envelope. As she pried open the letter, a fine white dust emanated from the opening and lifted in the air. Startled, Sally jumped to her feet, dropping the envelope. Glancing off her pants and crashing to the floor, the letter released its full contents. The fierce impact quickly formed the tiny particles of dust into puffy clouds about her feet. Frozen briefly in horror, Sally paused and then panicked!

With Sally's terrified screams all normality stopped. Everyone in the building flew into action or panic. Gwynn grabbed Sabrina and dove behind the medical table in room two. Dr. Taugney locked his door and cowered behind his desk. Several people spilled out of the waiting room into the parking lot, seeking refuge in their cars or running down the street. Jay instinctively turned and ran toward the entrance. Removing his conceal and carry, he cautiously opened the door and looked about. Tammy dove under her desk and dialed 911 from her cell phone. It was pure pandemonium as Tom ran down the hallway toward Sally. Turning the corner, Tom found her frozen and in shock. His eyes stared intently as the powder swirled in the air. Noticing Jay enter the lobby, Tom directed, "Call 911. It's a possible anthrax attack!"

"Roger," said Jay. "I'll secure the perimeter and make sure the patients are safe."

"Sally, listen to me. We need to get that substance off of you as soon as possible." Grabbing a patient's robe, Tom guided, "I need you to back up slowly and strip down to your underwear."

"Okay," Sally said unconsciously.

Scared and vulnerable, Sally did as she was told and walked with Tom back to room one, where he proceeded to clean her skin with antibacterial surgical soap. Sally was shaking like a leaf during Tom's frantic attempt to scrub every inch of her skin. In the meantime, Jay had managed to evacuate the building and secure the premises. Everyone on staff was rattled and dazed as they stood in the heat under the tall shade trees that lined Almond Street.

Christopher, Amy, Cindy, and the other sidewalk counselors had managed to assist all the fleeing clinic patrons who would accept their help. A small group led by Amy Dover was huddled on the corner praying for the Lord's intervention and the safety of everyone at the clinic. The counselors had come prepared for the hot day and had plenty of bottled water on hand, which they distributed to the nervous clients and the staff of

Rose & Taugney. In the pandemonium as they waited for the paramedics, police, and hazmat team to arrive, people reached out to each other. These two opposing sides blended together and helped each other get past the fear and shock of the morning's attack.

After Sally and Tom had been taken by ambulance to the hospital, the hazmat team commenced a thorough investigation. The police questioned everyone on the scene, both those who had gathered on the sidewalk to pray and those who had been inside the clinic. In short order, the whole thing was determined to be a hoax. The powder was nothing more than an ultrafine grind of dry dish soap and powdered sugar. Pissed and sweating, Taugney re-entered the clinic and demanded to see the note inside the envelope. The investigating officers promptly informed Dr. Taugney about the rules of evidence and asked him politely to step outside. Looking at the pile of Sally's clothes, anger took hold of Jim like a fever. Kicking over the nearest trash can, he flew into a rage, cursing all the way to his car. Driving past Christopher and the other intercessors, Jim rolled down his window and screamed, "You people are responsible for this madness! You think about that, Christopher!" Peeling out, Dr. Taugney gave the group a one-fingered salute and sped off.

Frustrated and saddened by the day's events, Christopher gathered the group of counselors and prayed, "Lord Jesus, forgive the person, or people, who through their frustrations and anger turned to terror instead of help, condemnation instead of grace, and hate instead of love. Father, watch over Tom and Sally and everyone who was inside the clinic today. Shower them with Your grace and mercy and use this terrible event for good—calm their fears and help them see acts of terror and the people who perpetrate them for who and what they are,

hushed

especially the terror that is inflicted on hundreds of little babies here at this clinic. Jesus, grant us favor, grace, and peace moving forward after this cowardly act. Amen."

chapter 17

Not My Will, but Yours

"I'm sorry, Mr. Jacobs, I don't know why I took the money," said Sasha, looking at the floor.

"Sasha, if you need money for something, all you have to do is ask, and we'll discuss it," assured Lucas. "However, I am going to ask that you work off the forty dollars next week at the sporting goods store."

"Okay, Mr. Jacobs."

"I'll pay you eight dollars an hour, sound fair?"

"Yes, sir."

"Good," said Lucas. "Tell me when you want to work next week, and I'll plug you into the schedule."

"Sir?" said Sasha.

"Yes."

"Why would you and your family want to help a person like me?"

"Because you need it, and because God's given us the ability to," replied Lucas.

"Did you know I got pregnant trading sex for drugs? I don't even know who the father is," confided Sasha. "I'm a mess, Mr. Jacobs."

"You think God doesn't know how you conceived, Sasha? He's the One who gave you this child," said Lucas. "He's not so much concerned with who you used to be, but with who you're going to become."

"Sir?"

"Pull up a chair, Sasha, I want to read you some verses and share with you a Bible story."

Sasha sat down at the kitchen table and stared at the beautiful flower arrangement that sat neatly by the wooden napkin holder and the salt and pepper shaker. She marveled at the peace and prosperity of the Jacobs family. They were like no one she had ever known. There was joy in their home and decency. They all helped each other, and nobody acted superior or entitled. They rarely spoke out of anger or used profanity. They were other-worldly. Returning from a trip to retrieve his Bible, Lucas laid it down next to Sasha and said, "Would you like a cup of tea or some coffee?"

"Tea sounds good," replied Sasha.

"Tea it is," said Lucas. "We have Earl Grey, Sleepytime, gingerbread spice, or peppermint."

"Whatever you want is fine," said Sasha.

"I'm partial to peppermint. Is that okay?"

"Sure."

As Lucas prepared the tea, Sasha wondered how she'd even arrived at this moment in time. After a year of sexual recklessness, living on the streets, and taking shelter in two drug houses, how had she made her way to the comforts of this middle-class family? Why had she stopped to talk with Christopher on the day of her appointment? How had he convinced her that she and her baby still had some self-worth? Somehow, his kindness gave her hope that day. She didn't know how or why she was here with Lucas, but she was glad she was.

"I thought you might like a slice of cheesecake to go with your tea," Lucas offered.

"Thank you."

"You're welcome," Lucas said with a smile. "Do you mind if we say a quick prayer before we look at the Bible?"

"No, I guess not," said Sasha.

"Father, open our eyes and our ears to what You are about to teach us from Your Word. Let it stimulate our minds, improve our character, and nourish our souls. We ask this in the mighty name of Jesus. Amen. Have you ever read the Bible before, Sasha?"

"Not much, and not for a long time," Sasha confessed.

"That's all right, sometimes it's best when it's fresh."

Opening to the Book of Psalms, Lucas read a portion of Psalm 139 to Sasha. As he read the Bible out loud, he could feel Sasha lean forward as she contemplated the words. Being four months pregnant, her body was just now showing subtle hints of the life inside. Placing her hands over her abdomen, she listened as the words of King David emanated from Lucas's lips: "*For you formed my inward parts; you knitted me together in my mother's womb. I praise you, for I am fearfully and wonderfully made...*" Sasha was struck by the poetry of the verse and the revelation that God indeed creates and forms every life in the womb. She had never really thought about life being from God—that He intentionally and purposefully created her. Still, she thought, how could God care for me? What did He know of her pain, disappointment, and struggles? Turning back a few pages, Lucas read from Psalm 127: "*Behold, children are a heritage from the Lord, the fruit of the womb a reward.*" This child didn't feel like a reward, more like a burden or a reproach, thought Sasha. How could God reward her? Why would God give her a gift in the midst of her sin and depravity?

"You see, Sasha? God sent you this child to bless you. It was within His will to allow you to conceive," Lucas instructed.

"Why? Why would God send a child to me? What hope is there for this child, for me?" asked Sasha. "After all I've done, why would He choose me?"

Looking intently into Sasha's eyes, Lucas said, "God is good, and He always has a plan for the good of all. He doesn't always give us what we want or even what we think we're ready for, but He always gives us good things. And children are one of His greatest gifts to us. In the midst of deep darkness and despair, God is working for our good—walking with us, leading us, giving us things we can't always see or understand initially. But over time He builds our character and forges in us endurance, hope, and joy."

"You think something good is going to come of this?"

"I certainly do!" assured Lucas. "Let me read you the Bible story I mentioned earlier to illustrate the point."

Leafing through the pages of his Bible, Lucas gave Sasha a breather and asked her how her cheesecake was and if she needed a warming for her tea. When she graciously declined, he took a bite of the moist cheesecake, swallowed, sipped his tea, and proceeded to read from the first chapter of Luke the story of Mary and her miraculous conception. Laying down his Bible, Lucas looked up at Sasha and said, "Mary was an unmarried, pregnant teenager in a culture that highly valued purity and virginity. She made the courageous choice to trust God, facing stigmatism, the unknown experience of pregnancy, and the potential rejection of her betrothed. She chose to trust in God's plan. In time, God rewarded Mary's faithfulness by blessing her with a happy marriage to her fiancé, respect among her peers and those that would come after her, and the privilege of raising God's very own Son, the Savior of the world."

"But I'm no virgin," blurted Sasha. "And I don't believe God's ever chosen me for anything!"

"He's chosen you to be a mother," Lucas rebutted. "While you and Mary conceived under different circumstances, you both made the choice to put God's plans ahead of your own, and that takes courage and faith. Sasha, sex is an act of our own will, unless there is abuse involved. But conception is always an act of God's. Think of all the times you've engaged in similar behavior but didn't get pregnant."

"I guess I never thought of it that way," said Sasha. "Still, I don't see how God can bring good out of bad. Mary was good and so was her baby, but I'm not good."

"Sasha, only God is truly good," informed Lucas. Smiling, he continued, "The Word of God tells us that we've all sinned and made mistakes. I've rebelled against God many times. But I know He's forgiven me and He will also forgive you. The Bible assures us that God came into our world and shared in our humanity and trials so He could help us, ultimately dying for our sins before we even understood we needed forgiveness or asked for it. God can bring good out of anything."

"You really believe that, Mr. Jacobs?"

"Yes, I do!" Looking at Sasha, Lucas felt the depth of her need and seized his opportunity. Without hesitating, he said, "Do you mind if I share with you the mission of Mary's Son, Jesus?"

"No, I don't mind," said Sasha.

Thumbing through his Bible, Lucas found the spot in Luke he was looking for and began to read: *"The Spirit of the Lord is upon me, because he has anointed me to proclaim good news to the poor. He has sent me to proclaim liberty to the captives and recovering of sight to the blind, to set at liberty those who are oppressed, to proclaim the year of the Lord's favor."* Lucas explained to Sasha that this was the mission statement of God's Son foretold hundreds of years before His coming—that Jesus came to seek and save that which was lost. Lucas went on to share that Jesus had come to earth from heaven for those people who had lost their way and made regrettable choices. He came to redeem and restore those who were and are broken.

"Perhaps your baby is the path to your redemption," Lucas said. "It's no accident that God has brought you here under our roof. He knows the plans He has for you and your baby."

"What plans, Mr. Jacobs? I can only see heartache and struggle for me and my child. Even adoption seems cruel and empty," retorted Sasha.

"Thousands of years ago God promised the Israelites release from those who had enslaved them, and this is what He said: 'For I know the plans I have for you, declares the Lord, plans for welfare and not for evil, to give you a future and a hope.' Your baby represents the future and brings hope, Sasha. Look at my daughter, Rachelle, and her little Jaleesa. God has done great things for them despite their struggles and the burdens of single parenting. It may not seem like it today or tomorrow, but God works out all things for good if we trust Him."

"I'm not like Rachelle, sir. She's so put together, so mature, so good."

"Yes you are—you just don't know it yet." encouraged Lucas. "No matter how dark our beginning, God can see to it that we finish in the light with victory and joy. Listen to these words of Paul, a great follower of Jesus Christ. Before Paul encountered Jesus, he persecuted God's followers through abuse, imprisonment, and murder, but afterward he did many wonderful things. He became one of the greatest believers in Christ and helped an entire region of people discover the freeing grace of Jesus." Finding the Book of First Timothy, Lucas read: "*'Christ Jesus came into the world to save sinners, of whom I am the foremost. But I received mercy for this reason, that in me, as the foremost, Jesus Christ might display his perfect patience as an example to those who were to believe in him for eternal life.'* Sasha, you can have a new life in Christ just like Paul. You were created by God, and the One who made you is calling out to you to believe in Him, to taste His promises, and to begin fresh with Him from this point forward. You can start over, Sasha. It's never too late."

"If this God of yours is real, I want to know Him," said Sasha. "But it's hard to believe He could love a low life like me."

"You're not a low life, Sasha. Your life has infinite value. The great thing about Jesus is that He loves us just as we are—right where we're at, and then He changes us into something better, something beautiful. May I read you one last story?"

"Okay."

"This is one of my all-time favorite passages from Scripture," Lucas beamed. "It's a great portrait of Jesus' love for the guilty and the broken." Turning to the Gospel of John, Lucas began to read: "*'The scribes and the Pharisees brought a woman who had been caught in adultery, and placing her in the midst they said to him, 'Teacher, this woman has been caught in the act of adultery. Now in the Law Moses commanded us to stone such women. So what do you say?' This they said to test him, that they might have some charge to bring against him. Jesus bent down and wrote with his finger on the ground. And as they continued to ask him, he stood up and said to them, 'Let him who is without sin among you be the first to throw a stone at her.' And once more he bent down and wrote on the ground. But when they heard it, they went away one by one, beginning with the older ones, and Jesus was left alone with the woman standing before him. Jesus stood up and said to her, 'Woman, where are they? Has no one condemned you?' She said, 'No one, Lord.' And Jesus said, 'Neither do I condemn you; go, and from now on sin no more.' Again Jesus spoke to them, saying, 'I am the light of the world. Whoever follows me will not walk in darkness, but will have the light of life.'* Do you believe that, Sasha? Do you believe Jesus is the Light of the world?"

"I want to," Sasha said with a tear in her eye. "It just so hard to accept that I could be loved like that after all the things I've done."

"You are loved, Sasha. Jesus' love is dependable. He doesn't change," affirmed Lucas. "Would you mind if I prayed and asked God to give you a sense of His love, to let you experience Him in a personal way?"

"I'd appreciate that," said Sasha.

chapter 18

Compassion

Sally gingerly pulled into the parking lot at the clinic. A month had passed since she had last worked, and a nervous fear began to creep up her spine as she turned off the engine. She knew the anthrax incident was just a cruel prank, but she couldn't shake the memory of her all-too-real fear and anxiety. Unable to move and trancelike, Sally began to shudder. Closing her eyes, she wrestled to gain control and relax. Slowly feeling the moment pass, she opened her eyes to the sight of Amy Dover standing before her car with a bouquet of flowers. Immediately looking away from Amy's gaze, Sally felt overwhelmed. Why her? Why won't these people leave me alone? Quickly grabbing her keys and her purse, she abandoned the car and walked briskly toward the front door of the clinic. On her way, she heard Amy call out, "These flowers are for you, Sally. We want you to know how sorry we are about the harm that was done..." Slamming the door behind her, Sally disappeared. Jay shouted something coarse at Amy and followed Sally into the clinic. Entering the lobby, he saw Gwynn standing behind Sally with her hand on her shoulder comforting her. Burying her face in her hands, Sally wept.

With anger welling up inside him, Jay stormed out of the building and yelled at the counselors, "What the hell is wrong with you people? Can't you show some decency and compassion?"

Meeting his flashing eyes, Amy said, "That's what we're trying to do every day, but especially today on Sally's first day back."

"Then why is she inside crying, Amy?"

"I'm so sorry, Jay. We're all sick that this happened to you and your coworkers."

"You're not sick about this," Jay said sternly. "This is what you and your people do—terrorize others! Why do you think Tom and Jim hired me?"

"I'm sorry you feel that way, Jay, but you know that's not how I and the others who regularly come to the sidewalk to pray and offer alternatives behave. We condemn what happened here as much as you do."

"Well, maybe you wouldn't do such a thing, but your side did!"

"And what side would that be, Jay?"

"Pro-life, right-wing, conservative religious zealots!" blurted Jay.

"Again, Jay, I'm sorry this happened to you and Sally and the others, but the only side I'm on is that of humanity and Jesus Christ. Out of respect for Sally and our sorrow over this cruel act, we're going to leave early today. Would you give these flowers and this card to her?"

"No."

"Come on, Jay. It's the right thing to do."

"No. She doesn't want anything from you."

"May I leave them on or near her car?" Amy persisted.

"Fine. I'll give them to her, but you must open up the envelope and show me the contents first."

"Certainly," Amy said, pulling open the envelope and slipping out the card. Satisfied, Jay took the items and said, "I don't know if she'll accept them, but I'll offer them to her before she leaves."

"Thank you, Jay. We're so sorry this happened to you all. God bless, and have a good rest of your day."

As Amy and the other counselors walked away, Jay looked at the flowers and wondered how someone as nice as Amy could be caught up in a movement that hated women and interfered with their choices. Looking closer at the card, he noticed it was homemade with a hand-drawn rose on the front. The artistic detail and subtlety of the drawing were beautiful and worthy of admiration. Opening the card revealed a Scripture written in the most striking calligraphy that read, "*Because of the Lord's great love we are not consumed, for his compassions never fail.... Though he brings grief, he will show compassion, so great is his unfailing love. For he does not willingly bring affliction or grief to the children of men.*" Across from the Scripture, the salutation was addressed to Sally, Tom, and staff. Out of curiosity and caution, Jay read the handwritten note before him:

We are deeply saddened by this calloused and brutal attack. No one should have to suffer such an expression of hatred! As those who stand for the rights of all human beings, born and preborn, we feel acutely the violation of your rights and security during this cowardly act. Our thoughts and prayers go out to you and yours, and we share with you the hope that those responsible for this act of terror and intimidation will be brought to justice. Please accept our most heartfelt sorrow during this difficult time, and know that if there is anything we can do to help you in the process of recovery, healing, or justice, we'd be glad to help.

Sincerely, —

hushed

Looking at the close of the note, Jay was touched by the handwritten signatures of Amy Dover, Christopher Thompson, Cindy Taylor, and over thirty others who regularly visited the sidewalk to pray. Gazing up at a single car that entered the lot, Jay felt alone and empty. What was it about these people who came to pray? Why did they faithfully come week after week to the public edge of Rose & Taugney?

chapter 19

To Serve and Protect

Snow crunched under Joe Tyndale's boots as he walked through the heavy forest. His breath unfurled before him like a scroll upon the winter landscape. Today's hike had taken a toll. Walking over the rough, frozen ground, his eyes intently scanned the wilderness. Watching the sun drop lower in the sky, Joe could feel his fatigue to the very bone. Fifty feet ahead, his dog, Wallace, sniffed and bounded through the freshly fallen snow, decomposing vegetation, and jutting rocks. It had been a long hike, and Joe's back ached from the unevenness of the terrain. Sitting down to rest and drink some water, he noticed he had been in this part of the forest before. It must have been a month ago, he thought. It all looks the same, and then it doesn't. Getting out his map to orient himself and mark off his progress, he heard the sound of crackling and crunching approaching from over his shoulder.

"Ethan, is that you?"

"Yeah, Dad. It's me."

"Find anything in that fallen timber back there?"

"No. It looks like it hasn't been disturbed in ages," said Ethan.

"Well, are you ready to knock off for the day and go home?" asked Joe.

"I suppose. It's getting bitter cold, and we've been at it for hours."

"I'm beat. Let's go home, get warm, and have a cup of hot brew."

"Sounds good, Dad," agreed Ethan. "Wallace! Wally! Come on, boy. We need to go."

Walking steadily out of the forest, father and son talked about the hunting season and bygone days. There was laughter and silence, soreness and serenity, slipping and sliding, and the enjoyment of a relationship forged in common blood and history. Ethan looked up to his dad, and it meant the world to Joe to have his son by his side, especially now that he had completed detective school and had joined the force in Eastbrook.

Ethan was only fourteen years old when Jenny Foster became the first girl abducted by the now notorious BQB. In all, seven other girls had shared her fate and fallen victim to the brutal rapist over the past seventeen years. With only six of the eight still alive and very few leads or pieces of good evidence, the cases had become an embarrassment to the department and a recurring source of fear for the people of Eastbrook—a fear that waned in between attacks and then resurfaced with abandon whenever a new girl was found. After a five-year period when no attacks occurred following the death of Kieu Lang, the people of Eastbrook had all but forgotten. But with an attack about every two years now, and the recent attacks on Rana Nadira and Tiffany Thompson, those fears had surfaced again in earnest. His father's dedication to the case and his years of service in law enforcement were the primary reasons Ethan became a detective. Joe's resolve and integrity had made an impression. Even though his father was highway patrol and had no direct involvement in or departmental clearance for the case, he had picked up two of the girls on Route 122. Witnessing firsthand how these beautiful girls had been tortured, he made up his mind—he wasn't going to pick up a third. Joe believed the rapist was committing his crimes somewhere in the hills, forests, and mountains that ran along Route 122, a theory he formed after he stumbled upon the BQB's third victim lying naked beside mile marker fifty-five just off the highway. Later, his encounter with Belia Lopez confirmed his suspicions. For Joe, there was no longer any doubt as to the region where the rapes occurred. He'd spent many years patrolling this lonely stretch of road, and he was convinced it was the perfect spot to come and go unnoticed. Over the past ten years, mostly alone until recently, Joe had been spending half of his weekends hiking the woods, hills, trails, and mountains on both sides of 122, hoping to find the sadist's lair, or him, or evidence that would lead to his apprehension. Using topographical maps and a grid-like approach, Joe had searched over eight hundred square miles in his pursuit of justice.

Reaching the SUV exhausted and cold, the two men unloaded their gear, put Wally in the back, and drove down the winding four-wheel road to 122. It was a cold day in mid-November, 2007. The air had become painful amid the frosted evergreens and bare aspens. The fading sky showed forth its last glimmer of light and hope as they walked out of the forest. Rolling over endless miles of white stripes, father and son sat in silence and pondered during their journey home.

Arriving at the house, Ethan transferred his gear from his father's car to his as the brisk night air reintroduced itself. Making haste he finished before the night chill reached his bones. Quickly ascending the steps in front of his boyhood home, Ethan gladly accepted a cup of hot coffee from his father and followed him to the family room. Taking a seat by the glow of the fire, Ethan asked, "What is it we're missing, Dad? Do you think we're wrong…that maybe he isn't local?"

"No, he lives here; he's in the state, more than likely

in Eastbrook. Half of the victims were from here, including the first, second, and sixth, and all were residing in the state," said Joe.

"The state and local police have spent a great deal of time since late '90 looking in the mountains and along the major interstates and trucking routes. They even spent several months after the first several attacks looking where we've been looking, Pop."

"He's here, Ethan," Joe affirmed. "What have the boys in your division come up with recently?"

"Nothing new. The girls' collective testimony is one of dizziness, disorientation, and repeated drugging. What little we've corroborated has been of almost no use to us. The girls remember a cold earthen structure, the smell of pine, a large white male, smells of an antiseptic solution, repeated rape and beating followed by thorough body cleaning, an aggressive vaginal rinse, the removal of all body hair, and being placed in a strange breathable bag for hours or days before waking up near a highway. Curiously, the girls have given several different testimonies in regard to his eye color. We think he's using color contacts. We haven't found any shoe or boot prints since the first case. The knife and rechargeable razor he's using haven't been found, and the most likely matches judging from the marks on the victims can be purchased anywhere, by millions. It's like he's a ghost, Dad. He always strikes at night or before bad weather, which works wonders to cover his tracks. The perp seems to have no priors. We can't find a DNA match with any of our collected fluids, of which we have precious little. He's psychotic and smart. We have no witnesses, no vehicle description, and no pattern, except the beauty of the victims."

"What do the girls have in common, besides looks?" asked Joe.

"Nothing that's obvious. They're all different ages,

socio-economic classes, and various races. Two were in high school, two in college, one a drop-out, three worked—all at different jobs. None of the victims knew each other. They all lived in different parts of the city or state."

"Did any of them attend the same school?"

"No, not to my knowledge, but I'm new to the team. I'll double check with Michaels this week," said Ethan.

"That sounds good, Son," said Joe rising as he went into the kitchen. "For now, we'll just have to keep praying and searching, something is bound to show up."

"Thanks for the coffee, Dad," Ethan said as he walked toward the front door. "I'll see you and Mom at church tomorrow."

"Sounds good. Get a good night's rest."

"You, too, Dad," Ethan said leaving the house.

Watching his son drive away and slip into the dark, Joe couldn't wrestle his mind away from the case and the unimaginable trauma these eight young women had been subjected to. He felt helpless and tired, and he wondered why it was so hard to halt evil. Exhausted and angry, he reached for a whiskey glass and began to pour some bourbon over ice—anything to help him sleep and deaden the pain. Slowly lifting the glass to his lips, Joe noticed the light refract off the glass and spill onto his leather Bible. Pausing, he chuckled to himself and mumbled under his breath. Making his way to the kitchen sink, Joe poured the liquor down the drain and returned to his Bible. Picking it up, he entered the family room and sat down by the dying fire.

Clicking on an end-table lamp, he opened his Bible near the middle, to the Book of Psalms. Perusing the pages in front of him, his eyes focused on Psalm 62. Joe began to read aloud:

"For God alone, O my soul, wait in silence, for my hope

is from him. He only is my rock and my salvation, my fortress; I shall not be shaken. On God rests my salvation and my glory; my mighty rock, my refuge is God. Trust in him at all times, O people; pour out your heart before him; God is a refuge for us."

Folding his hands, Joe prayed, "Forgive me of my sins, Jesus. Help me trust in You, Lord. Be my provision and my source. Thank you for reminding me that I don't need alcohol or distractions when I'm troubled. I only need You. Lord Jesus, guide me through Your Holy Spirit and honor my work. Help me and my fellow officers catch this man before he harms any more of Your people. Don't let any more of Your precious daughters suffer at his hands. Give us the victory over our enemies, Lord, and show us the path to apprehension. Speak to me, Lord! Thank you, Father, for Your loving Son. It's in His name I pray. Amen."

Turning out the light, Joe sat in silence, while the glowing embers flickered and faded to black. As the last ember died, he rose in the void and walked upstairs. Undressing, Joe stared out his bedroom window at the beauty of the night sky. The splendor of God's handiwork continually speaks of His majesty and presence, he thought. Walking to the bathroom sink, he brushed his teeth, sipped some water, and turned out the light.

The morning sunlight cascaded through the blinds, illuminating the dust like gently falling stars. Descending, the glowing specks melted into a dozen streams of light, shimmering like rippling water across the floor. There by the bed in the beams of light lay Joe's journal. It was perched awkwardly under his bedside chair with a pen marking the place it had last been opened. Rolling in bed to avoid the glare, Joe squinted hard and rubbed his throbbing head. Groggy and heavy from a rough night of tossing and turning as he went in and out of awareness,

Joe struggled to gain focus. Reaching, he discovered Maggie was already up. Feeling the physical impact of the day before, he proceeded to the shower and hope. It was there, standing under the water, that he vaguely remembered a dream.

Hurriedly, he toweled off, dressed, and began in earnest to locate his journal. Checking the nightstand, the bookshelf, his chest of drawers, and the edges of the cushion in his chair, Joe couldn't find it. Puzzled and exasperated, he returned to his search in earnest. Lying on the floor and peering under the bed, all he could see was a rifle case, a baby gate they used for the grandkids, a pair of socks, and an empty aspirin bottle. Moving around for a better look, he found it underneath the chair behind a polished maple leg and a throw pillow.

Opening up his journal to the pen place-keeper, Joe noticed the numbers 10, 8, 14 and the words "psalm, school, arrogance, dark, pictures, antique desk, and basement." As he struggled to recall the dream, he felt certain that this was a cryptic message from God about the elusive rapist, but nothing seemed to connect. Think, Joe, think! Joe stared at the words with purpose, but he could not conjure the dream. Deciding he needed a change of pace, he walked downstairs, greeted Maggie with a kiss, and poured a hot cup of coffee.

"Did I say anything to you about a dream I had last night?" asked Joe.

"No, you haven't had dreams in a long time, but you sure were rambunctious in the night," answered Maggie.

"I know. I think the Lord may be speaking to me again in my sleep."

"You and Ethan were up late. Did you have a rough outing?"

"It was cold, but nothing out of the ordinary," said

Joe. "I wrote down some scrambled numbers and several words in my journal last night, but I can't decipher any of it or recall the dream."

"What are they?" inquired Maggie.

"The numbers are 10, 8, 14, and then the random words 'school, pictures, basement, antique desk, psalm, dark, arrogant.'"

"Have you been looking at pictures lately of school desks or visited any dark basements?"

"No."

"Could the numbers be a combination of some kind?"

"Not any I can think of."

"A badge number?" suggested Maggie

"No, they're usually one to four digits," Joe responded.

"What were you doing before coming to bed last night?"

"Reading the Psalms," said Joe. "That's it maybe. Maybe the numbers are Psalms!"

"It's possible," said Maggie.

Getting his Bible, Joe went to his study and turned to the Psalms. Locating Psalm 14 first, he began to read: *"The fool says in his heart, 'There is no God.' They are corrupt, they do abominable deeds, there is none who does good. The Lord looks down from heaven on the children of man, to see if there are any who understand, who seek after God... Have they no knowledge, all the evildoers who eat up my people as they eat bread and do not call upon the Lord?"*

Intrigued, Joe turned back a page and discovered Psalm 8: *"O Lord, our Lord, how majestic is your name in all the earth! You have set your glory above the heavens. Out of the mouth of babies and infants, you have established strength because of your foes, to still the enemy and the avenger. When I look at your heavens, the work of your fingers, the moon and the stars, which you have set in place, what is man that you are mindful of him, and the son of man that you care for him? Yet you have made him a little lower than the heavenly beings and crowned him with glory and honor. You have given him dominion over the works of your hands; you have put all things under his feet..."*

What did this all mean? What was the Lord trying to tell him? Was the Lord telling him anything? Were the numbers even connected to the Psalms? Confused but determined, he pressed forward and focused his eyes on the last of the group, Psalm 10: *"¹ Why, O Lord, do you stand far away? Why do you hide yourself in times of trouble? ² In arrogance the wicked hotly pursue the poor; let them be caught in the schemes that they have devised. ³ For the wicked boasts of the desires of his soul, and the one greedy for gain curses and renounces the Lord. ⁴ In the pride of his face the wicked does not seek him; all his thoughts are, 'There is no God.' ⁵ His ways prosper at all times; your judgments are on high, out of his sight; as for all his foes, he puffs at them. ⁶ He says in his heart, 'I shall not be moved; throughout all generations I shall not meet adversity.' ⁷ His mouth is filled with cursing and deceit and oppression; under his tongue are mischief and iniquity.* **⁸ He sits in ambush in the villages; in hiding places he murders the innocent. His eyes stealthily watch for the helpless; ⁹ he lurks in ambush like a lion in his thicket; he lurks that he may seize the poor; he seizes the poor when he draws him into his net. ¹⁰ The helpless are crushed, sink down, and fall by his might. ¹¹ He says in his heart, 'God has forgotten, he has hidden his face, he will never see it.' ¹² Arise, O Lord; O God, lift up your hand; forget not the afflicted. ¹³ Why does the wicked renounce God and say in his heart, 'you will not call to account?' ¹⁴ But you do see, for you note mischief and vexation, that you may take it into** *your hands; to you the helpless commits himself; you have been the helper of the fatherless.* [15] *Break the arm of the wicked and evildoer; call his wickedness to account till you find none.* [16] *The Lord is king forever and ever; the nations perish from his land.* [17] *O Lord, you hear the desire of the afflicted; you will strengthen their heart; you will incline your ear* [18] *to do justice to the fatherless and the oppressed, so that man who is of the earth may strike terror no more."*

Dumbfounded, Joe laid down his Bible, closed his eyes, and prayed. Staring again at the words he'd written in the night, parts of the dream began to resurface. As he started to make connections, it all became clear. Walking excitedly back to the kitchen, Joe exclaimed, "Maggie, we're about to catch the rapist! I think he lives near one of our schools—in a dark basement."

"How do you know?"

"God has answered my prayers. He's told me in a dream!"

"How can you be sure, Joe?" Maggie asked.

"He's confirmed it in His Word, Psalm 10:8-14!"

chapter 20

Slippery Ground

Surely you place them on slippery ground; you cast them down to ruin. How suddenly are they destroyed, completely swept away by terrors! (Psalm 73:18-19, NIV).

Pulling into the parking lot of St. Luke's hospital, Ethan Tyndale reached for his badge, cell phone, and notepad. The brisk morning air hit his face like ice-cold water as he stepped out of the car. It was a freezing day in early January. Entering the lobby of Eastbrook's newest hospital, Ethan took in the view of a magnificent building featuring an all-glass foyer that showcased a breathtaking view of the mountains. In the center of the lobby, a fountain danced to streams of artificial light, soothing one's senses with the murmur of cascading water. Full trees of summer adorned the fountain, and everything felt alive, comfortable, and pleasant. Ethan basked in the warmth of the sunlight that poured through the glass. Making his way to the coffee bar, he ordered a latte and began to sip it slowly. Pleased, his thoughts carried him away to the mountains as his insides transformed to the same temperature as his freshly radiated skin. For a moment he was quite enjoying himself, but then he remembered he had work to do. Ambling over to the information desk, he rang the bell and waited for assistance.

"May I help you, sir?" said a voice coming from over his shoulder.

"Yes, I'm looking for Dr. Jacobs and the Birthing Center," said Ethan.

"Take the elevator to the left and go up to the fifth floor."

"Thank you."

"You're welcome," she said.

Ethan paused for a moment to check his notes and make sure he had everything he needed. Exiting the elevator, he walked down a short hallway to the nurses' station in front of the maternity wing. Feeling slightly nervous, he approached the counter and said, "I'm here to see Dr. Jacobs at nine o'clock."

"May I tell her whose calling?" asked the nurse on duty.

"Detective Tyndale of the Eastbrook Police Force," revealed Ethan.

"Let me buzz her, sir," said the nurse. "I'm sorry, Detective Tyndale, but she was called for an emergency delivery this morning at 4:30 a.m. She won't be available for at least another half hour."

"That's okay. I'll wait," said Ethan.

Sitting down and sipping his last third of latte, Ethan looked over his notes, a few photographs, and his prepared questions. He couldn't get over the brutality captured in the pictures—these beautiful women had been treated like disposable waste—their bodies swollen, bloody, and bruised. Unrecognizable forms of the women they once were. Ethan wondered how any had survived such a brutal assault. His mind was flooded with visions of Sundari Yosha, the second victim of the BQB, whom he'd tried to interview earlier in the week. Institutionalized, paranoid, fearful, and heavyset, she was nothing like the beauty she used to be. Her injuries had healed; no scar could be seen on her flesh, but her soul, her heart, her spirit—they had been crushed. Sentences would explode out of her mouth like firecrackers, leaving only fragments of disconnected thoughts. She could not make sense of the violence perpetrated against her. Her world was locked away, dark, and undecipherable. It was clear she hadn't been a victim once in the past, but rather, she'd been one every day since the attack. Ethan had hoped to gain some insight and information from his visit with Sundari, but instead he came away with only pity, anger, and despair.

Distracted by a tug on his pants, Ethan looked down and beheld a little boy pulling on his pant leg. "Can I help you with something?" Ethan asked.

"My car went under here. Can you move your leg?"

"Certainly. Anything I can do to help," Ethan said, stepping out of the way.

The little boy reached under the chair and strained to no avail. "I can't reach it."

Putting down his file, Ethan said, "Let me have a look." Lying flat on the floor, Ethan scanned the shadow of the chair and spotted the tiny, dark red sports coupe. Reaching with purpose, he grabbed the car and returned it to the smiling boy. "There you go," said Ethan as he handed the much-desired companion to the child. Taking off without saying a word, the boy was racing through imagined hills to the shiny racetrack city in the back of the room. Watching the boy play reminded Ethan of his own childhood and how much he had liked cool cars, fast tracks, and adventure. Jolted out of his remembrances, Ethan beheld a disheveled-looking man burst into the room.

"There you are, William! You've got to stay with me, buddy! You can't just run off like that! Grab your cars and come with me." Spotting Ethan, he said, "Sorry, it's been a long morning."

"No problem. He's just been happily playing here with the racetrack," assured Ethan.

"It's been a crazy night. My brother's wife had a difficult delivery, and he called me in to look after Will. I guess I'm not that good with kids," said the man sheepishly, but relieved.

"Who is?" comforted Ethan. "Everything work out all right with the delivery?"

"Yeah, it's fine now, but earlier it looked a little scary," the man confided.

"Sorry about the stress, but I'm glad to hear everything turned out well," Ethan said with a smile.

"Thanks for taking care of Will. My name is Robert," he said as he reached out his hand.

"Ethan. Nice to meet you, Robert,"

"Well, thanks for keeping an eye on William. It's time for him to meet his baby sister."

"Tell your family congratulations."

Turning to leave with William, Robert concluded, "I will, Ethan. Thanks again."

Sitting back down, Ethan started to think about his own desire for a family. He'd like to have a son someday and maybe a little girl to cherish and spoil. At thirty-one he still had time, but there were precious few eligible Christian women on the horizon. Much to the chagrin of his mother (she just knew her oldest would be married and providing her with grandbabies by now), Ethan had remained single. He felt he was ready to settle down, but he hadn't met the right woman. He wondered what she did. Where she lived. How old she was. What she....

"Detective Tyndale?" inquired Rachelle.

"Yes."

"I'm Rachelle Jacobs."

Flustered, startled, and entirely unprepared, Ethan uttered, "Wow, err, a, excuse me. It's nice to meet you, Dr. Jacobs, I'm Ethan Tyndale."

"Nice to meet you, Detective Tyndale."

"I'm sorry, you caught me a little off-guard. I...is there somewhere private we could talk?"

"My office is across the catwalk in the south building. We could talk there."

"Great," Ethan said motioning for her to lead. "After you, Dr. Jacobs."

As they walked, Ethan tried to collect himself and regain his focus. This, however, would be no easy task. He was completely overwhelmed by the presence of Rachelle. The only photograph he'd seen of her, other than those taken after her abuse, was a high school yearbook picture. The young girl in that photograph was pretty, but the woman now walking beside him, tired, without pretense, and dressed in unflattering medical scrubs, was exceptional. Her beauty could not be ignored. Reaching her office, Rachelle offered Ethan a seat and then gracefully sat behind her desk. "What can I do for you, detective?" asked Rachelle.

"I'm terribly sorry to have to do this, but I wanted to ask you some questions about your assault in 1994," Ethan said gingerly.

"I've already told the police everything I can remember," asserted Rachelle.

"I appreciate that, Dr. Jacobs, but I'm new to the case, and I need to clarify some specifics."

"I can give you a few minutes, but then I need to attend to my patients," Rachelle said firmly.

"A few minutes is all I'll need," assured Ethan. "What was the approximate date of your abduction?"

"August 25th, 1994."

"Can you tell me what you were doing prior to the attack?"

"I was checking a flat tire after leaving from my job to return home."

"According to my records you worked at Wal-Mart, is that correct?"

"Yes, I was a checker there, and I had just finished my shift."

"About what time was that?"

"Around twelve o'clock at night."

"Did you make any other stops before encountering the car trouble on Sixth Street?"

"No, I pulled over to look at the flat tire, and that's when the other vehicle pulled up with the really bright lights—that's the last thing I remember until…," Rachelle's voice cracked as she looked away. "I wish I could remember more, but I can't."

Noticing her discomfort, Ethan quickly pressed forward, "I have your address at the time listed as 1317 Helm Street. Is that correct?"

"I'm sorry. What did you say?"

"I asked if you were living on Helm Street at the time," reiterated Ethan.

"Helm Street?" asked Rachelle. "No, I was living at 1317 Elm Street."

Pausing, Ethan looked through his notes and asked, "You weren't living on Helm Street near the foothills at the time of the attack?"

"No, I was living on Elm Street."

"Isn't that close to the Academy?"

"Yes, it's about two blocks away."

"Where were you attending school at that time?"

"I wasn't," answered Rachelle. "I had recently graduated from Washington High School in California, and had moved here to establish residency so I could lower my tuition for the following fall semester. The awarded scholarship was good, but the costs were still quite high, so I deferred a year and settled in to work. I'd been accepted to the Academy—as part of their accelerated undergraduate program."

"How long had you been living in Eastbrook before the attack?"

"About a month," said Rachelle.

"To clarify, Dr. Jacobs, you weren't living on Helm Street at the time of the assault, but Elm Street."

"Yes, that's correct," affirmed Rachelle.

Recognizing what he'd just discovered, Ethan looked at Rachelle and said, "Dr. Jacobs, I think I have all the information I need for now. If I have any more questions, I'll contact you. I'm sorry to have interrupted your day at work, but I do appreciate your help."

"Is there something wrong, detective?" asked Rachelle.

"No, nothing to worry about. Thank you for your courtesy. I've got everything I need," said Ethan, rising from his seat. Hesitating, Ethan slowed down and said, "May I just say, Dr. Jacobs, how sorry I am for your assault, and how much I admire your courage. Here's my card. If you need anything or think of anything else that might help our ongoing investigation, please call my direct number. Thanks again for your time and cooperation."

"You're welcome, Detective Tyndale," Rachelle said, shaking Ethan's strong hand. "If you need any more information from me, don't hesitate to call."

"Thank you so much," Ethan said.

As Ethan left Rachelle's office, he looked back over

his shoulder for one final passing glance at Dr. Jacobs. Discovering her returned gaze, Ethan immediately looked away and hurried out of the office. Feeling embarrassed about being caught looking, Ethan chastised himself while he rode the elevator to the lobby. Stupid move, he thought, but her beauty had ensnared him. She was gorgeous and more than he had expected. Ethan's mind slowly began to drift from the captivating Rachelle to the case before him. Making his way to the car, he couldn't believe the investigating officers in '94 had made such a blundering error—an enormously significant clerical error. It was an easy enough error to make, but critical. Thinking Rachelle was a local Wal-Mart employee who lived fairly close to the first victim, they had failed to connect that two of the first three victims had ties to the Academy. Ethan couldn't wait to tell his father about this new development.

Driving through the streets of Eastbrook, he recalled his father's dream from a couple of months before about the rapist living near a school. He now knew that school was Eastbrook Academy. Picking up his cell phone, he called Terry at the station and asked her to run a check on every white male home owner or renter within a five-block radius—north, south, east, and west—of the Academy. This was the break they'd been looking for. Ethan could feel it in his bones. Maybe this was the link to finding one of the most brutal criminals Eastbrook had ever known.

Ethan parked his car and entered the station brimming with confidence and hope. He felt different about this lead. Maybe it was his dad's powerful dream. Maybe it was seeing how Rachelle had overcome. Maybe it was the clear and subtle mistake the police investigators and detectives had made in '94. Maybe it was wishful thinking or all of them mixed together. Whatever it was, he felt good for the first time in a long time. There was a noticeable jump and energy in Ethan's movements. He believed, now, more than at any other time, they were about to catch the Beauty Queen Butcher! Passing through the glass doors and past a uniformed officer at the front desk, Ethan briskly made his way into the building. The station was bursting with activity and focus, but not overwhelmed. Nodding to some and engaging others, he made his way to the Eastbrook detective wing and Terry.

"What have you got for me, Terry?"

Without looking up, Terry said, "Chomping at the bit, Ethan?"

"I think this is the big one, what do ya got?" pressed Ethan.

"The initial search pulled fifty potentials," said Terry.

"How many were between thirty and sixty years of age?"

"Forty."

"How many renters?"

"Fifteen."

"Of the fifteen, how many with records?"

"Two."

"How many of large build, say, plus six feet and 190 pounds?" inquired Ethan.

"Only six," revealed Terry.

"Of the six, how many records?"

"One."

"Good, we'll start with those six. Notify Michaels and Raintree to begin surveillance of the first four on the list, and I'll look in on these last two characters. See if any of the six works at or attended the Academy. Keep looking for distinguishing habits, repeat purchases, records, occupations, anything that would give us a connection, access, or motive," instructed Ethan.

"What, no thank you?" Terry retorted.

"You're the best; you know that. Steaks on me next week," said Ethan.

Returning to his car, Ethan located the men's places of residence on a map while he waited for the car to warm up. Looking at the street names before him, Ethan contemplated everything he'd read, heard, or seen regarding the elusive rapist—so much speculation, very little hard evidence, and now this break. He knew his dad's dream and their latest conversations had led him to this point. Reaching for his cell phone, Ethan selected his father's number from the list but before he could push the button, the ringer sounded. Answering, he heard the familiar voice of his father.

"Hey, Dad, I was just about to call you, greeted Ethan. "What's up?"

"Ethan, I've made a breakthrough!"

"What is it, Dad?"

"I've been looking at all the schools in the area to see if I could find any connections to my dream and I've discovered that the dorms at Eastbrook Academy are called, 'The Villages.'"

"This is incredible, Dad! You won't believe what's just happened to me!"

"Don't you see, Ethan, that's where he picked his first victim, Jenny Foster was a student there. But more importantly, the psalm God gave me says, 'He lies in wait near the villages.' Son, he lives near the Academy."

"Dad, I know. You won't believe this, but I just discovered that the first and third victims had ties to the Academy!"

"That's incredible news, incredible news. I've been praying for years for a breakthrough. This is it! This is it, Son!"

"Can you tell me from your dream the description of the rapist's place again?"

"I didn't get much, but I remember it looked like a dingy basement containing an old desk. And I had the powerful impression that he had photographs of his victims. I also felt he lived alone and that he lived close to a school. Ethan, I would start with the matches that live nearest the Academy."

"Thanks, Dad," said Ethan. "I think we're about to get him. Pray for me and the other detectives to be smart and safe."

"I will, Ethan. I will. Be careful, and call me when you have something."

"I will, Dad."

Ending the call, Ethan looked again at the map and determined the best place to start was the house on Ash Street, only two blocks from the Academy and three blocks from Rachelle's newly discovered former place of residence on Elm Street. Dialing Terry, he asked her to do some digging into the length of time the renters of suspicion had lived at their current residences and notify Jones to meet him for back-up. Ethan was nervous and excited, and he knew he was close. After bowing his head and uttering a prayer, he pulled out of the station and headed for Ash Street.

chapter 21

The Beginning of the End

Standing near the Ross Building with books in hand, Ethan took several concealed shots with his cell phone of H.T. disposing of the building's trash. The sun was penetrating on this calm, brisk day as Academy students walked to and from their classes. Dumping the trash, H.T. stealthily guided a used hypodermic needle into his pocket and walked away with the empty receptacle. Each day, Ethan was more and more convinced he had his man. Over the last couple of weeks, no other suspect had presented so intriguing a prospect. H.T. had worked at the Academy as a janitor and a groundskeeper since before Jenny Foster went missing. He routinely went for walks in the community after work, taking pictures of buildings and people. Earlier in the week, he had walked through the woods next to Swan Lake and taken several photos of an athletic, young blond girl as she practiced her figures and jumps on the reflective surface. He never socialized with anyone or went out on the town with a group. Every night, he was home by seven, and on the past weekend, he'd driven into the woods for a hike along Route 122. H.T. was well outfitted and perfectly rigged for a man who spent long hours in the woods. Ethan held back and shadowed his mark as well as he could until he lost H.T. in the ruggedness of the wilderness. Having spent hundreds of hours himself in the wilderness, Ethan realized H.T. was a true outdoorsman. Several things were clear: H.T. knew the woods, was a man of preparation, and was in excellent shape for a man in his mid-fifties. Heading back to the truck, Ethan watched from a concealed spot for H.T.'s return. Two-and-a-half hours later, the large man slipped out of the woods and into his dark-tinted truck. Ethan estimated that with the distance he'd traveled following H.T. into the woods and the time it took before he reappeared and drove home, H.T. must have hiked at least seven or eight miles in the cold January weather. No one could have fit the profile of the man they'd been looking for better than H.T.

The following morning, Ethan and a team of five investigators, accompanied by two search-and-rescue canines, entered the woods at the spot Ethan had lost H.T. and began hunting for the hidden rape chamber. It was cold as the breath of both man and beast intruded in the densely wooded forest. A little more than a mile from the road, the terrain jutted and slowed in the tightening timber. This part of the woods was a maze of confusion even in the dead of winter. It was a foreboding location, and Ethan began to wonder if there was any hope at all. Stumbling over rocks and cutting through the rough and knotted brush, the men pressed forward in stern determination. Time slipped away as the sting of frost dampened the will. Their efforts were fruitless. Frustration seized the weary group, and even the dogs seemed bewildered and lost. Why couldn't they catch a break? How was this man so lucky, so clever…so wicked? They all knew he had to be brought to justice, but when would they discover the key evidence?

With the day ending in defeat, the men felt numb and surly as they hiked out of nature's labyrinth. All was futility until the sharp bellow of Caleb, the team's powerful German Shepherd, cracked the evening. In the ebbing light of day the dog began to dig. Rushing to his side, Ted Raintree exclaimed, "What you got, boy? You found somethin', huh?" Peering down into the hard scratched earth, Detective Raintree saw the glint of metal and a flash of light. "Ethan, get over here! Caleb found somethin'. Come quick!"

Sprinting to Ted's location, Ethan paused to catch his breath and staring, inquired, "What is it, Ted?"

"An earring."

"I'll be damned if that isn't exactly what it is! Get Gibbs up here with the kit. We got ourselves something to process."

The team loaded up and left euphoric. Strange how giddy a weary group of men could become over a tiny earring, but then again it wasn't like most days over the years where "nothing" was the answer given when asked about the day. Hope, however, began to fade as the earring yielded zero forensic leads, and in the weeks that followed, no additional clues materialized. The location of the hidden chamber remained undiscovered even after hundreds of hours of collaborative investigation by several different members of the law enforcement community. The tightly swept ten-mile search area and surrounding forest was probed repeatedly, but like all the times before, nothing was discovered.

Even the positive identification of the earring by Rana Nadira, the seventh victim, yielded only pain. The retelling of Rana's assault during their interview sickened Ethan and left him more determined than ever. Rana was the first victim to report that her attacker had several crisscross scars on his left arm. In their struggle she had managed to rip his dark bodysuit and get a glimpse of his arm before he knocked her cold. When Ethan learned that the attack on Rana had left her permanently sterile, he could barely conceal his grief and anger. Her injuries and the latest solution the BQB was using to destroy any semen that remained in his victims led to a massive infection and, ultimately, a complete hysterectomy. Leaving Rana's apartment, Ethan had no words, no answers, no frame of reference, only pain—and then he thought of Rachelle. How could anyone survive an assault like this? How had Rachelle overcome the devastation? He wept for Rana and all the victims, but he couldn't take his mind off of Rachelle.

After a month of searching the woods, meeting again with victims, and continuing to come up short, Ethan was growing impatient. He believed they needed to move fast, and he worried that H.T. was beginning to sense he was being watched. Over the last month, H.T. had been sticking closer to home. He rarely took his walks in the community, and he hadn't visited the woods since Ethan first tailed him there. Deciding to strike before H.T. had any more time to sniff things out, and hoping he could discover a concrete link to the crimes, Ethan developed a plan.

The following week after H.T. drove away for work, Ethan queued Detective Michaels, who was waiting further up the road, to begin his tail duties and cautiously approached the front porch of the modest little brick house on Ash Street. Knocking on the door, Ethan waited for a response. When no one came promptly, he peered through the front-room window and saw an old woman with a walking stick move gingerly toward the front door. Returning from the window, Ethan patiently waited for the door to be opened.

"Mrs. Ety, I presume," greeted Ethan.

"Sorry," replied Mrs. Ety. "You'll have to speak a little louder, my hearing isn't as sharp as it used to be."

Clearing his throat, Ethan half-shouted, "Mrs. Ety, I'm Bill Hopkins with the utility company, and I've been authorized by the city to check your furnace and gas line. We've had some leaks in the area."

"I'm not having any problems that I'm aware of," replied Mrs. Ety.

"It's just a precaution, ma'am. Can I come in?"

"How do I know you're who you say you are?" asked the old woman.

"My truck and the uniform aren't enough?" offered Ethan.

"You never can be too careful. There are some dangerous people in our town," informed Mrs. Ety.

Standing in full view of the open door, Ethan processed that the steady gaze of Mrs. Ety hadn't changed one iota from their initial contact to now. "Ma'am, can you see me?" asked Ethan.

"I lost my sight quite some time ago," said Mrs. Ety.

"Would you like to have the utility company call you directly to confirm my employment with the city?"

"No, that won't be necessary. I suppose if you wanted to harm me, you'd have done it already. How long will this take?"

"No more than five or ten minutes to run the test, then I'll be on my way, ma'am."

"That sounds reasonable. Come in."

"Thank you, ma'am," Ethan said as he entered the house. "How do I get to the furnace, Mrs. Ety?"

"It's in the basement, but I haven't gone down there in years. That's Mr. Taylor's place. He rents from me."

"Is he home?" Ethan asked furtively.

"What's that?" said Mrs. Ety. Hearing Ethan repeat the question a little louder, she said, "I don't think so, he usually works during the day."

"Can I access the apartment from up here, or do I have to use an outside entrance?"

"Mr. Taylor is a very private man. I don't know if he'd like having you in his apartment without him being here," asserted Mrs. Ety.

Ethan raised his voice and said, "I can appreciate that, ma'am, but if there is a leak down there, it could lead to an explosion or asphyxiation. It will just take a few minutes, and I'll stick to my job. I promise, he'll never even know I've been here."

"The key to the door leading to the basement is over there on the key hook by the telephone." Having obtained the key, Ethan unlocked the door and proceeded down the stairs into the dingy, dark basement. Taking out his flashlight, he scanned the sparse apartment. It was neat and empty, save for a small sofa and an old television supported by cinder blocks and plywood. Its emptiness, no doubt, reflected the soul of the man who resided there, thought Ethan. Feeling a bit nervous, he exited the living room and walked slowly down the hallway toward the bedroom. The apartment possessed an eerie quality, like an old cemetery or a dark wood. As he opened the door to the room, his skin crawled and his breath became short. There before him was an old desk just exactly as his father had dreamed. His body gave a shiver as his eyes widened at the site. Cautiously, he entered the room.

The walnut desk was clearly an antique—probably mid to late 1800s, Ethan guessed. It was beautifully carved and meticulously cared for. Smooth lines and beautiful curves drew the eye to an ornate center carving of a single blooming rose just above the mirror. Sporting five drawers all with locks, four equally proportioned on the right and left with one long drawer in the middle, the desk was typical for the period and feminine. Hints of the black leather writing tablet carefully edged by polished walnut peeked out from under the disheveled mail that lay atop it. Standing over five feet high, it was supported by four artistically carved cabriole legs. Perhaps what set the desk apart more than anything was its presence in an otherwise rudimentary male apartment. Suspended for a time as he reflected upon his father's dream, Ethan returned to focus, slipped on his gloves, and approached the elegant desk.

As he suspected, all the drawers were locked. Being unwilling to force them open, Ethan began a quick search of the desk, bed, laundry hamper, and closet for the key. His search failed to yield what he sought, but it did lead to the discovery of several pornographic magazines in the closet, many of them depicting sadomasochistic behavior and simulated torture. Ethan, sensing he was running out of time, felt under the desk, making one more attempt to locate the hidden key. Coming up empty, his eye was drawn to a visible cut in the leather desk top. Deftly lifting the mail, Ethan made out the letter "W," which had been roughly carved into the leather. Proceeding gently to avoid detection as he lifted the mail, Ethan deciphered the beginning of a word cut into the leather writing tablet. There in this otherwise perfectly preserved charming desk was the crudely carved word: *whore*. Stepping briskly back from the desk as a piece of mail crashed to the floor, Ethan knew he had his man! Putting the fallen mail as best he could back in place, he stepped out of the room and briskly walked toward the kitchen.

To his surprise and delight, several marijuana plants lined the far counter. Situated under some glowing photo lamps, Ethan couldn't have been more pleased. Looking further at the knives in the drawers and in the block on the kitchen counter, nothing added to the already intriguing discoveries, but Ethan felt confident with the new round-the-clock surveillance of H.T. that he would soon be able to bust him for marijuana possession. And following the arrest, get a warrant to search H.T.'s apartment for the possession of even greater quantities of an illegal substance. All he needed now was a way in, and he believed the rest would take care of itself. After quickly glancing at Mr. Taylor's unremarkable bathroom, Ethan walked upstairs and addressed Mrs. Ety.

"Everything checks out, Mrs. Ety. Your furnace could use a cleaning, but other than that, everything looks fine," said Ethan.

"I told you there wasn't a problem," said Mrs. Ety.

"Yes, ma'am, you did," acknowledged Ethan. "But it's always better to be safe than sorry. Thanks for your time and cooperation. Have a nice day, Mrs. Ety."

"You too, young man."

Walking down the steps and out to his truck, Ethan called Terry and told her to prepare a written request for a broad search warrant on the suspicion of possession of illegal substances with intent to sell for 6673-½ Ash St. that could be expedited at a moment's notice.

chapter 22

Rescue

Knotted and nervous, Ruth sat in silence as the traffic buzzed. She hadn't experienced too many carefree days as a teen, and today was no exception. Looking over at Shondah, she uttered a silent prayer and shifted in her seat. Ruth was not where she wanted to be, and this was not how she hoped things would go for Shondah. Nevertheless, they were on their way to Rose & Taugney, a place she had already experienced firsthand. Ruth deeply regretted her abortion, and she couldn't believe her seventeen-year-old friend was about to make the same mistake, even after their lengthy discussions on the matter.

"Shon, don't do…"

"Ruth, I've made my decision! I just need you to support me, okay?"

Choking out the word "okay," a large tear released from Ruth's eye and rolled down her cheek. How could she do anything more than Shondah had done for her when she was sixteen? Despite what she knew, her opposition to abortion seemed hypocritical at best. It was now Ruth's turn to support her best friend. Conflicted and sad, she stared out the window, longing for the day to end. But that was just it; she knew from her own abortion that this day would never end. It had been over a year since she chose to end the life of her baby, and she was still haunted by the choice she made. Still, what could she do? Who was she? Amid the pain of her despair, she heard a Voice intone in her spirit, "Love keeps no record of wrongs. I have forgiven you, Ruth. Now go and love Shondah and her baby the way I have loved you. I will be with you, and I will send you help from the sanctuary!" Startled by the voice of God, Ruth began to silently intercede for her friend and the little one she was yet to know. "Dear Jesus, You are both Rescuer and Deliverer. Please deliver my friend, Shondah, from the hand of the Enemy and her child from the grip of merciless death. Show her the privilege of being a mother, and remove from her the power of fear. Jesus, intercede for us and send us the Holy Spirit to help us." Ruth's countenance began to change as she pleaded for the rescue of her friend and her baby. Flooded with the assurance of God's presence, Ruth discovered afresh her faith and the beginnings of hope.

As Shondah turned down 13th Street, Ruth's eyes lit up when she saw women praying on the sidewalk. Today, unlike the day of her abortion, people had come. She felt sure this was the help God had promised, and she intended to use it. Rolling down her window as they entered the parking lot, Ruth yelled out, "Pray for us— we need your help." Amy, sensing a strong move of the Holy Spirit, began in earnest to pray for the two teenage girls. Behind her an elderly Catholic woman named Vera joined the intercession, while Jael quickly approached the parking car holding out several brochures. Shondah, feeling betrayed snapped, "What the hell, Ruth? I thought you had my back!"

"I do, Shon, and I can't bear to see you do this."

"*You* did!"

"I know, and it's the worst mistake I ever made," confessed Ruth. "Nothing will ever take away the pain I feel over the loss of my baby. Even with my faith, I still don't feel forgiven sometimes."

"You know how my mother feels about sex before marriage," said Shondah. "She will never let me in her house again. I'll be dead to her."

"People can change, Shon. Look at *me*. You can't completely predict how your mom will react—maybe she'll surprise you, but I can tell you that this decision is permanent, and once you make this decision, it will never change."

"Just last year you told me they weren't babies yet, and that only wanted children should be brought into this world!"

"I lied to myself, Shon, and I lied to you. I know that now, and I'm sorry, truly sorry, but I'm telling you from my own experience that as soon as it's over, you'll realize the truth. Shon, don't live a life of regret, haunted by what might have been," pleaded Ruth.

"Enough! Stop! I see what you're trying to do, Ruth, but my situation is not like yours, and I've made up my mind! Let's just go before we're late," insisted Shondah.

Exiting the car, Shondah politely refused Jael's literature and her verbal offers of assistance. Deflated, Ruth got out of the car and followed her friend inside the clinic. Once inside, panic began to rise in Ruth as she faced afresh the memories of her own experience. How old would her baby be now? Sitting in the waiting room while Shondah checked in, she became flush and overcome with anxiety.

Willing herself to walk, Ruth said, "I need some air, Shon. I'm going outside."

"Okay, but don't be too long. I need you."

"I know. I'm just feeling a little dizzy. I'll come back in as soon as I clear my head."

Stepping outside, Ruth closed her eyes, took a deep breath, and arched her back in the morning sunshine.

The warmth penetrated deep inside her body, but the desperate nature of her circumstance left her cold and weary. Overcome by worry, she was interrupted by the sound of audible weeping. Startled, Ruth opened her eyes in bewilderment and saw Amy weeping loudly as she made intercession too deep for words. Overwhelmed, she heard Jael call out, "Sweetheart, come get some literature for your friend, and don't give up on a miracle. We're here for you and your friend. You can do all things with Christ who strengthens you. The Lord brought you here to be an instrument of rescue, and He won't fail you!"

As tensions were mounting at the clinic, Christopher was just getting away for his morning commitment at Rose & Taugney. Pulling up to Pastor Jim's, Christopher honked the horn and glanced at the clock—9:30. Initially not in a hurry, he began to feel an urgency to get to the clinic. Honking again, Jim appeared from his porch and got inside the car.

"That new wife of yours causing you to run late, is she?" teased Jim.

"Something like that, but I can't say I mind too much," said Christopher.

"How are things going with you and Anna?"

"It's great. We're still getting settled, but it's been awesome so far. I love being married to her."

"Nothing is better than young love," mused Jim.

"I'm glad you decided to come with me today, Pastor."

"It's only taken three years."

"I appreciate it still. I know you're a busy man. The flock always needs tending, right?"

"How are things going at the clinic?"

"It's up and down. The core group of intercessors and counselors is really strong, but it's a battle to get the leadership or the laity from most churches involved."

"Don't lose heart, Chris. It's tough sledding trying to motivate the people," encouraged Jim. "Keep praying and working, and God will bring the people. Just look at me—I'm coming today."

"True enough, Pastor," said Christopher. "I do have one cool story for you. One of my Catholic friends, Walter, who's frequently involved in pro-life work, recently shared with me a personal story I think you'll appreciate. Walter told me how his preborn grandchild had, in effect, saved the life of his son. Earlier this year, his son, Troy, who's now almost forty, was about to welcome his first child into the world, and realizing that he smoked too much and was in poor shape decided to change his ways—get in shape and quit smoking before the baby's arrival. When Troy started to work out on his exercise bike, he began to notice tightness in his chest and some mild discomfort. Initially, he dismissed it as shortness of breath due to all the smoking, but after a pitiful attempt at jogging, in which he could barely make it fifty yards, he decided to schedule a checkup with his doctor. The visit revealed a congenital defect in Troy's aortic heart valve that led to immediate open-heart surgery. After the surgery, the doctor reported that the valve had closed so much that if the problem hadn't been discovered when it was, Walter's son probably would have experienced heart failure and died within a month. If Walter's daughter-in-law hadn't been expecting, Walter probably would have lost his son. Isn't that crazy?"

"That's amazing, Christopher. It just goes to show that the impact and the purposes for every life are beyond searching out. Not bad, saving a life before you've even left the womb. How is Walter's son doing now?"

"He's recovering nicely, and the doctor said his future looks promising."

"That's great news. What a neat story."

Nearing the clinic, the two men saw the small group of huddled intercessors and, slowing down, began to look for a place to park.

By now, Jael and Ruth had developed a plan. They decided Ruth would try to help Shondah connect with her child by sharing with her the key fetal development markers that her baby had already passed. Selecting some valuable points from the brochure, the women prayed a quick prayer, and Ruth once again entered the clinic. Asking the Lord for boldness, Ruth sat down next to Shondah and waited for the proper moment. Feeling isolated and uncomfortable, the two friends sat silently in the crowded room. Three couples, a single woman, and a mother with her daughter all sat waiting for their names to be called and their lives to be forever changed. No one really looked at each other or spoke. It was deadly calm as their children and their children's children neared the day of their death. The people were a brooding, somber bunch, and not one of them felt truly happy about their choice.

"Are you feeling better?" asked Shondah.

"For the most part—the fresh air really helped," said Ruth. "You want to step outside and get a little air yourself?"

"With all those ladies outside, no thanks."

"They're nice. One of them gave me this brochure. Look." Shondah's eyes fell on a picture of a beautiful baby when Ruth handed her the pamphlet. In that moment, time stopped for Shondah. Everything faded from her field of vision but the image of a beautiful child, her child. Standing to her feet, Shondah muttered, "Oh, my God, what am I doing?" Dropping the brochure, she quickly walked out of the building and ducked behind a partition the clinic had set up for smokers. Followed immediately by Ruth, the two girls disappeared from view.

"What are you doing, Ruth?" Shondah said, trying to catch her breath.

"I'm trying to help you see the truth and avoid a mistake," asserted Ruth. "Did you know right now your baby is developing fingernails? She has already formed every major organ in her body. She has a heart that's been beating for six weeks. This is your baby, Shon! Don't throw her away."

"Where am I going to go after my mother tosses me out, huh?" pleaded Shondah. "You think Derek will take us in? He doesn't care about us!"

"I don't know. Maybe your mom won't throw you out. Maybe you could stay at my house, the church, somewhere."

"What about money, school? What chance do I have on my own?"

"What chance do you have if you live forever with the reality that you killed your child?" pleaded Ruth. "Don't be like me; don't make the choice I made!"

"I don't have a choice, Ruth. I hate it, but it's the best option for me."

"What about your baby? Is it the best for her?"

Pausing as if she heard Ruth for the first time, Shondah said, "You think it's a girl?"

"I don't know for sure, but I have a feeling. Come on, Shon, let's go home. We can work this out."

"No... no, I'm sorry, but there's no other way," Shondah said, moving abruptly past Ruth as she re-entered the clinic. Taking a deep breath, Ruth followed for a third time.

As the counselors and intercessors gathered to pray, Christopher and Pastor Jim approached the sidewalk. Christopher sensed immediately the gravity of the situation when he beheld the ladies' faces and the intensity of their prayers. Walking over to the group, he asked Jael what was happening. Jael quickly filled Christopher in on the two girls and their struggle for life. Pastor Jim, overhearing the conversation, asked the group to gather once again and pray. Holding hands, the small group entreated the Lord on behalf of Ruth, Shondah, and Shondah's baby. The words of their prayer rose like incense before the throne of God, and Pastor Jim began to weep. Infectious weeping soon took hold, and the group ministered as one through tears. During their prayers for courage, deliverance, wisdom, and the absence of fear, Pastor Jim heard the Spirit of the Lord speak in his soul, "Isaiah forty-nine, fifteen and sixteen." Looking at Christopher, he said, "Chris, open your Bible to Isaiah 49, verses 15 and 16, and when the girls come back out, read it to them. Be alert, and we'll continue to plead with the Lord in prayer." It was a verse that Christopher knew well. Turning to Isaiah, he prayed for the Lord to unleash the power of his living Word, which penetrates soul and spirit. While the group prayed and Christopher finished his intercession, Ruth once again walked out of the clinic and approached those on the sidewalk.

Motioning her over, Christopher said, "Ruth is it? My name's Christopher." Shaking her hand, he continued, "How can we help you and your friend?"

"She's conflicted, but I feel there's still hope. She's terrified of her mother's reaction to the news she's pregnant. She believes her mother, who is deeply religious, will abandon her and kick her out on the streets, especially when she finds out the father is a man who's mixed up in all the wrong things. A man who wants nothing to do with the baby," confided Ruth.

"What religion is her mother?" asked Christopher.

"She's a devout Baptist."

hushed

"If she's a true believer in Jesus and the teachings of the Bible, she won't abandon or disown her daughter. But even if she does, the members of the church I attend can help. We've established a financial fund for mothers in crisis, have host families that can provide lodging, and even have a job-training and placement program that can help your friend get back on her feet," informed Christopher. "Ruth, would you do something for me? Would you take this Bible to Shondah and read to her these two highlighted verses in Isaiah, chapter forty-nine?"

After reading the verses, Ruth looked up at Christopher with a smile on her face and said, "Yes, sir. Yes, I will."

"Great, let's pray before you go. Lord Jesus, thank you for Ruth and for her love for her friend. Please use her and Your Word to bring about deliverance for Shondah and her child. Smile on them with Your grace and mercy, Eternal Father. Amen."

"Amen."

Leaving with new determination, Ruth walked, with Bible in hand, toward the clinic. Opening the door, she noticed Shondah was no longer seated in the lobby. Looking in disbelief, she saw Shondah's back disappear through the door to the procedure rooms with Sally. Running to the door, she burst through and shouted, "Shondah, stop! I need to read you something." Startled, Sally yelled, "Gwynn, call security!" Boldly, Ruth shouted back, "Shondah Miriam Davis, don't you do this until you've heard the counsel of God." Sally stood dumbfounded as Shondah turned back to her friend and said, "Okay, Ruth." Bursting in from outside, Jay beheld the two friends standing in the hallway with the Bible open. No one knew what to do for a moment, until Gwynn suggested the two girls be taken into room one and given a moment of privacy. Everyone took a collective breath after determining that there was no immediate danger and that Shondah did indeed want to have a final word with her friend. In the quiet of the room facing the medical table, the two girls sat and read the words of the prophet Isaiah: "*Can a mother forget the baby at her breast and have no compassion on the child she has borne? Though she may forget, I will not forget you! See, I have engraved you on the palms of my hands; your walls are ever before me.*" Shondah began to weep. In that moment, she realized she could not forget this child conceived in her and that her own mother would not forget either, but even if she did, God would not! Rising, she grabbed Ruth's hand and said with new determination, "Let's go home." Tearfully rejoicing, the two girls walked out of the clinic and into the sun—a feeling of hope in their hearts and a gleam in their eyes.

Briefly exchanging contact information with Christopher, the girls got into their car and pulled out of the parking lot. Amy smiled and wept as she gazed at the weary smile of Ruth through the passenger window. This was a moment of victory and celebration that no one on the sidewalk would ever forget. But more than that, it was a moment when a wounded teenager stood in the gap for her best friend and saved one life from destruction and another from ruin. Joy unspeakable descended upon the counselors and Pastor Jim as they tasted the power of God and the rich, salty tears of joy.

chapter 23

Justice Brings Joy

When justice is done, it brings joy to the righteous but terror to evildoers (Prov. 21:15, NIV).

"*Blessed is the man who does not walk in the counsel of the wicked, nor stand in the path of sinners, nor sit in the seat of scoffers! But his delight is in the law of the Lord, and in His law he meditates day and night. He will be like a tree firmly planted by streams of water, which yields its fruit in its season and its leaf does not wither; and in whatever he does, he prospers.*" Closing his Bible, Ethan thanked the Lord for His divine intervention in the case against H.T. He knew without the providence of God and His favor, the department never would have caught the Beauty Queen Butcher or won the case against him. It had been a long nine-month battle since the arrest of H.T. for the kidnapping, rape, and assault of eight women and the murder of Kieu Lang. Still, the end of the matter was not nearly as long as the beginning. In all, H.T. had terrorized the people of Eastbrook for eighteen years—truly heartbreaking and remarkable. Stepping up to his mirror, Ethan began to shave and prepare for the victory celebration at his father's house. This was a conviction long sought and long anticipated by the law enforcement community. Several policemen and detectives had come and gone over the years, but everyone who played a significant role in the investigation along with those currently in the department were invited to attend, and Ethan expected a large turnout. He was looking forward to seeing his parents and the members of his department. Shaved, dressed, and ready, Ethan left for home.

Approaching the steps to his father's porch, he could hear the sound of joy and merrymaking as several silhouette figures moved like shadows across the blinds. Entering the warm, familiar house, Ethan was greeted by Captain Denton, Paul Michaels, and his father.

"There he is, the man of the hour," said Denton. "Nice to see you again, Ethan."

"Nice to see you, Captain," said Ethan. "How's retirement treating you?"

"A little better now that we got the BQB!"

"I can appreciate that, sir. He didn't make it easy on any of us, did he?"

"No, he didn't. He sure was a crafty weasel," interjected Paul.

"That he was, that he was," said Denton. "But he didn't get away from you, Ethan. You brought him down."

"I wouldn't say that, sir. It was a team effort. If it wasn't for the Lord's help, the department's perseverance, and the evidence uncovered during the drug raid, I'm not sure we ever would've got him."

"Can you believe he escaped the needle?" chimed Paul.

"I don't like to see anybody killed, no matter what the offense, but given the testimony about his childhood and the level of abuse he suffered at the hands of his mother, I thought the verdict of life without parole was just," reasoned Joe.

"I just look at the girls he destroyed and I just don't see how the state could let him live," Paul rebutted. "I mean he murdered the Lang girl, Thompson's still in a comma, and Nadira tried to kill herself not long after her attack."

"Well, at least it's over now, and he's off the streets," said Ethan.

"Agreed," followed Denton.

"So how's the fishing been lately, Captain?" Ethan asked.

"You didn't tell him about our last outing, Joe?"

"Haven't had the time," said Joe.

"Your father caught a brown an inch-and-a-half off the state record, and I caught a mess of good-sized brook and rainbow trout," informed Denton. "The river has been just outstanding this fall, and Timber Lake has been almost as good."

"I'm jealous," confessed Ethan. "Maybe this next weekend we can all hit the water?"

"I'd like that," said Denton.

"Let's plan on it," Ethan said. "Well, if you gentlemen will excuse me, I feel a drink calling my name."

"Good work, Ethan."

"Thanks, Captain," said Ethan as he turned and walked toward the kitchen.

Rounding the corner, Ethan bumped into his mother and Terry. The two were busy refilling the fruit and veggie trays and talking about the increased security and freedom they felt with the community's most notorious criminal behind bars and off the streets.

"Hello ladies, where can a fella get a drink?"

"Hello, Son," Maggie said, giving Ethan a hug. "The coolers are out on the deck. Help yourself to whatever you want."

"How's my favorite assistant?" asked Ethan.

Smiling, Terry responded, "Couldn't be better, boss. Your mom sure knows how to throw a party."

"Yes, she does," said Ethan with a wink.

All over the house, members of the department laughed, teased, and bantered about. Everyone was in high spirits now that the long, difficult campaign to bring this brutal man to justice was over. Around every corner and in little pockets here and there, people discussed the details of the case, the verdict, and their various opinions on H.T.'s sentencing. The photos, knife, and electric razor found at H.T.'s during the marijuana raid drew considerable attention, as well as the decision not to seek the death penalty. Many people were caught up in the revelation that H.T.'s birth mother had been as wickedly abusive to him during his childhood as he had proved to be to the girls he abducted. H.T.'s testimony and a few inconclusive but intriguing police reports painted a picture of a psychotic woman who repeatedly abused her son throughout his childhood and adolescence until her disappearance during H.T.'s sophomore year of high school. Struggling to make it in the fashion industry, Mrs. Taylor was a divorced mother who was away from home for days or weeks at a time, often leaving H.T. alone, tied up, or locked in the basement. When she was at home, she'd get drunk or hopped up on drugs and abuse her son. Her favorite form of abuse was forced stimulation and rape. The defense even produced some horrible photos of H.T.'s pelvic region which still bore the scars of her abuse.

But by far, the greatest topic of discussion was the critical DNA evidence that finally turned the trial in the prosecution's favor. Throughout the trial, H.T. maintained his innocence as the largely circumstantial case was presented. H.T.'s knife matched the one used to make the cuts and punctures in the victim's bodies, but no blood, hair, or DNA was found to connect it directly to the victims. He had pictures of every girl that was abducted in his apartment, except Rachelle Jacobs. Unfortunately, having pictures of these women in various public places didn't mean he'd abducted them or tortured them, especially when he had photographs of hundreds of the town's people and buildings in his collection. His razor also came up as a match for the type used to remove the girl's body hair, but failed to yield a single forensic certainty. H.T.'s physical fitness, medical syringes, needles, boot covers, possession of the chemical compounds necessary to anesthetize, and frequent visits and trips to the woods all created suspicion and gave him opportunity, but proved nothing. His truck, upon seizure, revealed a hidden sub-floor compartment under the rear cab bench seat big enough to hold a human being, but yielded nothing in terms of usable evidence. He had all sorts of connections to the crimes, but no concrete link. Everything came up clean. H.T. made no confession, and even up to the present no one knew where his secret lair in the woods was located. The girls who testified gave general descriptions of their attacker, but offered few specifics, and their collective testimony failed to convince the jury that the perpetrator's voice matched H.T.'s. Even the compelling written testimony submitted by Rana Nadira that the rapist had several crisscross cuts on his upper arm failed to prove conclusively that H.T. was the BQB. The defense rightly pointed out that many victims of childhood sexual abuse self-injure as a means of coping with their pain.

Just as the case began to look unwinnable for the prosecution, Rachelle Jacobs came forward with the one piece of irrefutable evidence H.T. hadn't destroyed—his daughter. Rachelle had left Eastbrook a month after her attack for California, and no one, including Rachelle, knew she was pregnant at the time. Choosing to keep the matter to herself and her family, no one outside the Jacobs family knew the source of her pregnancy. Everyone just assumed she'd gotten pregnant sleeping around during her first year of living apart from her parents' watchful eyes. After Rachelle came forward and tipped Ethan off, he and his colleagues went to work gathering the remaining evidence to prove the crime. Ethan and his team collected some of Jaleesa's hair after she had it trimmed by a local beautician, matched her conception within a week of her mother's attack, and proved through Rachelle's short residency in Eastbrook before the attack that the time frame was air tight.

The D.A. also presented several written statements from men who'd dated Rachelle over the years to attest to her habit of purity. Since character evidence was inadmissible under state law in cases of rape and incest, the prosecution chose to introduce another form of evidence called "habit evidence" in an attempt to establish that Rachelle had cultivated and demonstrated a habit of purity throughout her life. Her extensive volunteer efforts with various sexual purity groups in California and in Eastbrook helped further their claim. Rachelle's only two boyfriends in high school flew out to attest to her lifestyle of purity and to testify under oath that at no time did they have any kind of sexual relations with Rachelle. The resulting investigation proved that either H.T. had raped Rachelle Jacobs or that the two had had consensual sex. When Rachelle finally took the stand, the defense could not find one shred of proof that she ever knew Mr. Taylor or that he knew her. In fact, one of the defense team's most embarrassing moments came when they suggested that Rachelle's return to Eastbrook and the Academy was evidence that she'd suffered no severe trauma in Eastbrook in the past. In Rachelle's finest moment, she recounted eloquently her pain, therapy, faith, and the recovery work that bolstered her courage to return to the school she never got to attend as a sign to herself and her rapist that she was not going to let him win. Accompanied by her parents and her daughter, she vowed to face her fears and potential flashbacks and live! Her strength of character and bold pursuit of her dreams made a strong impact on the jury that day. Ultimately, the irrefutable DNA match between H.T. and Jaleesa Jacobs carried the day. Jaleesa Jacobs was more than a light in Rachelle's life, she was the linchpin of justice and the key to the apprehension of the most dangerous and disturbed man in the history of Eastbrook and Cascade County.

The officers and detectives at the party couldn't stop talking about the courageous mother and their lucky break, but Joe and Maggie knew better. They knew it was a miracle. Ethan knew it was a miracle, too. The providence and plan of God was obvious to anyone who knew the facts of the case and the events leading to Taylor's apprehension. Standing on the deck as the night sky revealed its brilliance, Ethan marveled at what God had done for him and for the people of Eastbrook. Overhearing a woman ask her friend if the little girl knew her father was the Beauty Queen Butcher, Ethan contemplated the difficulties that awaited Rachelle and her daughter and decided it was time to leave. Stopping to shake a few more hands and say goodbye to his mother and father, Ethan made his way to the door and the relief of the open road.

A half hour later, he arrived at the place he wanted to be most. Feeling a rush of gratitude and joy, Ethan bounded up the steps and knocked on the door. Waiting in the soft light of the porch, he could feel his heart race, and he knew he was in love.

"Hello, Lucas. Is Rachelle home?"

"Come on in, Ethan. She's out back."

Stepping through the patio door, Ethan found

Rachelle sitting by the fire pit gazing at the same brilliant sky he'd viewed at his father's place. "I've never seen anything more beautiful!"

"Nothing can compare to God's handiwork," replied Rachelle without looking back at Ethan.

"Agreed, but I wasn't talking about the night sky. The only thing more beautiful than the stars is you," said Ethan. "Mind if I pull up a chair and join you?"

"Help yourself," invited Rachelle. "I was hoping you'd drop by."

"I can't help myself. I know I just saw you on Friday, but you're intoxicating."

"I think someone had too much to drink at the party," teased Rachelle.

"No, ma'am. All I had was a soda and about a half a bag of pretzels."

"Did you bring any for me?" asked Rachelle as she looked at Ethan's empty hands. "You've got a lot to learn about women." Looking into Ethan's steady eyes, Rachelle smiled and said, "Ethan swings and misses—strike two!" Laughing, the couple settled into each other's arms and watched the angels in the night sky.

As Rachelle snuggled close, Ethan reflected over his recent blessings. He'd been dating Rachelle under the radar for the last couple of months. And he believed this was the biggest miracle of all to come out of the case against the BQB—his incredible fortune in meeting Rachelle. A woman he was otherwise unlikely to come across in his day-to-day life, faith being their only real connection. The fellowships they attended weren't exactly peas in a pod, not to mention their considerable physical distance from one another in the city. Ironically, the case had brought them together. From the start there was infatuation and longing, but there was something more. Ethan was smitten, and he was convinced their relationship was meant to be. Even his awkward and clumsy invitation to a first date, six months after their initial meeting at the hospital, had been graciously received by an intrigued and hopeful Rachelle. Ethan's desire for Rachelle was strong, and at times hard for him to control. Her beauty enticed and overwhelmed, but it was her strength of faith and her intimacy with Jesus that engaged him. In their short courtship, her heart had drawn him in, and he hoped one day to win it.

Looking down from her bedroom window, Jaleesa watched the two snuggle below with satisfaction. She enjoyed seeing her mother this happy. Ever since the two started dating, Jaleesa picked up a joy and a peace in her mother that she'd never quite sensed before. The relationship was good for her mom, and Ethan was different from many of the men who'd attempted to be in her mother's life. Ethan was special. He was a Christian, and he genuinely appeared to care for her mother—mind, soul, and body. Leaving the window and slipping into bed, Jaleesa asked God to bless their relationship, and if it was His will and not too much trouble, to allow them to marry. Clicking off her tiny lamp, she closed her eyes, and smiled.

chapter 24

Consultations

Beverly waited nervously for the doctor to return with the results of her pregnancy test. She'd had two children already, and she knew better than anyone what it meant to be late and what it felt like to be pregnant. Things were tight financially, and she desperately wanted to leave her husband, Robert, and move in with Tim, but this child would make things all but impossible. Her gut and her body told her she was with child, but she had to be sure. Hoping against hope that she wouldn't need to abort, Beverly fidgeted and waited and longed to be surprised. It was so unfair that God chose women to bear the children and men to beget them. If only Tim wasn't sterile, she could pretend that the baby was his and perhaps solidify their love. But in reality she knew Tim wouldn't want a child even if he could have one. He was already concerned about dealing with the lone child that still lived with her, even if it was only going to be on a part-time basis after the divorce. Anger burned in her soul at the thought of being pregnant again. Beverly hated getting fat, losing sleep, and having her sex life interrupted. Self-pity coursed through her veins. She hardly ever slept with Robert anymore, and when she did, she always took precautions. Why her? Why now? Life was an endless series of raw deals, she thought.

"I have good news, Mrs. Smith. You're pregnant," announced Soren.

"How can that possibly be good news?" exclaimed Beverly. "I want to schedule an abortion as soon as possible."

"May I ask why, Mrs. Smith?"

"I don't want it!"

"Surely you don't mean that. You're a healthy, beautiful woman, and any child would be lucky to have you for its mother," encouraged Soren.

"I'm broke. I'm leaving my husband, and I don't want it!" reiterated Beverly. "When can we schedule?"

"Mrs. Smith, news of this kind can be very emotional, and feelings can change from day to day. I suggest you take some time to think things over before you make such a life-altering decision."

"Dr. Ulf, I appreciate your advice, but the reason I came to you is that I've already spent a great deal of time considering this option, and I want to do it. Is there any reason we can't proceed with my choice?"

"Normally, I would say no, but, unfortunately, I have no openings for the next two weeks."

"How far along am I?" asked Beverly.

"From the looks of things, given all relevant information, I'd say you were about seven weeks pregnant. Not that far, but clearly carrying a healthy child."

"Would my risk be greater at nine or ten weeks?"

"Not substantially, but the cost would go up."

"Do you know any other doctor who could see me sooner?"

"No one I'd feel comfortable sending you to, and for all I know, their schedule could be as tight as mine," discouraged Soren. "Why don't you take a week more to think about it, and I'll tentatively schedule you for the first possible procedure date I have available."

"I'll take it, but I'm not going to change my mind, Doctor."

"Certainly, it's your choice, but I would look at all your options. Even adoption might be a plausible scenario," said Soren.

"I'm not going to have another one of Robert's babies, not anymore."

"I'm sorry to hear about your troubles, Mrs. Smith. The receptionist out front will see that you get scheduled, and if something in your circumstance changes, don't hesitate to call."

"Thank you, Doctor."

"My pleasure, Mrs. Smith," said Soren. "I do hope things get better for you in the future, regardless of what you choose."

"Thanks for understanding, Doctor Ulf."

"You're welcome."

As Beverly made her way out of the office, Soren stared at her with contempt. He couldn't stand to see a white woman abort, and, thankfully, very few chose his clinic. His clientele was typically the poor and the downtrodden. Women of means rarely came through his door. Not that Mrs. Smith was one of those necessarily, but she still came from good white stock. Nevertheless, thought Soren, if the bitch didn't come to her senses, he'd gladly abort. Perhaps he'd even push her toward permanent sterilization. Soren believed no one who didn't respect their own kind deserved to continue to procreate.

Dr. Ulf always insisted on handling certain consultations in person, but today was different; with the resignation of his most recent scheduler and Nurse V. out sick, he was stuck with the responsibility—a responsibility he loathed, but not one without its opportunities and joys.

Taking a quick sip from his flask, Soren was overjoyed that only one more appointment remained. Stepping out of his office, Dr. Ulf beheld a well-dressed African woman sitting all alone.

"Maskini, I presume? Mr. Johnson called and told me you'd be here. Come on back," invited Dr. Ulf.

"Thank you."

"Have a seat while I look up your test result," said Dr. Ulf. Maskini sat in silence staring at the doctor as he reviewed the findings. "The test was positive, Maskini. You are indeed pregnant."

Placing her hand over her mouth, Maskini gasped as a terrified look broke over her face.

Looking at her without feeling, Dr. Ulf said, "Mr. Johnson wants to abort, correct?"

Nodding, Maskini began to softly weep.

"These things happen unfortunately, but the good news is we have a solution. We can't have Mrs. Johnson finding out, can we? Frankly, it's a small price to pay in exchange for the benefits the affair affords you. You're a very lucky lady to be a mistress so well taken care of. I can attest to many a girlfriend who is not!"

Through her tears, Maskini begged, "Is there nothing I can do to change his mind, any other way to hide the baby—adoption?"

"I'm afraid not. Mr. Johnson was very adamant about his wishes if the test proved positive."

Horrified at the prospect of killing her baby, Maskini said, "Is there any other alternative, any group that can shelter me while I have the baby?"

"Sadly, no," Soren said abruptly. "Besides, choosing that course of action will destroy your relationship with Mr. Johnson."

"Can you help me, Doctor?" pleaded Maskini.

"I am helping you; this really is the best course of action. If you're worried about the embryo, don't. At eight weeks the embryo is little more than a mass of cells. It doesn't feel pain. It's not viable. You won't even remember the pregnancy a couple of weeks from now. In fact, as a favor to you and Mr. Johnson, I can take care of this problem tonight. In just a couple of hours you'll be back in your lover's arms."

"Is it really that simple?"

"Of course, it is. No hiding the pregnancy, no getting fat, no ruined relationships—it's the perfect solution. I see this all the time, and every time someone in your position chooses not to abort, the damage to their relationship is severe."

"How much will it cost?"

"Mr. Johnson assured me that he'd cover all expenses. All I need is your consent, and we'll get started."

"I know I should, but I'm afraid,"

"It's perfectly safe. I promise you won't feel a thing. I'll put you to sleep, and after the procedure is finished, you'll awake without any memory of the event. Trust me, you won't remember a thing."

"Okay, Doctor."

"Great. Sign here," Ulf said, sliding the paper across his desk. "Let's get you prepped."

Covertly slipping his digital camera into his overcoat, Dr. Ulf smiled and ushered Maskini across the hall.

chapter 25

Relief & Pain

Looking up from the morning paper, Tom poured a touch more cream in his coffee. There in front of him was the headline he'd always longed for: "Guilty!— Beauty Queen Butcher gets life!" Tom didn't know how to feel after eighteen years—he just knew it was over. The verdict couldn't bring Jenny back, nor did it fully satisfy Tom, but it did bring a measure of relief. He'd stopped following the case months earlier because it was too painful and angering. Nevertheless, he'd submitted his story to the prosecuting attorney in writing. Tom painfully detailed how the rapist's actions utterly destroyed Jenny and set in motion events that would forever alter both their lives. In the letter, he also passed along his recommendation for sentencing. Tom, understandably, wanted the death penalty. Life in prison, he thought, was too gracious for a monster like the BQB.

Scooping a few more strawberries onto his waffle, Tom felt odd and uncomfortable. There in the stillness of the morning, memories of Jenny came flooding back. Overcome with emotion, he was glad he'd taken the day off. As odd as it felt to be home from work, he knew he wouldn't be of any help to his patients today. Yesterday, when the verdict came in, he'd fallen to pieces and left the clinic. Taugney insisted Tom take a few days off. In fact, Tom was told he wouldn't be welcome back until

Tuesday. Consequently, this was the first Saturday he'd had to himself in ten years. Alone and acutely aware of it, Tom decided a drive might distract him.

Putting on his leather jacket and gloves, he grabbed his keys and stepped outside. There before him sat the latest object of his desire: a brand new blue ZR1. Smiling for the first time that morning, Tom thought to himself, *now this is why you buy a sports car, for days like this.* Tom had always wanted to own a Corvette, but he'd never dreamed he'd be able to afford one that cost over six figures. Business was booming, and the clinic had never been more successful. Tom's American dream machine was fast and ferocious. It had elegant lines and said all he wanted it to say about the status of the driver. He delighted in the newly purchased beast, and he loved driving it in the mountains through dark tunnels and around tight curves. Looking to escape, Tom could think of no better way to spend his day. Slipping into the driver's seat, he grasped the stick and turned the key making the engine thunder with greedy expectation. Pulling slowly out of the garage, the sun glinted off the dark-blue paint. Rumbling with ease to the corner stop sign, Tom looked both ways, put on his Revo shades, and then peeled out. Streaking toward the foothills, he gloried in the exhilaration of affluence.

As the miles passed, Tom noticed the fall day was not unlike the day of his proposal to Jenny. The air was crisp but pleasant. The trees were adorned with the rich colors of fall, while the sky was as clear as crystal. But the brightness of the sun as it showed forth its radiant brilliance was the one thing that jogged his memory most. Passing Metzger's farm, Tom marveled at the golden fields and how they'd been frozen in time. He loved this stretch before the mouth of the canyon. Here, the road straightened out for about twenty miles. Checking his radar detector, he opened up the throttle and felt the power of the beast. Watching the needle pass one-hundred-and-thirty miles per hour, Tom noticed the engine wasn't even in labor. Pushing the car further, he felt the rush of performance. Slowing down considerably as he entered the canyon, Tom still drove furiously, exceeded every limit and dodging every weekend traveler. Driving like a man possessed, he raced all the way to Timber Pass. Arriving faster than he ever had before, Tom parked and stepped outside. The view from the pass was always majestic, but today it was captivating. As the mountains, valleys, and hills faded into dark and light bumps on nature's loom, Tom took in the fresh air and began to feel his tensions release.

He loved the High Country Lodge. It was perfectly seated on the mountainside, affording great views of the endless ridges, timber, and bluffs that descended to the floor of the plain. The great hearth in the center of the structure crackled nine months out of the year with the flash of fire. Today the heat was welcome but not necessary. The service was good, if a bit slow, but the food was excellent. Tom loved their smothered mountain burrito and their delicious mud pie. He'd forgotten in his quest for success just how good it was to get away and take time to enjoy the simple pleasures in life. Enjoying his lunch and the breathtaking vista, Tom began to unwind.

Savoring his delicious meal, Tom's tranquility was broken by two young men who'd just been seated in the booth behind him.

"Heck of a nice day, isn't it?"

"I'll say, the fish were pounding my Adams fly."

"They get greedy this time of year. There's nothing like fishing just before the winter hits."

Tom's mind flashed to his love of fishing, a love he'd neglected over the past eighteen years. In his busyness, he'd all but forgotten the simple pleasure of a stream and the feel of a trout. His mind flooded with visions of his father and brother and the joys of youth. How great the times they shared! Interrupted by the waitress, Tom asked for some extra green chili and a refill. Taking a warm satisfying bite, he again tuned in to the nearby conversation.

"Did you hear about how they convicted the Butcher?"

"Completely remarkable! I can't believe the lady kept her baby after something like that."

"Yeah, she didn't tell anyone. She just went back home and had the baby—she didn't even give it up for adoption."

"Brutal courage!"

"The quirks in life, can you imagine? The worst possible insult and it turns out to be the very thing that brings your attacker down."

"Crazy how DNA works. It's now the silent partner in justice!"

"Does anybody know who she is or what she does?"

"No, the media never released any of the victims' names, and the judge kept a tight rein on public access. I heard he even brought the girls in to testify through a secret entrance into the courthouse."

"Crazy stuff!"

"Yeah, the balls on that lady..." One of the men snorted out a laugh. "I guess that didn't sound so good, did it?"

Laughing, the two men began to tease about the faux pas as Tom sat motionless. His mind was overwhelmed with the truth. How could it have happened three times—what are the odds? When did the victim come forward? How old is the child? How did the police find out? What irony! What horror! What regret! Hastily pulling out his wallet, Tom laid several twenty dollar bills on the table and quickly left the lodge.

Speeding down the canyon, Tom's mind swirled with emotion. The fluidity and precision of his machine no longer satisfied or mattered. He was bankrupt and raw. Could that have been Jenny? Should that have been Jenny? If Jenny had made a different choice, could they have stopped this monster earlier? Was he responsible? Hitting some loose gravel coming off a turn, the car skidded, whipping up a panicked cloud of dust before Tom regained control and pulled to a stop. Desperate and disillusioned, he fought his rising tide of regret. There on the shoulder under the shadow of the tall timber, he swore in furious anger. Gasping for relief as he melted from the depths of his soul, the face he saw was not that of Jenny Foster, but Jamie Goodwin. It had been a long time since he'd let himself think of her. Tom had worked so hard to bury his memories of Jamie. He'd had other girls since, but Jamie was the only other girl he'd truly loved besides Jenny. As memories flooded his mind, Tom could barely breathe. At last, he saw Jamie before him.

"Just go, Tom. Go," Jamie said through her tears.

"Jamie, these things take time. We'll be good again," pleaded Tom.

"You don't care about me, about us!"

"You know I do, Jay, you're just having a rough time."

"A rough time! We killed our baby, Tom!"

"No, we didn't! We got rid of something neither of us wanted and neither of us were ready for!

"You can lie to yourself all you want, but I'm through listening to your lies. I want you out of my life. It's over!"

"Why are you so determined to throw away what we have?"

"What we had, we flushed down the toilet. Now get out!"

"Jamie…"

"Get out. I hate you! Get out!" Jamie shouted.

Tearing himself away and back to the present, Tom's eyes burned with pain as the emotions of the past infected his soul. He'd lost Jenny, and he'd lost Jamie, but Jamie was his fault. He should have listened better, he should have pushed less. Why was he always trying to fix things? Why was he so afraid to love, to parent, to give, to trust? Shaking his head and cursing, Tom punched the steering wheel repeatedly until his knuckles bled. Exhausted and no longer willing to fight, he shifted into first and headed down the canyon. Nothing caught his eye and no pleasure was derived from his affluence, not even the orange brilliance of the setting sun drew his admiration. He was alone, and he knew tomorrow would be no different. Empty and cold, Tom finally pulled into his driveway. He wished he'd gone to work, he wished…

chapter 26

Hawaii

Jaleesa stood with her toes buried in the sand as the tide crashed against her ankles. She loved the smell of the ocean and the sound of breaking water. Though she'd only visited the ocean twice since she'd moved with her mother to Eastbrook, it always felt like coming home. Enchanted by the raw beauty of the islands, Jaleesa was in love with Hawaii. The white and black sand beaches, the green of the vegetation, the lush grandeur of the mountains, and the beauty of the valleys all captivated her soul. She'd never seen such breathtaking flowers or such clear water. This was a place marked by the hand of God, and she could think of no better place to celebrate a marriage equally marked.

Jaleesa felt truly blessed to be a part of her loving family. Her mother had never been happier. Her career and her growing relationship with Ethan were both sources of joy. Lucas and Aaliyah were still deeply in love and clearly the bedrock of the entire family. Rachelle's older brother, Keshon, was celebrating ten years of marriage to his beautiful bride, T'anay, and her cousins, Terrell and Hope, were adorable. It seemed the entire family was experiencing a season of joy and prosperity. Despite the acne of a sixteen-year-old, Jaleesa was enjoying life in high school and all the trappings that came with it. Each day she looked more like her mother, and it was apparent to everyone that she was becoming a beauty just like Rachelle. She could think of no better place to celebrate thirty-five years of marriage than this majestic island paradise.

Lucas and Aaliyah had decided to spend two beautiful weeks in Hawaii celebrating their thirty-five years of commitment, faith, and love, and for the two of them that couldn't be accomplished without including God's richest blessings in their lives: their children and their grandchildren. The trip, thus far, had been a true delight and a magnificent experience. Amid the grand views, succulent seafood, and pristine beaches, the laughter of family stood out. The simple joy of being together in fellowship is what made this anniversary one of their best. They marveled at the island waterfalls and the sunlit clouds that surrounded their private helicopter as they peered into the mouth of Kilauea, but the time watching Jaleesa, Terrell, and Hope bring their imaginings to life in the sand were the most precious. The impossible card game played below deck, while the cards slid back and forth, as they sailed to Molokai was every bit as stamped upon their minds as the dolphins that leapt in pace with their vessel's bow. Hawaii was indeed a place of enchantment and possibility, but without their children and grandchildren present, its richness would have been diminished, for they, too, were filled with enchantment and possibility.

Life was good, and Jaleesa knew it. A feeling of euphoria washed over her as she danced along the tide and took in the beauty of the beach. Looking back at her mother lying in the sun reading, Jaleesa was filled with appreciation for her and all the sacrifices she'd made. To be sure, Lucas and Aaliyah had always been a tower of support, giving Rachelle stability and financial provision, but it was her mother's hard work, determination, and character that had been critical in Jaleesa's life. She had great respect for her mother and the effort she had put forth as a single parent. Rachelle had made all the difference, and Jaleesa counted herself blessed. Looking down, the glint of a pearly shell caught her eye. Reaching, Jaleesa picked up the abalone and marveled at its radiance. The colors reflected the sun in a promise and invigorated her imagination. She sensed today would be another special day, and she couldn't wait for their next adventure. Walking toward her mother, Jaleesa soaked up the sun's heat and smiled.

"How's the water, baby?" asked Rachelle.

"Perfect!"

"You couldn't ask for a better day."

"It's lovely, Mama," said Jaleesa. "When do we have to meet Papa and Gammy?"

"After lunch, but we've got to leave soon if we're going to shower, dress, and catch the seafood special at the Island Cutter."

"I love their shrimp bisque," reflected Jaleesa.

"Me, too," agreed Rachelle. "What's in your hand?"

"It's an abalone shell I found. I've never seen one this perfect. It shows the most brilliant colors when you hold it at the right angle. It reminds me of the beautiful rainbows you see back home after it rains."

"You hold on to that, baby. I believe that shell holds a promise, just like every rainbow. God wants to do extraordinary things with your life, J.J. Hold fast to Him, and He'll bring a rainbow after every rain," advised Rachelle.

"Thanks for believing in me, Mama."

"I always have, baby."

"Help me pack up this beach bag, will ya?"

Dried from the sun, Jaleesa scooped up the volleyball

and water bottles, while Rachelle shook out the towels and grabbed the radio and suntan lotion. The temperature was a perfect eighty-three degrees as the girls walked back to the rented beach house. In the quiet of the house, Rachelle beheld her budding daughter. She was changing so fast. She could still remember the little girl who stood beaming in head-to-toe pink on the first day of school for her mommy's litany of photographs. The young girl who fell a dozen times before she steadied her bike and rode through tears the length of the street. Rachelle would never forget the streaked radiance on Jaleesa's face when she conquered. There had been so many memorable times—like the time Jaleesa fiercely grabbed her arm on the big roller coaster and screamed with terrified glee. The years hadn't always been easy, but the two shared an unmistakable bond and a kindred spirit, forged out of love, shared blood, and time. As Rachelle moved into the master bedroom, Jaleesa followed and made her way to the deck.

"It's so beautiful here, isn't it, Mama?"

"It's extraordinary," replied Rachelle. "You mind if I hop in the shower first?"

"Sure, go ahead."

Excusing herself, Rachelle walked into the master bath and pulled the French doors closed. Sliding the small drapes in place, she turned on the water and began to undress. As Rachelle slipped out of her one piece and prepared to shower, Jaleesa looked back and caught her mother's image in the mirror through a small gap in the curtain. Seeing afresh the scar on her mother's left breast and the jagged dimple in her side, Jaleesa winced. She'd seen it once before, but had never had the courage to ask about it. Turning her gaze away, she returned to the ocean. Certainly there were things about her mother that she didn't know, but how did she receive those injuries?

What had happened to her? Working up the courage to ask, Jaleesa waited. Fifteen minutes later, Rachelle entered the bedroom wrapped in a towel.

"Your turn, baby," said Rachelle.

"Did you leave me any hot water?"

"A little."

"Is that why you always wear a one piece on the beach?" blurted Jaleesa.

"Come again?"

"The scars, is that why you wear a one piece—to cover the scars?"

Pausing, Rachelle looked at her daughter and then at the floor. Understanding that this day could one day come, she answered, "I suppose that's part of it, but I've always been a big believer in modesty and mystery. Keeps 'em guessing!"

"How did it happen?"

"It was an event that happened after my senior year in high school."

"What kind of event?"

"I don't like to talk about it, J.J. It was a long time ago, and I'm fine now, okay?"

"Okay, Mama," agreed Jaleesa. "Mama…"

"Yes, baby."

"I'm sorry that happened to you," consoled Jaleesa.

"Thank you, sweetheart. Now you go on and take that shower so we won't be late."

As Jaleesa washed the sand from her body, she contemplated her mother's words and her injuries. She didn't understand fully, but she knew her mother had been wounded in some deep way. Perhaps one day her mother would share with her the truth. Or perhaps she never would. Some wounds are too deep to express. All she could do is accept her mother's wishes and pray. There in the midst of the water, she prayed for peace and for the grace to let her curiosity rest. Troubled, she asked God to bless her mother and heal her wounds.

After an enjoyable lunch and a spirited conversation about some upcoming shopping and a really nice handbag the two had seen the day before, Jaleesa and Rachelle headed for the harbor and their rendezvous with the family.

"Do you know much about Pearl Harbor, Mama?"

"I know a little. I know it happened in December. I know it was the Japanese who attacked the Pacific Fleet, and I know it was the beginning of our nation's involvement in World War II."

"My history teacher told me that the Arizona Memorial was a must see."

"That's where we're headed, J.J. Papa's always wanted to see it."

Arriving, Jaleesa and Rachelle walked to the visitor center and met up with Lucas, Aaliyah, and Uncle Keshon. T'anay and the children had decided to spend the day at a family fun center near their hotel with go-carts, mini golf, bowling, and laser tag. After exchanging hugs and small talk, the five of them entered the visitor center and took their time perusing the pictures, artifacts, dioramas, and historical documents that were on display. Keshon, who loved to build models as a young boy, took particular delight in the intricate display of Battleship Row. The harbor had been painstakingly exacted, and each ship was meticulously represented in its precise anchored position for the morning of the seventh. Rachelle and Jaleesa marveled at the photographic murals, as Lucas and Aaliyah stopped to chat with a Pearl Harbor veteran who still possessed a fire in his eyes despite all he'd seen in his eighty-plus years of life. The day was perfect, and Lucas was having the time of his life. A slight breeze blew through the open-air portion of the facility, making the afternoon every bit as splendid as the morning had been. The whole Jacobs clan was filled with excitement and awe as they stepped back into history.

"Dad, look at this picture. Can you believe the size of that explosion," said Keshon.

"Unbelievable what happened here. Many of those young men never had a chance. Amazing the power of the images they captured that day."

"What did the veteran have to say?"

"Paul was a navy corpsman who assisted in the rescue efforts that morning after coming home from the shipyard. He said he still remembers the men they lost, the fires, and the smell of burning fuel."

"That must have been so insane."

"I can't imagine being so young and having to deal with all the chaos, death, and fear," reflected Lucas. "Probably the most interesting thing Paul told me about was the 'black tears.' He said to look for them when we get to the Arizona Memorial."

"Black tears? What's that?"

"Apparently, the Arizona had over a million gallons of oil on board when she sank, and the ship still seeps a little bit of it to the surface each day. 'A fitting tribute to the fallen as the Arizona weeps for her slain,' he said."

"Wow, that's intense!"

"I know, I'd never heard of that until he told me," confessed Lucas. Glancing at his watch, Lucas noticed the time, "Hey, we're about to miss the show. Let's get the girls and head over to the theater."

When the documentary finished, Jaleesa had acquired a newfound appreciation for the gravity of Pearl Harbor and the ferocity of the surprise attack. The film captivated in a way no other documentary had for Jaleesa. Watching the attack unfold at the site where it actually occurred added a whole new dimension and richness to the historical reality. The stories of heroism inspired her—especially the exploits of Doris Miller, a navy cook on board the USS West Virginia, who helped his fellow sailors reach safety during the attack and who also manned a 50-caliber anti-aircraft gun, downing a Japanese warplane. Leaving the theater with her family, J.J. felt surreal gazing across the water at the brilliance of the USS Arizona Memorial. Walking to the dock to wait for the boat that would bring them out to the memorial, Jaleesa listened to her grandfather talk about the battle and the interesting tidbits he'd picked up over the years. She liked seeing Papa delight in the experience. Today, she understood better than ever his love of history. In this place, history came alive. The crowd was full of every race, creed, and color as people from all over the nation and the world gathered to take in the site and remember the men who fought and died at Pearl Harbor. As the throng of people vacated and then filled the ferry, conversations began to die, and a reverent hush soon fell over the crowd. Only the occasional whisper could be heard amid the lapping water and the steady drone of the engine as they passed the quarter-mile trip to the Arizona.

Entering the memorial, Rachelle and Jaleesa took in the names of the lost. Looming before them was a large white wall etched with the names of the fallen. Jaleesa's eyes focused on the inscription surrounded by the names that read: "TO THE MEMORY OF THE GALLANT MEN HERE ENTOMBED AND THEIR SHIPMATES WHO GAVE THEIR LIVES IN ACTION ON DECEMBER 7, 1941 ON THE USS ARIZONA." Looking at all the men's names gave this fellowship of death a personalized reality, and the girls began to feel the loss. Making their way to the side of the memorial, they gazed out on the rusted parts of the ship that showed above the water. Bumping against the side of a rusted, round shaft was a wreath of beautiful flowers now beginning to wilt. It was an awesome sight as the sun penetrated the water and revealed both hidden and still hidden parts of the massive ship that lay underneath. There was a power in this place, and one couldn't help but feel it—a mixture of longing, loss, and patriotism. Overcome with emotion, Rachelle looked up and saw the stars and stripes list in the breeze and curl like a tired soldier at the end of his first real look at war. Coming over to join them, Papa, Gammy, and Uncle Keshon took in the hallowed waters.

"Dad, is it true there are hundreds of sailors still entombed in the belly of the Arizona?" asked Keshon.

"From what I understand, of the eleven hundred and seventy-seven men who were killed in the attack, only two hundred and twenty-nine were recovered," informed Lucas.

"That's why this place holds such a powerful spirit," interjected Aaliyah.

"Amazing," said Keshon.

"It's the largest loss of life ever for one of our nation's warships," Lucas said.

"So sad, Daddy," uttered Rachelle.

"Yes, it is," responded Lucas. "So many young boys cut off before they'd really begun to live!"

"Look, Papa, it's the tears the veteran told you about. See?" pointed Jaleesa.

There in the water below, a thin streak of black was illuminated by the sun in the clear turquoise water. It rose to the surface like a whisper from the deep, uttering a mournful reflection of what might have been if men could learn to live together in peace and harmony.

As quickly as the Jacobs had witnessed the sob, it disappeared like a mist upon the wind. Silence passed between them as their souls filled with understanding. After a long pause, Lucas gathered his family and said, "How many more tears will we shed before man learns to love his brother?"

"It sure seems like the hardest lesson," said Aaliyah.

"No doubt," said Lucas. "Thanks for coming with me today. It's been a profound experience. I'm glad you all could be here to share it with me."

The next morning, Rachelle arose to find a note on her kitchen table that read, "Meet us at the Blue Lagoon for breakfast. We've reserved a table on the deck for nine o'clock, Dad." Picking up the phone, Rachelle called Keshon to inform him of the morning festivities. Graciously bowing out, he let Rachelle know that his family was bushed and they'd catch up with the tribe later that afternoon. Jaleesa was already with her grandparents, having spent the night with them.

Knowing her daughter was safe, Rachelle looked at the clock and realized she had more than an hour before she had to be at breakfast. Pleased, she rummaged through her luggage and pulled out a small worn Bible. Rachelle enjoyed her solitude when it presented itself, something she was afforded more and more now that Jaleesa was in high school and her medical career was well in hand. Relaxing, she fixed a cup of tea, and stepped out on the deck with her Bible. Looking out at the majesty of the ocean, Rachelle contemplated the Creator of time who could hold such waters in the palm of His hand. Smiling, she prayed to her Savior as the light danced on her face. He'd made all the difference in the dark places of life. Picking up her Bible, she read a few Psalms in the glow of the morning before moving to the shower and the rest of her day.

hushed

Arriving at the Blue Lagoon, Rachelle looked lovely in a beautiful red summer dress. Her deep black hair glistened in the sun as she walked out on the deck. She radiated joy after her hour of peace and her time with the Lord. Rachelle was excited about these last three days in Oahu and meeting her parents and Jaleesa for breakfast after a night apart, but when she appeared on the deck, it wasn't her family that she saw.

"Surprise!" Ethan bellowed.

Hugging Ethan, Rachelle said, "What are you doing here, and where's my family?"

"I asked them if I could steal a little bit of your time, and they graciously accepted," replied Ethan. "It appears I have you for the whole day if you'll take me?"

"You sly dog, I thought you couldn't get away from work."

"The captain owed me a favor, and I cashed in. Paradise was too much to miss, especially with the prettiest girl on the island. What do you say? You want to make a day of it?"

"Oh, I don't know," teased Rachelle. "Are you sure my parents and Jaleesa are okay with it?"

"You think I didn't ask? They said it would be their pleasure. They thought you could use a day to relax; besides, they knew I paid for my own ticket."

"When are you going back?"

"Same time as the rest of you. If I'm lucky, maybe I'll get to sit next to a sexy doctor on the way back."

"That'll depend on your behavior and if you can keep your hands to yourself."

"You know I'm always a first-rate gentleman!"

"Yeah, sure."

"Let's eat. The smell of the surf and turf is killing me."

"For breakfast? Are you kidding me?"

"It's going to be a big day. I'm gonna need a solid foundation."

As the two ordered breakfast, Rachelle flirted with Ethan and twirled her hair. She'd forgotten just how strong and handsome her man was. His hands, his muscles, his skin, his jaw, his eyes—it all went together nicely. But it was his heart she truly loved. He was funny and carefree, strong and playful, and yet he had integrity of soul. He was a man's man. His character and compassion were always present, even if he feigned otherwise. She was delighted he'd come. With the demands of detective work and his limited vacation time, she'd been convinced that there was no way possible for him to accompany her to Hawaii to celebrate her parents' 35th wedding anniversary. Still, here he was sitting before her grinning without a care in the world. Certainly, this day, and the rest of her trip, would be one to remember.

"I thought I'd take you shopping for a new suit and a sarong, and then we'd go snorkeling at a private beach."

"What's wrong with the suit I have now?"

"Nothing. You wear it well. I just think we can do better, especially with the selection offered here in Oahu."

"This isn't just a ploy to see me in all my glory, is it?"

"I won't deny there are certain benefits to going shopping with you. But no, Miss Jacobs, this is to ensure that the fit is suitable for snorkeling and that the crew of the catamaran I've booked keeps their eye on the water and me in the boat."

"Purely humanitarian," said Rachelle.

"Completely."

"Well, in that case, I'm in."

"How's your crab omelet?" asked Ethan. "It looks delicious."

Standing on the boat after a beautiful morning of

shopping and fun, Rachelle's mocha skin flashed like the water about her as she slipped on her flippers and prepared to enter the turquoise-enveloped reef. Her elegant yellow one-piece sizzled under the sun's rays, but it was hardly the draw. Moving in position, her long elegant muscles fluidly snapped to attention upon leaving the yacht and entering the water. She was a sight to behold as she swam graciously to the submerged reef. Undulating in the lapping pockets of water, Rachelle lost herself in the winsome coral. Below her, myriad colors swayed as a pattern of light and shadow played across the coral's face. She felt blessed to be in Hawaii and overjoyed now that Ethan had come.

Rachelle was right about the beauty beneath the waves. It was a whole new world, a different dimension, Ethan thought. He couldn't get over the diversity of species and the brilliance of God's underwater world. He'd been to aquariums before, but this was like nothing he'd ever seen, and the densely packed marine life was overwhelming. The eels, turtles, puffer, angel, and butterfly fishes, the blue-green algae, bright-red sponges, urchins, brittlestars, and anemones blended together like a deciduous forest molting in the autumn breeze. Out of the corner of his eye, Ethan caught sight of a school of yellow fish that raced beneath him and disappeared into the labyrinth of coral and reef that stretched as far as his eye could see. The life that teemed before them was inexplicable. As Rachelle beheld a beautiful angel fish and many other works of the Almighty she couldn't name, Ethan beheld her in the beauty of the water. She was everything he could have hoped for and all he wanted.

The carefree couple delighted as they swam and played among the hidden treasures of God's creation. The ocean was refreshing and the rays penetrating as they swam together and apart through the waters of the

Pacific. Taking respites to talk, laugh, and kiss amid their exploration, Ethan and Rachelle were enjoying to the full their romantic adventure and this season of courtship, discovery, and emerging love. Getting out of the ocean, the two toweled off and lay in the warmth of the powerful afternoon sun. Ethan, delighting in the occasional refreshing spray produced by the catamaran as it cut a path toward shore, exhaled with satisfaction.

Arriving at the harbor, Ethan helped Rachelle off the yacht and the couple walked hand-in-hand to the showers and their next big adventure. As Rachelle rinsed and dressed, she thought about Ethan and how much she loved him. From their very first contact at the hospital, she'd been attracted to him, but it was the man that she'd grown to know hiking through the woods, playing in the church volleyball league, walking in the park, fishing at the lake, and sipping coffee in between shifts that had captured her heart. The leadership he'd shown, both as a detective and in the church, had impressed her. She loved the way he closed his eyes and raised his hands during worship, even if he did sing a little off-key. His dedication to the Wednesday morning prayer group that gathered at six a.m. reflected his sincerity of faith—and she liked that. She respected Ethan. He was a good man and a good friend, and she felt things for him she'd never felt with anyone else.

Waiting outside the showers, Ethan smiled as Rachelle exited the structure in a t-shirt and jeans with her hair all tousled. Even then, she couldn't look anything but gorgeous. Her beauty was such that no matter what her state or how tired she was or how hard she'd worked out or how fierce the elements, she never failed to shine. Ethan was captivated by everything about her. Her character, her beauty, her strength, her discipline, her work ethic, her purity—she was worth more than rubies. He'd been looking for her all his life, and he hoped today she, too, was looking. Taking her hand and slipping a kiss on her cheek, Ethan walked Rachelle to a shiny BMW coupe he'd rented and opened the door for his girl.

"Nice wheels, ET. You spent a little cash on this endeavor," Rachelle teased.

"My girlfriend's a smug doctor. You've gotta pull out the big guns to impress her," Ethan retorted.

"Sounds like one of those high-maintenance types."

"You wouldn't know it if you looked at the way she keeps her hair."

"Maybe she's got you so bedazzled that she doesn't care how she looks."

"Maybe," Ethan chuckled. "Maybe."

"What's next, detective?"

"Speaking of detection, I think it's time we go on a little seek-and-find mission. You up for it?"

"Point me in the right direction, Sherlock."

"That's the spirit," Ethan blurted as he handed Rachelle an envelope and a map.

Taking the envelope from Ethan, Rachelle read out loud the handwritten note: "*Before we can dine, you need to look fine. So, before we can eat, there are some tasks to complete. With the genius you are, I know we'll go far! Use the map as your guide, and lead us on toward the tide. The X marks the spot of your first discovery.*"

"Nice note," Rachelle mocked.

"Don't let me down," said Ethan. "You got what it takes, navigator?"

"What are you up to, Mr. Tyndale?"

"Just trying to have a little fun, Ray."

Looking at Ethan suspiciously, Rachelle playfully

punched him in the shoulder and said, "I know you. You're up to something! This better not be one of your practical jokes."

"No jokes, Ray, just a bit of fun before dinner."

Studying the map, Rachelle guided Ethan to the proper exit and a small strip of beach. Stepping out of the car, she watched the ocean surge and spray every time it rhythmically contacted the rocky shoreline at the north end of the white sand beach. With the sun setting lower in the sky, she wasn't surprised to see a diminished crowd on the beach, but to not see anyone came as quite a shock. Moving further up the beach she discovered a small ornate wooden box, no bigger than a child's lunch pail.

"I've found it, Ethan. This is it," she exclaimed. Excited but cautious, Rachelle peered into the box (she still remembered the time Ethan had hidden one of those spring-loaded lizard toys in a similar gag). Opening it slowly, she discovered yet another note. Looking up at Ethan, she remarked, "This is a wild goose chase, isn't it?"

"No, every spot has a reward. Read the note."

Gently unfolding the paper, she read: *"If you avoid the spray, you'll be sorry today. Look to the pool, and you'll find a jewel."*

"You know this is my only pair of dry clothes?"

"Hey, a little water never hurt anyone, especially an old beachcomber like yourself," said Ethan. "I think if you watch your step, you'll manage it. Or, if you'd rather, we can just move on to the next discovery."

"You're enjoying this, aren't you?"

"Man's gotta have a little fun, especially when he cashes in his vacation time and buys an overpriced ticket to Hawaii!"

"You know you just couldn't stand to leave me unguarded on the beach!"

"A man does have to keep a close eye on his assets!" chimed Ethan. "Times a wastin', little lady."

Rolling up her pant legs, Rachelle grabbed a handful of sand and without warning flung it in the direction of Ethan's face. Ducking most of the debris and spitting out the few grains that reached their target, Ethan started out after the instigator and yelled, "You're in trouble now, lassie!" Rachelle, already in a full sprint, laughing and bounding over the cooling sand, was well out of reach. After a few close calls and a stumble, Ethan finally corralled his lady and spun her high through the air. Laughing and out of breath, the two held each other close and enjoyed the moment. Rachelle looked perfect as the descending sun glimmered off her silky hair. Stealing a kiss, Ethan took his love by the hand and led her through the mist of the crashing surf. Hopping from rock to rock, Rachelle searched diligently for the hidden treasure. Peering ahead, she spotted the perfect little pool nestled inside a large rock formation. This is it, she realized; this is the spot described in the note. Timing the tide perfectly, she leapt onto the rocks and moved swiftly to the spot. Looking into the rippling three-foot-wide pool, she saw a little green box rocking in the bottom of the depression. Extracting it from twelve inches of water, she scurried back to Ethan and the safety and dryness of the beach.

Opening the box, she sighed, "They're beautiful, Ethan. The exact pair I wanted from the ski lodge last Christmas. I didn't think I'd ever see them again."

"I knew you liked 'em. Besides, those emeralds will look great on your cute little ears."

"They're absolutely beautiful," beamed Rachelle. "Thank you, Ethan."

"You're welcome, Ray," Ethan said, hugging Rachelle. "Is that the only thing in the box?"

"There's more," Rachelle said excitedly. Returning her attention to the box she spotted the crumpled note. "Ah, yes, the next discovery." Unfolding the note, as the sky began to show forth its color, she read: *"Get back in your car, for the next stop is not far. Continue up the road past the public commode. Turn left at the light or risk the troubles of night. Follow the sugar cane field to mile marker eight. And there enter in—your reward will be great. Hurry and arrive before the sun sets, or risk being filled with lasting regrets."*

Looking at the golden streaks upon the ocean, Rachelle knew her time was short. Jerking Ethan's hand, she urged, "Let's go, ET. Let's get a move on. This is gettin' good!" Rushing quickly to the car, the two hopped inside and sped off to the cane field.

Arriving at the sugar cane field, Rachelle used the hand-drawn map and accompanying pace estimates to guide her to the next piece of the puzzle. The dense, tall cane would have been almost impossible to navigate if it weren't for the small paths in between rows and those cut by the farmers for access. Walking through the field was both eerie and beautiful as the cane whistled in the evening breeze. The now-fading sun dappled and streaked the narrow paths through the thick crop. Ethan followed Rachelle closely as she made her journey through the maze. Wide-eyed as she walked among the tall grass, Rachelle marveled at the splendor of the evening sun as it played in the field. Reaching the junction of two paths, she stopped dead in her tracks. There before her, glinting in the few remaining beams of light, was an elegant string of pearls tied delicately to a group of stalks by a red ribbon. Rachelle gasped with delight at the beautiful discovery.

"Now I know you're up to something. These are gorgeous," exclaimed Rachelle.

"What, I can't dote on my girl?" I've always thought you'd look stunning in pearls. I just thought I'd bring a little paradise to paradise, that's all."

"I don't know what to say, Ethan."

"Say you love me," whispered Ethan.

"I do," responded Rachelle, leaning in for a kiss.

"Maybe I should buy you jewelry more often," teased Ethan.

"Well, it can't hurt," confessed Rachelle. "I almost forgot—the note!"

"Read it."

"Thanks for the sugar, Sugar!" Looking up with a smile on her face, Rachelle said, "You're unbelievable. Could these get any cornier?"

"I couldn't resist—go on, read the rest."

"With your jewelry in place, we need to finish with grace. So it's off we go to a place you know to put on your best and discover the rest. So take us back to your hut with a view. 'Cause I've got another surprise for you."

"We better get going. It's getting hard to see," reminded Ethan.

As the two walked joyously out of the sugar cane field in the dimming light, they heard the sharp sound of a stalk snap in the distance. Ethan thought nothing of it until he saw Rachelle shudder and freeze. Her sense memory kicked in, and in the dying glow of the evening's light, the woods flashed before her eyes and the muffled sound of snapping beneath the feet of a monster. A look of horror emanated from her face. Frozen, Rachelle looked in the distance with trepidation and fear. Lunging to her side, Ethan put his arms around her and held her close.

"It's all right, baby. I've got you, I'm here. Hold on to me. I'll keep you safe."

Coaxing her frozen body out of its shock, Ethan quickly led Rachelle out of the maze of grass and into the BMW beside the road. "It's okay, you're safe now. We're going home." Realizing his error in judgment, Ethan chastised himself in his mind. Stupid, so stupid—why had he picked a sugar cane field in the lateness of the evening to hide the necklace? Idiot! As the car sped away, Rachelle began to breathe. Placing her hand on her chest, she closed her eyes, issued a silent prayer, and began to work on calming down.

"I'm sorry I freaked out back there."

"It's my fault. I don't know what I was thinking choosing a spot like that. I'm so sorry, Rachelle. Will you forgive me?"

"It's not your fault, Ethan. It's nobody's fault."

"It's somebody's fault," blurted Ethan. Frustrated, Ethan sighed and said, "I'm sorry. I feel terrible."

"That hasn't happened in a long time. I'll be okay," Rachelle encouraged as she put her head on Ethan's shoulder. Placing his hand on her thigh, Ethan patted her leg while the last glimmer of light faded from the night sky. Arriving at the beach house, Ethan walked Rachelle up the steps and safely guided her inside. Putting her comfortably onto the couch, he made sure she was relaxed before he went to the kitchen to obtain a glass of water for the woman he loved.

"I hope this doesn't spoil the rest of your plans, Ethan?"

"No they can wait. It's important that we take care of you first. Is there anything I can do to make you feel more comfortable or safe?"

"I think I need a moment in my room. Would you stay out here and wait for me?"

"Of course. Take all the time you need. I'll be right here."

"Thanks for supporting me, Ethan, and thanks for today. You've always been so good to me."

Excusing herself, Rachelle walked into her room, closing the door behind her. Turning on the sink, she could still feel her fear as she washed her face. Ethan felt miserable. The biggest night of his life and he'd unwittingly put Rachelle in a position to remember the terror of the past. How come he didn't think things through better? Why did it have to happen tonight? Looking up at the mirror, Rachelle beheld the words she had written on the glass the day before: *For God has not given us a spirit of fearfulness, but one of power, love, and sound judgment. So don't be ashamed of the testimony about our Lord, or of me His prisoner. Instead, share in suffering for the gospel, relying on the power of God.* Tears came to her eyes as the Scripture ministered. Closing her eyes, she prayed and thanked God for His encouragement, grace, and empowerment. Finishing her prayer, Rachelle looked over at her bed and there sitting on top was a beautiful box wrapped in a red sash with a note on it. This must have been the next phase in Ethan's plan, she thought. Moving to the bed, she sat down on the edge and slipped the note out from underneath the sash. Opening the envelope, she read: "*My darling, Rachelle. You are my pearl of great price, and I wanted you to know how special you are to me. Please accept this final gift and meet me down on the beach for a firelight dinner. I love you, Ray. You bring me joy. Ethan.*"

As her tears began to strike the page, she knew the night must go on. Rising, she gathered the gift, wiped her eyes, and entered the bathroom yet again.

Leaving his self-condemnation and worry behind, Ethan sat on the couch and prayed for Rachelle. He pleaded with God to heal her heart and mend the brokenness. They seldom talked about her attack, but they both knew it cast a shadow at times. He loved Rachelle, and he'd do whatever he could to make her happy and keep her safe, but he knew that only God could truly heal her wounds and bring her peace. So it was to the Great I Am that he committed his request. With eyes closed and lips moving in supplication, he heard the door open. Looking up, Ethan blinked in amazement. Standing before him was Rachelle in her final gift—a beautiful strapless white chiffon dress that fit her perfectly. Her size-six frame and full figure commanded attention, but the glow on her face swept him off his feet. She seemed utterly different from the terrified woman he'd escorted home. The woman standing before him was luminous and bold. Ethan could feel Rachelle's courage like a sharp wind on a winter day. This was the woman he loved, the girl he knew, and the one he'd first met at the hospital. She was nobody's victim!

"You look stunning in that dress," praised Ethan. "I knew it would look great on you, but this…" Rising to meet her, he said, "Do you like it?"

"I love it, and I love you," Rachelle said, giving him a hug. "Let's go down to the beach."

"Are you sure? Because…"

Putting a finger to his lips, Rachelle said, "Ethan, let's not let the past define us."

Beaming, Ethan took Rachelle's hand and walked her out to the secluded beach behind the house. A glowing bonfire lit up a lone table and chairs. An elegant tablecloth listed in the evening breeze as the sound of the gentle surf pulsed to nature's rhythm. The brilliant canopy of stars dulled as they neared the fire and the heat of its welcome. Pulling out Rachelle's chair, Ethan offered her a seat, pushed in her chair, and lit the center candle. Ethan poured each of them some water and retrieved two halibut entrees from the temperature-controlled grill behind the table.

"I took the liberty of ordering your favorite: grilled halibut, rice pilaf, steamed vegetables, baked potato, and, of course, ample tartar sauce," Ethan said with a smile.

"It looks delicious. Thank you."

"You're welcome. Shall we pray?"

"Please."

Taking Rachelle's hand in his, Ethan prayed, "Heavenly Father, thank you for life and for this wonderful food we are about to partake. Bless it to our bodies and forever guard our health. Thank you for the gift of Rachelle and the beautiful person she is. Lord, thank you for this night and our time together. May it be truly blessed. Amen."

In the light of the fire, Ethan and Rachelle enjoyed a delicious meal and each other. As the evening wore on, neither party remembered the incident at the sugar cane field. Laughing and exchanging glances, the two were caught up in the moment, their love for one another, and being together. Satisfied and confident, Ethan invited Rachelle for a starlit walk along the beach. Walking hand-in-hand, the lovers strolled past the gleaming white water that flashed in the moonlight at each crest of a wave. The sound of the ocean was majestic and beckoning, while the heavens showed forth like ivory on an ebony grand piano. It was a magical night preceded by an almost flawless day. Making their way back to the fire, Ethan and Rachelle stood and warmed themselves with its remaining heat.

"There's one more gift I want to give you," Ethan

said, looking into Rachelle's attentive eyes. "The gift of us." Holding her hand in his, Ethan took a knee and pulled out a diamond that sparkled in the firelight. Beholding the beauty of her soft, yet stunning, eyes, he said, "I bought you the emerald earrings because they have unparalleled beauty, like you. I bought you the pearls because you're one of a kind, like your daughter, Jaleesa. And I want you to know I will always love you both, like the pearls that you are. Nothing would make me happier than for us to be a family. Rachelle Jacobs, will you marry me and be my bride, my forever friend?" With joy in her eyes, Rachelle settled to her knees, and smiling at her beloved, said, "It would be my honor to spend the remainder of my days with you. Yes, Ethan, I will marry you!"

chapter 27

Discovery

Jaleesa lay on the floor staring at a photo of her soon-to-be family. She was glad that Ethan had proposed and that he would now be taking on the role of Dad in her life. She'd liked Ethan from the start. From the beginning of his courtship with her mother, he'd always sought to include her, making her feel valued and important. She respected and enjoyed Ethan. But the anticipation of having a full-time father in the house made her wonder even more about her own dad. Why had he abandoned her? Why had he left Rachelle? Where was he? Who was he? As a little girl, much of these things had never occurred to her, but now in her teen years she began to wonder about her beginnings and a relationship that seemingly never was. Shuffling through several other photos, Jaleesa decided to place the one of the three of them in the center of her scrapbook page entitled "Fun in the Sun." Looking at the recent pictures of their trip to Hawaii brought it all back. She had many fond memories of that place, but none better than the day Ethan and Mark, the soon-to-be best man and a long-time friend of Ethan, arrived on the island to ask Lucas, Aaliyah, and Jaleesa for Rachelle's hand in marriage and set up the romantic day of the proposal. Mark was indispensible in the background as Ethan pulled off his grand day. Ethan had impressed everyone when he genuinely sought the family's blessing before proposing to her mother, a gesture that meant the world to Jaleesa. She loved the romance of the event and the thought of her mother being spoiled and swept off her feet by her long-awaited prince. She could think of nothing her mom deserved more.

The dawn of new love taking wings in the shadow of a great marriage made the final dinner on the island held in honor of Lucas and Aaliyah all the more special. It was a remarkable two weeks and a powerful and profound experience for Jaleesa. This is what it's all about, she thought as she looked at a photo she'd taken of the two couples. This is the way courtship and marriage are supposed to be done. She was impressed, for sure, and not lost on her was the role faith in a loving, powerful, personal God had played in it all.

Holding a picture of the Arizona Memorial in her hand, she remembered other things she'd learned there, too—lessons of sacrifice, honor, duty, and courage. She had come to appreciate a life lived for others and the sacrifice required to ensure people's liberty. She admired the young sailors who fought against great odds to defend their shipmates and their country, and the ultimate role their generation played in making a stronger nation and a better world. She had learned about evil, as well, and the lives it takes. How suddenly the enemy is upon us and how quickly one can be swept away by terrors. Life is short, she thought, and she intended to make the best of hers. Sorting the rest of her pictures and memorabilia from Pearl Harbor, Jaleesa glanced at the clock and realized it was almost time for Wednesday evening fellowship. Putting down the pictures, she put on her jacket and went downstairs to wait for her friend, Sally, and a ride to church.

Having arrived at FSO, the girls mingled with the other high school students as they prepared for the evening activity. Jaleesa smiled when Christopher announced they'd be picking teams for capture the flag. She loved competition, and she knew she was fast. When the dust settled after thirty minutes of play, her side had won. Laughing and waiting for her turn at the water fountain, Jaleesa's eyes lit up as Christopher hobbled by in defeat.

"You should have played on our side, Pastor Chris," taunted Jaleesa. "An old man like you needs the protection of speed."

"That's what I recruited Miles for," Christopher said, breathlessly. "I didn't know he was going to scrape up his leg."

"Always go with a Jacobs, Pastor."

"Next time, I'll choose more wisely," reflected Christopher. "I'll see you girls upstairs for praise and worship."

"See ya there, Pastor."

Jaleesa loved going to church and fellowshipping with friends. For Sinners Only was a good church—a place of joy and acceptance where she always felt welcome. It was a great place to grow in God, and she felt blessed to be a part of it. After a time of joyful worship, Jaleesa sat down next to Sally and Miles for a time of teaching that would change the direction of their lives.

Standing in front of the group, Christopher seemed more focused than usual. Getting the students' attention, he began, "Will you join with me in a moment of prayer?" Jaleesa felt Christopher's intensity as he bowed his head and prayed: "Lord Jesus, we come before You tonight in expectation of the good things You're going to bring to us through Your Word and Your Holy Spirit. We ask that You would come and minister in this place. Father, forgive me and this body gathered here our sins and speak through me Your truth tempered by grace. Amen."

"Amen," echoed various voices from the small crowd

of students.

"Tonight's message is one close to my heart and one I believe this group is mature enough to hear," said Christopher. "Tonight we're going to begin a series on the biblical doctrine concerning the sanctity of human life, abortion, and the Christian's role in society. For the next month, our group will be looking at what the Scriptures reveal about life, the medical discoveries regarding fetal development in the womb, personal testimony from those who've experienced abortion—my friend Cindy Taylor is going to come and share with us—and the things we can all do to make a difference in our church, schools, and community.

"What we're about to discuss can be intense, and if at any point you feel you need to excuse yourself, please feel free to do so. Our discussion tonight is not about passing judgment or pointing the finger, it's about raising our awareness and giving all of us the proper foundation for living responsibly. For we have a responsibility to be good to our neighbors, and I believe that starts with properly recognizing the value of every human person.

"If you're uncomfortable with a teaching on abortion or you've been involved with an abortion in some way, I want you to know you're not alone. Abortion affects us all—whether we realize it or not. But it's never easy to talk about or face. It's a serious matter, and it can be painful, disturbing, and overwhelming. If you've had an abortion in your past, Jesus wants to forgive you. There isn't a person in this room who hasn't sinned, repeatedly, myself included. The Bible tells us that we've all sinned and come up short of God's glory. But the good news is Jesus came to bear our sins and our burdens so that we wouldn't have to. If anyone is burdened tonight by abortion or anything else, give it to the Lord and let Him heal you. There is no sin God can't or won't forgive if we lay it before Him and ask Him to.

"While abortion is the focus of this lesson, it cannot be overstated that abortion always occurs after people's sexual choices and behaviors. The many consequences of sexual activity, including pregnancy and STDs, is something we all need to consider before engaging in sexual relations. But even more importantly for us as Christ followers, God calls us to purity, self-control, and abstinence until marriage. If anybody here is struggling with dating relationships, pornography, or purity, talk to someone and pray with me or the other staff members before you leave tonight. There's help here. There's hope in Christ. Let's allow God into these important areas of our life. If we've stumbled, we can ask God to reorder our steps and set our feet on a new path to purity and self-control. We need to invite God into our struggles and allow Him to redirect our passions. No one is perfect sexually; everyone struggles with impure thoughts, urges, and sexual desire. In fact, our desires are strong and God-given, so we need to be gracious with ourselves and others as we grow unto maturity. Always be willing to be a person of forgiveness— forgiving ourselves and others when we stumble and fall. But don't settle for sin; resist it through God's help and the help of His people. When we trust God with our sexuality, He promises to bless us. If we follow God's path, one day, God willing, we'll discover incredible union and sexual fulfillment in the sacred bond of marriage. Listen to me, guys: Self-respect, self-control, and purity are the best ways to prevent abortion from entering our lives.

"If anyone is sitting here thinking, what does abortion have to do with me? I hope tonight we discover the answer to that question. God asks us all to love, help, and protect our neighbor, and abortion is a great threat to our neighbors all over the world. Let tonight be a time of awakening. May we see abortion for what it is tonight, and may this time set our hearts on fire to love our neighbors and the least of these.

"I know this series is going to be intense, and that many emotions will be stirred, so I've asked Melanie, Keith, and Sandy to be available for personal prayer and counseling. If at any time during this teaching anyone needs to be excused, get prayer, or talk to someone on staff, please take the opportunity to do so. This evening may bring conviction to some and awakening to others, but it is not about condemnation. So let's journey down this road and see what the Lord brings.

"We're living in a time of crisis in America. For the past thirty-eight years, our nation has allowed the destruction of over fifty million human beings in their mothers' wombs. The reality of abortion has stripped all the generations under forty years of age by twenty-five percent. Look around tonight. Look at the people in this room, and realize that only three quarters of us have made it out of the womb alive. Along with divorce and promiscuity, abortion has wreaked havoc on the American family and the bedrock of our civilization. Nothing in the history of the world has inflicted more damage on us as a people than abortion. It threatens the very fabric of our existence and all that God has for us in this life.

"If you brought your Bibles, please turn with me to Colossians one, verses fifteen through twenty." Opening his Bible, Christopher began to read:

> *He is the image of the invisible God, the firstborn over all creation. For by him all things were created: things in heaven and on earth, visible and invisible, whether thrones or powers or rulers or authorities; all things were created by him and for him. He is before all things, and in him all things hold together. And he is the head of the body, the*

church; he is the beginning and the firstborn from among the dead, so that in everything he might have the supremacy. For God was pleased to have all his fullness dwell in him, and through him to reconcile to himself all things, whether things on earth or things in heaven, by making peace through his blood, shed on the cross.

"Did you hear it, young people?" asked Christopher rhetorically. "Jesus and Jesus alone made you! Genesis one, twenty-seven tells us, 'God created man in his own image, in the image of God he created him; male and female he created them.' This may come as a surprise to some in this room but Darwin got it wrong. We did not come from apes; we came from the One who made both men and apes. Jesus, our passage says, made everything. The Bible teaches that each of us is distinct, set apart, and that there's no one else like us in the whole universe. We are all unequalled and planned by God from the very foundations of the world.

"Guys, build your life on Scripture and let it define you. Let God define you. Don't let the world tell us who we are. Only God can tell us who we are! The Great I Am says we're made in His image, fashioned by His very own hands. He made us. He wants us, He loves us, and He's got a destiny for each one of us to fulfill.

"Listen to what God told the prophet Jeremiah." Opening to the book of Jeremiah, Christopher read:

"'Before I formed you in the womb I knew you, before you were born I set you apart; I appointed you as a prophet to the nations.' Before we were born, God had a plan for us. While we were still developing in our mother's womb, he had a destiny and a mission for us to accomplish. Maybe it's playing sports with character and grace or writing beautiful music; maybe it's leadership; maybe it's research

or teaching or building things or finding a cure for various diseases; maybe it's telling the world about Jesus, raising a family, or being a blessing to our parents, friends, neighbors, and world. Whatever it is, God wants us to discover it and use it to bless Him and His people. Every life has value—yours, mine, everyone's!"

Pausing, Christopher surveyed the room while he let his words sink in. Sensing he had their attention, he continued, "On this last point society doesn't disagree, do they? Look at all the programs we've developed inside and outside the church to help and assist people. We all believe in the value of human life, don't we? Sadly, the truth is we don't in America. More than thirty years ago, our Supreme Court decided to avoid and ignore the question of when life begins in the womb. Devaluing all life and erasing the legal humanity of all people in the womb. Before we travel down this road any further, let's pause and watch a short clip of a baby in the womb. Let's allow this visual testimony to weigh in on the debate. As this brief video showing a baby's journey in the womb plays on the screen, think about God and His marvelous plans for you and all of us."

While the video rolled and the ultrasound images played, a young girl started to softly weep. In the dim light of the room with the audible sound of a fetal heartbeat pulsing, the young girl now sobbing got up and started to leave. Melanie, moving quickly toward the girl, put her arms around her and gently guided her out of the room. Silently, Christopher prayed for her and grieved for all the others who shared her pain.

Returning his attention to the youth before him, he studied the young people as they watched the images on the screen of an unmistakable human being. When the video finished, Christopher turned up the lights and asked, "How many of you have seen an ultrasound image before?" Very few hands went up. "Isn't it amazing?"

"I think it's beautiful," said Sally.

"Me, too," echoed Jaleesa.

"How many of you have heard a teaching on the value of human life and abortion before?" asked Christopher. Less than one-quarter of the group raised their hands. "How many of you have heard that the Bible is silent on the issue of abortion?" A few students raised their hands. "Let me assure you tonight that that's simply not true; nothing could be farther from the truth. If the Bible is silent on the issue of abortion, then it is silent on almost everything.

"Keith is handing out a list of Scriptures that reveal what the Bible says about life in the womb and how that applies to the critical issue of abortion. Please take time this week to look up these verses and be ready to discuss them next week. Read them. If you have a pen, underline Psalm 139:13-16; Exodus 21:22-24; Genesis 4:1; Job 31:13-15; Galatians 1:11-16; Luke 1:41-44; and Acts 3:1-19. People often fail to grasp what the Bible communicates about abortion because they get tripped up looking for the word 'abortion,' but if they would pay attention to what the Scriptures teach us about life, creation, personhood, or when life begins, they would discover a wealth of information. They would encounter words and phrases like: 'womb,' 'with child,' 'begotten,' 'conceived,' 'fruit of the womb,' 'offspring,' and they would uncover just how thoroughly the Bible treats this question.

"When we study the Bible with an eye toward life, we discover that life is intentional, sacred, and fully alive the moment God creates it. There is so much to say about this topic, but I sense there are already some things brewing in your spirits and some questions you may want to ask. So I'm going to open up the floor for your questions, and we'll see where the Holy Spirit leads."

Raising his hand, Miles asked, "How many babies did you say have died in America because of abortion?"

"Sadly, more than fifty million babies, gone, or to put it another way—a hundred thousand every month, over three thousand every day, one-hundred-and-thirty-seven every hour, or roughly two babies every minute. These abortion statistics are so shocking and overwhelming they can be difficult to process, but as you look over your handout this week, take time to meditate on these numbers and feel the weight of our national loss."

"I had no idea it was that bad," responded Miles.

"You're not alone, Miles," affirmed Christopher. "Because abortion is so seldom talked about most people don't know how common it is."

"My health teacher said that scientists don't know when life begins. Is that true?"

"It's not true, Sally. It's misleading. Scientists and those in the medical community have known for quite some time that human life, biologically speaking, begins at fertilization: the joining of sperm and egg. When conception occurs, a unique human set of DNA is created that never existed before and will never exist again."

"I heard the President say that he didn't 'want his daughters to be punished with a baby if they got pregnant before they wanted to,'" chimed Whitney.

"We need to pray for President Obama to change his views on abortion. The conclusions he's come to are terribly unfortunate, but let's examine his comment. First of all, his comment reveals that he knows the conceived embryo or fetus is a baby. Sadly, the President chooses to be confused about children in the womb, pregnancy, and his Creator," Christopher responded. "If he'd read his Bible with an eye toward human dignity and human worth, he would refrain from making such biblically ignorant comments. Psalm 127 reveals that children are a gift from the Lord. It says the fruit of the womb is a reward. Babies are not a punishment, they are a reward! They're not created in a vacuum or by the evolutionary process, but by Almighty God. Our culture talks a lot about children in the womb being wanted, but the Scriptures reveal that babies aren't wanted or unwanted, they are *given*. And I can assure you, every child the Lord gives He wants."

"Pastor Chris, if this is such a great problem and so clear in the Word of God, how come we haven't heard more about it?" asked Jaleesa.

"Discussing abortion is difficult and uncomfortable. Sadly, most people try to avoid it."

"I've grown up in this church, and I've only heard this mentioned a few times. Why haven't we spoken about this more?" followed Jaleesa.

"I believe we need to speak about it more, which is why we're going to spend the next four youth nights discussing it," responded Christopher.

"My family has visited several churches over the years, and I've never heard this discussed at any of them. Do you think most churches don't see this as a problem or believe it's none of their business?"

"Unfortunately, several churches take their cues from society and the culture rather than the Bible. Some churches, pastors, and organizations have been fighting abortion from the beginning, and some for a short season, but sadly many more have shied away from getting involved."

"How can that be? I've always thought the church was a light to the world—God's representatives on earth?"

"Tragically, the opportunities for forgiveness, restoration, and healing are withheld from many in our fellowships because of the silence from many pulpits. Silence in our congregations often leaves people isolated and alone as they face this difficult choice. Before or after abortion, silence can be deadly."

"How can we make a difference?"

"I'm glad you asked that, Jaleesa," said Christopher. "We can cherish every life, save sex for marriage, and be an advocate for the life message in our circle of influence. One of the most important things we can all do is to be supportive and encouraging to our friends who find themselves facing an unexpected pregnancy. Often, we just need to listen to their stories, be accepting, and let them know we're there for them."

"I've heard a couple of abortion rumors at school, but if the numbers are as large as you're saying they are, who's having these abortions?" asked Mike.

"In our country, everybody, Mike," said Christopher. "What I mean by that is that every race, religion, and gender has participated in abortion. You can't find a group that hasn't been touched by abortion. Any group you want to look at has, at some level, participated in abortion, and we're all guilty of allowing it to continue in our nation. None of us is clean. Legalized, modern-day abortion is the greatest affront to human rights in the history of the world. In fact, the abortion rate for the church is almost the same as the non-churched."

"Are there any groups that have been affected by it more than others?" asked Mike.

"African Americans are being devastated by abortion. The last figures I read reported that while blacks make up less than 13 percent of the population, they account for over 30 percent of the nation's abortions. If this continues, the black population may never recover; even immigration may not be able to offset the loss."

"Are you saying that the black community is being destroyed now more than at any other time in our nation's history?" recoiled Jaleesa.

"Tragically, yes. That's what the research indicates," confirmed Christopher.

The rest of the discussion went dead for Jaleesa as she grappled with the wholesale slaughter of black America. She couldn't believe what she was hearing. Her people, who had fought so hard for racial equality, justice, and their rightful place in America, were once again being destroyed. She was aware of the death toll for inner-city blacks, but nothing prepared her for a loss like this. Roughly tabulating the numbers in her head gave her chills; the thought of around 380,000 black babies being killed each year haunted her. She was in shock, and she couldn't bring herself back to the discussion.

During Christopher's closing prayer, Jaleesa quietly made her way over to Sandy. As the two retreated for prayer, the remaining students mingled after the message, discussing what they had heard. Christopher went across the hall seeking the young woman who had left earlier with Melanie. Finding them in the second room where he looked, Christopher eased his way inside the door and waited until the girls finished their prayer. Wet tears dappled Tasha's face as she looked over at Christopher. Approaching the two women, Christopher sat down and looked in Tasha's downcast eyes.

"Tasha, how can I help?" asked Christopher in a calm and comforting manner.

Speaking through tears, Tasha blurted, "Oh, Pastor Chris, I always feel like people in the church are going to judge me. It's like I can't forget what I've done, and I feel so guilty and unforgivable."

"Tasha, we're all fallen and sinful, but none of us is unforgivable," asserted Christopher. "That's the good news of the Gospel; Jesus came to redeem that which was, and is, unforgivable, sinful, and broken."

"But my sin isn't a little lie, Pastor," retorted Tasha with despair.

"Tasha, my sins haven't been little lies either. But it's not about our sins or their frequency; it's about our Savior and His power to deliver us. The Enemy of our souls wants us to dwell on our sins, Tasha. He would like nothing more than to lead you down a path of self-condemnation and leave you there. Satan accuses, Tasha, but God forgives and liberates! You are loved and highly valued by God, not to mention your parents, your friends, and us. May I share with you a verse from the Gospel of John?"

Tasha nodded.

"John 10:10 says, 'The thief comes only to steal and kill and destroy. I came that they may have life and have it abundantly.' God is a life-giver, Tasha. He wants to lift the burdens of our sin, teach us the truth about sin, and give us the tools to recognize and resist sin as we move forward in the freedom He provides. Satan has already stolen the blessing of a child from your life, and now he's seeking to destroy your life in the aftermath. Don't let him! You are a precious child of God, Tasha, despite the sins you've committed. I know your baby is in heaven cheering for you to continue your walk with God, waiting for you to join him or her in heaven one day."

"My child can't possibly be cheering for me in heaven! How could my baby love me after what I've done?"

Looking softly into Tasha's tortured eyes, Christopher spoke with deep conviction, "Your child has been perfected like the Savior. Those who enter heaven with God are utterly new. They've been completely transformed. Your child holds nothing but love for you, Tasha. Jesus came while you and I were lost sinners. He came and died to pay our debt and set us free. As sinful as we are before we come to Christ, and at times afterward, all of heaven longs for us to come to the One who can make us new, come to the place they now reside. Confess your sins to the Lord, Tasha, and let Him restore your soul and set you free."

"I have confessed, but I still don't feel free!"

"Tasha, let me pray for you; let's seek the Lord together. Will you do that with me?"

Weeping, Tasha said, "Yes."

"Tasha, look at me." Making eye contact, Christopher spoke with confidence, "Jesus loves you. He loves you!" Taking hold of Tasha's hands, Christopher continued, "I want you to start the prayer and confess your sins to God, pour out your heart to Him, and then I'm going to pray for you, okay?"

"Okay, Pastor."

Holding hands in the silence with Melanie's arm wrapped around her, Tasha timidly started to pray, "Father God, I'm sorry…" Tears began to cascade over her cheeks as she heaved and wheezed with emotion. Choking through the tears, she continued, "I'm sorr… sorry I… I ki… ki… killed my baby." Sputtering to breathe, she strangled out, "Please, please forgive me." Collapsing under an avalanche of tears, Tasha fell into Melanie's lap as both girls wept.

Silently interceding for Tasha, Christopher waited for what seemed like an eternity to pray, but when he was moved, he prayed, "Dear Jesus, Holy and Righteous Lamb of God, fall afresh on my dear sister, Tasha. Accept her prayer for forgiveness and set her heart at liberty once again. Create in her a clean heart, O God, and renew a right spirit within her. Restore unto her the joy of Your salvation—cleanse her of any guilt and shame, O God.

We pray in the mighty name of Jesus, that the words Paul wrote in Romans eight would take root in Tasha's soul: 'There is therefore now no condemnation for those who are in Christ Jesus.' And again he writes, 'If God is for us, who can be against us? He who did not spare his own Son but gave him up for us all, how will he not also with him graciously give us all things? Who shall bring any charge against God's elect? It is God who justifies. Who is to condemn?' God, remind us in this moment that nobody loves and forgives like You. O merciful God, look down on us, Your wayward children, and turn our wailing into dancing! We thank You for Tasha and the work You're going to do in her life. Move gracefully in her and through her by the power of the Holy Spirit to accomplish all You have for her. We thank You in advance for her healing and all the good You're going to bring out of this tragedy. We pray for her protection from the lies and the schemes of the Enemy, and we ask that You guard her heart. Lord, speak to Tasha's heart the assurance that we're here for her every step of the way. She has our support and the support of everyone in this group. Shower her with Your love and grace and grant us the wisdom and the resources to assist her in recovery. We pray these things in the mighty name of Jesus, that name that is above every name. Amen!" Looking into each other's eyes, the three hugged and encouraged one another in the Lord.

✶✶✶✶✶✶✶

Staring up at the mechanism that moves the goalie, Christopher didn't see Miles walk in to the rec. room. Loosening the nut on the metal shaft that extends to the fixed goal keeper, he noticed some large feet moving toward the table. "Hey, Miles, you wanna give me a hand with this?"

"How'd you know it was me, Pastor?"

"I don't have any other kids with size-17 feet," teased Christopher.

"Oh, yeah," reflected Miles. "Hey, while you're at it, you should fix the warp in the corner."

"And lose my advantage? You've gotta be joking."

"I thought you believed in fair dealing, Pastor?"

"Mostly," quipped Christopher. "So what brings you by, Miles?"

"I need to talk to you about something that's been troubling me."

Sliding out from under the table and gaining his feet, Christopher said, "Shoot, I'm listening."

"Ever since our last youth night I've been stirred up about this whole abortion thing, and I need to get something off of my chest. I can see now just how big it is, and I want to get involved, but I feel so hypocritical…"

Interrupting, Christopher said, "Is this about your struggles with pornography?"

"No,"

"Oh, well good, I'm glad to hear it. How's that been going lately anyway?"

"I'm doing better, not perfect, but better. Going to morning prayer with the men has really helped. It keeps me grounded. But what you said to me when we first talked about it is what's stuck with me the most. When you said the Christian life wasn't so much about abstaining, but obtaining—that really got to me. Reaching for all God has for me and not cheating myself or my future wife out of the reward that will be ours for walking in greater purity really spoke to me. I want God's best for me in every area of life, Pastor."

"You continue to nurture that desire, Miles, and I believe you will," encouraged Christopher. "Keep your eyes fixed on Jesus and where He's leading you to be of help to others and you'll find you experience greater victory and have less time to fall into sin."

"I'm going to do that, Pastor Chris."

"Good, so what is troubling you then? It's certainly not the game last week, 150 yards, two touchdowns, and ten receptions. That was tight!"

"I did have a pretty good game, didn't I?"

"Yes, you did!"

"No, it's not football but I guess it's kinda related. Earlier this season one of my teammates got his girl pregnant, and he didn't want nobody finding out, so a bunch of us pitched in to help pay for the abortion. What you shared last week just rocked me, and I'm sick about my involvement in this abortion thing."

"I'm sorry that happened to you and your friends—that's a tough thing. How come you didn't come to me with this when it was happening?"

"I don't know. I guess I didn't think it was that big of a deal at the time," confessed Miles. "But I see now that it was."

"It's never easy, Miles, but it's good when the Spirit brings conviction. I'm glad that you came to talk with me about it, and that you're owning up to your part of it. That's the first step to freedom," said Christopher. "You know you can always come to me with anything, right?"

"I know, Pastor Chris. I knew you'd be the one to talk to about this. I knew you could put things into perspective for me," Miles said with relief.

"Your buddy and his girlfriend probably need you now more than ever."

"What do you mean?"

"The aftermath of abortion can be difficult to manage, and they're going to need your support and love going forward. Just like how you feel today—at some point their biggest need is going to be forgiveness."

"But how can I help them when I was a part of the problem?" asked Miles.

"Because you've already established a relationship with them, and because, to some degree, you've been involved and can empathize. Miles, God uses us to comfort and help others the way we've been helped and comforted. Remember all the times I've shared with you guys about my struggles in college with my temper and how angry I was at God over the death of my sister?"

"Yeah."

"Well, think about it. God used some key people in my life to set me on the right path, and He wants to do the same things for you. If you'll allow God and His people in, He'll set you free and then use you to help others. God does some of His best work through broken and reformed people. I mean, if you were a thief who was under the conviction of stealing, would you rather talk to a reformed thief about how to quit or a guy who's never stolen a thing in his life? God never wastes our stumbles and hurts if we give them to Him, and often He uses them to bring about good in the lives of others. Don't ever buy into the lie that you're not worthy of service because of something you've done. You're a great kid, Miles, and God's going to do awesome things through your life."

"Thanks, Pastor Chris. That means a lot."

"Let's pray before you go," offered Christopher. "But I also want you to seek the Lord this week about how He wants to use you in this. Ask the Lord what you can learn from this and how He can use you to make a difference."

✶✶✶✶✶✶

The following weekend, Jaleesa awoke to the smell of fresh roasted coffee and her mother's delicious cinnamon rolls. Easing out of bed, she found her slippers and gathered the courage to stand. Walking down the hall to the bathroom, Jaleesa turned on the shower, brushed her teeth, and stepped inside. She was nervous about today, but she knew she had to go. She had to see for herself the reality of abortion at the clinic's door. Christopher had invited her to the beginning of a round-the-clock prayer effort at the local Planned Parenthood. This would be a good chance to see the movement up close, get connected, and decide if this was a place God might use her. Still, the thought of being ridiculed, hated, and standing on the doorstep of death and great evil made her apprehensive and uncomfortable. There under the water, she prayed for courage—that God's peace and His presence would be with her. Having made her peace with God, she stepped out of the shower and dressed for the day. Pulling back the curtains from her bedroom window, she peered out at the beautiful mountains rising in the distance. The air was so clear the mountains looked like they'd been freshly painted. Jaleesa loved nature's majesty. Sighing deeply, the words of Romans echoed in her head: "For since the creation of the world God's invisible qualities—his eternal power and divine nature—have been clearly seen, being understood from what has been made..." "I see You, God. I feel You, God," she whispered under her breath. Grabbing her cell phone and keys, she descended the stairs and entered the kitchen.

"Cinnamon rolls, Mama?"

"Hot out of the oven, just like you like 'em."

"I better have me one of those, and a big glass of milk," delighted Jaleesa. "Are you sure you're okay with me going to the clinic?"

"I trust you, sweetheart. Besides, God will protect you," reassured Rachelle. "Stick with Chris and everything will be fine. When are they coming to pick you up?"

"Should be in the next fifteen minutes," informed Jaleesa.

"Well, sit down and enjoy your breakfast until they get here."

After finishing her last bite of warm, melty cinnamon bliss, Jaleesa rinsed her plate, loaded it in the dishwasher, and walked to the bay window in the front room. Looking out like a little kid waiting for her playmates, the anticipation crawled in her belly. Thankfully, it didn't take long for Christopher and Miles to arrive. Miles Johnston had taken Christopher to heart when he'd said one of the things the students could do to make a difference was to come to the sidewalk and pray. Miles' popularity and status at school as one of the best athletes on campus, being a football and basketball star, made Jaleesa all the more impressed with him. He was handsome and strong, and now it seemed his character was also an enticement. Getting in the car, Jaleesa made eye contact with both men, thanked Christopher for the ride, and settled into the back seat. As Christopher talked about what to expect and prayed for their safety, Jaleesa's nervousness began to subside. She began to relax as the city rolled past her window. Looking out the glass, she marveled that a city this lovely and normal could conceal so great a villainy.

Parking a block away from Planned Parenthood, the two rookies followed the veteran toward a small crowd of people gathered on the sidewalk. It was a brisk day in the middle of winter, and all was cold and stark as they approached the clinic. Nearing the crowd, Jaleesa could hear lively chatter, laughter, and the sound of camaraderie. To her surprise, the people gathered on the sidewalk were full of life. They bantered with one another and shared stories of hope and goodwill. One older man turned to Christopher and beamed, "It's great to see you, young man. How are things at R & T?"

"They're well," Christopher responded. "We could always use more people, but they're well."

"Isn't that the truth—in the Lord's timing, the crowds will come."

As the men were talking, a loud voice boomed out of a passing car. Yelling out his open window, the driver screamed, "Get a life you ignorant jackasses!"

Immediately, Miles yelled back, "We hope so!"

Several in the group chuckled at the newcomer's brashness and wit. But Christopher used the incident as an opportunity to explain to Miles and Jaleesa that it was not their practice to engage those who drove by and heckled.

Noticing Father Rick Ramsey, Christopher brought Miles and Jaleesa over to meet the priest. "Father, I want you to meet my friends, Miles Johnston and Jaleesa Jacobs," introduced Christopher.

"Nice to meet you," greeted Fr. Rick, shaking their hands. "Are you two part of Chris's youth group?"

"Yes," responded Jaleesa and Miles, almost on top of one another.

"Eager bunch aren't they," Fr. Rick said to Christopher. "Well, it's wonderful to have you come to Mass and prayer. I hope you'll come again," invited Fr. Rick. "If you'll excuse me, I have to begin the Mass."

As Father Ramsey moved to the front of the group for Mass, Jaleesa and Miles took their place among the crowd. It was a brief sacrament in which Father Ramsey spoke insightfully about the broken body of Christ and how it speaks a counter message to the message of abortion. Jaleesa was intrigued by the ceremony and the beauty of its presentation. It was not unlike her previous

experiences with Holy Communion at church. The revelation that Jesus' body was broken for all humankind
as the atonement for sin was not new to Jaleesa, but the
revelation that abortion breaks the body of an innocent
life for the perceived benefit to an individual or society
was. Fr. Rick's message resonated deep within her. She
had never thought of it that way before, but when Father
Ramsey spoke the words, "Christ says, 'My body broken
for you,' abortion says, 'the baby's body broken for me,'"
she wept. She saw even more clearly the wickedness of
abortion and its antithetical relationship to Jesus. When
the Mass ended and the people dispersed along the sidewalk facing Planned Parenthood, Jaleesa and Miles took
their place behind Christopher near the driveway.

A few cars had already passed the group during
Mass, but now the parking lot really started to fill up.
Christopher informed his guests that Saturday was one
of Planned Parenthood's busiest abortion days. As people prayed, read their Bibles, and attempted to connect
with clients about their babies and their options, Jaleesa
stood mesmerized by what she saw. Angry clients; sullen
clients; profane clients; embarrassed clients; brazen clients, girls her age; mature women; affluent couples; people living off the streets; men; women; fathers; mothers;
friends; siblings; every race, ethnicity, or creed seemed
to be represented at the doors of Planned Parenthood.
Some had come for birth control, counseling, or exams,
but most had come to end the life of their baby. Their
emotions were mixed and varied on the way in, but more
uniform on the way out. Leaving, they depicted a collective lethargy, sadness, and bewilderment. Something
profound had happened inside. Perhaps more profound
than they knew, but the wound was evident on most.
Jaleesa couldn't restrain her tears as the reality of abortion paraded past her eyes. This was a fellowship of pain

the likes of which she had not seen before. Her greatest shock, however, was the arrival of Maggie Adams, the clinic abortionist. Earlier in the morning when her vehicle approached, Christopher informed Jaleesa and Miles that the abortionist was pulling in. Driving hurriedly past the three of them, Jaleesa caught a glimpse of this professional, well-groomed woman of around fifty. Watching as the car disappeared around the building, she was stunned. A moment later, Maggie's heels echoed off the pavement while she ran into the clinic. Mixed with the hard clack of Maggie's heels, Jaleesa heard a voice shout, "Don't do this, doctor. You *know* they're babies." All went silent as Jaleesa grappled with what she'd just witnessed. Slowly gathering her faculties, she turned to Christopher and said, "She's black!"

"Yes," responded Christopher. "Regrettably, no race is without its share of people who are involved in abortion."

Arriving home after a full morning, Jaleesa thanked Christopher for treating her to lunch, and then slipped silently upstairs to her room and solitude. Sinking into her favorite beanbag, she clutched a soft teddy bear and wept. Her mind swirled with thoughts and emotions wrought from the morning's education at the clinic. *What provoked my mother to act so out of character and have sex before marriage?* And then a terrible thought leapt to her mind: *Is that why I've never known my father? Did he want me aborted?* In the silence, Jaleesa wondered and wept.

chapter 28

Neighborhood Watch

Fred sat in the kitchen with his paper, perusing the morning's headlines. Last night's car crash had claimed the lives of five individuals. The President was preparing to address the nation about the economy and our involvement in the Middle East. And the market and the unemployment numbers were both slightly up. Flipping to the box score in the sports section, he noticed his team had won last night's game in the bottom of the eleventh, 8-7. Smiling to himself, he was glad he'd decided to DVR the game. The victory marked five wins in a row. The team was hot, and he looked forward to enjoying the satisfaction of victory without all the suspense. Sipping his morning Dr. Pepper, he read the editorials and the smattering of articles about his favorite athletes and the grand old game. Looking out his window as the morning rays filtered through his large oak, he heard the familiar voice of Christopher reading the Scriptures: *"You have lived on earth in luxury and self-indulgence. You have fattened yourselves in the day of slaughter. You have condemned and murdered innocent men, who were not opposing you."* Tossing his paper hard on the table, Fred rose and muttered, "Ah, these knuckleheads ruin every Saturday!"

Walking into the room and noticing her father was visibly irritated, Lilly inquired, "Something wrong, Dad?"

"Did I wake you? I didn't realize you were up. I thought with your flight last night you'd…"

"Don't sweat it, Dad. I'm an early riser these days," assured Lilly. "You seem a little off. Are you okay?"

"Oh, it's these idiot protesters and their obnoxious proclamations. I wish they'd shut up and go home! They're worse than the punk kids who used to loiter around the joint when it was a convenience store. At least they'd buy their liquor, have a smoke, and then leave, but ever since the doctors moved in, these religious wackos disturb my peace for hours on end!"

"How long have they been protesting?"

"Several years now," grumbled Fred. "I'd move if it wasn't the last place I'd shared with your mother, God rest her soul."

"What are they protesting?" asked Lilly. "They must be pretty dedicated to endure in their cause for so long."

"Oh, I don't know… the killing of babies, I suppose."

"It's an abortion clinic!" Lilly said, alarmed.

"More like a women's center or a reproductive health center," clarified Fred.

"Dad, if they're killing children over there, I'm glad those people are standing outside!" retorted Lilly. "Have you ever stopped to think of the reasons why they might be out there? Maybe one of the reasons they stand out there all alone and shout so loudly is because people like you and me never listen to their cries and assist them. I'm sure most of them have more enjoyable things they could be doing. When was the last time you woke up on a Saturday and said, 'Gee, I think I'll go down to an abortion clinic and awkwardly try to make a difference in some stranger's life instead of going golfing or fishing or watching the game?'"

Stunned by his daughter's passion, Fred remained

quiet for a moment and then said, "I'm sorry, Lilly. I didn't know you felt so strongly about it."

"Well I do, Dad!" Lilly exclaimed, still hot with passion. "In fact, your grandson wouldn't be here if it weren't for people like that."

Concerned now, Fred inquired, "What are you saying?"

"Just forget what I said."

"No, I want to know!"

"Fine, I'll tell you. Ten years ago I almost aborted Tim. I went to a similar clinic back home in San Diego, and if it weren't for the compassion and courage of the people outside, I would have aborted Tim."

"Oh, God, Lilly. I never knew."

"Well, you do now."

In the awkward silence that developed, Fred and Lilly heard clear as a bell the irate voice of Sharry Edles. Bursting forth from her house, screaming profanity as she approached Christopher on the sidewalk, Sharry was in full attack mode. She'd held her tongue on many occasions, but not today. Fixing her gaze on Christopher and clearly ready for a fight, she squawked, "What the hell do you know about it? This is a women's issue, not a man's! Don't you have anything better to do than to torture vulnerable young women and subjugate them with your patricidal bullshit?"

Turning to face his accuser, Christopher retorted, "I'm here to do just the opposite, ma'am."

Stunned and realizing her mistake, Sharry said, "I meant patriarchal, dammit! What you're doing is outrageous and beyond offensive."

Abruptly and full of fire, Christopher responded, "What they're doing offends me! Every day fifteen-hundred men are killed in the wombs of their mothers by these deceiving beasts. Don't you dare tell me I have no cause in this fight! Every one of these babies who will die here today came about from the union of male sperm and female ovum!"

"Go to hell, you idiot!" shouted Sharry, as she turned to leave.

Hearing in his mind the words of Proverbs ("A gentle answer turns away wrath") and realizing his impassioned error, Christopher pursued Sharry and said, "Ma'am, please ma'am… I'm sorry I yelled at you. I owe you more respect than that. I apologize."

"I don't want your apology. I want you to go home!"

"Can I help you in some way?"

"Yeah, you can help me by leaving!" mocked Sharry.

"I'm not leaving, but I can answer your questions and help you understand why I, and the others here, feel compelled to come."

"I know why you and the others come. It's because you're sick in the head."

Refusing this time to take the bait, Christopher said, "I'm sorry you feel that way, ma'am. If you need my help for anything in the future, please don't hesitate to ask. Again, I'm sorry for my anger earlier."

Sensing there was no longer going to be a fight and unable to think of anything to say, Sharry turned and walked back to her house.

Fred stared out his window, perplexed, trying to grapple with all he had just witnessed and discovered. Noticing his daughter heading for the door, he said, "No, Lilly, let her be. She's just a wounded woman, and she needs some time to process. The man on the sidewalk doesn't need you to come to his defense; he knows why he's there."

"I suppose you're right, Dad," reflected Lilly. "I think

I need a break. It's been a stressful morning. I'll tell Tim to take a shower and get ready to go to the zoo."

"Sweetheart…"

"Yes, Dad."

"I'm glad you told me the truth. You helped me see things differently today, and I'm grateful."

"I'm sorry I got so agitated."

"Don't apologize, Lilly. You were right."

chapter 29

Belia's Dream

"Mommy, follow me. Come to my side, I need you here," said the voice through the mist. Belia could not see as the clouds enveloped her whole body. Her feet, silk nightgown, and head were totally enveloped. "Mommy, come to me," the voice beckoned.

"Where are you?" Belia asked.

"I'm here," she heard.

"I can't see you, my love," said Belia. "Show yourself!"

"Soon," rang the gentle voice. "Follow me."

Belia hesitated in the confusion, and then a light penetrated the clouds and illuminated a path. Walking quickly in pursuit of the voice, she felt the cool of the cobble stones beneath her feet. Suddenly, she was upon a beautiful village basking in the sun of a summer morning. Belia felt so warm in the light. Joy and ecstasy poured upon her. Pleasure filled her being, and she began to sing. Unable to contain herself, she danced and leapt and shouted for joy. All around her the sleepy little town was coming to life with the sounds of merrymaking and gladness. The sun shimmered off the cobblestones and glinted off the dew that clung to the boxed flowers resting underneath the village windows. Young lovers held hands, children played, old men read the paper, and everyone breathed easy in the morning glory. Belia was so enamored with the charm of her new surroundings that she forgot how she'd come to this place or what she'd been doing.

Skipping and beholding the risen sun, she remembered as the voice far away in the distance called, "Discover me, Mommy."

Turning her attention to a side street from whence the voice had come, she followed. Walking farther, darkness crept in. Feeling heavy oppression and fear, she desperately cried out, "Speak to me!"

Echoing off the dark walls of the city, the voice rang out, "I'm waiting for you on the other side, make haste to come to me."

Feeling the urgency of the moment, Belia broke into a run. As she passed quickly over the cobble stones, the street became darker and darker, till all was black. Overcome by a sudden lethargy, she slowed like one facing a strong wind. The stones became rough and then course and then sharp. Looking down, she could no longer see her legs or the road, but she began to feel a sticky-wetness about her feet. Terrified, she froze. Trembling, she reached down to touch the soles of her feet. Brushing through the wetness she slowly raised her hand to her face and smelled blood. Tasting a small portion, she confirmed the horror of her discovery. Panic filled her mind as she flailed in the dark. At first she touched nothing, but then she began to feel a menacing, haunting, brutal presence. She shrieked and cried out, but no one came to her aid. Panicked she screamed for help. Nothing! No one! She was alone. The darkness brushed her face and began to crush her body. Belia's pain was sharp and radiating as she was repeatedly grabbed, stabbed, and torn. Her throat closed, her eyes lost their sight, and her heart melted within her as her body succumbed to the vicious attack. Desperate and terrified, Belia eked out, "Save me."

The voice cried out with longing, "Come to me... Come to me!"

Gathering what little strength remained, Belia rose to her feet, and ran toward the beckoning voice. Making great haste, she ran and ran and ran until she crashed through an earthen wall and landed in a meadow. Gone was the blood, the pain, the dark. All that remained was light and joy and peace. Gazing at the beauty of the meadow, she smiled and made her way to her feet.

Carried on the Wind past a stream, Belia heard the sound of the voice as clear as ever proclaim, "Here I am, come and abide with us."

Looking to her right, she beheld a Priest dressed in white with His arms outstretched. His smile was warm and inviting. As natural as a little child, Belia ran into His outstretched arms. Delighting in His embrace for a long time, she felt tears of joy well up in her eyes. Pulling back to look at her, the King said, "Welcome home, my daughter. I've been waiting for you."

Beaming, Belia responded back, "It's good to be home." Taking her hand, her Father walked her through the meadow to an enormous tree and a little boy who sat at its base.

Compassionately meeting Belia's eyes, the Man said, "Belia, I'd like to introduce you to your son, Mateo."

Gazing at the child gave her chills. The beautiful little boy was the spitting image of his father. Overcome, Belia gasped and awoke in the dark with a shriek that roused her husband.

Sobbing in the dark, Belia cried out, "Oh, Jose! I killed our son! I killed our son!"

"Belia. Belia, baby. What are you talking about?"

"I saw him. I saw him!"

"Saw who?"

"Our son… I killed our son!"

"That's nonsense. We've never had a son."

"Yes, we did!"

"Belia, you're dreaming! It's just another one of your nightmares from that animal in your past, but they got him, baby. They put him behind bars forever."

"I need God, Jose. He showed me in a dream that the child I aborted was ours."

"Belia, that's impossible!"

"No, it's not! Remember the week before I was abducted? We made love for the first time that Saturday night. That's when it must have happened, that's when I conceived," lamented Belia. "I've given you two daughters, but I've never given you a son. Oh, Jose, how miserable am I? I need God, Jose. We need God!"

"You really believe this, Belia?"

"I do. I saw it. I know it in my heart! We need God, Jose, or we'll never see our son in heaven."

"Belia, even if this is true, you couldn't have known. How could you know?"

"I should have. Maybe at some level, I did," Belia said. "He has a name, Jose. Our son has a name—it's Mateo."

"Mateo. Really, Mateo? That's crazy…what are you saying?

"I'm not crazy, Jose!"

"Okay, okay, I believe you. You know it's funny, but I've always liked that name."

"I want to start going to church, Jose."

"All right, let's go to church," Jose said holding Belia. "Belia, if what you say is true, then you have given me a son…a son."

chapter 30

The Truth

Standing in Ethan's office, Jaleesa read the various plaques and clippings on the wall. A walnut plaque, proudly displayed in the center, read: "Eastbrook Outstanding Detective 2010—for outstanding work and bravery in the face of danger, we salute Ethan Tyndale, Eastbrook Police Department." A nearby clipping read: "Eastbrook detectives break up downtown drug ring and remove blight from our community." Looking at all the other articles and accolades made her proud that Ethan was her stepdad. It had been a little awkward having Ethan in her life on a permanent basis, but moving into a new house after the wedding and spending more one-on-one time had helped. Overall, Jaleesa was enjoying her new family. The joy Ethan brought to her mother was undeniable, and that always made Jaleesa smile. Continuing to read, her eyes fell on the headline: "Newcomer, Detective Ethan Tyndale, proves crucial in the apprehension of the BQB." Reading further, she saw the words: *serial rapist condemned by DNA evidence obtained from an anonymous girl he fathered during one of his brutal attacks.* Intrigued, Jaleesa moved closer to the article as Ethan entered the room. Noticing the article his daughter was reading, Ethan quickly spoke, "What's up, J.J.? Sorry I'm late; I got held up by the captain. We were discussing a new lead in a case we're pursuing about some armed robberies."

"You helped apprehend the BQB? He was one of the worst criminals in the history of Eastbrook, right?"

"Yeah, but that was a while ago," Ethan said dismissively.

"Not that long ago," challenged Jaleesa. "Who's this girl the prosecution used to nail him?"

"Hey, you want to get some mozzy sticks? I'm starving."

"Won't that kind of spoil our workout?"

"Well...ah, yeah. I meant afterward. You know, after we're done at the gym," Ethan sputtered. "Let's get going. We're running late as it is, and we're supposed to meet your mom at Canino's for dinner."

"I guess we can just get the mozzarella sticks there."

"Yeah, sure."

As Jaleesa jogged on the treadmill at the club, she wondered why Ethan had acted so strange and evasive in his office. She had rarely seen him flustered, and it was obvious something was bothering him. About what she couldn't tell, so she ran and breathed and pondered. Finishing her workout, she made her way to the girls' locker room. Getting off the scale, Jaleesa headed to her locker and began to undress when she heard the familiar voice of a classmate.

"Looking good, J.J., but then you always do," teased Whitney.

"Hey, Whitney. What's up?"

"Nothing much, I'm just trying to keep my shape like you," said Whitney. "I wish I had skin like yours though. It's so light and smooth, not like this dark color of mine."

"I think your skin is beautiful. It reminds me of my mother's."

"Trust me, you've got the better look, but then everything you have is better. Look at your hair, so silky and straight. It's a far cry from this woolly head of mine," said Whitney.

"Whitney, don't say that about yourself—you're beautiful. God made you perfect just the way you are."

"There you go again talking about God."

"I can't help it," Jaleesa said. "It's the way I was raised. Hey, you want to come with me to the hot tub?"

"No thanks. I've got a cycle class in five minutes," said Whitney. "Who was that man you came in with?"

"That's my dad."

"Well, that explains it!"

"Explains what?"

"Why your skin's so beautiful. You're the perfect combination of light and dark."

"Oh, he's not my biological father. He's my stepdad."

"Funny. Sure looks like somebody white was your father," remarked Whitney as she headed toward the restroom. "Have a good one, J.J."

"You, too, Whitney," said Jaleesa, grappling with what she had just heard.

Sitting in the warm undulating water, Jaleesa pondered the words now echoing in her head—"Sure looks like somebody white was your father." Could it be—could her biological dad be white like Ethan? Is that why Mom is attracted to Ethan? Has she always preferred white men? Who was her father? Why didn't he want her? Why does Mom never talk about him? What mystery is she hiding? Is she deeply ashamed about her sexual past? Does she regret having me? Is my father still around? Do I know him? She needed to know. She had to know.

Dinner was uneventful as the three sat and made small talk while they ate their pasta. Rachelle's day was busy. Ethan's was routine and full of paperwork. But Jaleesa's day, a day that should have been busy with school, the club, and her normal routines, was now awash with mystery, speculation, and anxiety. She couldn't take her mind off her biological father. She tried to engage in the banter, but it was clearly a sideline gig. Noticing her daughter was unsettled, Rachelle asked, "Are you okay, J.J.?"

"I'm okay; I'll talk to you later about it."

Concerned and nervous, Ethan asked, "Did anything happen at the club while we were there?"

"No. I'm fine."

"You know you can talk to me, too, if you ever need anything, right?"

"I know. Thanks, Ethan."

"Still, some things are better discussed woman to woman, true?"

"Yeah."

"All right, who's ready for dessert?"

Entering Jaleesa's room for the nightly prayer, Rachelle sat on the edge of the bed and asked, "So, what's bothering you?"

Buying time to work up her nerve, Jaleesa asked, "Could you get me a glass of water before we talk?"

"Sure, baby. I'll be right back."

Walking downstairs, Rachelle contemplated her daughter's evasiveness and developed a growing concern. Reaching in the cabinet for a water glass, she wondered what was troubling Jaleesa? Was there a health issue, girl problems, a boy, an incident at school or the club? Was she feeling awkward around Ethan, or worse yet, had Jaleesa seen or heard something when she and Ethan had been intimate? Swirls of various possibilities roamed through her mind. Looking up, she noticed Ethan standing by the kitchen table and asked, "What happened today? Can you think of anything that might be upsetting her?"

"I'm not sure what's going on. When she arrived at the station after school for our normal trip to the club, I got detained. When I finally entered my office, I found her reading a clipping I have posted about the BQB."

"You have a clipping up?"

"I'm sorry. I'd forgotten it was up. I don't know how much she read or even what the article says anymore, but I changed the subject as quick as I could, and we left. As for anything else that might have happened, I can't think of anything. I don't know what's troubling her. It could be anything."

"Well, thanks for telling me."

"Ray, I'm really sorry if I've created a problem for you."

"It's okay, honey. I'll deal with it."

Ascending the stairs, Rachelle tried to prepare her heart for anything. Crossing to the bed, she forced a smile and handed Jaleesa her water. Once again sitting on the edge of the bed, Rachelle took a deep breath and asked, "Okay, J.J., what's up?"

"Mom, who's my real dad? Why don't you ever talk about him?"

"Oh, sweetie," said Rachelle. "I knew this day would come, and I've never been sure of how to tell you the truth,"

"Why, Mom?"

"It's complicated."

"He didn't want me, did he?"

"I don't think so, J.J."

"Did he ask you to abort me?"

"No, sweetheart."

"Is he dead?"

hushed

"No, he's not dead."

"Do you know where he is?"

Hesitating, Rachelle made up her mind to tell the truth. Looking softly at Jaleesa, she said, "Yes."

"Well, where is he then?"

Taking a deep breath, Rachelle said, "He's in prison."

"Prison!" blurted Jaleesa. "What for?"

"Jaleesa, honey, you're my daughter, you're beautiful, and I love you more than life itself, and that's all that will ever matter. What I'm about to share with you will be difficult, and I'm sorry I never shared it with you earlier, but I didn't know how. There's really no easy or gentle way to say this, so I'm just going to say it. The reason I've never talked about your biological father or told you about him is… is because you were conceived in rape."

"What! What are you saying?"

"I'm sorry, J.J., so sorry…"

"Who raped you?"

"Jay, please…"

"Who raped you, Mama?" Jaleesa persisted. "Is that why Ethan was acting so strange? Were you raped by the BQB?"

"Yes, baby," muttered Rachelle through tears.

"Oh, my God! Oh, my God!" Jaleesa shrieked, running from the room.

Ethan rushed upstairs as the bathroom door slammed and two women, in separate rooms, began to wail. Not knowing what to do, he put his head in his hands and prayed, "Oh, Lord, minister peace in my house and comfort Your brokenhearted daughters. Help me be a support and an anchor in the days ahead, and lead us in the way of grace." Carefully entering Jaleesa's bedroom, he put his arms around Rachelle and held her as she sobbed. Her tears gave rise to his, and he wept with his love for all

248

her pain and the pain of her child. Weeping gave way to silence and silence to stillness.

In the flow of time, Jaleesa returned to the room and beheld her wounded mother. Moved by compassion, she uttered through tears, "That's why you have the scars. I'm so sorry, Mom. I'm so...sorry!" Gathering strength as Jaleesa struggled to breathe, Rachelle fixed her eyes on her precious daughter and said in all the strength she could muster, "Jaleesa, you're my pearl of great price! I'll never regret having you, my beautiful daughter!" Grabbing Jaleesa, they embraced and wept in each other's arms, while Ethan wept and prayed to the Lord.

chapter 31

Pride

Looking down the street, Jaleesa noticed a tall, muscular man exit his car and walk around to the passenger door to open it for a young woman. Stepping out of the car, the young woman took his hand and the two proceeded, at an even pace, down the sidewalk. Moving their direction, Jaleesa offered a silent prayer and approached the couple with a smile on her face. Mustering her courage, she held out a fetal development brochure and said, "Did you know your baby's heart is already beating? Would you like to come with me and see an ultrasound of your baby?"

Looking Jaleesa straight in the eye, the man said, "We're not here for an abortion. We're here to purchase birth control."

"I understand, but did you know this facility kills thousands of innocent children every year?" inquired Jaleesa. "Why support an organization that kills children with your finances?"

"Look, lady, it's cheap! Besides, what do I care if they kill children?"

"Excuse me," Jaleesa recoiled.

"I've killed people and children while serving my country," retorted the man. "Take your pious crap and go home!"

Staring him in the eye with deep conviction, Jaleesa said, "I'm sorry you feel that way, sir. Disregard for any life is a tragic state of being…"

"Buzz off ya silly…"

"Donald Brown," sharply interrupted his companion. Glaring at Jaleesa, the man turned away his gaze, and the two walked onto the property and never looked back.

Jaleesa stood bewildered and amazed by what she'd just witnessed. It had been months since she'd learned the identity of her biological father and longer still since she'd been awakened to the ravages of abortion upon society, but this was another shock—to think a soldier, who's supposed to defend the weak and protect people's freedom, could be so callous to the slaughter of innocent children was beyond her. Standing there pondering the matter, it occurred to her that perhaps his view, more than others, could be understood for he had been dulled by the ravages of war. But was the average citizen who lived a life of relative ease and security any different? In fact, the routine indifference many displayed on the sidewalk day after day and week after week boggled her mind. She couldn't understand why so few cared when so great a multitude was being lost daily to the human race. Things were so messed up! How could America, parents, and the church care so little for children and their neighbors in distress? What was wrong with people? Why had they lived with this lie for so long? Interrupted in her thoughts, she heard Christopher say, "Are you all right, J.J.? What was that all about?"

"The man was so indifferent to murder; he had lost all respect for life," Jaleesa said unconsciously.

"Did he threaten you?" asked Gail.

"No, not really," answered Jaleesa.

"If you ever feel threatened or uncomfortable, just

back away from the people and come grab one of us, okay?" instructed Christopher.

"Yeah, okay, yeah, it was just odd, that's all," said Jaleesa. "I think it's good when there are more of us out here though. Thanks for coming, Gail."

"You'd think being a trial lawyer, I'd be up for anything, but it's totally different being on this side of the equation," confessed Gail. "I'm just so nervous being out here."

"Nonsense, you've done great," reassured Christopher. "Remember, we're just out here to pray and offer assistance to any who will receive it. If either of you feel uncomfortable at all, just pray and let me or Amy or Cindy handle it."

After Jaleesa's difficult exchange, the day ground like so many before, as the morning wore on and the heat of summer began to rise. It seemed as though traffic at the clinic was lighter than usual, and for that everyone rejoiced. Those who did come largely slipped into the clinic without fanfare. Few took the literature, despite Jaleesa's attempts to inform them that their baby's heart was beating at 22 days after conception or that at six weeks a baby's brain waves could be recorded. Some slammed their car doors, others ran into the clinic, still others stood smoking behind the partition or staring with contempt at those who had come to offer help and rescue. It was another typical day in a forgotten tragedy. No one from the outside world seemed to notice or care. Sure there was the occasional wave and honk of a fellow supporter of life or the prolonged honk and single-finger salute of an angry citizen, enraged that people would dare offer an alternative to abortion or intervene at the final moment of decision. But for the most part, society at large gave very little thought to any of this.

In the quiet moments when Jaleesa found no more

words to pray, she reflected on the past year and all she had discovered. Even with the whole family in group and individual counseling, Jaleesa continued to hurt over her entrance into the world. She ached over her mother's past injuries, felt hatred and heartache for her biological father, and couldn't fathom why God chose to send her to earth during the brutal rape of her mother. Life was a mystery. Certainly, God was at times. Nonetheless, she believed she was created for a purpose, and part of that purpose she'd discovered was to come to this sidewalk and plead with God and others for the rescue of their babies. She longed to see parents alter their course and forgo the damage of abortion. She even prayed for the deliverance of Tom Rose and Maggie Adams. Despite her difficulties, Jaleesa had always felt close to God, and she believed He was good, that He worked for the good, and that He had good plans for her and her family. Time had begun to heal some wounds, but the most difficult ones, the deepest scars, she knew only God could heal. And she believed He would in His timing. Trusting her pain to God, she made her petitions, and rested in Him to supply her strength.

The soldier and his girlfriend hadn't exited the clinic, and Jaleesa now knew what she suspected all along: They had not come for birth control after all, but for an abortion. A tear formed in her eye as she contemplated the beautiful baby lost to such an attractive couple. Who could their child have been, and who would they become now that they shared a horrible secret—an ever-present fellowship of death? How many precious people had been lost in this desperate way? And how many holes were left in the hearts and minds of the men and women who had consented to such a choice? Jaleesa shuddered to think of the cost. As hard as it was to reckon the truth, it only strengthened her resolve to press on—to try to make a difference. Hearing the clack of heels, she looked over her shoulder and took in a woman the likes of which she had never seen.

Crossing the street in high heels and the shortest mini skirt one can imagine, Blair Adams approached. She was brash and arrogant and without apology. Her half-shirt halter barely held her breasts in place, and it was clear that she intended to leave very little to the imagination. Blowing Christopher a kiss and gesturing in a lewd manner, she yelled out, "Let me know when you want some, Chrissy! It's on the house!"

Fixing his eyes on hers, Christopher calmly replied, "I'm praying for you, Miss Adams. Let me know when you want to get serious and leave your life of sin."

"Oh, I'm serious, honey, serious about making you feel gooood," Blair said brazenly as she entered the clinic.

Jaleesa stood stunned by the brash vulgarity. Amy never even opened her eyes, Cindy chuckled, and Christopher turned to Gail and said, "Ouch, she's a handful. Pray with me, would ya?" Inside the clinic Blair checked in and sat down in the waiting room. Not bothering to cross her legs, her red lace panties were in full view of Sally. Embarrassed and looking away, Sally hoped that Blair would be called soon. This was yet another part of her job that she loathed, and unbeknownst to any in the clinic, Sally was already preparing to leave. For too many years she had sat behind the counter and watched the weak give way to the strong, and the defeated to defeat. Her hands weren't clean, and she knew it. Thankfully, Gwynn arrived quickly and called Blair to the back. Entering room one, Blair playfully hopped up on the table and bubbled out, "Should I put my feet in the stirrups?"

"That won't be necessary, Miss Adams," said Gwynn

flatly.

"Okay, I guess I'll just make myself comfortable while I wait for the handsome doctor!"

Unimpressed and cold, Gwynn said, "You do that; he should be along in a couple of minutes."

Ten minutes later, Tom entered the room and stated, "You're roughly nine weeks pregnant, Miss Adams."

"When can we schedule, Doctor Tom?"

"There's the problem, Blair, we can't," said Tom earnestly.

"What do you mean?"

"I mean this is your third time, and I won't do it," asserted Tom. "You want to talk sterilization in the future, I'm your man, but I won't continue to aid you in your irresponsibility!"

"Come on, Tom, you know I might want to have kids some day," teased Blair. "I need this; I've got clients to serve."

"Not from me, not anymore."

"I'll give you a freebie right here on the table."

"Get out, Blair!"

"Come on, Tommy, you wanna play doctor and nurse?"

"Goodbye, Blair," dismissed Tom, as he started to leave. Pausing, he said, "You know I like the way you give it to the crazies, but I just can't be a party to this anymore. You need to take better precaution or get sterilized, but I'm through coming to the rescue."

Walking out without hesitation, Tom left Blair all alone. Staring at herself in the mirror as her mascara began to run, Blair experienced a moment of self-loathing. She hated what she had become, but then again, she hated everything. Wiping her tears and straightening her skirt, she deftly removed her panties, took a deep breath, and exited the room. Walking past Tom's office, Blair stopped, uttered a few choice words, and hurled her underwear at Tom's face. Leaving the clinic with her head held high and giving her best runway performance, she bellowed, "Call me, Christopher."

Looking over his shoulder, Christopher encouraged, "Jesus will never give up on you, Blair, and neither will I. Anytime you want to break free, we'll be here."

"Fat chance, preacher man," refused Blair as she rounded the corner and disappeared.

Turning to Gail, Christopher proclaimed, "Would that they were hot or cold, there's still hope for Blair." Making his way toward Jaleesa, Christopher expressed, "I'm sorry you had to witness all that. Blair is a very troubled woman, and she can be quite a handful the first time you encounter her. What am I saying? She's a handful every time you experience her! Anyway, it's getting late, and we need to get you back home. Gail said she's going to stick around and catch a ride with Amy. Do you mind if we say a quick prayer with them before we go?"

"Not at all; let's do it," agreed Jaleesa.

Back in his office, Tom sat contemplating his day. It hadn't been very pleasant to this point, and it was only going to get worse. Taugney had recently sold his remaining interest in the business and left Tom the sole owner. It was now his clinic and his alone. More than ten years in the making, Tom had finally reached his goal. Jim Taugney was no longer part of the equation. Their only contact now would be the occasional fishing trip or golf outing. Normally, this was a great source of pride for Tom, but today he felt only irritation. This was the lone day in the next two months that the marquee technician could show up to change the sign from Rose & Taugney to the singular Rose Clinic. Tom dreaded being exposed to the hecklers while he approved the workmanship and signed off on the completed project. Still, how bad could it be; he'd heard it all before.

Tom took a deep breath and entered the parking lot to behold the new sign. Pleased by what he saw and the short amount of time it took the technician, Tom praised the workman and offered to finish the paperwork in the cool of his office. Just as he was about to re-enter the clinic unscathed, he heard a familiar voice speak in a soft tone, "We're praying for you, Doctor Rose." Turning, he beheld the face of Gail Godfrey. Without processing, Tom said, "Hey, Counselor, what are you doing here?"

"Praying," replied Gail timidly.

"Praying!" Tom said indignantly. "What are you, some kind of saint now?"

"No, Tom, you know better than anyone that I'm not a saint, but I have changed since I found faith in Christ," said Gail.

"That's rich," mocked Tom.

Gail looked at the ground for a moment and then responded, "You know, Tom, even saints have a past, but more importantly, I believe every sinner has a future. The real question is what kind of a future? Mine is getting better, Tom, and so can yours."

"Unbelievable," muttered Tom as he walked off toward the door of the clinic.

"I'm praying for yours, Tom, I'm praying."

chapter 32

Paradigm Shift

The sanctuary was half empty when Jaleesa arrived and took a seat near the back. The event had only gathered a modest crowd. Even though it had been well advertised on the main Christian radio outlets, few people had paid any attention. The keen observer might have picked up on the gathering through the many small posters placed at several local coffee houses and churches, but the event was easy to miss and ignore. Jaleesa heard about the evening from Christopher and Amy and had decided to attend at the last minute. Uncomfortable but curious, she came. After a few introductory remarks by the pastor representing the home church, the attendees rose to sing "Amazing Grace" and "O Holy Night," a song Jaleesa felt was a bit odd for a summer gathering but nonetheless a classic. As the Christmas carol came to a close, Amy Dover took the stage.

"Welcome to our gathering tonight! This is going to be a blessed and inspirational evening. On your way in this evening I hope many of you noticed the beautiful artwork that lined the foyer. Those paintings and drawings are just a few of the talents displayed by our guest speaker, Talitha Swanson. She is an award-winning artist, musician, and author. Her book, *Light in the Darkness*, is remarkable, and I strongly encourage everyone to pick up a copy before they leave. I had the great privilege of hearing Talitha in Boston, and my life has never been the same since. We are in for a tremendous blessing tonight. Would you join with me in prayer before we hear from the dynamic Talitha Swanson?" Closing her eyes, Amy began to pray, "Father of Grace, Light of Truth, descend on us this evening. Show us afresh the path of life and leave us breathless at Your mercy, love, and purposes. We humbly acknowledge Your supremacy, and we bow at Your glorious feet. Bless Talitha, and anoint her words with power! Thank you, Father. It's in the great name of Jesus we pray. Amen. Without any further ado, it is my privilege to introduce Talitha Swanson."

Crossing the stage, Talitha slowly made her way to the piano. She was a small, unassuming woman who walked with a noticeable limp. She couldn't have been much over five feet tall, and nothing about her appearance commanded attention. That is until she sat down to play. In the stillness of the sanctuary, her piano thundered and whispered with all the power of a storm—calm and robust, blistery and ebbing. Her talent was at once evident, and the room sat captivated by her abilities. As her last note intoned, the audience erupted in applause. Smiling, Talitha nodded, brushing her hair away from her face.

Making her way toward the podium, she bowed for one last ovation. Standing with her Bible before her, Talitha gazed at her audience and said, "Children of God, it is a great privilege to speak with you tonight, and I believe Almighty God has a word for us this very evening. Before we begin, let's beseech the Lord in prayer. Father of all, I humbly ask for Your best tonight. Open our eyes, unstop our ears, and instruct our hearts. Grant us spirits that will not take offense. Open our minds and help us surrender our wills. Show us the path of life and lead us in the way everlasting. Restore our souls with Your forgiveness, grace, and truth. We bless You, Jesus, and we thank You for everything You are and everything You're about to do. Amen."

Looking up with purpose in her eye, she exclaimed, "Glory, the Spirit of the living God is in this place! I want you to know how humbled I am to be here with you all and how much I enjoyed your singing. I love Newton's "'Amazing Grace,'" God bless that sainted sinner who proclaimed with his very life the essence of redemption. I greatly appreciated the fervor with which you sang "'O Holy Night,'" a song I request to be sung every time I address an audience because it speaks so powerfully of Christ, redemption, and life. I can attest that when Jesus Christ appeared in my life, my soul felt its worth. How about you? He gave me a thrill of hope, respite from my weariness, and the breaking of the night with the dawn of a new and glorious morning! Tonight, I fall on my knees and I can hear the angel voices sing over Him as He sings over us. Zephaniah 3:17 assures us that the Lord is our mighty One who will save, a Savior who sings over us—a God who quiets us with His love—a God who delights in us, His children. God knows our needs and our weaknesses. Behold our King! In all our trials, He was born to be our friend. And in His name, all oppression shall cease. Hallelujah! May we tonight behold our King!

"Ladies and gentlemen, I praise God that I'm standing before you this evening as your invited guest. The purposes of God are beyond searching out, and it's only because of Him that I can share my story—because, you see, there was an attempt on my life even before I was born. It's a miracle of God that I'm alive today! According to the prevailing societal mindset I shouldn't even be here. I'm a survivor of a chemical abortion and our tragic national holocaust against the preborn. It is only by God's grace that I stand before you.

"To tell my story is to delve into the rare and the uncomfortable. Tonight we're going to look at abortion and its lamentable justification using the trauma of sexual violence. Journey with me this evening and discover how in the name of Jesus we can find worth, purpose, healing, deliverance, and the impetus for action. Every time I speak, I'm mindful that we are all helpless sinners, that Christ is our great Savior, and that my audience is filled with hurting people, especially those women with whom I share a kindred grief.

"Because of the nature of my story, I often attract wounded and broken people, young and old, the curious and the argumentative, and the victims of abuse, violence, and rape. If you're hurting tonight, God loves you. If you're wounded tonight, God hears you. If you're angry tonight, God understands. If you're lost tonight, God knows right where you are. And if you're confused tonight, He's not. Jesus said in Matthew 11:28, 'Come to me, all who labor and are heavy laden, and I will give you rest. Take my yoke upon you, and learn from me, for I am gentle and lowly in heart, and you will find rest for your souls.' Jesus came for the broken and the wounded, and He atoned for and healed all brokenness through His own wounding and brokenness on the cross. Hallelujah!"

Pausing, Talitha took a sip of water and cleared her throat. Smiling, she continued, "My story, like all people, began in the epoch of space before time in the mind of a Genius, a Lover, a Giver, a Father, and a Friend. The Holy Scriptures proclaim in the Book of Ephesians that God chose us to be His adopted children before the foundation of the world. In His grace we've been chosen to be His people. Everyone in this room was chosen by God to exist, even before time began. Paul preaches in the book of Acts, *'God who made the world and everything in it, since He is Lord of heaven and earth, does not dwell in temples made with hands. Nor is He worshiped with men's hands, as though He needed anything, since He gives to all life, breath, and all things. And He has made from one blood every nation of men to dwell on all the face of the earth, and has determined their pre-appointed times and the boundaries of their dwellings, so that they should seek the Lord, in the hope that they might grope for Him and find Him, though He is not far from each one of us; for in Him we live and move and have our being, as also some of your own poets have said, 'For we are also His offspring.'* For the glory of God, for the purpose of our calling, for relationship, for love, for good works, and for joy, our Father chose to send us to earth in His way and in His timing.

"On a humid July night in the back of a minibus, God elected to send me to my mother as five wayward college boys repeatedly raped and assaulted her. As devastating as the violent rapes were on my mother and as painful as it was for me to discover the truth about my beginnings, does that mean I don't belong on this earth? Did the manner in which I was conceived determine whether or not I existed? Does the intention or manner of anyone's conception validate or invalidate their existence? Conception is a mystery outside of human will or control. How often have I heard, as I'm sure many of you have as well, that those of us conceived during sexual assault are unwanted, a punishment, the product of wicked men, a painful reminder of brutality, or a heavy burden! By whose definition?

"Listen, children. Who determines who we are? Only God and ourselves! When I discovered that this unknown man who hurt my mother was not my first father, but instead only part of the process God used to bring me forth, I began to see from a broader perspective. When I saw through Scripture that I was a planned, intended, and wanted child of God, my whole world changed! My paradigm shifted, and I began to see myself and my conception circumstance in a different light. I saw, like Peter, that what God has instituted and made clean, no one could call unclean. Only God opens and closes the womb. I saw that I was a gift given on the heels of depravity, that God works all things together for good, and that while people are granted the freedom by God to choose wickedness, God is equally free to bring beauty out of ashes. Hallelujah!

"Children, the knowledge of who we are, and whom we belong to, should set us free! Shouldn't we consider Him who has dominion over life and death? Who are we, the creatures of the Creator, to decide that killing an innocent is an acceptable answer to sexual violence, or anything? Or that getting rid of God's greatest earthly gift is a benefit to a wounded and broken mother. The Sacred Writings proclaim children are a gift from the Lord. Glory! How many times when the pro-choice movement speaks of this brutal crime against women and a resulting conception do they identify the child in the womb as the product of the father, but when they talk of the so called 'routine' abortion, the child is now the product of the mother or an insignificant part of her body. Oh, father of lies, we're done listening! Listen instead to God, dear children. He declares through the Prophet Isaiah, '...you whom I have upheld since you were conceived, and have carried since your birth. Even to your old age and gray hairs I am he, I am he who will sustain you. I have made you and I will carry you; I will sustain you and I will rescue you.' Regardless of how you were conceived or how deep your wound, God wants you! God wants all of us! People, hear me tonight. God

Almighty purposely created you, He loves you, and He wants you here.

"Mothers and fathers, if you were encouraged to abort, forced to abort, or desperately chose abortion after your attack, God wants you to know that He loves you, too. God is grieved over what happened to you, and He wants you to know that He has been and still is working for your good. He wants you to come boldly to the throne of grace tonight. He's calling you to forgive and be forgiven. He wants you to confess with the confidence of David, 'Deliver me from the guilt of bloodshed, O God, the God of my salvation, and my tongue shall sing aloud of Your righteousness. O Lord, open my lips, and my mouth shall show forth Your praise. For You do not desire sacrifice, or else I would give it; You do not delight in burnt offering. The sacrifices of God are a broken spirit, a broken and a contrite heart— These, O God, You will not despise.' God wants your heart that He might deal with your heartache. He wants to take your fear, self-condemnation, and sorrow, and replace it with faith, hope, and love. Won't you let Him this evening?"

At these piercing yet gentle words, several women in the crowd began audibly weeping. Hearing the release of emotion in the church, Talitha called out, "Daughters and sons, please gather around these, your sisters and brothers, and lay your hands upon them and begin to pray for them. The Scriptures teach us to weep with those who weep. And again it proclaims, 'Blessed are those who mourn, for they shall be comforted.' Pray for each other, children, with groans too deep for words."

Jaleesa was weeping as she laid hands on the beautiful woman beside her. Through the sobs, she heard her confess, "I destroyed my baby boy because I thought he was the product of rape. Forgive me, God, forgive

me! I see now that he was God's child and my child."
Jaleesa silently interceded and wept as the woman made
confession. Gently, Jaleesa asked the wounded woman
her name.

"My name is Belia."

"May I pray for you, Belia?"

"Yes," she said.

"Lord, You love Belia so much; she is the work of
Your hands, the intention of Your will, and a receiver of
Your grace. Shower her with love and peace and speak
deeply to her heart that You have removed her sins as
far as the east is from the west, and that if she confesses
her sins, which she's done here tonight, You are faithful
and just to forgive her and cleanse her from all unrigh-
teousness. God You've made Belia beautiful, and I'm sure
her child in heaven is beautiful, too. Give her a sense of
his place there and his eager desire for her. Jesus, thank
you for my sister, Belia. Love her and bless her always in
Christ. Amen."

"Thank you," Belia said, wiping her tears. "Can I
pray for you?"

"I'd be honored," invited Jaleesa. "You can pray for
my mother, Rachelle, and that I will always honor her
and give her the respect she deserves."

"What's your name, sweetheart?"

"Jaleesa."

After a lengthy interlude of prayer, Talitha performed a few more brilliant songs and finished her talk.
It had been a powerful night and a powerful time, and
Jaleesa was grateful she had come. She was deeply moved
by Talitha's efforts to locate and meet her biological
mother. Jaleesa loved that Talitha's full name was Talitha
Koum Chasia which meant "Little Girl Arise—protected
by the Lord." And it was clear from her testimony and

the many twists and turns along her journey that she had indeed been protected by God. Despite the emotion of the evening and the heaviness of the topic, everyone who attended left encouraged and filled with new hope. The thing that lingered most for Jaleesa was Talitha's desire for the redemption of her biological parents and the wayward father she never found. Talitha's heart to forgive along with a passage she shared from Ezekiel, inspired Jaleesa. The words of the prophet still echoed in her heart:

> *The soul who sins shall die. The son shall not bear the guilt of the father, nor the father bear the guilt of the son. The righteousness of the righteous shall be upon himself, and the wickedness of the wicked shall be upon himself. 'But if a wicked man turns from all his sins which he has committed, keeps all My statutes, and does what is lawful and right, he shall surely live; he shall not die. None of the transgressions which he has committed shall be remembered against him; because of the righteousness which he has done, he shall live. Do I have any pleasure at all that the wicked should die?' says the Lord God, 'and not that he should turn from his ways and live?'*

This passage, more than any other, spoke to her soul. Imaginings of her own biological father pervaded Jaleesa's thoughts as she left the gathering. What about his soul—his life? Didn't he need Jesus, too? Was it possible through Christ's power to love even this man? Reading the poem inscribed on her newly purchased bookmark, which depicted a painting by Talitha of a beautiful baby boy peeking out from under a blanket, Jaleesa realized the evening had helped her turn a corner in her understanding

and grief. Meditating on Talitha's words, Jaleesa knew
what she needed to do:

Carried on the Wind,
How did my life begin?
With a word from Him!
Slated for the tomb,
How did I escape the womb?
With a word from Him!
Abandoned in a car,
How did I get this far?
With a word from Him!
Unwanted from the start,
How did I keep my heart?
With a word from Him!
Unloved, except by the One above,
How did I discover love?
With a word from Him!
If you don't know
The way to go,
Get a word from Him!
No matter how deep the sorrow,
He's holding forth a better tomorrow.
With a word from Him!

chapter 33

The Visitor

Tom blinked the tiredness from his eyes. He'd recently finished a very long week at the clinic and endured an even longer prayer campaign by the opposition. The efforts of Christopher's group and many other pro-lifers had taken its toll on his career. Tom was frustrated, disillusioned, and tired. This wasn't the first time he'd considered abandoning the whole abortion component of his business. He was weary of the tension, the controversy—the rhetoric. He longed for peace and a hassle-free life. He'd already made plenty of money, and the revenue from his other services and delivery fees were more than enough to keep him comfortable. But every time he'd considered it before, he'd rejected the idea because he knew he provided a vital service to women. Tom prided himself on the fact that no patient of his had ever been seriously injured or killed during a procedure, a fate that, he knew all too well, was experienced by many other women who chose to visit less competent and conscientious physicians. Jenny was always before him, and he knew it was his calling to protect others like her from a similar fate. If he was honest, however, he'd admit that most of the women he'd helped since he'd chosen to practice abortion didn't come close to Jenny's circumstances—but they all had their reasons.

Hearing the loudspeaker squawk that passengers from Phoenix flight 88 could now claim their bags from carousel two, Tom moved into position. It had been four years since he'd seen Jonathan and seven years since Max had moved the family to Arizona so he could teach at a small college. Max and Sandy had arranged for Jonathan to stay with Tom for six weeks while they traveled Europe as part of an extensive history grant from Max's college. Max needed the time and the personal experience to complete a doctoral project concerning the history of European resistance and rescue during the Holocaust. Max had always been fascinated by the history of the twentieth century and, in particular, the Holocaust and World War II. Unfortunately, not enough money was available to bring both Jonathan and Kaitlin along, so it was decided Jonathan would stay behind and spend the time with his uncle in Eastbrook, the place of his birth and the holder of many fond memories.

Tom took a seat near carousel two and watched it move in a slow and unending circle. He was excited to see his nephew. If only he wasn't so tired and bogged down at work. Having arranged for a two-week break in the middle of Jonathan's visit, Tom told himself he could make it. He'd been looking forward to this break with all his heart, a chance to go fishing, camping, and just plain bumming around in the city and the surrounding areas. He wondered how Jonathan had changed over these last four years and how much he'd grown. Startled out of his meditations, he heard a familiar voice say, "Mind if I take this seat, old man?"

"Old man my… Give me a hug, you rascal! How was your flight?"

"It was good, Uncle Tom. How are things?" beamed Jonathan.

"Same ole same ole," offered Tom. "Come on, let's get out of here. I've got a little surprise for you, Jon-Jon."

"You're starting to gray, Uncle T. I sure hope this doesn't mean the end of the road!"

"Ah, youth!" said Tom. "I can see this summer is going to involve some good humbling."

"We'll see about that, my pong's improved since the last time we played."

"Good, maybe this time I'll use my right hand!"

"So, what's this surprise you have for me?"

"You'll see."

Making their way through the concourse, it was obvious the two had missed each other. Their playful banter evidenced a deep bond of affection. Jonathan had grown into a handsome young man, possessing wavy blond hair and a smooth tan. His complexion showed the gleam of youth, and his smile was warm and inviting. Tom already knew he was smart, but the handsome, confident young man walking beside him was a revelation of the person he'd become while away in Arizona. Leaving the terminal, Jonathan breathed in the freshness of the air and gloried in the pleasant Sunday afternoon. Making their way through the parking garage, Jonathan stopped in his tracks as he took in the shiny, new red 2012 ZR-1.

"No way!" celebrated Jonathan. "This baby is yours? I've got to start studying for med school! Is she fast?"

"You tell me," invited Tom as he threw Jonathan the keys.

"Are you serious?" said Jonathan in disbelief. "I only got my permit a couple of months ago."

"Yeah, why not? I trust you. Go ahead. Let's see what she can do, shall we?"

"Oh, Uncle Tom, this is sweet! Maybe we should go

pick up some babes? We appear to have all the necessary equipment," teased Jonathan.

"Well, we've got the car, but not much else!"

"Speak for yourself, old man."

"No, Jon, I was speaking for you!"

"Oh, Uncle T, you know I'm a handsome devil!"

"I can see the sun hasn't damaged your perception!"

Jonathan eased the car out of the lot, stalling only once. The drive to Tom's was pure fun as both boys acted like school friends, joking, laughing, high-fiving, and generally acting immature. Tom loved it, and he loved his nephew. He wondered what it would be like to have his own son. If he did, he'd want him to be like Jonathan. They spoke of Max, Sandy, and Katie and how excited they all were to take the trip to Europe, about Jonathan splitting time between Tom's place and Grandma Rose's place, Tom's successful practice, and all the cool things they planned to do during his visit. It was a great reunion, and Jonathan loved the car!

Waking up the next morning, Jonathan discovered a note on the fridge. Tom had left instructions on how to find and work things around the house, where to locate the golf clubs if he fancied a morning round of golf or a trip to the driving range, the code to the pool and spa, and any contact numbers he would need for locating Tom while he was away at work or Grandma if he wasn't available. It was a teenager's dream to be at such a cool place with all the comforts of adulthood. The only drawback was the friends Jonathan had left behind. He thought about trying to catch up with some of his buddies from before he left Eastbrook, but he was only nine years old at the time and didn't know where to begin. So Jonathan settled in for a summer of privilege and the adventure of the unknown.

hushed

That night while eating at Tuscany House, Jonathan said he'd like to see Tom's work and then maybe bum around Old Town Eastbrook for a couple of hours. He also suggested they grab lunch at Joe's. The burgers at Joe's were the best in the state, and Jonathan could still remember their flavor. Grilled to perfection, the double cheeseburger was the best he'd ever tasted. As Jonathan recalled, the cheese on the Joe's double was truly exceptional; it had the perfect blend of American, Swiss, and parmesan cheeses. Tom couldn't refuse, and besides, Tuesday was a non-abortion day and, as a result, a non-protest day. Tom figured it was the best time to let Jonathan see the clinic. Tomorrow was set, but the night was still young, so the boys went out for a little friendly bowling and some root beer floats.

The next day, Jonathan regretted his decision as Tom yanked him out of bed at seven a.m. for breakfast and a run before the drive to the clinic. Jonathan had missed the trees, the temperatures, and the mountains of Eastbrook. It was the ideal city, in an ideal location, and he still regarded it as home. Jonathan shared a kinship and a mystical bond with the place of his appearing, and he felt it. He couldn't believe how much he remembered and how much the city had changed, even in the old parts. Everywhere he looked it seemed there was new construction. The city had gone on without him, and there was plenty for the living. Pulling up to the clinic, the modest single-story building showed forth a sprinkling of sun through the green leaves of the giant trees that lined 13th. Looking up at the sign, he joked with Tom about his name being in lights. Jonathan teasingly asked where the red carpet was as he exited the SUV—to which Tom promptly said something about not being a smart....

Inside the clinic, Jonathan was introduced to Megan, the new receptionist, Gwynn, Tammy, and April—a new

OB-GYN Tom had hired to help share the workload at the clinic. She was fresh-faced and eager to take on the world. Maggie Adams had recommended her, and Tom knew she'd be a perfect fit. The clinic was clean and typical, but nothing overly impressive, and Jonathan felt a twinge of disappointment in the facility after seeing the lavish place his uncle lived. In fact, he wondered if the whole clinic cost more than Tom's 'Vette and his music/theater room put together. Tom had bragged the night before about his B&W speakers that cost thirty thousand dollars apiece, speakers that no doubt sounded phenomenal, but for sixty grand? Nonetheless, it was cool that his uncle was a doctor and had his own medical clinic. After touring the facility and spending some time in Tom's office looking at all the books his uncle had read, Jonathan was ready to leave. Walking past Megan and a few women waiting in the lobby, Jonathan stopped to inform her that he was headed out and to please remind Tom that he'd meet him at Joe's for lunch.

The weather was comfortable as Jonathan made his way to Eastbrook Records, a shop that had been in Eastbrook since the early sixties. The shop, a second-generation family affair, was brimming with character and history. Eastbook Records was a local treasure that still sold vinyl records and turntables for the purists as well as CDs, DVDs, and Blu-rays for the general public. Jonathan loved old music, bargain deals, and the rare item one could find at Eastbrook Records. The store and the music each had a history and a novelty that delighted his soul. He remembered fondly the days in his past when he'd spent time with his father and Tom poking around in this unique store for the hidden treasure or forgotten musician—his father still owned a rare Beatles LP that they found here. After about an hour of searching and a rare Stevie Ray Vaughan find, Jonathan left the record shop and headed for Sports Works and his other love, baseball. Sports Works sold all the latest sporting equipment and clothing, but it also had a section that celebrated sports history. They sold rare items, collectable posters, cards, memorabilia, and the like. It didn't take Jonathan long to find the baseball cards encased in protective glass. Salivating over a 1951 Bowman #165 Ted Williams that he knew he couldn't afford, Jonathan waited for assistance.

"Welcome to Sports Works," said the man behind the counter. "What can I do for you?"

"How much for the Seaver?" asked Jonathan.

"Which one, the '69 Topps #480 or the '71 Topps #160?"

"The year the Miracles won the Series," said Jonathan.

"'69 it is. This one's in very good condition so it's priced at $35," informed the man.

"Cool, I'm also interested in the Ruth, Aaron, and Mays card."

"You've got a good eye, that's one of my favorites, too," echoed the man. "1973 Topps #1! It also costs 35 dollars."

"I'll take 'em," said Jonathan confidently.

"Anything else I can get for you?" asked the clerk.

"No, seventy dollars is already too much, but I love baseball history," said Jonathan.

"I can see that," affirmed the man. "Well, you won't be disappointed with these. Thank you for your purchase, and have a good day."

"I will. You, too."

As Jonathan left the counter, a young woman walking toward the counter caught his eye. Turning his attention to some autographed football posters hanging on the wall, Jonathan lingered to satisfy his curiosity and take a better look. She looked to be about 5'7" or 5'8" with long black hair, flawless skin, and a beauty that drew the eye. Trying not to be obvious, Jonathan stole little glances whenever he could.

"Hey, Hank, have you seen Lucas around?" Jaleesa asked.

"No, I haven't, J.J.," replied Hank.

"I checked in the back, and they haven't seen him either," Jaleesa said with disappointment. "I guess I'll check the main floor. If you see him, would you tell him I went to Jefferson Park?"

"Sure thing, J.J.," assured Hank. "I hope you find him."

"Thanks, Hank, have a good one."

"You, too, J.J."

As Jaleesa turned and walked out of the memorabilia section, Jonathan confirmed his interest. She was absolutely captivating! Jonathan was lured in—he just knew he had to know her. Following at a distance, he watched as she chatted with a few more clerks and ultimately made her way out of the building. There was an air of grace about her as she walked down the busy commercial street of outdoor shops and businesses. Continuing to follow, he felt silly, determined, and compelled as he pursued the young beauty. Walking at a safe distance, Jonathan felt confident his presence had been undetected. Impulsively, he followed Jaleesa, never thinking about what he would say to her or how she would react or if she had a boyfriend. It was like he was caught in a trance or a tractor beam. Before long, they'd arrived at Jefferson Park. Keeping his distance, Jonathan watched J.J. make her way to the park fountain. Slipping off her shoes and rolling up the bottom of her capris, she approached the fountain and flitted along the edge of the pulsating water. She moved with such grace and freedom, looking charmingly appropriate among the small children running through the water in their summer playfulness. Jonathan slipped unnoticed onto a nearby park bench and watched for several minutes as Jaleesa and the children enjoyed a moment of play. Sensing he had nothing to lose and desperately wanting to get to know her, he drew near to the fountain. Approaching from behind and slightly out of Jaleesa's view, Jonathan said, "Looks like fun."

Turning in the direction of his voice, Jaleesa looked at the handsome young teen and said, "It is. You should join us."

Pleased and not knowing what else to say, Jonathan replied, "All right then, maybe I will." Taking off his shoes and wiggling some life into his toes, he crept up on the water and cautiously placed his foot over a dormant jet. A moment later when a blast of water riddled the sole of his foot, he jumped back and exclaimed, "Geez, that's cold!"

Laughing, Jaleesa said, "Mountain water's a little different from back home, I take it? You're not from around here, are you?"

Looking at Jaleesa with a smile on his face, Jonathan retorted, "Just been away for awhile, but I adjust quickly," and with that he charged the water. Leaping through the ice cold spray and dodging little children, Jonathan whooped and hollered and laughed as his body and face took the brunt of the fountain's merciless assault.

Clapping her hands in appreciation of the gallant charge, Jaleesa hollered, "Way to go, California!"

"That's not where I'm from, but it's warmer there, too," said Jonathan. Dripping wet and looking a bit silly, he skirted the fountain and said, "I'm from Arizona, and my name's Jon."

"Pleased to meet you, Jon. I'm Jaleesa."

chapter 34

Crushed in Spirit

"Lord, use me today to be a light in the midst of darkness. Forgive me my sins and help me forgive others who've offended me. Fill me with Your Holy Spirit and allow me to be an instrument of help, encouragement, and rescue. Walk with me Jesus that I might conduct myself in a manner that evidences You. Protect me and all those at the clinic today from the Evil One. End abortion, Lord God, and set at liberty the captives for Your name's sake and glory! Help me to be a neighbor to the broken and a help in time of need. Thank you, Jesus, for loving me and all Your people. Amen." Finishing her prayer, Cindy Taylor arose and picked up her Bible. Opening to the thirty-second Psalm, a psalm she'd made a habit of reading during recovery and still one she continued to declare up until this day, Cindy began to intone:

> *Blessed is the one whose transgression is forgiven, whose sin is covered.... I acknowledged my sin to you, and I did not cover my iniquity; I said, 'I will confess my transgressions to the Lord,' and you forgave the iniquity of my sin.... you are a hiding place for me; you preserve me from trouble; you surround me with shouts of deliverance.*

"Amen, Lord, let it be so!" she proclaimed. After quickly brushing her teeth and putting on her lipstick, she made her way to the kitchen to prepare her husband's lunch for his upcoming day of work, one of the many ways she served her husband as an ongoing testimony to him about the presence of Christ in her life. It had been a difficult marriage for both of them, but Cindy held fast to her faith. She believed that through love, sacrifice, serving, and her example, she would one day win her husband without a word. Finishing his lunch with a simple note about her hope for his day and her love for him, she picked up her car keys and headed out the door.

Arriving at the clinic, Cindy was pleased to see Amy, Miles, and Jaleesa already on the sidewalk. It was a typical summer Thursday, and everything felt familiar and routine. Getting out of her car, she could still hear the last song that played on the radio in her head. Walking down Almond St., she quietly sang:

"…you're covered with the fingerprints of God
Never has there been and never again
Will there be another you
Fashioned by God's hand
And perfectly planned
To be just who you are
And what he's been creating
Since the first beat of your heart
Is a living breathing priceless work of art"

"Hey, Cindy, how's it going?" asked Jaleesa.

"Good. It's a beautiful day, isn't it?" replied Cindy.

"Gorgeous, but it never quite warms up quickly enough for me in the early morning," said Jaleesa.

"Trust me, in an hour you'll be wishing for the cool."

"I suppose you're right."

"Hey, how was Talitha last week?" asked Cindy.

"She was amazing, and her testimony just blew me away."

"I'm sorry I missed her," Cindy said. "Did she talk about her son, Samuel?"

"No, she didn't, but maybe that's because we spent a lot of time praying and ministering to the wounded people in attendance."

"That sounds like Talitha," said Cindy. "Still, it's such a powerful part of her testimony."

"Was he a miracle baby or something?"

"Yeah, after her mom was raped, she was given a hormonal drug called DES which was used in the '70s to treat women with various conditions, but one of its uses was for the purpose of preventing pregnancy after rape, like today's so called 'emergency contraception pills.' But it turned out that DES caused various birth defects, which is why Talitha still walks with a limp. Not only did the chemical damage Talitha's foot, it caused her to be infertile. So after years of trying to have a baby with her husband and researching what the Scriptures taught about life's beginning and purpose, she started to camp on the story of Hannah and began to pray for the healing of her barrenness. And five years ago, she conceived and gave birth to a baby boy who, naturally, she named Samuel."

"Holy cow, that's an awesome miracle of God! What a testimony to God's role in the conception of new life!" exclaimed Jaleesa.

"Yeah, so powerful," said Cindy. "I'm surprised she didn't share that with you guys at her talk."

"She did share about finding her biological mother during her college years and leading her to Christ," Jaleesa said. "That must have been where she learned about the reason for her handicap as well as the story of her conception and abandonment after birth."

"What an awesome witness she is," reflected Cindy.

"I know. I just loved her."

The two women abruptly ended their conversation as they noticed a lone woman approach the clinic. She was thin and pretty with a melancholy air about her. Ignoring their offer of help, she passed without a word and continued into the clinic in silence and despair. Immediately, the girls began to pray. The oppression and disillusionment on the young woman's face was evident. She seemed past the point of return, but knowing God is mighty to save, the counselors pressed forward in fervent intercession. Miles read the Word, while Amy, Cindy, and Jaleesa gathered to pray. With great travail they prayed for the thin woman, but after an hour passed with no hint of her release, it became clear that she would not choose life this day. Others had entered into a similar fate on this summer morning, but Cindy couldn't get the thin woman off of her mind. She felt a strong move of the Spirit regarding the young woman and started to intercede anew for her healing and release from all that bound her. Cindy gently rocked as she prayed under the large oaks, "Gracious Father, release this daughter from the sins that bind her, the relationships that are a hindrance to her, and the guilt of bloodshed. Lord, deliver her! Come in Your power and give me the grace to minister healing and reconciliation in her life. Use me as an instrument of compassion and rescue. Amen."

Not long after the noon hour, the thin woman, for whom they'd all prayed so earnestly, exited the clinic and walked toward Cindy. Miles and Jaleesa had been replaced by a Catholic couple from Saint Michael's who were currently engaged with Amy in prayer for another couple that seemed to be reconsidering their choice for abortion. Cindy felt in her spirit the acute nature of the young woman's aloneness as she approached. Compelled, Cindy said, "Ma'am, Jesus wants me to tell you that you're not alone and that He loves you now more than ever." Stiffening, the woman averted her eyes and briskly passed Cindy on the sidewalk. Following meekly behind, Cindy implored, "Let Jesus help you. He loves you. He loves you!" Almost breaking into a run, the woman made it an additional fifteen feet before falling to her knees and uttering the bitterest sound Cindy had ever heard. As she burst forth in tears, Cindy ran to her side and, kneeling, held the fragile child as she wept. Rocking the woman as if she were a newborn babe, Cindy whispered, "God's here. He loves you, and He forgives you! His love for us is unrelenting!"

Looking up through tears, the woman said, "He'll never forgive me."

"Let Him heal what's broken. He can do it," encouraged Cindy.

"Nothing can save me now."

"You're wrong. His grace is sufficient," said Cindy. "I know because He did it for me." There on the sidewalk, the women entered a sorority of grief, a fellowship of suffering, and the beginnings of grace.

Driving home after an emotional morning shift, Cindy mourned the loss of Stacy's child, but she gloried in the prospect that Stacy would not be lost as well. She was filled with hope because of the work God had done that morning on the sidewalk. She knew the hard work was yet to come for Stacy, but with Stacy's contact information and her promise to accompany Cindy to the next post-abortion recovery class offered at Eastbrook Pregnancy Care, there was real hope. Hope for healing,

hushed

wholeness, and freedom. Praising the Lord, she recalled the psalm that says, "Yahweh, if You considered sins, Lord, who could stand? But with You there is forgiveness, so that You may be revered… Israel, put your hope in the Lord. For there is faithful love with the Lord, and with Him is redemption in abundance."

chapter 35

The Park

Lincoln State Penitentiary looked drab and dusty, sitting alone in the dry valley behind the Illapah Range. It was the state's most notorious maximum-security prison, reserved for heinous offenders and psychopaths. Sitting ninety miles west of Eastbrook, it took a little over two hours to reach by car. The valley was awash in morning sunlight as Jaleesa descended from the pass in her maroon Honda Civic, a gift Rachelle had given her on her seventeenth birthday. She was nervous to be sure, but she'd prayed about this for weeks, and she knew it was something God had placed on her heart to do. Gathering courage as she listened to Talitha Swanson's latest CD, she repeated a proverb the Lord had impressed her with earlier in the week: "The wicked flee when no one is pursuing, but the righteous are bold as a lion." With adrenalin pumping, she approached the lone facility.

The protocol for prison visitation was more intense than Jaleesa expected. Waiting for her first-time visitor request to be approved by the prison and H.T. was torturous and nerve-racking. The request forms she was required to fill out were long, and the processing of her ID and social security number moved at a snail's pace. She wondered briefly if H.T. would even agree to see her—a stranger. Did she look at all like him? Could she keep it together—keep her emotions in check? Was this a mistake? Fighting back her questions and her doubt, Jaleesa chose to remain undeterred. She didn't know what to expect, and her nerves were starting to get the best of her, but she resolved to trust the Lord to make a way. Jaleesa had come too far to turn back now. Despite her mixed emotions, she was close to answering some long-awaited questions and satisfying a curiosity she couldn't deny. *Who was this man with whom she shared DNA?* Being notified that H.T. had indeed consented to see her, Jaleesa was informed of her rights and the stipulations of the visit by the superintendent and the lead security officer. She was greatly relieved to hear that security glass would separate her from H.T. and that at no time would physical contact be allowed between her and the prisoner. After finalizing her paperwork, she was led through a metal detector, searched with a wand, and told to leave all personal effects in the waiting room, except for her Bible, which she had already had cleared by prison security. With her preparation over, she paused for prayer before she began the long walk to the secured visitor room. Summoning her courage, she entered the room and approached the man seated behind the glass.

"Hello, I must have died and gone to heaven," cackled H.T. leeringly. "To what do I owe the pleasure, Miss?"

Looking him square in the eye to cover her nerves, Jaleesa said, "Soul business. I've come to share the Gospel of Jesus Christ with you, Mr. Taylor."

"Oh, thank you, Jesus!" exclaimed H.T. "At least the good Lord had the sense to send a fresh little thing like you to do his work."

"Mr. Taylor, from what I understand, I'm the first and only visitor you've ever had. Maybe you should try not to offend me."

"Whatever you want, darlin'. I'm just happy to look!"

"Mr. Taylor, has anybody ever shared with you about Jesus?"

"Nah, the religious crowd never gave a damn about me."

"I'll make a deal with you, Mr. Taylor. If you'll clean up your language and stop the filthy-old-man routine, I'll come and visit you twice a month."

"All right, sister, I'm not promising anything, but I'll play along."

"Good. Let's start with the basics," said Jaleesa. "Do you know why you exist, Mr. Taylor?"

"To pleasure myself!" H.T. said with a smile. Immediately seeing he'd elicited no response from his guest, he retreated and said, "Beats the hell... excuse me, I guess I don't know, young lady."

"Well, that's why I'm here, Mr. Taylor, to share with you God's story and give you an opportunity to know Him, to know the power of His resurrection, and to help you answer questions like the one I just asked."

"Are you serious? You're joking, right? You couldn't possibly care about me," said H.T. "You're just here on some kind of religious mission to earn points with God and somehow absolve whatever guilt you must have!"

"No, Mr. Taylor, my guilt's already been taken care of by Jesus at the cross. Nothing I could ever do will earn His gift, and nothing bad I've ever done can keep me from it! You see, I've entrusted my life to Him, and once He's been entrusted with someone, He never loses them. Nevertheless, I do strive to live according to what He taught, and He instructed us to visit those who are in prison," Jaleesa said as she met H.T. square in the eyes to establish she was not one to shrink back.

"I've never read the Bible. Is it a good story?"

"The best," answered Jaleesa. "It's God's story, and

our story, our truest story. Let me give you a taste, Mr. Taylor, and let's see if the Bible can't answer that question I asked you a minute ago." Opening her Bible to the Gospel of John, Jaleesa read: "*In the beginning was the Word, and the Word was with God, and the Word was God. He was in the beginning with God. All things came into being through Him, and apart from Him nothing came into being that has come into being. In Him was life, and the life was the Light of men. The Light shines in the darkness, and the darkness did not comprehend it.*" "Does that speak to you, Mr. Taylor?"

"No ma'am, but you do," flirted H.T.

Ignoring H.T., Jaleesa found another verse, "Let's try this one, '...*in the Lord, neither is woman independent of man, nor is man independent of woman. For as the woman originates from the man, so also the man has his birth through the woman; and all things originate from God.*' Do you see it now, Mr. Taylor?"

"See what?"

"The reason you exist?"

"I don't see how I'm going to get answers like that from a book. All I'm hearing so far is light and dark, beginnings, and words."

"Forgive me, Mr. Taylor, I should have started with a prayer. Do you mind if I say a quick prayer before I share this next verse?"

"Whatever floats your boat, darlin', but I doubt it'll help much," H.T. said proudly.

"Lord Jesus, open Mr. Taylor's ears. Send the Holy Spirit to help him hear Your truth and receive Your love. Amen." Remaining in First Corinthians, Jaleesa flipped ahead and read: "*... 'yet for us there is but one God, the Father, from whom are all things and we exist for Him; and one Lord, Jesus Christ, by whom are all things, and we exist* *through Him.'* So I'll ask you again, Mr. Taylor, why do you exist?"

"I suppose, according to what you just read, I exist for God," responded H.T.

"Exactly, Mr. Taylor, you were created for God, and while you may not have known it or lived it in the past, Jesus is reaching out to you today. He wants you to discover Him and the plans He has for the rest of your life. Jesus is offering Himself to you as a free gift. Through Jesus you can receive a new life, forgiveness of your sins, life in heaven after your earthly death, and freedom from whatever binds you."

"What's your name, little lady?" inquired H.T.

"You can call me J.J."

For the next several minutes, Jaleesa read the Scriptures and shared Christ with her biological father until he became irritated with her persistence and requested to return to his cell. Maintaining her composure while H.T. left the room, Jaleesa let out an audible groan and doubled over at the sound of the closed prisoner door. All she'd held back spilled forth. Feeling a huge dump of emotion, she wept over the state of this man who, until today, she'd never known. Jaleesa knew before she came that it would be tough to share the Gospel with her biological father and even tougher to love him, but she was convinced she needed to try. She was a mess now, but she was relieved she'd held her own during the visit. Gathering herself slowly, she made her way out of the visiting room. One thing that gave her solace—she was glad she didn't look like him. Her mind was a jumble as she fought for composure. Despite their shared DNA, H.T. remained largely a stranger. Her visit had been hard and somewhat awkward but she was glad she'd come, and resolved to continue until the Lord lifted her burden or H.T. no longer entertained her visits.

Leaving the prison, she asked security if they would give H.T. a small pocket Bible she'd purchased for him. The prison staff assured her they would offer it to him, but that there was no guarantee he'd accept it. Jaleesa understood and left its delivery and destination in the Lord's hands. During her weeks of prayer before visiting, she'd highlighted several passages about God's love, forgiveness, and grace in the small Bible. She trusted God to use it to speak to this lost and wounded man.

Arriving in Eastbrook after a long return trip of reflection and grief, Jaleesa decided to drive to Jefferson Park and unwind. It was there that she usually felt her heart restored and her mind released. She loved the old park with its mature trees, small pond, fountain, and festive activities. There was always something going on at the park. Taking in the familiar, Jaleesa watched as several merchants milled around selling their food, candies, and products. Strolling past the water, she found a nice spot to sit beneath a shade tree and watch the ducks. It was impossible to believe that H.T. was her biological father, but she knew it was true. She didn't know what she'd received from him, but she gathered from her brief encounter it wasn't much. He was devoid of faith, crass, and perverted, and these were not things she exemplified or struggled with. Her issues were more in the vein of perfectionism and anger, but graciously the Lord, her mother, therapy, and her strong family support system had brought her through much of what ailed her. Her deepening faith had blossomed over the last year as she grappled with the many ironies of her life. Jaleesa had come to understand through the revelation of her conception and her time spent with Christopher learning God's view of the sanctity of human life just how blessed she was. She saw clearly that she'd been given much and that much was required of her, so it was from this conviction that she purposed to reach out to her biological father in accordance with Micah 6:8 (*He has showed you, O man, what is good. And what does the Lord require of you? To act justly and to love mercy and to walk humbly with your God.*).

Hearing the rapid sound of approaching footsteps, Jaleesa looked over her shoulder and caught the returned gaze of Jonathan Rose.

Smiling a weary smile, Jaleesa said, "Getting a little afternoon run in, are you?"

"Yeah," said Jonathan, panting. Taking a moment to catch his breath, he added, "You look a little down, Jaleesa, is everything all right?"

"I'm okay, I just had a bit of a rough morning."

"You want to talk about it?

"Not really."

"Okay, but I'm going to have to ask you to stop coming to my park unless you're going to get some ice cream with me?"

"So this is why you run, you got a sweet tooth, do ya?"

"No, I play baseball in a competitive league in Arizona, and I've got to stay fit, especially since I'm missing part of the season this summer while my folks are away."

"You staying with family here?" asked Jaleesa.

"Yeah, my uncle lives here, and I'm staying with him until my parents get back from Europe."

"Why didn't you go to Europe with your parents?"

"My dad's a professor, and the college could only pay for three out of the four of us to go, so I stepped aside and let my sister go."

"That was nice of you," said Jaleesa.

"Yeah, I suppose so, but I like Eastbrook and my uncle's a pretty cool guy."

"That's good, what's he do?"

"He's a doctor."

"Oh, yeah? My mom's a doctor. What hospital does he work at?"

"He delivers babies at General sometimes, but he's also got his own clinic."

"What's the name of his practice?"

"You've probably never heard of it, it's called Rose Clinic."

Trying to hide her shock, Jaleesa said, "Your uncle is Tom Rose?"

"Yeah, you know him?"

"Of course I know him."

"Wow, I didn't think he was that big in town," beamed Jonathan.

Obviously perturbed, Jaleesa said, "He's well known because he's one of the biggest abortionists in the city!"

"I wouldn't know about that. I mean, he probably does some, but… how would you know anyway, have you had…"

"No, I haven't had an abortion! I know because I regularly stand outside his clinic. I go there twice a week and try to encourage his clients not to get abortions and instead to keep their babies or give them up for adoption," Jaleesa said defiantly.

"Sorry, I didn't mean to offend you or anything, but I can tell you this—my uncle's a good man, and whatever you think he's doing, I'm sure it's perfectly legal and safe."

"Safe for whom?" Jaleesa demanded.

"Well, for whomever he's treating," said Jonathan.

"I can tell you this right now, it's never safe for the babies!" Jaleesa said sternly.

"I'm sure he's not hurting babies. He's an obstetrician for god's sake,"

"You don't have any idea what he does, do you?"

"Well, sort of…"

"Well, I think you better find out!" challenged Jaleesa. Sensing she'd let her passions go too far as Jonathan recoiled, Jaleesa backed off, slowed her motor, and collected herself. "I'm sorry, Jon, it's been a long day and I just think I'm a little short tempered right now. Will you forgive me for getting wound up?"

"Yeah, okay. I didn't mean to offend you or anything."

"Me, neither," said Jaleesa. "Can I apologize by treating you to some ice cream?"

"No, I can get my own," assured Jonathan.

"Please, I'll treat. I'm just not myself today, and I want to make it up to you."

"Okay, ice cream sounds good."

"Good, it's settled. Let's go to Cream Works," suggested Jaleesa.

"Fine by me, they make the best in town," said Jonathan with a smile.

chapter 36

The Grass Withers, the Flower Fades

Sitting with her arms folded wearing a pair of gray sweats and a hoodie, Blair waited apprehensively for the doctor. Her eyes were still black and blue behind the large dark sunglasses she wore, and her whole right side was sore to the touch. This was the first time in three-and-a-half weeks she'd felt well enough to go to the doctor. She'd been roughed up a couple of times before turning tricks, but never like this. The man who beat her was strong and merciless. He'd driven them to the perfect out-of-the-way spot with no witnesses and no escape. She should have known by his behavior not to get in the car with him, but she needed the money, and she figured she could handle herself. It was a miracle she hadn't miscarried due to the beating she received, but even that bit of good fortune had eluded her. Blair had never carried a pregnancy this far, and she was desperate to terminate. Perhaps Dr. Rose was right, she thought, maybe she should get sterilized. She probably wasn't ever going to have any kids, and, besides, who would want to start a family with a used-up thing like her?

Entering the room, Dr. Ulf sat behind his desk and appraised the situation. He hadn't treated a white woman in a while, especially one that was hiding more than an unplanned pregnancy. Blair's body language was slumped and weary. Despite her efforts to cover up, Blair looked hollow and defeated. Glancing at her file and then back at her, Ulf said, "Why the hood and the glasses? Why the disguise?"

"I don't want anyone to know I've come here, and I heard from a friend you're very discreet," answered Blair.

"Did someone hurt you, Miss…?"

"Blair, I prefer just Blair."

"Did someone hurt you, Blair?"

"It's a rough world sometimes, ya know."

"What do you do for a living, Blair?"

"Let's just say I provide services people need."

"People or men?"

"A lot of my clients are men, but, ya know, they're not the only ones with needs."

"I see," said Soren. "I estimate you're around seventeen weeks pregnant, which will cost roughly nine hundred dollars. Do you have that much in cash?"

"Yes."

"Good, I'll inform the nurse, and she'll get you situated," said Soren.

A few minutes later, Nurse V. walked Blair to the only private procedure room Ulf afforded in his facility. He kept it for the rare inspection and the higher-end client. Soren was crafty, and he knew that a client of means could make trouble if they saw or experienced too much. He was confident Blair wasn't one of those, but he suspected she had a big mouth, and he didn't like to mix the races, even when he was entertaining white trash. Ulf hated white women who sold themselves, but they were still obliged to more decency than the dirty rabble that filled the ghettos. Looking forward to his evening, Ulf smiled. He knew it would be busy and lucrative. Reviewing his list of clients and the gestational ages of their fetuses, he calculated he'd pocket around ten grand.

With a full stable of minorities upstairs and Little Miss Prostitute on the main level, it was going to be a night to remember.

Walking into the private room, Ulf smiled at Nurse V. and moved into position. Seeing that Blair was well sedated, Dr. Ulf looked up at Nurse V. and, making a lewd gesture with his forceps, said, "Looks like we've finally got someone who gets around more than you, Vi."

"Screw you, Soren."

"Well, I guess I could consider it."

"In your dreams, Doc!"

"Since you're not interested in a little bump and grind, why don't you go check the other girls? I've got this well in hand," said Ulf.

"My pleasure," said Nurse V. derisively.

With Nurse V. gone from the room, Ulf stopped mid-procedure to take some photos of Blair. Lifting her shirt, he was disappointed to discover her coloring. Her bruised skin, still inconsistent after the attack, ruined his shot. Her body normally would have had potential, but alas, its current state was just a turn off. Soren felt enraged as he considered all the men who'd used this vessel and all the waste Blair had allowed herself to become. Her condition was far from ideal, but he resolved to make the best of it. Soren possessed a disturbing mixture of desire and loathing for Blair. Unhappy, he managed to capture a few shots that might work. Sitting back down, Dr. Ulf resumed dismembering Blair's child. As he worked, he contemplated hurting Blair. Maybe he should tie the slut's tubes or perhaps damage her ovaries. Regrettably, he hadn't the time, but he consoled himself with the knowledge that perhaps she'd contract Chlamydia or gonorrhea from his oft-infected instruments—something to teach her a lesson—to give her pause about her filthy lifestyle.

The thought of a painful parting gift made him smile. Pausing to regain his composure, Soren cleared his mind and applied himself to the task at hand. Concluding his work quickly, his rage began to simmer. Finishing, he knew he was ready for the stable of sluts and miscreants upstairs. Soren, gazing at Blair, rose and shook his head, what a waste, he thought. Ascending the staircase, Dr. Ulf entered his large upper room. He was delighted to see that Tia had delivered. Grabbing her struggling preemie, Ulf raised his scissors and to his great relief and satisfaction ended the tiny life. As the little one convulsed in his hands, he knew the fun had just begun.

"Hey, Vi, looks like the fat one here is about to pop. Why don't you take this dead fetus downstairs, and on your way up swing by and check on the whore?"

"My feet are killing me tonight. Can't I wait till we've got two or three to take down?"

"You think I pay you to just sit here? Get going. Besides, the whore probably needs to be moved to recovery and then dismissed."

"Man, you're ugly tonight. She's a human being, Soren!"

"Yeah, she's also a whore! Now move your ass."

Nurse V. was tired and worn down by the drudgery of her daily duties. She often thought about leaving Reproductive Freedom, but where else could she work with her meager education and no license? She'd worked hard and endured much to pocket fourteen dollars an hour. She didn't like handling the dead fetuses, but as long as they weren't twitching, it wasn't too bad. Packing the deceased male fetus in the basement freezer, Nurse V. pondered how many more boys were being aborted lately than girls. A curious trend that seemed strange, but then again she'd seen gender runs before, a trend that seemed to cycle and ebb up and down over the years. Washing up, she felt relieved to be away from Soren and decided it was a good time to take a cigarette break.

Standing under a bright canopy of stars, Nurse V. felt relieved. Taking long, slow drags on her cigarette, her nerves began to calm, and her tension eased. Soren had been especially ugly and irritable the last couple of weeks after finalizing his fourth divorce. The financial strain of all his past failures and this latest debacle clearly had made him unbearable, making a man with an already short fuse extra volatile. Ulf's clinic was again an unhappy place to be—it was hard to come to work right now but she'd been down this road before, and she knew Soren's mood would pass as soon as he found a new partner. For now, she just needed to put it out of her mind and not take anything too personally. Stamping out the glowing butt on the ground, Nurse V. noticed the heavens and thought, my God, they're beautiful.

Opening the door to Blair's room, Nurse V. found Blair lying on the table unconscious and struggling to breathe. Running up the stairs, she shouted for Dr. Ulf, "Soren, Blair's still unconscious and her lips are turning blue!"

"What?"

"Blair's lips are blue!"

"What the hell did you do this time? Grab her admission form and meet me downstairs!"

Running as fast as she could, Nurse V. retrieved the two small pieces of paper that had been partially filled out on Blair. Realizing she had never bothered to read them, she hurried to Blair's room where she discovered Dr. Ulf frantically engaging in CPR. Timidly, Nurse V. gently laid the papers next to Soren and rushed out into the hall. Returning promptly with an old oxygen canister covered in a thick layer of dust, Nurse V. hoped to be of some assistance. But as she approached the table, Soren thrust out his arm and shoved her against the wall. Hitting hard, she dropped the oxygen tank and let out an audible gasp of pain as her body smacked hard against the concrete surface. Having successfully revived Blair, Dr. Ulf turned on Nurse V. and shouted, "You stupid, incompetent fool, she's an asthmatic! Even a normal dose of Demerol and diazepam wouldn't be warranted in her case, but you practically drowned her in the shit! You've really outdone yourself this time, Vi! Dammit, would it hurt to read the forms once in a while? I've had just about enough of your lazy ass! Well, don't just stand there, dammit, help me move her to the car," demanded Ulf.

"I'm so sorry, so..."

"Sorry, my ass!" shouted Soren. "This isn't the first time you've screwed up! Drive her to General and dump her in front of the ER. Do it quickly and wear a hood and glasses. Maybe without plates and disguised no one will finger you. Whatever you do, don't you dare leave a trace that leads back to me!"

"I know. I won't."

"She's a heavy bitch, isn't she?" grunted Soren as he helped Nurse V. relocate Blair.

Lifting Blair's limp, lifeless body off the table and into a wheelchair, Nurse V. noticed her dilated empty pupils and shuddered with fear. She'd run other patients to the hospital before, but Blair was the worst in recent memory. Glancing away from Blair, she saw Soren pocket his lighter. This was all so wrong, but backing out now wasn't an option. Watching the trash can flare with the diminishing evidence of Blair, she felt chills run up her spine.

Assisting Nurse V. to the car, Dr. Ulf shoved Blair's awkward body into the back seat of a beat up Chevy Cavalier with an old Kansas plate on the front of the vehicle and no rear plate on the back. Looking at Nurse _hushed_

V. sternly, Soren instructed, "Remember, after you drop her, you don't come back here for two days. Take the car to the abandoned lot near Pecos and use the chemicals in the trunk to wipe it down."

"I know the drill. I won't fail you," assured Nurse V.

"You better not, because this time it's your neck on the line!" said Soren. "Drive fast; she doesn't have long."

★★★★★★★

"Push Liz, push!" exhorted Bob. "You're almost there, baby, bear down. You can do it!"

"Aaaaaaa, I can't," screamed Liz. "It hurts!"

"Breathe, baby, breathe," encouraged Bob.

"Liz, he's starting to crown," said Tom. "Just give us one more good push, and he'll be here. Rest for three seconds, take one more deep breath, and give me your last best push."

Breathless, Liz sucked in as much air as she could muster and then exerted with all her remaining strength, "Aaaaah…Mmmmm...Aaaaaa!" Hearing the cry of her newborn babe, Liz laid back her head and gasped as tears of relief and joy dappled her cheeks.

"He's beautiful, Liz. Our boy is beautiful!" exclaimed Bob with great joy.

"Congratulations, Mr. and Mrs. Davis. You have a healthy little boy," said Tom. "Dad, you want to cut the cord?"

"Absolutely!"

Watching with satisfaction, Tom delighted in the experience of birth and the happiness it brought to new parents. Handing the newest Davis to the nurse and returning to complete his care of Liz, Tom began to feel his fatigue. It was late, just after midnight, and Tom was glad Liz's labor had been relatively short. It was a successful,

298

clean delivery, and he was eagerly looking forward to his return home. After determining that things were well in hand and answering a few final questions, Tom noticed his hospital pager was flashing. Reluctant to respond, Tom returned the page and proceeded to the ER.

"What's going on, Mitch?" asked Tom.

"We had a women dumped out front about an hour ago. She's in bad shape, but we managed to get her breathing again. I think she's suffered a stroke and probably has some brain damage. When we finally looked her over, it was clear she was the victim of a botched abortion," informed Mitch.

"Miserable hacks!" blurted Tom.

"Normally I wouldn't ask, but since you're here, would you mind performing an emergency D&E? I'm pretty sure there are some retained fetal parts?"

"Yeah, I'll do it."

"Thanks, Tom, she's back here."

"Let me splash a little cool water on my face and scrub up, and I'll be there in a minute."

"Sure."

chapter 37

Safely Wounded

*A voice is heard in Ramah, weeping and great mourning,
Rachel weeping for her children and refusing to be comforted, because they are no more (Matt. 2:18 NIV).*

Cindy Taylor paced back and forth in front of
Eastbrook Pregnancy Care. Looking again at her
watch, she noticed it was already ten o'clock. She prayed
and paced, and then she saw Stacy's car enter the parking
lot. Relieved, Cindy walked toward the car and smiled.

"I'm glad you found it," greeted Cindy. "I'm so glad
you came."

"Sorry I'm late. It's been a hard morning," confessed
Stacy.

"Don't worry about it. We always get started a bit
late anyway," Cindy said. "Let's go inside and get some
tea."

Cindy held the door for Stacy and then ushered
her down a long hallway to the staircase. Walking up
the staircase, the women engaged in small talk about the
weather and the mild temperatures. Arriving one flight
up, they made their way down another hallway and into a
modest conference room that overlooked a beautiful garden. Coffee and tea, along with some little danishes, were
set out on a draped table for the women's enjoyment. As

Cindy stopped to pour some tea and grab a couple of treats for the two of them, Stacy walked past the chatting women to the window overlooking the garden. Normally she would have been intimidated by the strangers in the room and her nervousness about the gathering, but the garden enticed her. It held a strange attraction for her, and she forgot about everything as she stared out the window. A slight smile emerged on her face as she watched a beautiful monarch move lithely from one flower to the next. Rising on the wind, the butterfly swiftly crossed the fountain that flowed in the middle of the garden. Captivated, Stacy could almost hear the water as it cascaded over the lip of its pedestal and down into the pool below.

"Beautiful, isn't it?" mused Cindy.

"Yes, it is. Is it maintained by the pregnancy center?"

"Yes. Alethea, our group leader, suggested it fifteen years ago, and with the help of the center, local churches, and private individuals, it was funded and landscaped. The center and the moms have maintained it ever since."

"It's just lovely."

"Ladies, we're running a bit behind today, so let's gather around our circle for prayer and then we'll get started," chimed Alethea. Waiting for the women to take their seats, Alethea smiled warmly at Stacy and said, "Welcome, I'm Alethea."

"Pleased to meet you. I'm Stacy."

"Why don't you sit next to me so I can keep an eye on Cindy—she has a tendency to need to be reined in."

"I don't think I'm the one who gets blustery," said Cindy. The girls let out a collective laugh, and Stacy felt a brief release from her growing tension.

"Let's pray," Alethea said. "Merciful Savior, we come before You today humbled by Your grace and forgiveness, and we ask for the power to forgive, both others and ourselves. Holy Spirit, we invite You to come and mend what's broken in us and around us. Jesus, show us afresh Your redemption and Your resurrection power. Heal our wounds, cleanse our minds, renew our thoughts, and set our feet upon Your Rock! Temper our words, rule over our spirits, and keep us ever-protected from the accuser by revealing to us how we are hidden in You. Hear us, Jesus, as we pray now the prayer You taught us to pray…" Finishing the Lord's Prayer the women uttered a hearty "Amen" and settled in for another time of fellowship and healing. "Ladies, we have a newcomer to the group, the beautiful Stacy, and so I'd like to go over the group rules and allow each of you to introduce yourselves before we begin. Cindy, would you start us off, please?"

Handing Stacy a small booklet, Cindy pointed to the opening paragraph and proceeded to read: "This is a covenant fellowship of caring sisters, redeemed sinners, and daughters of God. We exist for the betterment of one another, the forgiveness of sins, and encouragement unto Christ. We will not gossip about nor slander anyone in the group. We will listen and love without judgment. We will encourage one another and pray for each other. We will admonish, but only in a spirit of grace and acceptance. Nothing shared in the group will be revealed to others not participating in the group. We will espouse the principles, commands, and precepts of Christianity, and we will agree with Scripture that he who the Son sets free is free indeed! We will respect each individual, her privacy and her person, and we will acknowledge that all involvement in the group is voluntary. We agree to these guidelines and bind ourselves to them for the duration of our time together. All in agreement please say, we will."

Collectively, the group echoed, "We will."

Laying down her booklet, Cindy began, "Hello, my

name is Cindy, and I had my first abortion twenty years ago and my second and final abortion fourteen years ago. And I know I'm forgiven by the blood of Christ and my acceptance of His sacrifice for my sins. It's been a blessing and a privilege to be His adopted daughter."

"Hello, my name is Tasha. I'm still working on forgiving myself and others. My abortion experience has left a deep wound in my heart, but through the love of my pastor and his encouragement to join this group I'm beginning to heal."

"Hello, my name is Joan, and I aborted twins five years ago. This is the first time I've felt safe enough to share my heart and been able to talk about it with others."

"Hello, my name is Chau. I was forced to abort my baby at gunpoint and I'm still trying to forgive the father and myself. Please pray for me to be delivered from my anger."

"Hello, my name is Amanda, and I aborted my only child thirty-five years ago. I'm still trying to come to grips with my decision and forgive myself."

"Hello, my name is Simone. I've been clean and sober for six months. Prior to that, I spent several years after my second abortion sleeping around, doing drugs, and drinking. I don't ever want to return to that lifestyle, and with God's help, I believe I won't."

"Hello, my name is Gail. I aborted my baby twelve years ago in order to advance my legal career. I've regretted my decision every day since."

"Hello, my name is Renata, and I aborted my third child six months ago. I've also worked in a brothel, and until my recent encounter with Jesus Christ, I ran a chain of sexual novelty, apparel, and pornography stores. But, praise God, who gives us the victory, I'm beginning to feel and see things differently."

Hoots and hollers went up from various women in the group and Cindy and Alethea sounded a hearty and harmonious, "Amen!"

"Hello, my name is Alethea. As most of you know, I've consented to three abortions. The first was at the urging of my mother to keep my father's reputation from being tarnished as a prominent minister in our town. The next was to cover up an illicit affair, and the last was because my husband and I were without health insurance, and we were afraid we couldn't afford to pay for the birth and subsequent costs of raising a child. I have lived with shame, regret, and self-loathing for the better part of twenty years, but thanks to God's wonder-working grace, I'm now living forgiven and free!"

Stacy looked away from Alethea as she concluded her remarks and fidgeted with her blouse. Gathering courage and feeling that silence would draw more attention than confession, she slowly offered, "Hi, I'm Stacy. I had my first abortion five weeks ago. I have so many confusing emotions, and I'm not entirely sure why I came. But I wanted to come because Cindy invited me here and because she's been so kind to reach out to me."

"Welcome, Stacy," the group responded.

"Thank you for sharing, Stacy, we are so happy to have you in group today," said Alethea. "I want to start by reviewing last session's key verses from Second Corinthians: *'Blessed be the God and Father of our Lord Jesus Christ, the Father of mercies and God of all comfort, who comforts us in all our affliction so that we will be able to comfort those who are in any affliction with the comfort with which we ourselves are comforted by God.'* Amen! It's great to know God is a comforter, isn't it? He longs to be merciful to each and every one of us. God brings us comfort through His Word, His Holy Spirit, and His people.

How did last sessions' study impact you, and what in particular brought you comfort?"

"I was deeply moved by the verses from Micah chapter seven and the thought that God delights to show us mercy. Something I've had trouble extending to others, and especially myself, God happily gives all of us upon repentance. It gave me tremendous peace to contemplate my sin of abortion being cast by God into the depths of the ocean. Reading the statistics on the volume of water in the ocean and its incredible depth pressure really added to the Scripture's imagery for me. It was powerful and comforting to imagine my sin imploding under the pressure of God's grace!" Gail testified with a tear in her eye.

"I've always felt like David in the 51st Psalm when he said, 'For I know my transgressions, and my sin is ever before me,'" intoned Amanda. "I've always found it a tremendous struggle to forgive myself, and that passage in Zechariah 3 was extremely liberating—to realize that the high priest, a holy man, was covered in sin akin to excrement while facing Satan's brutal condemnation, and still Christ defended this man and cleansed him from all iniquity. That brought me comfort."

"I just want to say I love this group and the support you all have given me during this time. Through prayer, God's Word, and the loving support of this body, I've begun to experience some real breakthrough and receive comfort," voiced Joan. "Even a passage like Psalm 139, which used to cause me unbearable guilt and shame, I now have begun to see in a new light. I see that I, too, am a miracle of God, fashioned by His very own hands for a purpose—and that God has, still does, and always will love me as much as my babies. Take the verse in Romans chapter nine we looked at about the twins, for instance.

Years before, if I'd have noticed that verse at all, I would have felt burdened by the declaration of the preborn twins' innocence, but reading it this past session, I felt joy that my babies passed their time in innocence and that they most certainly must be enjoying great fellowship with God."

"Praise God, sisters, I see the Holy Spirit at work in you," exclaimed Alethea.

"I'm pissed at God!" blurted Stacy. "Where was He in my passions, in my pastor, in our relationship? All God did was abandon me to a terrible choice—left me all alone, as His cowardly clergy knocked me up, pressured me, and left me alone to abort! Even this had to be done in secret—his reputation couldn't be marred by being seen at the clinic! No, there was no comfort for me."

Reaching out to Stacy and clasping her hand, Alethea said, "No, child, God never leaves us or abandons us, but He does allow us to go our own way. He loves you, Stacy, and He always has."

"No, He doesn't!" Stacy said defiantly.

"Yes, He does," rejoined Alethea.

At that moment, Cindy put her arms around Stacy just like she had on the sidewalk, and whispered, "Yes, He does, Stacy. Jesus loves you."

One by one, the women in the group left their seats and gathered around Stacy. Placing their hands on one another and Stacy, they began to intercede for their wounded sister. Stacy stiffened briefly and then melted in the outpouring of grace. Pouring out their hearts through prayer, many declarations of God's love were spoken over Stacy, as she surrendered to the truth and the women who'd experienced a similar pain. And then in the stillness of prayer, the demure voice of Tasha broke through: "'...if I have a faith that can move mountains, but have not love, I am nothing. If I give all I possess to the poor and surrender my body to the flames, but have not love, I gain nothing. Love is patient, love is kind. It does not envy, does not boast, it is not proud. It is not rude, it is not self-seeking, it is not easily angered, it keeps no record of wrongs. Love does not delight in evil but rejoices with the truth. It always protects, always trusts, always hopes, always perseveres. Love never fails.' God's love will not fail you, Stacy. His love conquers all!"

chapter 38

A Challenge

Jonathan dressed in his best summer shorts and shirt, brushed his teeth—twice, and put on a dab of Tom's cologne. Fiddling with his hair for the umpteenth time, he decided he wasn't going to look any better. Still, he was pleased with his tan and his overall look after a week of camping and fishing with his uncle. The sun and the hiking had done him good, and he was looking fit. It had been a good trip, but he was happy to be back from the mountains. Amid all the fun of swimming, fishing, and boating, he couldn't get Jaleesa off his mind. He'd never seen anyone more captivating or confident. Jonathan hoped for more than summer love or distraction, but he'd take whatever he could get. Hurrying out to the garage, he contemplated driving the 'Vette to the park for the ultimate statement. But then he visualized the wrath of his uncle if anything happened to the car, plus the unsure effect it could have on Jaleesa. She didn't seem to be the type that was impressed by money or possessions, so taking the 'Vette could backfire. Opting for Tom's tricked-out mountain bike, he made his way to the park.

Arriving there, Jonathan locked up the bike and set off to find Jaleesa. The park was crawling with activity, from Little League baseball to Frisbee to soccer to the little kids running in the playground. It was a great day to be outside, and people were everywhere. The energy was palpable, and Jonathan was excited about the prospect of spending more time with Jaleesa. Making his way past the outdoor pool, he approached the volleyball pits and spotted her playing at the net. Her legs were long and elegant, and every time she rose for a spike, her muscles flashed and glistened in the sun. She was a picture of beauty in motion. Watching her play, Jonathan was delighted to be back in Eastbrook. She was even lovelier than he remembered. As the sand flew from Jaleesa's winning spike, he stood and clapped as she and her friend walked around the net to congratulate their opponents.

"You were devastating out there," said Jonathan. "Have you been playing volleyball long?"

"Since I was five," Jaleesa said proudly. "Jon, I'd like you to meet Sally. Sally, this is my friend Jon."

"Nice to meet you, Jon," said Sally.

"You, too," said Jonathan.

"Hey, J.J., I've got to split and get my little brother from the pool," said Sally. "I'll catch up with you later."

"Okay, Sal. Have a good one… Hey, Sal, killer digs today."

"You know it! See ya around, jackrabbit."

"Jackrabbit?" inquired Jonathan.

"She always calls me that, because I've got hops," said Jaleesa.

"I'd say that's fair, you did sport some spring out there," agreed Jonathan. "You afraid you're going to burn or something?"

"What do you mean?" asked Jaleesa.

"Well, all the other girls were wearing bikinis, but you're wearing a T-shirt and shorts."

"You worried I can't compete," said Jaleesa. "Think I might have trouble getting a date?"

"No," Jonathan stuttered.

"My mom taught me the importance of modesty and it stuck with me. Besides, it lets me focus on the game and not my outfit. I'm dying for a drink. You wanna get something cool?"

"Sure."

Finding a lemonade vendor on the opposite side of the lake, the two grabbed a couple of cool drinks and some pretzels. Jaleesa led Jonathan to a cozy spot under some tall shade trees with a great view of the paddle boats. Lying back, she wiped the sweat from her brow and said, "Man, it's hot out here today!"

"Temp read 88 when I was riding over on my bike."

Sitting up and savoring a long swallow, Jaleesa said, "Boy, that sure tastes good."

"Does the trick," agreed Jonathan.

"So how was your fishing trip?" Jaleesa inquired.

"Great! We had lots of fun, caught some fish, and did a ton of hiking. I forgot just how awesome and rugged the mountains are here. We spent an entire day just hiking to Arapaho Falls."

"I've been there, it's gorgeous."

"Yeah, three hundred feet of falling water, and the runoff this year is especially high," Jonathan said excitedly.

"That must have been great," said Jaleesa. "What else did you do?"

"My uncle's got an awesome telescope, so we did some pretty cool star gazing. When you get that far away from civilization, the stars really stand out."

"My grandfather says there is a star for every person ever created. The Bible sometimes calls angels stars, and he believes every star is someone's guardian angel."

"Huh—that's cool."

"Something your uncle wouldn't know about," Jaleesa said without thinking.

"What do you mean by that?"

"I'm sorry," Jaleesa retreated. "Sometimes my mouth runs ahead of my mind."

"Are you still bothered by what my uncle does for a living?" asked Jonathan.

"I'm sorry, really. I shouldn't have said anything."

"No, it's okay. I had a talk with him about what you said, and he said that people like yourself are well-intentioned, but that you just don't understand the truth about fetal development or viability."

"What?" blurted Jaleesa.

"He said that in the early stages of pregnancy the embryo is no more than a potential life, a collection of cells, plasma. That your side sees it as a baby from the beginning, and that's why you get so impassioned, but he said fetuses are not viable until around twenty-four weeks in the womb, and, even then, premature babies often struggle to survive outside the womb."

"Maybe you and your uncle should read an embryology textbook," Jaleesa quipped.

"You know, I don't even know why we're talking about this…but I think it's kind of crazy for you to be lecturing my uncle about embryology. He went to school for a decade to study pregnancy and birth and works every day in the field!"

"You're not the only one who knows a doctor, Jon. My mom's an OB-GYN just like your uncle, and I can assure you, every human embryo is a living, self-generating being from the moment of conception. Zygotes and embryos will never become something other than what they are: *human beings*!" asserted Jaleesa. "Your uncle lied to you, Jon, and maybe that's how he can do what he does—maybe he's lying to himself."

hushed

"How dare you call my uncle a liar! He's a great man, one of the best men I know."

"I'm sorry, Jon, but what I said is true. If you don't believe me, check out one of your uncle's embryology texts or go visit the library."

"Wow! Take care of yourself, J.J."

"Jon, wait… I'm…"

chapter 39

Blind Side

Slowly reaching over for his glass of water, Christopher took a few sips and returned the glass gingerly to his bedside table. Returning to his book, he began to read: "'This yer young-un business makes lots of trouble in the trade,' said Haley, dolefully.

'If we could get a breed of gals that didn't care, now, for their young uns,' said Marks; 'tell ye, I think 'twould be 'bout the greatest mod'rn improvement I knows on,' —and Marks patronized his joke by a quiet introductory sniggle.

'Jes so,' said Haley; 'I never couldn't see into it; young uns is heaps of trouble to 'em; one would think, now, they'd be glad to get clar on 'em; but they arn't. And the more trouble a young un is, and the more good for nothing, as a gen'l thing, the tighter they sticks to 'em.'"

"Wow, how prophetic!" blurted Christopher.

"What did you say, honey?" Anna hollered from the baby's room.

"I'll tell you when you're done changing Alex."

Moments later, Christopher's lovely wife, Anna, entered the bedroom with little Alex on her hip. Even in the midst of personal hardship, juggling work and family, she was a radiant beacon of strength and support for her husband. Placing Alex under some dangling toy keys suspended from his play set, Anna turned to Christopher and said, "How's your pain, do you need some more medication?"

"No, I feel okay for now," assured Christopher.

"You sure?"

"Yeah, I'm fine."

"Well, you do seem to have more strength," said Anna. "What was it you said a minute ago?"

"I was just commenting on the book I've been reading. I'm amazed at the parallels between our struggle for the rights of the preborn and the movement to abolish the slave trade. Now that my eyes are better, I'm reading the book Jael brought me in the hospital. It's powerful the similarities in the causes."

"What's the book?"

"Uncle Tom's Cabin."

"Isn't that a classic?" asked Anna.

"Yeah, I think so, but I don't think too many people are reading it today, and if they are, they're missing the point. I'm only a little of the way into it, and it already is speaking to so much that is going on in our nation with abortion and the oppression of the preborn."

"I remember the title from high school, but I never read the book. Isn't it about slavery?"

"Yeah, but my point is that in 1852, when the book was published, African slaves were treated as property and today we treat preborn children as property—my body, my choice—and all that garbage."

"Didn't you say something about prophecy though?"

"Yeah," Christopher said excitedly. "The part I was just reading is about two slave catchers bemoaning the trouble they've had with slave mothers concerning slave children, and how the slave mothers make their jobs doubly difficult when their children are being separated from them or threatened. So in their conversation, the guys are saying how wonderful it would be if the slave mothers didn't care about the welfare of their offspring, a thing we greatly encourage today through abortion. And it struck me how prophetic Stowe's comments were."

"Sounds like an interesting read."

"Definitely. It's good," said Christopher. "It just goes to show that no matter what form of oppression one looks into, be it the Holocaust, or slavery, or sex trafficking, or some other form, one sees that the justifications for subjugating one group or dismissing another are often the same; they have the same pathology—the victim is dehumanized, objectified, and manipulated out of selfishness, greed, prejudice, and pride! The Scriptures once again prove true: 'You will know them by their fruit'—as constant and as unchanging as the love of God is, so, too, the lies of the Evil One!"

"Was that the doorbell?" asked Anna.

"Sounded like it."

"I'll go check."

Making her way downstairs, Anna wetted her finger and rubbed some dried baby food off of her shirt. Opening the door, she was greeted by Pastor Jim. "Hello, Anna. How is Chris today?"

"He's better, but still in pain," informed Anna. "Come in, Jim. He'll be glad you stopped by."

"How's little Alex?"

"Curious and fussy just like his daddy," teased Anna.

"Ah, so you're juggling two babies," Pastor Jim chuckled.

"Chris is upstairs. Let me grab Alex and tell Chris you're here."

"Sounds good."

Walking back upstairs, Anna opened the bedroom door and made sure Christopher had all he needed before entertaining company. Grabbing some empty glasses and a dish off the night stand, she quickly whipped up the few clothing items that were lying on the floor and drew the curtain leading to the master bath. Leaning down to gather up little Alex, Anna said, "I'll send Pastor Jim up. If you need anything, ring the bell."

With great difficulty, Christopher eased up on his pillows and awaited the entrance of Pastor Jim.

"Hey, there he is—the great prayer warrior of Eastbrook!" Pastor Jim said with a smile.

"Hey, Jim, thanks for stopping by."

"You look great. You look a lot better than you did a week ago at the hospital," said Jim. "How are you feeling?"

"Better, thanks," Christopher said. "My eyes are back to normal now that the swelling has subsided, and my arm doesn't hurt at all since it was cast. Unfortunately, my ribs are a different story. They still hurt when I breathe."

"Still, you look so much better than when I first arrived at the hospital," reiterated Jim. "You're lucky the man living next door to the clinic came out with his shotgun when he did or those thugs could have killed you."

"God was watching out for me, that's for sure."

"Indeed, he was," said Jim. "We've missed you at church, but don't worry, Keith has filled in marvelously during your absence."

"Yeah, I better get back or I'll be looking for a job, won't I?"

"Nonsense, you've got a place with us as long as you want one."

"Did you guys find a safe place for June?" inquired Christopher.

"We did, and I also told Ethan to be on the lookout for Bobby and Tony Cabrea."

"I wish I could be more certain it was them. But with the pepper spray and the initial blow from the bat, I wasn't completely sure what was happening. It sure sounded like Bobby though," said Christopher.

"Ethan's trying to get the surveillance tape from the clinic, but they're saying they weren't recording during non-business hours to save money—like I believe that," Jim huffed. "Unfortunately, the man who scared off your attackers only saw their backs and the black hoodies they were wearing."

"As long as June and her baby are safe, that's all that matters."

"We need to get these guys before they hurt someone else, Chris," asserted Jim. "Do you remember anything else about the attack?"

"Sadly, no," said Christopher. "I normally don't go to the clinic alone, but last week I showed up early to pray before our fall prayer campaign, and out of nowhere they attacked me. They must have been watching me or following me or something because one minute I was silently praying, and the next thing I know an arm reaches around my face with pepper spray and a baseball bat cracks hard against my ribs. As I fell to the ground, I was able to get my right forearm in front of the next swing, which unfortunately broke my arm, but then all I remember is hearing a voice that sounded like Bobby Cabrea's curse my name and the feel of a hiking boot crash into my forehead. After that I blacked out, but I gather they only got a couple more hits in before Frank Leeland came out of his house with his shotgun."

"Are you sure it was the Cabrea boys?"

"I'm not sure," confessed Christopher. "But Bobby did threaten June and me three weeks ago when she decided against his wishes to keep the baby. And then last week after June fled to our church seeking safe harbor, your secretary told me she saw him loitering in the parking lot and asking questions. It's a good bet it's him."

"Ethan said the police are conducting a routine investigation. Supposedly, Bobby left for a hunting trip the day before the incident. But he's not buying it. He said he'd try to do some digging, but, much to his displeasure, the department seemed to be dragging their feet on this one. Also, only one local news station chose to report the incident," informed Jim. "All the other media outlets have simply ignored the whole thing. It makes me so mad, the hypocrisy! When the clinic was threatened during the anthrax hoax it was wall-to-wall coverage about the volatile nature of the pro-life movement, but when someone from our side is attacked, it barely makes the news."

"Well, God never promised us an easy time of it on this earth, did He?"

"No, He didn't, but it still infuriates me!"

"True enough, Pastor," said Christopher. "It seems there's always a price to be paid in the cause of Christ and the pursuit of justice."

"I reckon so."

"I trust you're taking care of things out there while I'm on the mend?"

"You know I am," assured Jim. "I've instructed that no fewer than three people be out there at any given time, and everyone has been encouraged to carry cell phones. Ethan told me the police are going to increase their patrols of the clinic during business hours. And I've also asked the elders and the men in the church to accompany any women who have signed up for prayer times during the campaign."

"Thanks, Jim, I really appreciate it."

"Hey, I better let you get some rest, but I'm greatly encouraged by your speedy recovery. The whole church will continue to pray for you, Anna, and Alex."

"Thanks again, Pastor. And thanks for stopping by."

"It's my pleasure, Chris. We're all proud of your efforts at the clinic and your service to Christ. Oh, I almost forgot, we rescued a baby and her mother yesterday at the clinic. Another mother and her child saved from the grip of the Evil One!"

"That's incredible news, Jim, awesome news!"

"Glory to God, Chris, you can say with Paul that your power is from God and even though you have been pressed hard on every side you have not been crushed."

chapter 40

The Song of the Redeemed

"*Posterity will serve him; future generations will be told about the Lord. They will proclaim his righteousness to a people yet unborn—for he has done it.*" Lucas closed his Bible and looked fixedly out his study window on the blooming flowers. The care and diligence Aaliyah had given to their yard and garden was paying off. It was a true labor of love. One she had nurtured with patience and strength. Lucas delighted in the springtime when nature revealed its waves of rebirth and new life. It always refreshed his soul and renewed his energy. Lucas loved almost everything the hand of God had made, especially when it had been well cared for by His people. Breathing deeply, he closed his eyes and prayed, "Jesus, Holy Lamb of God, there is none like You! Forgive me my sins and fill me afresh with Your Holy Spirit. Protect my granddaughter and all of us down at the clinic today. Bless, Christopher with a full and speedy recovery from his injuries. Use us to fulfill Your purposes. Have Your way, Lord, and may Your will be done. Amen." Returning his gaze to the garden, he heard a knock at his door.

"Come in."

"Hey, Papa," beamed Jaleesa. "Are you ready to go?"

"Yeah," Lucas grinned as he grabbed a handful of M&Ms. "You want some chocolate?"

"Papa, you've got to cut back on those things," Jaleesa scolded. Then smiling, she said, "Yeah, sure, give me some."

Sharing a moment forged in memory, the two laughed and embraced. Lucas loved his granddaughter more than he could express. She was a light in his life, and he couldn't bear to risk her hurt. After the attack against Christopher, he had made up his mind to accompany J.J. whenever she visited the clinic. She was too precious to leave unprotected. A long-time intercessor for the cause of life, Lucas had never felt the compulsion to intervene at the clinic, but for Jaleesa's sake and safety, he decided to go. Walking arm-in-arm out of the study, they headed toward the darkness of abortion.

Arriving at the clinic, Lucas and Jaleesa drove past four intercessors and a lone sign that read: "God thinks you're beautiful, and so do we." Parking the car, they approached the sidewalk and greeted the faithful.

"Hey, Lucas, It's great to see you," said Leon.

"Good to see you, Leon."

"How's the store?"

"Good. Business is steady; we can't complain," Lucas answered. "How are you doing, Leon?"

"Awesome! My wife just gave birth to our fifth daughter and eighth child overall," beamed Leon.

"God bless you, Leon. That's wonderful news. How is Sharon doing?"

"She's good, especially now that we're back in Eastbrook close to family. Her mother has come up for a month to help out and take care of things till she gets back on her feet."

"That's wonderful. It's so nice to be close to family," said Lucas. "Hi, Amy. It's good to see you again."

"You, too, Lucas. Are you going to be at Early Morning Prayer tomorrow?" asked Amy.

"Hopefully. I've really been enjoying it," Lucas replied.

"How are you this morning, J.J.?" asked Amy.

"I'm good. It's great to have Grandpa here with me."

"Yes, it is," said Amy.

As the group was getting reacquainted, two cars pulled into the lot of Rose Clinic. Jaleesa quickly snapped into action and fished in her jacket pocket for some fetal-development brochures. Holding them out over the landscape berm as the car doors opened, she said, "May we help you today? We can adopt your baby. There are options, alternatives, and help available. Talk to us and let us help you."

Lucas observed his granddaughter with pride as she tried to engage the people and offer them assistance. But his pride soon became dismay as person after person ignored her, dismissed her, insulted her, and refused her information. The long slow parade of people who passed before his eyes took a toll on his spirit—beautiful girls, lonely girls, and mothers—angry men, timid men, anxiety, fear, poverty, wealth, shame, arrogance, hostility, tears… It was more of a revelation than he bargained for, and his heart began to break. Praying for the ending of abortion at home in his study was far different from praying in front of clinic doors. The reality here was visceral. Looking down the street, Lucas saw a young girl step out of a truck and slowly move forward. He could barely see the man in the driver's seat, but he knew something was wrong. She couldn't have been more than seventeen or eighteen, and her walk was tragically familiar. She was wounded both inside and out. Fear and pain were evident on her face as she neared the driveway. Her body language was one of defeat and suffering. Meeting her eyes, Lucas saw a pain he'd seen only once before. It was a pain he would never forget! Moving around the counselors in a fog, the girl passed the group without a word of acknowledgment. Tears of empathy swelled over Lucas's cheeks. This strong, tower of a man began to weep. Coming to his side, Jaleesa put her arms around him, and said, "It's okay, Papa."

"No, it's not okay, baby doll, none of this is okay!" asserted Lucas. "Pray with me, J.J., pray with me for the mothers and their babies."

As granddaughter and grandfather prayed, Amy joined the group, and the three interceded in one accord. After a final amen, the group hugged, and Lucas began to pace back and forth from one end of the clinic property to the other. Amy fell to her knees and wept as she prayed. Jaleesa wiped her tears and approached another young couple walking up the sidewalk. Pleading with God for a miracle, Lucas tried to rise above his disillusionment, and then he heard a Voice in his spirit. A still small Voice spoke, "Sing, Lucas, sing!" "What should I sing, Lord?" The Voice responded with joy, "Sing your favorite!" Lucas, filled with new hope, walked to the edge of the sidewalk near the door to the waiting room and cleared his throat. Quietly feeling the music in simple faith, he boldly began to intone:

"I AM the Lord, I'm the Almighty God
I AM the One for whom nothing is too hard
I AM your Shepherd and I AM the Door
I AM the Good News to the bound and the poor."

Lucas's voice rose like the distant roll of a lightning storm, and then exploded with a clap as four powerful fluid I AM's resounded with joy.

> "I AAAMMMM; I AAAMMMM;
> I AAAMMMM; I AAAMMMM."

Some in the nearby houses must have said it thundered.

> "I AM the Righteous One and I AM the Lamb
> I AM the ram in the bush for Abraham
> I AM the ultimate sacrifice for sin
> I AM your Redeemer, The Beginning and the End."

Gathering strength, Lucas bellowed the refrain with great authority! The beautiful long I AM's reverberated with a power that couldn't be missed. In the clear of the morning, all was hushed but the vibrato of this magnificent voice.

> "I AM Jehovah and I AM the King
> I AM the Messiah, David's offspring
> I AM your High Priest, I AM the Christ
> I AM the Resurrection, I AM the Life."

Amy began to rock back and forth in the Spirit as she wept tears of joy. "I AAAAAMMM's" repeated with thundering sustain like the mountains of God. Leon and the other counselors stood frozen, while Jaleesa glowed with familiarity and pride as the song swept like blazing fire over the dew of the morning.

"I AM the Bread, I AM the Wine
I AM your future so leave your past behind
I AM the One in the midst of two or three
I AM your Tabernacle, I AM your Jubilee."

Lucas's booming a cappella penetrated brick and mortar, and the words began to divide flesh and spirit. Tom laid down his instrument as the powerful voice began to shake everything that could be shaken. Everything shook, even the trees. Like a hushed opera house at the apex of a roaring solo, two more I AM's rolled thunderously on the wind and then broke into bursting impassioned verse.

"I AM hope, I AM peace, I AM joy, I AM rest
I AM your comfort and relief from your stress
I AM strength, I AM faith, I AM love, I AM power
I AM your freedom this very hour
Jesus said that, 'I AAAAAAAAAMMM!!!'
I AM hope, I AM peace, I AM joy, I AM rest
I AM your comfort and relief from your stress
I AM strength, I AM faith, I AM love, I AM power
I AM your freedom this very hour."

In the presence of the bride and the Groom, Lucas didn't skimp on the good wine but finished his crescendo with a host of I AM's, each one stronger than the last.

When the last note intoned, a profound silence descended on the clinic. There in the reverential void, Amy leapt to her feet and sounded a battle-cry yell that shattered the stillness. On cue, her fellow counselors erupted in euphoric praise. Leon, compelled by the Spirit, grabbed his Bible and read in a clear, deep tone: "'*Even now,*' *declares the Lord,* '*return to me with all your heart, with fasting and weeping and mourning.' Rend your heart and not your garments. Return to the Lord your God, for he is gracious and compassionate, slow to anger and abounding in love, and he relents from sending calamity."* Another long moment of silence passed, and nobody seemed to move inside or outside the clinic. All was eerily still. The only sound that could be heard was the wind. Those present could hear the sound of it, but they could not tell where it came from or where it went! A minute later, the door opened with a creak and a young couple stepped out into the sun, their faces streaked with tears. Guiding his companion gently toward the car, the young man smiled at Lucas, nodded his head in admiration, and drove away. One by one the clients emptied the lobby—no words were spoken. And then she came—running and sobbing straight into Amy's arms. Collapsing on the sidewalk, she cried, "I can't keep this baby! He'll kill me! Please, God, help me." Weeping and weeping, she repeated, "I can't. I can't."

Amy held her tight and proclaimed, "You can't, but Jesus can. He will care for you. And I will care for you and your child, until you can!"

Softly, Amy began to sing over the young girl. In the distance, her father exited his truck and began to move with great haste toward his daughter. His eyes glistened with fire, and his steps thudded with rage. But just as quickly as he had come, Lucas and Leon rushed to meet him and stood in his path. Halting, he knew he'd never touch her again. She had been rescued. God and his people stood to fight for her. Slinking away, he left—cast out and undone!

chapter 41

Why?

Henry struggled to control his breathing as he crouched behind a large boulder. Pulling his shirt down to cover his nakedness, he tried in vain to ignore the burning. He had to get away, but where could he go? The forest seemed so dark and foreboding behind him—it beckoned and terrified all at the same time. Why couldn't he just perform? Why couldn't he please her? Why did she hate him?

"Henry, I know you're out there," said his mother in a playful tone. "Come back in here. I bought your favorite treats and those movies we like to watch together. Mommy found a new girl. She's very exciting!"

Henry hunched lower as the dusk began to fade. Looking up he saw a star through the pines and wished he could be one—so high—so far away—so untouched.

"Henry," called her voice with a shrill impatience. "Dammit, child! Don't make me come get you!"

She was getting closer, and he knew he needed to escape now—to run deeper into the woods, but he was frozen. The approaching darkness and his fear of the unknown paralyzed him. If only he had courage, he thought. If only he was strong, he would run and run and run. Feeling the pits and ridges of the rock, Henry leaned around the edge and looked for his mother. She was nowhere to be seen. Peering to his right the wood invited in the flicker of remaining light. Cautiously turning to his left, he caught the flash of skin as her hand slapped down hard on his face. Tumbling back, she was upon him.

"There you are, you little bastard!" She fumed as she grabbed a fistful of his shirt with her free hand. Cocking her arm with all her uncanny strength, she clinched her fist and drew blood striking young Henry flush in the mouth. "You don't want to obey? You don't want to do what you're told? Well, we'll see about that. I want to trust you, Henry. I want to be good to you. But you're going to have to earn it. This little stunt has just cost you some freedoms. If this happens again, boy I'll... Now get your ass back in the house."

"Mom, I don't wanna."

"Shut up! Shut your mouth! I'll decide what's best for you...what's best for you...what's best for you..."

H.T. awoke with a start to the darkness of his cold cell. Sweating, he felt the sting of tears, but he dared not show any weakness. Not here. Not in this place. He couldn't be sure the hour, but judging by the stillness, it must have been late. Easing up on an elbow, he reached under his cot for the small Bible J.J. had given him. Clutching it close to his chest, H.T. lay in the void and thought of the lone person who had shown him any kindness of late, perhaps the only person who had ever shown him any kindness.

✯✯✯✯✯✯

Breakfast was tasteless and tepid, but H.T. had grown used to the loss of many things. Sitting alone, he began to feel his mood brighten. J.J. was scheduled to visit, and it couldn't have come at a better time. Joyful, he could no longer dismiss or deny the importance of her visits. His drab existence had improved since knowing her. She was so vibrant, innocent, and alive. She was a taste of a life he'd never known. A world he'd only guessed at. He couldn't explain it, but he enjoyed her company, even if she was overtly religious. And after a night of terror, he looked forward to seeing her.

Walking down the long corridor to the visitor chamber, H.T. felt a mixture of sadness and joy. He hadn't asked *why* in a long time, but today he wanted to know, why.

"Good morning, Mr. Taylor," Jaleesa said with a smile.

"Morning, J.J.," replied H.T. "How was the trip?"

"A bit chilly, but pleasant," said Jaleesa.

"I trust your breakfast was more pleasant than mine," H.T. said with a smirk.

"Bacon and eggs with the perfect golden hash browns," beamed Jaleesa.

"Ah, stop you're killing me!"

"I thought people went to prison just for the food?"

"Yeah, right!"

"So, what's new?" inquired Jaleesa. "I haven't seen you for three weeks."

"I had a nightmare earlier this morning about my mother."

"I'm sorry. That sounds terrible."

"She used to beat the hell out of me. The things she did are…," blurted H.T. through clinched teeth. Looking away to gain his composure, he continued, "Why did God let that happen to me? Why didn't He help me? If He's so loving, why does He let little children suffer abuse and torture?"

"I'm sorry that happened to you," Jaleesa said with empathy. "That must have been awful. You want to tell me about it?"

"No, it's not worth tellin'. Besides, there are things

you don't need to know about."

"I can't imagine. Have you ever told anybody about your childhood?"

"Childhood! What childhood?"

"I mean about the abuse."

"Nobody to tell," H.T. muttered looking at the floor. "When I was younger, I always backed her lies out of fear, and when I got older, well, let's just say she stopped hurting me."

"Have you ever thought about forgiving her?" Jaleesa asked calmly.

"Forgive hell!" H.T. spewed. "You still haven't answered my question. Why? Why is God so absent?"

"I don't know if there's a sufficient answer to explain the why of our pain on this side of heaven, Mr. Taylor. But I know God isn't the one who hurt you," said Jaleesa. "God hates wickedness and sin."

"But to allow children to suffer?"

"Jesus spoke often of His love for children. He told His followers who didn't think He had time for children not to hinder them from coming to Him. Children are precious in God's sight, and He wants all people to treat them well. In fact, He issued a stern warning to anyone who would lead a child into sin. He said it would be better for that person to be drowned in the sea with a heavy stone than to face His wrath." Pausing to let her words sink in, Jaleesa continued, "Jesus said His kingdom belonged to little children. If your mom had known God and His power, she would have treated you differently. She would have treated herself differently. If your mom would have understood her worth and your worth, she would not have done those things to you. But don't confuse her actions with God's. He's not the one who hurt you."

"But He didn't stop it," asserted H.T. "A good God

would have intervened."

"I know it seems so at times, but God's gracious gift of freedom allows people the choice to act out of love or hate—to do good things or evil things."

"If it's all about us, why bother with God at all?"

"Because it's never been just about us, it's always been about God and us. He made us to have relationship with Him, and one day we're all going to have to give Him an account for the choices we made and the way we lived."

"So, according to your faith, my mother is going to have to answer for the things she did?"

"Yes, she will."

"Good," H.T. said with a grin. "I hope she gets what she deserves!"

"If we all get what we deserve, it won't be pretty for any of us," said Jaleesa. "God's standards for righteousness are so high none of us can attain them. Only Jesus lived a life sufficient to remove our sins—my sins, your sins, your mother's sins."

"Let me get this straight," said H.T. "You believe God allows us to choose, ultimately makes us pay, but in the meantime leaves us alone to stew in our pain!"

"I believe Jesus was right there in the midst of your pain. Maybe that's one of the reasons He suffered so much at the cross—to let us know we're not alone when we suffer. Mr. Taylor, Jesus cared enough for you and your mother to die on that cross. He cared enough to atone for everyone's sin with His own blood."

"So God's a sadist. He enjoyed watching His children suffer so much that He decided to join them?"

"No, Mr. Taylor, He joined us because our sin and our suffering broke His heart," Jaleesa said in a soft tone. Opening her Bible, she continued, "The prophet Isaiah foretold long ago this word about Jesus and what He came to do for us: '*The Spirit of the Lord God is on Me* (Jesus), *because the Lord has anointed Me to bring good news to the poor. He has sent Me to heal the brokenhearted, to proclaim liberty to the captives and freedom to the prisoners...to give them a crown of beauty instead of ashes, festive oil instead of mourning, and splendid clothes instead of despair. And they will be called righteous trees, planted by the Lord to glorify Him. They will rebuild the ancient ruins; they will restore the former devastations...*'"

"What good did that do me in my hour of need?" asked H.T.

"I don't believe your hour has passed," said Jaleesa. "It's no accident that I'm here sharing with you the gospel of Jesus Christ. This very day you can invite Jesus into your life and begin to heal."

"But where was Jesus when I needed Him the most?" pressed H.T. "High-sounding words and speeches are great when life is pleasant, but in the midst of pain and horror, they're of little comfort!"

"True, if they're just words, but Jesus is more than words; He's a Person—a Person who's been there all along, whispering to you, inviting you to fellowship with Him."

"You don't know what she did! What I experienced! You couldn't begin to understand!" H.T. erupted.

"You're right, Mr. Taylor, I can't know or under-stand," Jaleesa softly confessed. Allowing a moment of calm to settle, she gathered her thoughts, took a deep breath, and, looking at H.T., continued, "But Jesus does understand. He knows what your mother did just as surely as He knows the things you've done. What about the people you hurt? Were your actions so different from hers?"

"My actions were because of her!"

"So, what you did was okay? You don't owe your

victims the same debt that she owes you? What if she hurt you because someone hurt her first? Is she then not responsible for how she treated you?"

"What do you know of what I've done?"

"I read your case, Mr. Taylor. There's hardly a person in this region who doesn't know what you've done. All those young girls you hurt, some of them my age. What about them?"

"Why are you here? Do you come here to see me suffer? Is my imprisonment not enough for you? Is that it?"

"No…" Jaleesa tried to interject.

"Is it some sick crush on bad men? Some morbid fascination with me? With my crimes? Do I turn you on? Get you all worked up?"

Standing in disgust, Jaleesa bit her lip and gathering the most composure she could muster uttered, "I think we're done for today. If I'm up to it, I'll visit next week. Perhaps my absence will give you time to reflect upon the conditions I set for my visits. Good day, Mr. Taylor."

chapter 42

The Trial

Mr. Michaels approached the witness and asked, "Mrs. Kunto, when was your abortion at Reproductive Freedom performed?"

"It was performed the evening of October, 11th, 2008," answered Maskini.

"Can you tell the court and the ladies and gentleman of the jury who performed your abortion?" followed Mr. Michaels.

"My abortion was performed by Dr. Ulf."

"Is he in the courtroom today?"

"Yes."

"Would you be so kind as to point him out, please?" encouraged Michaels.

Raising her finger with assertive defiance, Maskini pointed directly at Dr. Ulf. The clean and profession-al-looking doctor sitting at the defense table never flinched.

"Mrs. Kunto, I want to thank you for your brav-ery and your willingness to come to court today and face the defendant," said Mr. Michaels. "I want to apologize for any additional harm or pain your testimony may cause you, but I want you to know, Mrs. Kunto, you're a hero for being willing to testify. Again I apologize, Mrs. Kunto, but could you look at these lewd photographs and identify the woman in these pictures?"

"That is me in the photographs," confessed Maskini with her head down.

"Did you consent to having these photographs taken?"

"No," she whispered.

"Did you even know these pictures existed until you were contacted by the Eastbrook Police Department and the D.A.'s office?" asked Michaels.

"No, no, I did not," Maskini said as she looked away.

"The prosecution would like to admit these photographs into evidence and have it noted that they were obtained from a computer memory card found during the raid on Dr. Ulf's clinic." Turning back to Maskini, Mr. Michaels asked, "How did it make you feel when you discovered Dr. Ulf had taken these highly inappropriate photographs?"

"Objection. The patient's feelings aren't relevant to the facts of the case," barked Donaldson.

"Overruled. The witness may answer," stated the judge.

"I was shocked and appalled! I thought the doctor was there to help me, not exploit me!"

"Mrs. Kunto, would you describe for the jury the trouble you and your husband have had getting pregnant since your abortion?"

"Objection. Mrs. Kunto's struggles with fertility have no bearing on this case," interrupted Donaldson.

"Overruled. I want to hear where the prosecution is taking us."

"We have been trying for three years, ever since we got married. I've been to five different specialists trying to get pregnant. Just last month, I underwent a procedure to remove some scar tissue that had built up in my fallopian tubes. The damage my reproductive organs suffered at the hands of Dr. Ulf during the abortion was extensive," Maskini said, fighting back her tears. "I'm still hopeful that one day we will have a child, but so far nothing has worked."

"Thank you, Mrs. Kunto. You've been most courageous and helpful," said Michaels. "I have no further questions. Your witness, Counselor."

Approaching the witness, Mr. Donaldson pulled out a piece of paper and handed it to Maskini, "Mrs. Kunto, do you recognize the following consent form?" asked Donaldson.

"I don't know," answered Maskini.

"Is that your signature?" pressed Mr. Donaldson.

"Yes."

"Would you read the first paragraph for me, please?"

"I *Maskini Zahra* give my consent and authorization for an abortion procedure on this date of *October 11th, 2008*, freely and voluntarily after consulting with Dr. Ulf. I understand that while abortion is a common surgical procedure, it can carry some risks, including infection, bleeding, perforation of the uterus, cervical lacerations, and, in extremely rare cases, even death. The consequences of said complications have been explained to me and are an acceptable risk to me," read Maskini.

"According to this document, Mrs. Kunto, you were aware of the risks involved in the abortion procedure and chose to undergo the operation anyway," said Donaldson.

"The complications were never discussed with me," said Maskini. "I was assured by Dr. Ulf that the form was a formality and that the procedure was safe, or I would not have signed!"

"Do you normally have a habit of signing things you don't read?"

"No."

"Then what are we to believe, Mrs. Kunto?" pressed Donaldson.

"I don't know," said Maskini.

"I think you knew what you were doing. I think you needed to cover up an affair you had with a married man. You needed to protect yourself and your lifestyle, and you knew very well what you were doing. Isn't that right, Mrs. Kunto?"

"Objection. The circumstances around Mrs. Kunto's pregnancy are not on trial here," said Mr. Michaels.

"Sustained," ruled the judge.

"I have no further questions, your Honor," said Donaldson.

"You're dismissed, Mrs. Kunto. You may step down from the witness stand," informed the judge.

"Your Honor, the prosecution calls Dr. Tom Rose to the stand," said Michaels. After Tom was seated and sworn in, Michaels approached the stand. "Would you please state your name and occupation for the record?"

"My name is Tom Rose. I'm a licensed OB-GYN. I run Rose Clinic, a family planning clinic in the community of Eastbrook."

"Thank you, Dr. Rose. What sort of services do you provide at your clinic?" asked Michaels.

"We offer a full complement of services ranging from obstetrics and gynecology to mammography, abortion, and pregnancy testing," Tom answered.

"How long have you worked at this practice?"

"I've worked at Rose Clinic for more than a decade."

"Are your abortion services a rare part of your clinic practices, or are they more routine?" asked Michaels.

"Four out of the six days we're open we deal with abortion in some capacity, either scheduling or procedures," answered Tom.

"So would it be fair to say you are an expert on abortion?"

"Yes, you could say that," said Tom.

"Over all the years you've practiced, Dr. Rose, how many abortions would you say you've performed?"

"I don't know, fifteen maybe twenty thousand."

"Is it common to have serious medical complications result from abortion?" followed Michaels.

"No, by and large, abortion is a minor surgery achieved with very little difficulty. I personally have a very low complication rate, one of the lowest in the profession," Tom said confidently.

"Have you performed any second-trimester abortions?" asked Michaels.

"Yes, several."

"What's the latest gestational age you've performed an abortion?"

"Twenty-two weeks," said Tom.

"Is there a reason for that, Doctor?"

"If you're asking if there is a legal reason for that, the answer is no, not in our state," said Tom.

"Then why stop there, Dr. Rose. Is it just a matter of coincidence?" probed Michaels.

"No, I set my own limit there. I believe after twenty-two weeks it's harder to guarantee the safety of my patients, and I also know from my work in obstetrics that some premature infants can survive outside the womb after twenty-four weeks gestation with the proper care," clarified Tom.

"How would you feel about abortions performed in the thirty- to thirty-eight-week range?"

"Objection, your Honor. How the witness feels about legal late-term abortions is entirely irrelevant to the case," interrupted Donaldson.

"Sustained! Move along, Counselor," said the judge.

"Dr. Rose, are you familiar with the details surrounding the death of Katherine Fields?"

"No, I'm not, but I did hear that the paramedics found her dead when they arrived at Dr. Ulf's clinic."

Handing Tom a coroner's report, Mr. Michaels asked, "In your expert medical opinion, what caused the death of Mrs. Fields?"

"Objection. Dr. Rose never examined Mrs. Fields," squealed Donaldson.

"Overruled. The court will hear his opinion," stated the judge.

Taking a moment to look over the report, Tom responded, "Sepsis and cardiac arrest following uterine perforation and a massive blockage caused by retained fetal parts from the botched abortion of a thirty-two-week-old fetus."

"Dr. Rose, I understand you have some experience with another alleged victim of Dr. Ulf's named Blair Adams. Is that correct?" asked Michaels.

"Yes, I was working at Eastbrook General on the night she was dropped in front of the ER," said Tom.

"Dr. Rose, did you perform an emergency D&E abortion on Blair Adams the night of July 14th at Eastbrook General?"

"Yes."

"Will you inform the jury about what you discovered that night during your operation?"

"Miss Adams was in a coma following an overdose of Demerol and diazepam. Drugs, I should add, that are rarely administered today due to their many negative consequences. I was called down to the ER after I'd finished delivering a baby on the maternity wing. After a brief examination, it was determined by the ER staff that Miss Adams had been dropped out front following a botched abortion. When they had reestablished her breathing and stabilized Miss Adams, I was called in to finish the abortion and prevent any further complications from occurring. Without this second procedure, the resulting infection and bleeding certainly would have killed Miss Adams. During the course of my work, I pulled out an almost complete fetal skull and a partially dismembered leg. Miss Adams had also sustained several severe lacerations to her cervix, which I tended to," recounted Tom.

"Thank God you were there, Dr. Rose," exclaimed Mr. Michaels. "In your professional opinion, how old was the fetus inside Miss Adams?"

"The fetus looked to be between sixteen and eighteen weeks."

"Is there any reason for a physician to use general anesthesia during an abortion under twenty weeks?"

"Yes, in some rare cases," answered Tom.

"What kind of cases?"

"In cases like uncontrolled epilepsy, agitated psychosis, or perhaps rape, but local anesthesia is to be preferred because the risks to the patient increase under general anesthesia. There is a greater risk of perforation, bleeding, and death from aspiration of vomitus."

"Have you ever used general anesthesia in your practice?" asked Michaels.

"I've used general anesthesia less than a dozen times in all the years I've been performing abortions. All the rest of my procedures were conducted using local anesthesia," confirmed Tom.

"Would you ever use general anesthesia on an asthmatic patient?"

"No, I would avoid it at all costs; the risks would be too great. In reviewing Miss Adams' case, that was the grossest form of negligence I discovered. The average person under that much Demerol and diazepam would probably stop breathing, too, but an asthmatic? Miss Adams is in a nursing home today because of Dr. Ulf's medical malfeasance. She's lucky to even be alive!" Tom said angrily.

"Objection," Donaldson demanded. "Dr. Ulf hasn't been convicted of anything. The witness is engaging in pure speculation."

"Sustained. The jury will disregard the last thing Dr. Rose said, and his comment will be stricken from the record," ruled the judge.

"Dr. Rose, is this the worst case of abuse and negligence you've seen by a peer who performs abortions?" redirected Michaels.

"From what I've seen I wouldn't consider Dr. Ulf a peer, but yes, it ranks up there. This is why my profession gets a black eye, this kind of incompetence and brutality. Whoever was responsible for the condition of Miss Adams was a monster," Tom said emphatically.

"Thank you for your testimony, Dr. Rose."

Driving home, Tom was exhausted and angry. More and more of these hacks were showing up around the country, clinicians who only cared about the bottom line. But Dr. Ulf was a different animal altogether; he was a butcher, a monster, and a psychopath. Tom hoped the jury would convict and that another sad chapter in the abortion industry would be closed. Both sides had been responsible for atrocities in the abortion struggle, but this one hit close to home. Why hadn't he done just one more abortion for Blair? How did this monster go undetected in the city of Eastbrook? Tom had met Ulf a few times over the years at various pro-choice or professional gatherings, and he'd never suspected such villainy. By all accounts, he seemed like just another normal guy. Tom's mind raced as he thought about his bizarre life of late. He thought of Blair's broken body and his own donation that made it possible for her to get nursing home care. The clinic's empty lobby after Lucas's impassioned song. He'd lost women to the sidewalk counselors before, but nothing like that had ever happened. In fact, he'd never even heard of anything like that happening before. It reminded him of the stories he'd been told as a child after Mass, stories that were otherworldly, even miraculous. He couldn't explain it, but there was an abundance of self-doubt and discontent in his soul lately. And then there was Jonathan. It pained him every time he thought about it. He could still see him sitting there at the kitchen table, textbooks spread before him, ashen and cold.

"How can you do it?" Jonathan said bewildered. "How can you destroy babies?"

"What are you talking about?"

"You lied to me, Uncle Tom," asserted Jonathan.

"I've never lied to you, Jon."

"Their heart beats at day twenty-two, their central nervous system begins to form in week three, they have measurable brain activity after six weeks, and from day one, they're a self-directing, genetically complete organism! You told me they were just potential life, undeveloped non-viable embryos. They're babies, Tom! Growing babies! Your own college medical texts say so. How could you lie to me? How can you do what you do?"

"Jonathan, it's more complicated than that..."

"Is it?" interrupted Jonathan. "I bet the reasons for the Nazi Final Solution were complicated, too!"

"What! My God, Jonathan. Listen to what you're saying!" Tom said exasperated. "Where is this coming from? Is it about that girl?"

"No. It's about the truth!"

"What truth?" challenged Tom. "You think these textbooks tell the whole story? Let me tell you about what I've experienced and seen."

"You mean, like this?" Jonathan said as he placed a medical waste bag on the table containing the partially dismembered skull of a 17-week-old fetus. "Yeah, I wondered if the books were overstated, so I checked your trash at the clinic. Don't talk to me. Don't talk to me ever again!" Stomping out the door, Jonathan yelled, "I'll spend the remainder of my time at Grandma's."

"Jonathan, hey! Jonathan, come back here!"

Tom hadn't seen his nephew since the ugly exchange, and their parting weighed heavily on his mind. It grieved him deeply that he'd lost his nephew's trust. In Jonathan's passion and haste, he hadn't been allowed to explain about Jenny and the need to keep abortion safe—or the fact that abortion had been deemed legal and constitutional by the Supreme Court long ago. He knew his nephew was too young to understand everything that was going on and all the complex reasons why abortion was needed. Still, ever since Jonathan's parting, something crawled in his belly and tugged at his soul. Perhaps Jonathan was right. Perhaps it was just that simple. For the first time since losing Jenny, Tom allowed himself to consider the plain truth of medical science and embryology. Evidence that continued to grow stronger in the wake of Roe v. Wade as medical advancements and new technology made clear. Today it wasn't so easy to maintain the intellectual distance he normally felt regarding fetal development. Doubt about the justifications for abortion crept in, and Tom couldn't deny what he already knew. What was happening to him? He never let himself think this way. He had needed to see things differently for so many years, but today all he could see was the *truth*!

chapter 43

The Least of These

When the Son of Man comes in his glory, and all the angels with him, he will sit on his throne in heavenly glory. All the nations will be gathered before him, and he will separate the people one from another as a shepherd separates the sheep from the goats. He will put the sheep on his right and the goats on his left. "Then the King will say to those on his right, 'Come, you who are blessed by my Father; take your inheritance, the kingdom prepared for you since the creation of the world. For I was hungry and you gave me something to eat, I was thirsty and you gave me something to drink, I was a stranger and you invited me in, I needed clothes and you clothed me, I was sick and you looked after me, I was in prison and you came to visit me' (Matt. 25:31-36 NIV).

Worship music resonated through the foyer as Christopher and Anna prepared a table for the newest pro-life petition that sought to amend the state constitution. They knew this was something easy and simple the body of Christ could do to advance the cause of life: sign a petition and then vote in the affirmative that human life begins at conception. Something the Bible clearly teaches and science confirms. But even this would be difficult, thought Christopher. The previous measure had failed because too few Christians had voted for it. Apparently, their fears about possible restrictions on certain forms of birth control and the loss of abortion services for difficult cases involving rape or incest outweighed the daily loss of more than 3,000 innocent American children. Some people even voiced concern that women would be prosecuted for a miscarried pregnancy, something so bogus and illogical Christopher couldn't believe anybody would be taken in by it. Why couldn't churchgoers see that abortion is completely incompatible with biblical doctrine and a Christian worldview? Christopher knew the answers implicated and exposed the church, adding to its shame, but he refused to give up on the body of Christ. He was determined to press forward working, teaching, and sowing the seeds of truth and grace until the church understood its sacred role and took up the cause to defend the least of these, God's oppressed children in the womb. Looking over at Anna as she set out the petitions gave him hope. He was so blessed to have found her. Their marriage was a joy, and Anna, more than anyone else in recent years, had kept him going. Christopher smiled at his wife and sat down to write a large sign that read: Pro-Life Petition.

Approaching the table, a well-dressed woman holding a latte inquired, "What's this about?"

"This is a petition designed to define the term 'person' in our state constitution to include every human life from conception forward," answered Anna.

"Under any circumstances?" clarified the woman.

"Yes."

"Well, I understand what you're trying to accomplish, but there are exceptions," said the woman.

"What do you mean by exceptions?" asked Anna.

"It's got to be legal in cases of rape," asserted the woman.

"That's certainly a tough consideration," Anna said gently. "There is great pain and violation in rape, but I don't believe it's the right solution to destroy the child conceived by such an attack."

"Well, I guess you'd have to be there to understand!"

"No doubt, it's impossible for anyone to understand how an individual feels and deals with such a violation of their person, but I've met some women who've experienced a pregnancy following an attack, and their comments don't seem to support the conventional wisdom."

"And what's that?"

"That abortion makes things better. I've talked to women who have aborted after a rape, and most go on to describe how their abortion didn't alleviate their pain. In fact, their testimonies revealed that abortion actually added to their pain because they eventually felt like they had victimized another innocent person following their victimization. I've also met a few women who decided to keep their children or give them up for adoption following a rape, and they have found their decision to be a very rewarding, if not healing, experience," said Anna.

"I guess I hadn't thought of it that way, but I still don't want to sign your petition," asserted the woman.

"That's okay. Thank you for taking the time to come and check it out," said Anna. "Is there anything else I can help you with today, anything you'd like me to pray about?"

"No, thank you. Have a nice day," said the woman as she departed toward the service.

"You, too," said Anna.

"I think you handled that well, honey," encouraged Christopher.

"I don't know. She was probably hurting, and I'm not sure that was the right approach."

"I think you did fine. Let's keep her in our prayers and make a point over the next several weeks to get to know her. If all goes well, maybe we can invite her to our small group."

"Okay, yeah, that sounds good."

"Let's go sit in the service, and then we'll duck back out before it ends."

The couple entered the sanctuary as the last few lines of "How Great Is Our God" rang out from the crowd. Finding their seats, they settled in for the announcements, Holy Communion, and the greeting of their neighbors. Christopher and Anna loved their home church and all the relationships they had built there. It was a place of joy and fellowship with many good people, outreach opportunities, and sound teaching. But it had also been a place where the teaching of the sanctity of human life had been neglected and at points forgotten, a cry and a passion that burned in Christopher's heart and now resonated equally as strong in his chosen bride. Laboring diligently in the cause for life, Christopher had seen many ups and downs and many efforts come and go in his church. And today he hoped and prayed against experience for a great participation in the current ballot measure to clearly define human life properly as beginning at fertilization.

As Pastor Jim started to speak, Anna continued to think about her exchange with the woman in the lobby. Was she insensitive in any way? Should she have communicated more effectively or clearly the biblical message that God creates every life? Should she have been so bold as to ask directly if the woman had been touched personally by sexual violence in her past? Could she even help someone who'd endured such a tragedy? What would she say? How should she respond? What was it like to experience such pain and suffering? It was so hard to overcome this justification for abortion—this stronghold of the Enemy—and get people to see that the rape scenario was an emotionally charged tool to keep the nation from addressing the plight of thousands of preborn babies scheduled for abortion. She knew God hated rape and all evil, but she also knew God created every human life as a gift. Admittedly, there was mystery, but this much she knew: The Bible was clear in its teaching that every person is fearfully and wonderfully made—that we all have value and purpose before God. Anna knew God formed each one of us—that He played His divine part in conception. God was unmistakably the Author of life. As a woman, she felt acutely the fear and the agonizing feelings rape created, but the truth of God's Word stood larger still. She had come to accept that while God deplored the sinful, wicked act of rape, He sometimes allowed the womb to open to new life for reasons only He could know. Confident in Scripture that the fruit of the womb is a reward and that all children are a blessing, Anna had made peace with the reality that on rare occasions God chose to give beauty for ashes in the form of a pregnancy soon after the brutal crime of rape. Grappling with her thoughts, she understood afresh why this was so seldom discussed by people—it was painful and emotional, and there were no easy answers.

By the time Anna checked back into the sermon, Pastor Jim was in the heart of his message about the persistent widow of Luke 18. Tuning in to the message, Anna discovered a reason to smile.

"Did the widow pray? You bet she prayed, and she did it often with fervor, but she also took action in the civil arena," proclaimed Pastor Jim. "The widow wore the judge out with her persistent, perpetual coming. She returned again and again and again until her concerns were answered and justice was done. Ladies and gentlemen, every generation has their mission and their causes. For the widow it was justice against her adversary. For the early church and even unto today it is the spreading of the Gospel. George Muller took up the cause of orphans and prayer. Amy Carmichael cared for the downtrodden and sexually enslaved in India. For Harriet Tubman it was the Underground Railroad, for Martin Luther King, Jr. it was civil rights, and so on. Every age has had its heroes, patriots, martyrs, and ministers. People who left a mark, loved the Lord, and changed the world! My family and I love to watch the movie about William Wilberforce made a few years back, entitled *Amazing Grace*. For those of you who haven't seen the picture, it depicts Wilberforce's long impassioned struggle in the British Parliament to abolish the slave trade. A fight that spanned the last forty years of Wilberforce's life, with the complete abolishment of slavery throughout the entire British Empire coming just three days before his death. Wilberforce gave his finances, his energy, his health, and his life for this most noble and humane cause. At the close of his book, *Real Christianity*, he wrote, 'I find it necessary to affirm that the problems we face nationally and internationally are a direct result of the decline of faith and morality in our nation. My only hope of a prosperous future for this country rests not on the size and firepower of our military, nor on the wisdom of its leaders, nor on the spirit of her people, but only on the love and obedience of the people who name themselves after Christ, that their prayers might be heard and for the sake of these, God might look upon us with favor.' It is with this same hope that I must appeal to you, the people of Christ, to rise to the challenges in our generation. Our mission is to spread the Gospel to all people, and this includes our newly conceived brothers and sisters in the womb. The psalmist wrote, '*This will be written for the generation to come, that a people yet to be created may praise the Lord. For He looked down from the height of His sanctuary; from heaven the Lord viewed the earth, to* hear the groaning of the prisoner, to release those appointed to death...' David, witnessing the taunt of Goliath, proclaimed, 'Is there not a cause?' Today, I tell you, we have such a cause! Abortion is a monster standing in our land, taunting the armies of the living God. Taunting us for over forty years, and hoping we will remain in our ignorance, apathy, or fear. I for one am tired of being afraid! Tired of my all too frequent silence! I pledge to you this day that I will not, and we as a body will not, shrink back from such a cause as this. Today, like Wilberforce, we can sign a petition that declares that life begins at conception, and then in the next election, we the people can vote it into law. But, Pastor, I hear some of you saying, this is a political issue. Humbly, I tell you, no, this is a human rights issue and a biblical issue, for how can we claim to love the least of these and not defend the most innocent among us? Abortion is an affront to the character, plans, and purposes of God! To my shame and to the shame of the American church and the American body politic, we have resided too long in the shadows and allowed this atrocity to flourish! It's time for the collective church, and by that I mean all the denominations, institutions, and individuals who follow the teaching of Jesus Christ and the Bible, to wake up from our inexcusable slumber, repent of our apathy, indifference, and cowardice, forgive ourselves and those among us who've committed, procured, and performed abortions, and push back this darkness! Join with me today in taking a stand for life, and like the persistent widow, let's come today, tomorrow, and every day until justice is done!"

As Pastor Jim left the pulpit, the audience erupted in cheers, hoots, and applause. There was a palpable energy and enthusiasm in the room and everyone present felt this was a turning point in the life and history of For Sinners Only. A glorious moment when a page had been turned, a mantle accepted, and a cause engaged. As the people streamed out of the service after the close of worship, very few left without signing the petition. The lines were long and the chatter lively as the believers gathered to proclaim what they all knew: God alone is the Author of life, not man. He has made us all from conception, and from that point forward life is sacred.

******

Sitting beside Sosi's bed, Ethan finished reading the morning passage from Romans 13, "*Let no debt remain outstanding, except the continuing debt to love one another, for he who loves his fellowman has fulfilled the law. The commandments, 'Do not commit adultery,' 'Do not murder,' 'Do not steal,' 'Do not covet,' and whatever other commandment there may be, are summed up in this one rule: 'Love your neighbor as yourself.' Love does no harm to its neighbor. Therefore love is the fulfillment of the law.*"

"I've always loved that passage," said Sosi. "I can hear it so much better now that I have these new hearing aids you bought for me. Isn't technology amazing?"

"It sure is," said Ethan. "I'm glad you like them. Rachelle and I just wanted to bless you with a gift, and we thought a boost in hearing would be just the thing to brighten your day."

"God bless you, Ethan. You've been so kind to me."

"It's my pleasure, Mrs. Ety. Can I get you anything else before I leave? Perhaps water your flowers?"

"They do look a little wilted, don't they? Why not? A little water always helps."

As Ethan watered the flowers, Sosi let out a sigh, and said, "It's a miracle to see again. Now that I can see, I'm once again overcome with beauty."

"The things these doctors can do today are incredible, aren't they? What would our lives be like without them?"

"They're a blessing, a blessing straight from heaven," declared Mrs. Ety.

"Hopefully, that will perk them up," Ethan said. "Rachelle wanted me to let you know she'll check in on you on Tuesday, and I'll be back on Friday, okay?"

"Thanks again, Ethan. I always look forward to your visits."

"No trouble, Mrs. Ety. It's a pleasure to be here," Ethan assured, taking Sosi's hand. "Take care now, and I'll see you later in the week." Gently squeezing her hand, Ethan turned and headed for the door.

"Goodbye, Ethan," uttered Sosi as he walked away.

On his way out of the building, Ethan stopped at the front desk to request that Sosi be given another blanket and some fresh flowers. He had grown fond of Mrs. Ety in the years since their first encounter, and he felt it was an honor to tend to her in the nursing home. Unbeknownst to Sosi, Ethan and Rachelle had paid the lion's share of her bill ever since she was placed in Eastbrook Eldercare. It was something they had the means to do and something they delighted in. As Ethan stepped out into the Sunday afternoon light, he noticed Christopher approaching.

"Hi, Chris. How are you doing?"

"Good, Ethan. How are you?"

"I'm fine. I was just heading home. Hey, that sermon was great this morning, wasn't it?"

"Pastor Jim really stepped it up, and it helped, too. We got a lot more signatures, and the people seemed eager to get behind this most recent effort."

"That's great, Rachelle and I are always praying for the ending of abortion and your work at the clinic," said Ethan. "You look good. How've you been feeling since the attack?"

"Better, thanks," said Christopher. "How's the investigation coming?"

"Slower than I would like, but I think we're closing in on having enough evidence to arrest Bobby Cabrea and charge him with assault and battery."

"That'll be good, Ethan."

"Hey, I don't mean to hold you up," said Ethan. "Who are you seeing?"

"A girl I know from the clinic."

"She get in a terrible accident or something?"

"She was one of the victims of that wicked abortionist who's on trial for murder."

"Uh, that's awful," Ethan said sympathetically.

"It's a tragedy," said Christopher. "I've been coming on Sunday afternoons to read her the Bible and sit with her. She's in a terrible state of paralysis, but I think there's hope for her to finally place her faith in Christ—let God transform her life."

"We'll start praying for her," said Ethan. "What's her name?"

"Blair, Blair Adams."

chapter 44

What Fellowship Does Light Have With Darkness?

The aspens showed forth a brilliant yellow as Jaleesa descended the pass toward Lincoln State Penitentiary. Beautiful colors of fall surrounded the road with a rich vibrancy that made her smile. Taking in the crisp air, Jaleesa's spirit leapt with joy as she beheld the wonders of her Creator. She'd been coming to visit H.T. for months with mixed results, pain, and travail, but today seemed different. Jaleesa felt a fresh wind of the Spirit, and she dared to believe that today would be the day of her biological father's redemption. Perhaps the time had come for his release from darkness. As Jaleesa rested in the sweet Spirit of the Lord, the radio began to play "Amazing Grace." Taking it as a sign that H.T.'s redemption was drawing near, she wept. Jaleesa had come to know that H.T. was a man of great brokenness as well as wickedness, but she also knew that no one was beyond the grace of Christ and the power of His cross, the definitive work in history that freed all believing people from the power of sin. It had been a hard journey for Jaleesa, but her initial anger and contempt for her biological father had slowly turned to compassion and love. She had experienced Christ's forgiveness several times in her own life, and she'd come to see that through God's power, she, too, could forgive. Driving into the valley, Jaleesa beheld the ebb of life on the valley floor. Seeing the drab prison in the distance, she prayed again for H.T. and his release from the power of sin and death.

The preliminary process before visiting H.T. was no longer an unfamiliar burden to Jaleesa. It was a routine she took in stride, even making friendly conversation with the prison staff. She had come to know and like many employees of the prison. The lead security officer and Jaleesa had forged a respect for one another, and those who worked in the prison were dumbfounded by her continued presence. They couldn't believe a smart, attractive, young girl like Jaleesa routinely visited the state's most brutal serial rapist. Several of the guards had inquired about Jaleesa's faith during her months of visitation and had acquired a new appreciation for Christianity as practiced by this young woman. Jaleesa had noted how her witness had impacted many at the prison, and she was glad for it. The walk to the visitation room, likewise, no longer seemed torturous or daunting for Jaleesa, but it still carried some uncertainty because she never knew which version of H.T. she would encounter—the surly, perverse man or the calm and engaged man who seemed intrigued by her and what she had to share, thirsty for the perspective she would bring. Entering the secured visitor room with Bible in hand, Jaleesa noticed that H.T. was smiling as she approached.

"Hey, sister, how was the ride up?" asked H.T.

"Beautiful, Mr. Taylor," Jaleesa responded. "The fall colors are just marvelous this year."

"You know I miss the mountains and the trees; that's the one thing I dearly miss," said H.T.

"Did you know the Bible is full of references to the mountains?"

"Yeah, I read one I liked the other day. 'Let the mountains bring peace to the people...' I think it was Psalm 72."

"So you have been reading the Bible I left you."

"Sometimes," H.T. confessed.

"I like Amos 4:13, which says, 'He is here: the One who forms the mountains, creates the wind, and reveals His thoughts to man, the One who makes the dawn out of darkness and strides on the heights of the earth. Yahweh, the God of Hosts, is His name.'"

"Still trying to convince me there's a God who loves me, are you?"

"Don't you want to be free of all your pain and experience the liberation that comes through letting Jesus pay for your sins?" implored Jaleesa.

"Nothing will make me free. I'm in this hole for life!"

"Life? Don't you know that life continues beyond the grave? Don't you realize you can be forgiven and live free with God? Jesus taught that we are all slaves to sin and that no one bound, no slave belongs in the house of God, but sons and daughters are another matter. Rightful children belong in God's house and reside forever. So, if Jesus, the Son, adopts you and makes you His child, a fellow heir, you will no longer be a slave but free, truly free!"

"Free! Tell that to these walls!"

"If you give your life to Christ and let His work on the cross pay the debt of your sins, then walls cannot hold you, Mr. Taylor. No child of God is ever bound! He'll take your spirit to a place of peace and even joy. You'll once again ride on the mountains of God in the secret places of your heart until that glorious day when you meet your Redeemer face to face."

H.T. sat up a bit straighter, "How can some man, some teacher dying on a cross save me from my sins, my crimes—my judgment?"

"Not just any man, Jesus is the righteous Son of God who came to take our place, die for our sins, and show us the way to redemption."

"You speak in a language I don't understand," confessed H.T. as he leaned toward the glass. "But real life doesn't work that way. Once you're broken and bound, nothing and no one can set you free. I'm in here because my mother abused me, and I in turn abused others."

"I know your mother hurt you terribly and it seems impossible to forgive, but with Christ's help, you can. He wields a power that is like no other. Mr. Taylor, you won't understand God or His power until you surrender to Him."

"And you know this power?"

"Yes."

"How?"

"Because I surrendered to God and asked Him to live in me. I've experienced great things with God. He's helped me forgive people I thought I could never forgive."

"When has anything gone wrong in your perfect young life, J.J.? When have you ever been wronged or needed to forgive anyone?"

"I've had to forgive you."

"Me? What for? Cracking wise?"

"No, for hurting my mother."

"Excuse me," said H.T., bewildered. Pausing to connect the dots, he uttered, "Who are you?"

"I'm your biological daughter, Henry; I'm the daughter of Rachelle Jacobs."

"What?" blurted H.T. as he stood up "How dare you come here!"

"I'm sorry, Henry... "

"Sorry! Coming here—pretending to be my friend!"

"I needed to know who you were, and I knew if I told you who I was, I'd never get the chance," said Jaleesa.

"I knew you were too good to be true, that this whole faith thing was a con," said H.T. with fire in his eyes. "You want to know about this great God of yours. I'll tell you who He is. Your mom wasn't like the other girls. No— she was different. Oh sure, she begged and pleaded like all the rest, but she also prayed to God! She prayed that Jesus would shield her, protect her. She even asked God to forgive me, but that didn't rescue her, did it? No, it didn't rescue her! Your God is a fraud, J.J.!"

"She didn't need to be rescued, Henry, you did! You were the one in trouble, and you still are. Don't you see, Henry, God is still working to answer my mother's prayers. He is a God of longsuffering, mercy, and forgiveness. Even now, God is offering you a chance to repent—be forgiven and in turn forgive those who've hurt you."

"You really don't know what happened to her, do you?" sputtered H.T. "If you did, you'd know she was the one who needed to be rescued."

"She was rescued, Henry, just not in the way you think," declared Jaleesa. "God rescued her before, during, and every day since your attack. It's only by Christ's grace and peace that she's been able to stand and endure the hardship you inflicted. Jesus walked her through her valley of the shadow of death. Don't you see, Henry, God has granted her the victory!"

Stumbling back from the glass, H.T. stared at Jaleesa in a state of shock and unconsciously muttered, "Who are you?"

"I'm a child of God, sent to offer you a way out from the dark place where you live. Jesus offers real hope, your only hope," asserted Jaleesa. "Won't you come to the cross of Christ?"

"Leave me, J.J."

"Henry, Jesus loves you! He loved you enough to die

for you and all your sins. He's the only One who can forgive you. And more than that, He wants to!"

"Leave me," Henry said wearily.

"Henry, I know you sense God's hand in this moment and His power at work. Why else would He send me? Think of Rachelle, Henry. It's because of her that I stand here today. She has demonstrated the more excellent way of love. In your pain you responded to abuse with more abuse. She responded to abuse with forgiveness and love!"

Henry grappled furiously with the weight of her words and offered no response. Staring in disbelief, he looked at Jaleesa in utter defenselessness.

"I forgive you, too!"

At the sound of Jaleesa's tender words, Henry slid down the wall at the back of his booth and started to sob. Crumpling against the wall, Henry eked out the words, "I'm sorry." Tears coursed down his face, blurring his ability to see his daughter.

Moved by the Spirit, Jaleesa flipped to Isaiah, and said, "Listen to your Savior. He declares, *'It is I who have declared and saved and proclaimed, and there was no strange god among you; so you are My witnesses,' declares the Lord, 'And I am God. Even from eternity I am He, and there is none who can deliver out of My hand; I act and who can reverse it?'* Confess your sins, Henry, come to the cross. Come to Jesus. Let Him heal your hurts and forgive your sins."

Not knowing Henry had been reading that very passage from Scripture earlier in the day, Jaleesa was surprised by his spontaneous and tearful confession. Henry seemed so small crumpled against the wall. He was a mess, but beautiful. The broken, muffled words that poured from his lips seemed wholly unnatural, and of course they were. A broad smile of thanksgiving broke over Jaleesa's face as Henry uttered the words, "Forgive me, Jesus. I surrender to You. Please forgive me—for all my horrible sins." Mighty tears flowed as the old passed away and all became new. Henry joined the throng of the redeemed, and the Lord had done it!

✶✶✶✶✶✶✶

Jaleesa didn't know how she'd arrived outside the prison. Had she run, floated, skipped—walked with dignity? She couldn't say. Leaving the prison after Henry's confession was surreal. She was euphoric, drained, and stunned. Falling to her knees outside the prison gate, Jaleesa praised the Lord. She had witnessed the miraculous and nothing could quench her joy. She felt so alive—so blessed—so whole! Gathering herself and feeling a little foolish, Jaleesa quickly made her way to her car and left. Reflecting on the miracle as she drove, she knew this was a moment of destiny and deliverance that no one could have purposed but the great God of eternity. Driving out of the valley, she thought of her mother and the critical role she had played in this moment in time. Flashing back to a recent conversation the two had shared in the kitchen after a breakthrough session of therapy, Jaleesa recalled afresh her mother's words and the powerful example she had set. Her decision to love was still reaping a harvest.

"How did you survive, Mom?"

"I knew I was loved. It was the love of God and the love I'd received from my parents that sustained me. No matter what he did to me, he couldn't touch that revelation of love and self-worth I'd found in Christ! When I was tempted to believe I was worthless and dirty by his words and his abuse, I heard in my spirit the voice of my Savior saying, 'You're worth everything to Me. I've already made you clean. You are mine and I know my

own!' Somehow I knew whose I was and who held the future, and it wasn't him. Later, when the pain hit hard and my sadness deepened, it was Mom and Dad, my close friends, and prayer that pulled me through. But you know what helped me the most?"

"What, Mom?"

"You," Rachelle confessed. "Carrying you gave me daily proof that I wasn't like him. Feeling you grow inside me changed my life. Caring for you confirmed I was different from my attacker. I was not what he said I was. He was a taker, but I chose to be a giver. I found tremendous worth in loving you. You assisted me in recovery."

Tearfully, Jaleesa threw her arms around Rachelle and exclaimed, "I'm so blessed to have you for my mother!"

As tears flowed from the memory, Jaleesa ascended out of the valley and up the mountain toward home. Toward her mother and all that was good and beautiful and pure in her life.

chapter 45

Revelation

Slowly, it meandered on the air, following an uncharted path to an unknown destination. It was delicate, intricate, and utterly beautiful. Nothing seemed more brilliant or pure. It was unspoiled and full of purpose. Tom gazed in enchantment while the tiny flake fell from the heavens. Snow sometimes fell in autumn, but this was an unusually beautiful blanket of white. With three or four inches already covering the ground and more to come, it was shaping up to be a slow Tuesday at Rose Clinic. The sidewalk and the parking lot were empty, devoid of any stirrings, as the staff relaxed in the calm of the morning. At the normally bustling clinic, it was nice to have a slow day with no protest and no patients. Today was going to be a good day, Tom thought. Continuing to watch his snowflake descend to its final destination, where it mingled with the rest of its kin and watered the earth, Tom smiled. He had always enjoyed the snow, but ever since Jonathan was born, it held a special place in his heart. As he thought of his nephew and the day of his birth, Tom felt an unwelcome twinge of pain. His heart was saddened over their recent fallout, and he wasn't quite sure how to fix it. Hearing a knock on the door, he pulled himself away.

"Come in," said Tom.

"I thought now would be a good time to bring you the mail so you could add it to the pile from last week," teased Megan.

"Oh, goody," said Tom. "You're right, though, it is a good day to catch up."

"I hope it doesn't snow all day. I'd like to get home in one piece."

"I think it'll slow down," comforted Tom. "Still, it's beautiful, isn't it?"

"Yeah, I love the snow. I just don't like driving in it," Megan replied as she left the room.

Tom studied the pile of mail on his desk and then the snow. Facing the mail was the last thing he wanted to do, but he knew it needed to be done. Sifting through the heap, he began to separate the bills from the solicitations and the payments from the miscellaneous ads. He hated sorting mail, but it was a job he'd insisted on doing ever since the anthrax scare at the clinic. Sally was never the same after that, and he often wondered if that was really the reason she'd left. She'd said she just couldn't do it anymore, but she never said exactly what it was she couldn't do. Lifting a bill from Eastbrook Medical Supply, he paused as he touched a handwritten letter. The clinic didn't receive many of these, and when they did, it was always an uncomfortable moment of caution. Tom and his staff had received all sorts of nasty hate mail over the years, and most definitely a personal letter drew suspicion. But there was also the occasional letter of encouragement or a thank you mixed in. Holding the envelope up to the light, nothing looked out of the ordinary to Tom. Surveying the envelope a second time, he was about to pitch it in the trash when the name on the return address caught his eye: Shawn & Morgan Waters-Daley. The name was vaguely familiar, but he couldn't place it. Deciding to satisfy his curiosity, Tom reached for his letter opener and sliced open the envelope. Unfolding the letter, he began to read:

Dear Dr. Rose,

I'm writing this letter from a place of deep sorrow. My beautiful wife of eight years took her life earlier this month, leaving me and my two young sons to pick up the pieces. My wife, Morgan Waters, sought and obtained an abortion under your care over twelve years ago. Please understand, I'm not blaming you for her death. I'm not even sure why I'm writing you, but I feel you need to know or perhaps I just need to tell you. I guess I'm hoping my story can help you understand the long-term effects abortion can have on those involved in an abortion decision.

Morgan and I were both under the age of twenty when we sought our abortion. The pregnancy was ill-timed, unexpected, and neither of us felt we were at all ready to raise a child. Deciding not to face the moral judgment and ostracism Morgan believed she'd be subjected to by her family, we chose to abort in secret. I believe now this was a terrible mistake because once a secret, always a secret. The internal burden and pressure of hiding a secret from everyone over the years tore Morgan apart. This dark secret just festered in our lives. Ironically, it turned out that her parents and several others knew about our "secret" abortion, but nobody knew how to talk about it. Sadly, nothing was ever said until after the funeral.

I knew something had changed in Morgan right after the procedure, but I dismissed it as inconsequential. For the next two years, we went through many ups and downs and experienced the gamut of emotions from relief to shame. But then for a time we were good again, and the light broke through. We married, I started to climb the career ladder, and Morgan settled in to raise our two sons, who were born a couple of years apart during the first three years of our marriage. At the writing of this letter, they are five and seven. They are deeply troubled and confused by the loss of their mother, especially little Jake.

Early on in the marriage, I realized Morgan was haunted by her abortion decision. She had recurring nightmares, panic attacks, and even flirted with self-mutilation for a time. Her deep mood swings and irrational behavior brought us to the brink of divorce on more than one occasion. It became unavoidably clear that Morgan's pain and her self-hatred were increasing as time went on. In a last-ditch effort to save our marriage, I scaled back my hours at work, and we reached out for help. With professional counseling, the help of friends and family, more time together, and a renewed commitment to church, we began to repair Morgan's wounded heart. I even discovered through the process just how hurt I was over the loss of my firstborn child. After eight long years of heartache and struggle, we began to turn a corner, and I dared to believe our nightmare was coming to a close. For the next eighteen months our life together blossomed. Looking back now, I view that short season as a gift, a glimpse of what life could've been like if we'd made better choices or had more information given to us about the potential psychological impact of our abortion decision.

Unfortunately, the last six months of Morgan's life were filled with renewed nightmares and drinking. And then the bottom dropped out. My wife took our boys to the mall and, while tending to Kevin, lost track of Jake, who's always been a strong-willed adventurer. Morgan didn't know Jake's whereabouts for over thirty minutes until mall security located our son in the back of a large arcade. Her time of uncertainty and panic would have been difficult for any parent, but for Morgan it was catastrophic. Her heart broke, and she plunged headlong into a tailspin. In the note she left the next day, she wrote, "Every day I live with the guilt of killing one of my children, I will not be responsible for the death of another. It's time I remove the only worthless person in the equation, ME! I'm sorry, Shawn, but I know I'm no good to you or the boys. You're better off without me. I mustn't delay. I've always been a coward, and if I don't do it now, I'll mess this up, too. Goodbye. Me." She was a much lovelier person than she ever gave herself credit for. If only she could have received how much we loved her. I'm sorry to burden you with this knowledge, Dr. Rose, but I don't know what else to do with it. I hope it helps you in some way and allows you to bring better care to your patients. Perhaps it will stir something in you like it has in me.

Respectfully, Shawn Daley

Putting aside the letter and staring at the falling snow, Tom saw it now—the truth he'd always avoided: it's not our pains or our circumstances that define us; rather, it's how we respond to them. Deeply troubled, he picked up his coat and walked to the front desk. The empty lobby before him echoed his heart, and he knew he needed to change. Looking blankly at Megan, Tom said, "Megan, something has come up, and I'm leaving for the day. If something needs immediate attention have

Tammy or April handle it. Locate and pull the file on Morgan Waters. I need to look at it. I also need a statistical total of all the abortions I've performed since we opened the clinic. Thanks, Megan. I'll call you from the road in a couple of hours."

"Is something wrong, Dr. Rose?" asked Megan.

"Yes," Tom said as he walked out the door.

Leaving the parking lot on full autopilot, Tom headed for the interstate. As the miles passed, he flashed back to Jenny, Jamie, Jonathan, and a host of others he'd lost. He didn't even notice that the snow had stopped and that the sun was now penetrating the gray. So lost in his thoughts, it was a wonder he noticed anything. But he did notice the trees as he neared his destination. They gleamed in the penetrating light as the melting snow dripped from their leaves like the dew of the morning. Under the weight of the wet snow, many leaves broke free and fell, their kaleidoscope colors gently falling to the earth as the trees shed their clothing. Tom hadn't turned down this road in over twenty years, but it felt like yesterday. Pulling into the lot at the foot of the trail, he sat in the stillness and worked up his courage. The great puzzle of life never failed to surprise, he thought. Of all the misplaced or missing pieces, he certainly hadn't seen this one coming. The picture he'd built wasn't working and maybe it never had. It was time to change—time to make amends.

Exiting the car, he began his journey. Walking the path, he could hear her laugh, see her smile, and almost touch her hair. She was lovely, and something told him he'd never get over her, but he knew he had to let her go. Approaching the lake, his breath lifted like incense, a peace offering from his soul. Beholding its beauty, Tom fell to his knees. The lake seemed untouched by the world—timeless and unspoiled. Gazing out over the waters, a tear formed in his eye. Kneeling in the sun, his whispered words floated on the wind, "Please forgive me, Jen. I realize now how greatly I failed you. I let my own fears and prejudices get in the way of loving you and the little one inside you. Forgive me, my love—but I can't go on like this. I've got to let you go—forgive me!" Tom paused in silence for some time and let the sadness pour out of him. Looking out at the water, he uttered, "Goodbye, Jenny" and turned away.

Returning to his car, Tom pulled out his cell phone and called the clinic. Waiting for Megan to pick up, he felt a mixture of relief and pain. He knew this was only the beginning of unburdening his soul.

"Thank you for calling Rose Clinic, this is Megan, how can I help you?"

"Megan, it's Tom. Did you get the information I requested?"

Driving down the canyon, Tom turned at the first fork in the road and made his way to Our Lord of the Pines Chapel. It was a mountain parish he'd never visited, but he figured any church would satisfy. It was a beautiful chapel set against a deeply wooded hill. The small sanctuary was flooded with the dancing colors of stained glass as Tom approached the cross. Kneeling beside the front pew, he crossed himself and uttered a silent prayer. A loose floorboard creaked in the stillness of his meditation, and Tom turned to look.

"May I help you, my son?" asked Father William.

"I'd like to make confession, Father," said Tom.

"Please take a seat," directed Father William.

With Tom seated in the pew, the priest sat gently next to Tom and gave this stranger his full attention. Once Tom was ready, they began. Tom started his confession with the customary but long unuttered words, "Bless me Father for I have sinned. It has been nineteen years since my last confession..." Moving forward he uncovered the familiar—impure thoughts, covetousness, fornication, and the like. Digging deeper as he went, Tom confessed to potentially hurting an unknown number of women and performing twenty-four-thousand, one-hundred and twenty-two abortions, a number he'd arrived at through Megan's tally over the phone and an additional assumed thousand under the direction of Maggie Adams at Planned Parenthood. To this point in his confession, Tom had been rather composed and matter of fact. And then he confessed, "I also aborted my only child." With these words, he sucked in his breath and began to sob in a convulsive, uncontrollable manner. His composure now gone, Tom crumpled into the vestments of the priest in utter devastation over what he had wrought. Wailing through an avalanche of tears, Tom heard the distant voice of Father William. Opening his eyes through a flood of regret, he noticed for the first time the embrace of the old priest. This loving and gentle man was comforting him. Him—an abortionist, a killer! Burying his face in shame, he could barely breathe. Holding Tom as he sobbed, the priest shed a tear of solidarity and proclaimed, "Jesus is far greater than the sin of the whole world. He forgives you, my son. He forgives you completely! Let Jesus bear your past, and purpose from this day forward to live for Him." Holding Tom until his tears subsided, the gentle priest looked compassionately into his eyes and said, "Come walk with me, my son, and let's talk deeper about how to unburden your soul."

chapter 46

New Beginnings

Stacy stood facing the fountain, holding her token in the morning light. The sweet smell of budding lilac bushes filled the air with a pungent aroma, and everywhere one looked the garden was decked with blooming irises and tulips of every color. The spring greens of the bushes and trees made a spectacular canopy for the sun to breach, but the fountain stood unclouded as the rays descended. Glimmering under the water were the names. The bottom of the fountain was covered with shiny silver and gold tokens bearing the names of babies lost to abortion. Peering into the pool, Stacy looked past the shimmering flickers of light and witnessed the names: Tina, Matthew, Ronny, Susan, Joe, Gail, Tasha, Shelby, Tony, Ariel, Tom, Angela…. Closing her eyes, she took a deep breath and then looked at the glassy token in her own hand. The inscription read: NOAH 2013. Kissing the token, she offered a silent prayer and tossed her token in the pool of water beneath the flow of the fountain. Turning before it reached the bottom, she walked toward Cindy.

"I'm so proud of you, Stacy. You've come so far," Cindy said as she gave Stacy a hug.

"It's hard," confessed Stacy. "But it's strangely comforting to give my baby a place of rest and a name."

"This way you can always come visit whenever you want," said Cindy. "I like to visit when I've had a difficult day or after something reminds me of my babies and what I've lost. This beautiful place always reminds me that they're with their Savior in a far more beautiful place."

"Thanks for coming, Cindy."

"I wouldn't have missed it."

****

The prison yard was full every Saturday, but this beautiful spring day seemed to bring every available and able-bodied prisoner into the yard. Men were playing basketball, walking, lifting weights, and gathering throughout the high-walled and heavily guarded exercise yard. It was a treat afforded the inmates of Lincoln State Penitentiary only once a week. A small taste of the freedom they once knew. Soren slowly walked through the yard, nervous and afraid. He'd only been incarcerated for two weeks, but already his time had been ugly. Noticing a group of men playing chess, he cautiously approached and watched the action from a distance.

"Nice move, Henry," said one of the men. "You been reading up or somethin'?"

"Being the new prison librarian does have its advantages," quipped Henry.

"Yeah, who'd you smooch to get that gig?"

"What can I say? God likes me," said Henry.

Seeing Soren out of the corner of his eye, Henry took note of this newcomer, a sad-looking man. Returning to his game, he castled and waited for his opponent's next move—which came in the form of Rocco Dawson. Surrounding Soren from the rear, Rocco and his boys swooped in to intimidate and claim another victim. Looking up from the board and locking eyes with Rocco,

Henry proclaimed, "Hey, Rocco, he's with me."

"All right, Henry, but you're not going to be able to save 'em all," said Rocco through a menacing glare.

As Rocco and his thugs dispersed, Henry walked over to Soren and extended his hand, "Henry Taylor."

"Soren Ulf."

"Pleased to meet you, Soren."

****

Arriving at Planned Parenthood, Tom parked his car across the street and looked at the gathering crowd in front of the clinic. He still couldn't believe he was taking part in the rescue efforts on the sidewalk. Each time out he felt his awkwardness—joining a place and a people he had despised for so many years. Nevertheless, he felt compelled to come. Tom knew better than most the price abortion exacted, and he needed to give back. Getting to know Christopher, Amy, and the others he'd primarily seen through glass, Tom had completely changed his perceptions of who they were and what they were about. Their kindness and graciousness had made an impression. From the start, Tom had felt accepted and cared for by these affable people. This, remarkably enough, was where he now belonged. Taking a deep breath and exiting the car, Tom crossed the street and joined the large group of people.

"Hey, Tom, glad you could make it," said Christopher. "I thought with your talk coming up later today you wouldn't be here."

"No worries, I'm all set for that," Tom said confidently. "Hey, J.J., how's it going?"

"Good, now that I'm almost finished with high school," Jaleesa said excitedly. "I have less than three weeks to go before I graduate!"

"Good for you! Have you thought about what's ahead?"

"I've had some offers, but I might take my grandfather up on a summer trip to Europe and a year of hands-on business experience working at the store before I head off to school."

"It's probably a wise choice. Getting a little real-world seasoning before you head off to school is always good," said Tom.

"Yeah, besides I think he wants me to stay home for another year."

"A year working can really clarify what you want in life. Have you heard from Jonathan lately?"

"No, he just wrote me the one time," confided Jaleesa. "Is it getting any better between you two?"

"A little. I finally convinced him to take a backpacking trip with me next month. Hopefully, it'll give me another chance to apologize and show him I've changed. I…"

Just as Tom was about to divulge further, Rachelle and Ethan walked up along with Amy. "Dr. Rose, have you met my mother, Rachelle, and her husband, Ethan Tyndale?"

"Sorry to say I haven't," said Tom as he shook their hands. "Your reputation precedes you, Dr. Tyndale. I've heard only good things. Mr. Tyndale, it's a pleasure. I've admired your detective work over the years."

"Thank you for your kind words, Dr. Rose," said Rachelle. "Jaleesa has talked about you often in recent months. She's been greatly moved by your change of heart."

"Well, thank you, but I didn't get here on my own. I had a lot of people praying for me over the years."

"Haven't we all?" said Ethan.

"I suppose so," said Tom. "Well, it appears congratulations are in order. When is the baby due?"

"We're expecting in July," said Ethan.

Looking at Rachelle as she gently caressed her tummy, Tom said, "I can see where Jaleesa gets her beauty from. You're the most radiant pregnant woman I've ever seen."

"Thank you," Rachelle beamed. "I thought I was beginning to look a little fat."

"Not at all," said Tom.

"Hey, Amy, what's up with little Luke? I haven't heard him make a peep," inquired J.J.

"As soon as I placed him in the stroller, he just crashed," said Amy.

"Can I sneak a peek?" asked Ethan.

"Sure. Be gentle."

"He's absolutely beautiful," said Ethan as he lifted the blanket and pulled back the stroller canopy. "Is the adoption official now?"

"Yep. We completed it last week," Amy said with a broad smile.

"How's his mother?" asked Rachelle.

"She's doing okay. She's in a neighboring state receiving counseling and the care she needs to face her difficult past."

"That's so important. I know counseling helped me," said Rachelle. "Have you been able to stay in contact with her?"

"Yes, I contact her twice a week, and the adoption agreement grants her access to Luke along with scheduled visitation rights."

"Ladies and gentlemen, may I have your attention. Mass is about to begin," instructed Father Ramsey.

As the people huddled together, Christopher observed that this was the largest gathering he'd ever seen

at a Mass in front of Planned Parenthood. To his amazement, there must have been in excess of three hundred
people on the sidewalk. Amid them were prominent
members of the Eastbrook City Council, businessmen,
doctors, lawyers, police personnel, firemen, pastors,
school teachers, construction workers, and teens. Smiling
at Amy, Christopher began to sense that God was doing
a new thing. He was beginning to make rivers in the
desert, a way in the wilderness. The pro-life harvest had
always been plentiful, but today the workers didn't seem
so few. The word of Lucas's miracle rescue, Tom's change
of heart, Pastor Jim's important leadership in motivating and galvanizing some of the local clergy into a new
Pastoral Coalition for Life, and the efforts of the impassioned youth at FSO led by Miles Johnston and Jaleesa
Jacobs had all made a difference. Christopher smiled as
Father Ramsey read from the Bible:

> *Seek the Lord while he may be found; call upon
> him while he is near; let the wicked forsake his
> way, and the unrighteous man his thoughts; let him
> return to the Lord, that he may have compassion
> on him, and to our God, for he will abundantly
> pardon. For my thoughts are not your thoughts,
> neither are your ways my ways, declares the Lord.
> For as the heavens are higher than the earth, so are
> my ways higher than your ways and my thoughts
> than your thoughts. For as the rain and the snow
> come down from heaven and do not return there
> but water the earth, making it bring forth and
> sprout, giving seed to the sower and bread to the
> eater, so shall my word be that goes out from my
> mouth; it shall not return to me empty, but it shall
> accomplish that which I purpose, and shall succeed
> in the thing for which I sent it.*

Truly, God's Word had not gone out empty, for it had rescued many, redeemed Tom Rose, and forged a new movement that was growing by the day.

At the close of Mass, Christopher was pleased to see that Cindy and Jael had arrived as well as Lucas and Aaliyah. It was a glorious day, and he felt the power of God as the people came. Pastor Jim took the lead in forming a human chain that would begin a walk around Planned Parenthood and prayerfully declare the promises of God. Behind him Christopher, Father Ramsey, and Tom took their place. Tom smiled as he looked over at Sally—it was fitting that the two of them were working together again. Opening the Scriptures as the people began to move, Pastor Jim declared from the front of the pack, *"For the Lord is good; His lovingkindness is everlasting And His faithfulness to all generations..."*

****

Tom made his way into St. Francis Medical Center and the office of Dr. Charles Ferguson. He'd been invited to speak to the residents about medical ethics and abortion. It was an opportunity he appreciated, and a way for him to urge and equip the next generation of doctors to respect the life of all their patients, both born and pre-born. After a brief period of socializing and a kind introduction by Dr. Ferguson, Tom stepped up to speak.

"Thank you for inviting me to speak today, Dr. Ferguson; it's a pleasure to be here. My name is Dr. Tom Rose, and I've been practicing obstetrics and gynecology here in the community of Eastbrook for more than a decade. I spent a great many of those years, until recently, performing first- and second-trimester abortions. Procedures that I now deeply regret—procedures that destroyed many children and, I'm sure, negatively impacted the mental health of many of the women I cared for. Today, like me many years ago, you face the difficult decision of whether or not to provide abortions. Yes, abortion is legal, controversial, and complicated, but the decision on whether or not to provide abortion services shouldn't be. As physicians, our goal should always be to provide our patients with the utmost care, skill, and professionalism. When we strip away all the rhetoric, arguments, politics, and tangential scenarios in the abortion debate, the physician, and by extension, the public, is left with just one question: Who are the preborn? Are they persons or potential persons? Are they human or non-human? Are they sustainable, viable embryos and fetuses under normal conditions or not? Embryology, fetology, and medical science declare: Yes, they are full human persons from the moment of fertilization. The zygote is not going to become a new human being—it *is* a new human being! My fellow physicians, this is truly the key question and the one we must face. The evidence that these embryos are indeed human is longstanding and overwhelming. Ponder what you have learned to this point about embryonic and fetal development, fetal surgery, and prenatal care. Is it reasonable to believe that unless a pregnancy is wanted, we have only one patient? Is it ethical to disregard one life in heeding the desires of another? Our job is to care for all of our patients in any given situation.

"In light of this you might well ask, 'Dr. Rose, if the evidence is so strong that life begins at the fusion of sperm and oocyte, then why did you perform abortions?' The answer, I believe, is the same for everyone who has ever been faced with a tragedy, a difficult dilemma, or a crisis—in that moment a person usually asks how is this going to affect me? So often in a crisis or tragic circumstance our thoughts naturally center on ourselves or our partner. We can't easily see what's hidden or far off, future consequences seldom come into view, and all we can think of is the now. How do we fix it? How do we alleviate our present pain? For the man and woman facing an ill-timed, unwanted, and unexpected pregnancy, this is acutely true. In their state of confusion, fear, and unrest, we in positions of trust and authority need to be the voice of calm, assurance, and reason. We need to gently guide our patients to the truth of medical science, discussing all the options that will benefit both the parents and the child in utero.

"Before I began my practice, I experienced such a tragedy. My fiancée was raped and became pregnant. In our distress and pain, we sought to abort, never fully contemplating the many possible outcomes of such a choice. None of our friends or colleagues in the medical profession discouraged us, and so we scheduled our abortion. Tragically, my fiancée died as a result of complications following the botched abortion. In the aftermath, I vowed to be the best abortionist I could be so that no other woman would ever be hurt or killed during an abortion procedure. Thus began my career as an abortionist. Over the years, I've encountered other botched abortions, and I always felt good when I was there to halt the damage or save a woman's life. But today I realize that even this wouldn't be necessary if the women victimized by these crimes of gross negligence hadn't sought or been encouraged to seek an abortion in the first place. I've come to the conclusion that abortion is always the wrong decision. Through the grace of God and the help of many people, I have come to realize abortion is a flawed and failed procedure that kills developing babies and damages women. Simply put,—abortion flies in the face of everything medicine tries to achieve. Our art is one of help, of healing, and of life not death! I implore you as you begin your careers to learn from me and see abortion for what it is before tragedy strikes in your own life and the lives of others. I allowed a personal tragedy in my life to cloud my judgment and hide the truth. It doesn't matter how safe the procedure is for the woman, how informed she is about the practice, or how much care or concern we extend to her during it if what we're doing harms another. As doctors, we are charged with preserving, protecting, and healing if possible all our patients. In all my years of seemingly perfect service and safe abortions, I now realize that none of them were so. Every time I performed an abortion, I killed one person and potentially wounded another. I've learned much over the past twenty years, and I understand now that we can't avoid suffering and pain, life's cruelties and consequences, but we can avoid becoming monsters. Ladies and gentlemen, resolve today to be physicians who do what is right, even in the midst of adversity. Be healers, be compassionate, and use your skills to be agents for good in the world!

"It is in that spirit and tradition that I would like to lead you in the classical text of the Oath of Hippocrates. If you will turn to page seven in your packet, you will find it there. Many of our medical schools no longer use the oath, or, if they do, they use an altered version, but this fifth-century BC declaration got it right. All those who so desire, please stand and join with me in reciting the vow:

'I swear by Apollo the physician, and Aesculapius, and Hygeia, and Panacea, and all the gods and goddesses that, according to my ability and judgment, I will keep this Oath and this stipulation—to reckon him who taught me this art equally dear to me as my parents, to share my substance with him, and relieve his necessities if required; to look upon his offspring in the same footing as my own brothers, and to teach them this art, if they shall wish to learn it…. I will give no deadly medicine to anyone if asked, nor suggest any such counsel; and in like manner I will not give to a woman a pessary to produce abortion. With purity and holiness I will pass my life and practice my art.... Into whatever houses I enter, I will go into them for the benefit of the sick, and will abstain from every voluntary act of mischief and corruption; and further, from the seduction of female or males, or free-men and slaves.... While I continue to keep this Oath unviolated, may it be granted to me to enjoy life and the practice of the art, respected by all men, in all times! But should I trespass and violate this Oath, may the reverse be my lot!' Thank you for reciting the Oath with me and for allowing me to come and speak with you today," concluded Tom. "At this point, I will open up the floor for any questions you may have."

"Dr. Rose, how do you feel about abortion being performed in cases of fetal disability?"

"I was never very comfortable with it when I performed them, and today I'm wholeheartedly against it," answered Tom. "I feel we should extend the same care to those in utero as we do to those with disabilities after birth. Certainly, the art of fetal surgery continues to grow and amaze. But regardless of the treatments we employ, we should never forget that every patient we serve is wholly deserving of our best."

"What about medical circumstances that threaten the life of the mother?" challenged a young resident. "Surely you're not against abortion in cases of hemorrhage from the placenta or ruptured membranes that may lead to severe infection and life-threatening sepsis if the uterus is not evacuated—and what about an ectopic pregnancy?"

"As you know, medical science, techniques, and procedures are always evolving and what is medically impossible today may become possible tomorrow. I have come to the conclusion that our guiding principal in all situations should be to do no harm. But there are currently cases, some of which you've pointed out, where the life of a preborn baby may be lost as we attempt to save the mother. Given this admission, in all my years of practice, and this corresponds with the testimony of many other doctors who work in the field, I have never encountered a single case in which the baby's life had to be ended in order to save the life of his or her mother. I have, however, experienced firsthand a mother's life that was lost due to the taking of her child's life through abortion. While both scenarios are rare, they can and do happen. The point at issue being that abortion performed to save a mother's life is an extremely rare event and not indicative of the larger abortion question. More importantly, the loss of a child under these extreme circumstances would be the result of trying to save the mother's life, not the intentional destruction of the child's."

"So, would you say you're for abortions in extreme circumstances?" followed the resident.

"Certainly not, I'm decidedly against all forms of abortion," reiterated Tom. "Abortion should only be considered as a last resort when all other options have been exhausted. But I recognize there are rare medical complications that call for difficult actions in moments of life and death circumstances. We must do everything in our power to save both mother and child."

"How did your staff take the news when you informed them that you would no longer be performing abortions?"

"Most were relieved and very receptive, but I did have a few staff members resign. Some of my staff had experienced very damaging harassment and attacks against their family and persons in the past from aggressive protestors, and they were unwilling to forgive or abandon their perceived mission for the emancipation of women. There is no denying there have been some ugly incidents of violence on both sides of this issue. I myself have received hate mail and death threats over the years, but I don't believe these violent acts are the norm or central to the issue itself. And after more than ten years of abortion practice and honest thoughtful reflection, I can't see how abortion emancipates anyone, especially not the children developing in the womb."

"Dr. Rose, you said that several people helped you see the truth. Will you elaborate on that? Was it your peers in the medical profession or family?"

"There were a few doctors and colleagues that had challenged me over the years, but nothing significant. My journey was a complicated process of realizations, but perhaps my biggest awakening came at the hands of a teenager. My nephew, Jonathan, challenged me to look afresh at embryology and medical science. As I began to look again at fetal development, I realized that every child I'd aborted was potentially someone's Jonathan, and it broke my heart. My nephew has changed and blessed my life on more than one occasion and I cannot imagine what my life would be like without him——."

✱✱✱✱✱✱

The next morning, Tom awoke with the sun. Taking a long walk around the grounds of his gated community, he felt a peace he'd never experienced. Returning to his house, Tom stood sipping some coffee in his nearly empty living room as he gazed at the beautiful golf course below. The house was only a month away from new ownership, and he was relieved to be rid of it. His house, like his sports car, no longer held any attraction in his life. They were painful reminders of his past, and he wanted no part of them. Finishing his coffee, Tom ascended the stairs for a shower and the day ahead. Showered, shaved, and packed, Tom headed for the door and the bank.

Strolling into his local branch, Tom requested to see a private banker and was ushered into a nearby cubicle. Settling into a comfortable chair, he felt an energy he hadn't experienced in years. Smiling, his eye was drawn to a photograph hanging behind the banker's desk. It was a beautiful image of a sunlit path surrounded by brooding, dark storm clouds. The image couldn't have been more appropriate, he thought. Tom knew what it was like to live in the storm and from now on he vowed to walk in the light.

"Good morning, Mr. Rose, how can I assist you?" asked the banker.

"I need five hundred dollars in cash and a cashier's check in the amount of $500,000," requested Tom.

"I'm happy to take care of this for you, sir," assured the banker. "Just let me verify the funds are collected, and we'll get started."

"Thank you," said Tom.

"Everything appears to be in order, Mr. Rose. Who would you like the cashier's check made payable to?"

"Make it payable to Shawn Daley, please. And could you write on the memo line that the funds are to be used for the future needs of Kevin and Jake Daley."

"Certainly, Mr. Rose," said the banker. "Are you getting ready to take a trip?"

"Yes, going to New York City."

"I love New York. Are you going for business or pleasure?"

"I'm not sure yet. I'm going to find a woman that I never should have left," confided Tom.

"Well, I wish you the best of luck, sir."

"I appreciate that. Would you be so kind as to mail the cashier's check to the following address along with this letter?"

"Certainly, Mr. Rose."

"Thank you."

As Tom walked out of the bank, he could barely contain his excitement. It was a beautiful day to be alive, to be filled with dreams for the future and the promise of...

The references in this work to the great American classic *Uncle Tom's Cabin, or, Life Among the Lowly* are deliberate. May it remind readers, the church, and the nation of our past, the power of abolition, and how far we have strayed from the times and beliefs of Mrs. Stowe. Perhaps it's time to introduce a new Uncle Tom. In no way does this imply that this contemporary work is on an equal footing with Stowe's classic novel, and I strongly encourage all my readers to read her enduring work afresh. *Uncle Tom's Cabin* still speaks today with a power and a resonance that shouldn't be ignored. In 1852, Stowe wrote to a vastly different nation than the America of today, a nation that, by and large, viewed itself as a Christian nation. This novel, in like manner, is aimed at the modern-day body of Christ in America—however large or small that remnant may be. It is my contention that the Christian community must face the issue of abortion soberly and with grace in our own house before we can effectively help our nation return to its senses and compassion in the arena of abortion. Like Stowe's novel, the story presented here is essentially a Christian work, but I invite people from all walks of life to invest their time reading the book—hopefully finding it thought-provoking, challenging, and motivating. Stowe also courageously addressed and challenged a deeply divided nation when she wrote *Uncle Tom's Cabin*. And after forty years of legalized abortion resulting in the death of around fifty-five million preborn citizens,

America is once again deeply divided. We are truly living in yet another time that calls for concerted action and abolition. At our best, America is a nation that struggles to achieve ever-increasing heights of freedom, tolerance, and the protection of human rights to those born and, hopefully, soon to the preborn. Furthermore, it is my fervent belief that if Harriet Beecher Stowe were living today, she would write something similar to *Hushed*. Her sincere faith and her heart for "the least of these" and those hurting would compel her. After all, speaking through the character of St. Clare, she wrote, "My view of Christianity is such...that I think no man can consistently profess it without throwing the whole weight of his being against this monstrous system of injustice that lies at the foundation of all our society; and, if need be, sacrificing himself in the battle. That is, I mean that I could not be a Christian otherwise, though I have certainly had intercourse with a great many enlightened and Christian people who did no such thing; and I confess that the apathy of religious people on this subject, their want of perception of wrongs that filled me with horror, have engendered in me more skepticism than any other thing." Someone once commented that "Harriet Beecher Stowe was exceptionally effective at bearing witness." In that spirit, I humbly suggest that there are still grave evils in the world worth fighting. May *Hushed* be yet another cry to a culture whose conscience appears to have been seared with a hot iron.

Much of the content for the narrative comes from my own personal experiences with sidewalk counseling and pro-life ministry. Additional inspiration for this work was derived from personal friends and peers in the pro-life movement as well as my research in the pro-life/pro-choice arena. Several of the insights, truths, and thoughts expressed in this work have been articulated before by those who have preceded me in the pro-life effort. A special note of recognition goes to Fr. Frank Pavone who, to my knowledge, was the first to express the words attributed to Fr. Rick in chapter 27— "Christ says, 'My body broken for you,' abortion says, 'the baby's body broken for me,'"

While most of the characters presented in this novel have their counterpart in reality, none of those invented should be inferred to be actual persons living or dead. For those characters modeled after people I have encountered personally, fictitious names and characteristics have been invented to protect their privacy. Similarly, the dialogue and events are invented or reimagined. Those familiar with Philadelphia abortionist Kermit Gosnell will, no doubt, recognize that some peculiarities and abortion methods connected to the character Soren Ulf were taken from the grand jury report released in January of 2011 investigating Gosnell and others who worked for him. His methods and practice at the "Women's Medical Society" are a matter of public record: *www.phila.gov/districtattorney/PDFs/GrandJuryWomensMedical.pdf*. To watch a compelling documentary on Gosnell go to *www.3801lancaster.com*. Several other aspects of the character, Soren Ulf, have no connection to Gosnell, but represent an amalgamation of the worst attributes (uncovered so far) of the abortion industry and its eugenic roots. Admittedly, Gosnell is not your average abortionist, but in a profession where the killing of innocent children is the main object can we be surprised when such psychosis arises? Stowe may have said it best when she wrote, "Talk of the abuses of slavery! Humbug! The thing itself is the essence of all abuse!" And certainly this rings true for abortion. Abuse, culminating in death, is the very definition of abortion. For those readers interested in a frank discussion of abortion malpractice (pregnant women abused or killed by their abortionist) during legalized abortion in America, I recommend the graphic and highly disturbing book, *Lime 5*, written by Mark Crutcher (*www.lifedynamics.com*). It may also interest the reader to investigate the many potential medical and psychological complications that can result from abortion. Two good books about the topic are: *Women's Health after Abortion: The Medical and Psychological Evidence*, by Elizabeth Ring-Cassidy and Ian Gentles and *Real Abortion Stories*, edited by Barbara Horak. If you or someone you love is struggling with the after-effects of abortion, please seek out professional post-abortive care and counseling. Two good organizations to start with are: Care Net, *www.care-net.org* (a national network of pregnancy resource centers) and The Elliot Institute, *www.afterabortion.org* (information, post-abortive resources, and links to other resources).

****

It is my sincere hope that this novel compels individuals both inside and outside of the church to learn the truth about abortion. Study its impact on post-abortive men and women. Educate yourself about the medical discoveries concerning embryonic and fetal life. Search the Scriptures to understand God's view. And become aware of the staggering number of abortions done in our nation each year. Equip yourself with knowledge, and then join the pro-life movement by standing against this atrocity in your home, your church, and within the civil arena. There is so much we can do, but nothing will change unless we, the people, care enough to do it.

If you're not sure how to begin being a voice for the voiceless, start with these suggestions: Pray often for the ending of abortion, for pro-life efforts, leaders, and initiatives. Engage in peaceful protests and clinic prayer and rescue. Support pro-life petitions, legislation, and candidates. Never vote for a pro-choice politician or initiative. If a president, congressperson, or judge is for the killing of innocent children, does it matter what else they stand for? Volunteer your time in pregnancy resource centers or pro-life organizations. Teach your children and others about self-control, waiting for marriage, purity, and responsibility. Get involved with adoption agencies or consider adopting needy children. Offer assistance to women and men facing a difficult pregnancy—open up your home to them or offer to pay their medical expenses. Give financially to those pro-life ministries, politicians, pregnancy centers, organizations, and adoption agencies that are effective and achieving success locally and nationally. Educate your peers, family, and friends through speaking, writing, and teaching. Pass out your favorite pro-life book to others and encourage them to read it. Always be willing to help a relative, friend, co-worker, or neighbor make the right choice about abortion. Finally, apply your own creative ideas. Work in any capacity that will bring about the abolition of legalized abortion in America.

To all those who work, support, and labor on the side of "choice," I'm praying for you. May you discover the truth and may Jesus set you free. It's never too late to choose a different road and discover new life (John 3:16-17; Romans 10:9-13).

Like abortion, rape is a heinous act of violence perpetrated against women, children, and men, with by far the greatest number of victims being women. While the central rape scenarios depicted in this novel are in the statistical minority (research reveals that the vast majority of rapes are perpetrated by male family members, boyfriends, or acquaintances who knew their victims), they nonetheless represent possible rape trauma events, and are perhaps the imagined cases many people conjure when presenting the argument for providing abortions in cases arising as a result of rape or incest. In our misconceptions, fear, prejudice, and revulsion over rape, we in society often fail to deeply examine the argument for abortion following rape and its many possible negative outcomes and long-term repercussions for the mother, her child, and our society.

Instead of abortion, a better societal response to the unique event of pregnancy following rape or incest would be to provide compassionate, supportive care for victims of sexual assault, rape trauma counseling, and assisted help with parenting or adoption options. Most importantly, increased and improved efforts to diminish acts of sexual violence before they occur through education, awareness, effective law enforcement, and criminal prosecution should be pursued with vigor. Society needs to assist victims of sexual violence through their recovery with support, unconditional acceptance, compassion, and access to professional rape trauma therapy. In addition, society must work hard to reduce religious or cultural stigmas that often come with pregnancies outside of wedlock and respectfully celebrate and support mothers who choose to parent or seek adoption for their children. It's imperative that we support, encourage, financially assist, and provide helpful resources to these survivors. Violence against innocent preborn children is not a cure for sexual violence or its effects. In fact, there is mounting evidence to suggest that abortion may add to the sexual assault victim's trauma in innumerable ways, despite the erroneous conventional wisdom that abortion will somehow alleviate a victim's emotional pain or assist her in recovery. Our goal in society should be to diminish and remove acts of violence against others, not encourage them.

If you or someone you love is struggling with the after-effects of rape, please seek out professional rape-trauma therapy and counseling. Two good organizations to start with are: RAINN (Rape, Abuse, and Incest National Network) *www.centers.rainn.org* or 1-800-656-4673 and Find Christian Counselor *www.findchristiancounselor.com* the largest and most comprehensive network of Christian counselors, counseling pastors, and therapists with Masters or PhD level training and degrees. If you are a victim of sexual assault, the number one thing you need to know and believe is that the rape, molestation, or attack *was not your fault*, but rather the deliberate choice of your attacker (Deuteronomy 22:25-26). They and they alone are to blame!

In our culture, some still believe that rape and abortion are primarily women's issues, but this is a grave mistake and a great falsehood. Since around 98 percent of rapes are perpetrated by males and every conception requires a male, it is ludicrous to believe that these issues concern only, or belong exclusively to, the female gender. On the contrary, these issues belong to every member of the human race. But especially men because of the critical role we can play in prevention, support, protection, and rescue. Not to mention the fact that therapists, doctors, abortionists, clinic workers, pro-life advocates, pro-choice advocates, politicians, judges, pastors, preborn babies, family members, and so on can be, and often are, *male*. In fact, men are one of the biggest keys to addressing these issues and solving these problems. For far too long, many men have remained in the shadows, abdicating their responsibility by refusing to get involved with these issues out of apathy, ignorance, or agreement with these atrocities. Men, it is time to stand up and be counted—our calling is to protect women and children and advocate for them by promoting their equality, rights, and freedom (Malachi 2:15; Ephesians 5:25; Colossians 3:19-21; 1 Timothy 5:1-2; 1 Peter 3:7-12). No male has a right to sex by force, misconduct, or intimidation, and no male should ever quietly or collaboratively participate in the destruction of his own children or anyone's children. Just as no female should perpetrate rape or participate in the destruction of her own children. Rape and abortion are bedfellows of atrocity that must be opposed and defeated. And it's up to all people of good will to do their part. We can all be a part of the solution through our love, advocacy, forgiveness, and protection. Be a person who loves and cares for your children as only you can. Teach them through your words and actions their worth and the importance of defending the rights of others. Be a protector and defender of others, especially the weak. If you are a man, resolve to be a protector who will champion the rights of all people, especially women and children. Furthermore, we all need to take ownership of our sexual practices and accept any results thereof. Only by doing this can we live responsibly and protect our neighbors. Cultivating sexual responsibility is imperative. It behooves us as people of compassion to examine our attitudes, words, and actions regarding sexual violence and abortion. Let's do our best to represent our values and our Creator by being God-fearing, woman-honoring, man-honoring, child-protecting, forgiving, and loving *human beings*.

If you would like to learn more about rape, rape statistics, or how to become an advocate for rape victims, please go to *www.rainn.org* and click the link: "get involved" or read the selected books provided here in the Recommended Books and Resources section. Thankfully, the latest rape statistics are showing that the incidences of rape are declining in our nation. That's the good news. The bad news is that still many rapes go unreported and, therefore, the data is incomplete, something rape and abortion share in common—incomplete data. But with more than a million U.S. surgical abortions performed every year and countless more chemical abortions (RU-486; the morning-after pill); one could not really say that abortion is in decline—and this must change.

In closing, let me leave you with the words of a courageous woman who in sharing her abortion testimony uttered words I have never forgotten: "I know two things that would have kept me from aborting my baby all those years ago. First, if abortion had been illegal. And second, if the father of my baby had supported me and encouraged me not to abort." And similarly, a couple once shared with me, "If when we'd arrived at the abortion clinic someone would have been there and offered to help us and given us alternatives, we would not have proceeded with our abortion." May you and me and all of us be that someone, and may abortion once again become illegal and unthinkable in America!

Pro-Life Books

Alcorn, Randy, *ProLife Answers to ProChoice Arguments* (powerful defense of the pro-life position)

Brown, Harold O. J., *Death before Birth* (a Christian theology professor who co-founded the Christian Action Council (Care Net) brilliantly articulates the pro-life position)

Ensor, John, *Answering the Call* (pro-life appeal to love one's neighbor)

Grant, George, *Grand Illusions* (exposé on Planned Parenthood)

Klusendorf, Scott, *The Case for Life* (pro-life apologetic)

Last, Jonathan V., *What to Expect When No One's Expecting* (an engaging discussion of demographics, society's current attitudes about children, and underpopulation)

Miller, Monica Migliorino, *Abandoned* (an account of pro-life activism, civil disobedience, and clinic rescue and protest before the 1994 FACE law—this book contains graphic images of aborted babies)

Morana, Janet, *Recall Abortion* (the co-founder of Silent No More shares the stories of women who've lived through abortion)

Patchen, Joel, *Love is for Eternity* (pro-life devotional)

Pavone, Fr. Frank, *Pro-life Reflections for Every Day* (brief daily reflections from the Director of Priests for Life)

Peretti, Frank E., *Tilly* (pro-life fiction)

Resler, Roger, *Compelling Interest*
(the story behind the *Roe v. Wade* decision)

Sproul, R. C., *Abortion: A Rational Look at an Emotional Issue* (an examination of the ethical implications of abortion)

Willke, John, Dr. and Barbara Willke, *Abortion Questions and Answers*
(comprehensive abortion Q&A, informative)

Former Abortion Industry Personnel Who've Become Pro-Life

Everett, Carol, *Blood Money*
(former clinic director's testimony)

Johnson, Abby, *Unplanned*
(former director of a Texas Planned Parenthood)

Nathanson, Bernard N., M.D., *The Hand of God* (former abortionist's testimonial)

Sidewalk Counseling

Bereit, David and Shawn Carney with Cindy Lambert, *40 Days for Life* (inspirational stories documenting a nationwide prayer and fasting effort in front of abortion facilities)

Verwys, Mary Waalkes, *Wednesday Mourning*
(sidewalk counselor's testimony)

After Abortion Healing

Burke, Kevin LSW, David Wemhoff, and Marvin Stockwell, *Redeeming a Father's Heart*
(men share their abortion experiences and healing)

Cochrane, Linda, *Forgiven and Set Free*
(abortion recovery Bible study for women)

Cochrane, Linda and Kathy Jones, *Healing a Father's Heart* (abortion recovery Bible study for men)

Fredenburg, Michaelene, *Changed* (an open compassionate look at the emotional aftermath of abortion)

Reisser, Teri, M.S., M.F.T. with Paul Reisser, M.D., *A Solitary Sorrow* (working through the emotional aftermath of abortion)

Surviving Abortion

Shaver, Jessica and Gianna Jessen, *Gianna* (pro-life advocate who survived a saline abortion)

Fetal Development

Tallack, Peter, *In the Womb* (embryonic and fetal development)

Rape Awareness, Trauma, and Recovery

Atkinson, Matt, with contributions by many survivors, *Resurrection after Rape* (rape-therapy workbook)

Hislop, Bev, *Shepherding Women in Pain* (understanding and helping women who've experienced trauma)

Meili, Trisha, *I Am the Central Park Jogger* (a story of rape, severe trauma, and recovery)

Scott, Kay, *Sexual Assault: Will I Ever Feel Okay Again* (a Christian's journey through rape and recovery)

Rape and Incest from the Pro-Life Perspective

Ezell, Lee, *The Missing Piece* (a mother's story of rape, pregnancy, adoption, and a later reunion with her daughter who was conceived from the rape)

Reardon, David C., Julie Makimaa, and Amy Sobie, editors. *Victims and Victors* (a large study of rape and incest victims who did and did not choose abortion)

Surviving Sexual Abuse

Marx, Victor, with Wayne Atcheson and James Werning, *The Victor Marx Story* (the incredible true story of a martial arts expert who overcame childhood physical and sexual abuse)

Vredevelt, Pamela and Kathryn Rodriguez, *Surviving the Secret: Healing the hurts of Sexual Abuse* (faith-based recovery providing insights about both the abused and the abuser)

Overcoming Wounding and Shame

Cloud, Dr. Henry, *Changes That Heal* (healing through the process of becoming more like our heavenly Father as we strive to imitate Christlike behavior)

Rodriguez, Kathy, *Healing the Father Wound* (overcoming the hurts of poor or abusive fatherhood, and understanding the critical role of fatherhood)

VanVonderen, Jeff, *Tired of Trying to Measure Up* (breaking free of a Christian works mentality through understanding the power of shame vs. grace)

Grieving the Loss of a Child or Loved One

Simons, Eldyn, *The Dawn of Hope* (grieving the loss of a loved one)

Sittser, Jerry, *A Grace Disguised* (grief and recovery from a sudden tragic loss)

Weirsbe, David W., *Gone but Not Lost*
(grieving the death of a child)

Rescue and Courage

Gilbert, Martin, *The Righteous* (stories of courageous
rescue and faith during the Holocaust)

Mayer, Jack, *Life in a Jar* (the story of Irena Sendler and
the Kansas teens who brought her recognition)

ten Boom, Corrie, *The Hiding Place* (courage and rescue
in the face of Nazi persecution)

Wilberforce, William, *Real Christianity*
(a discussion of authentic faith)

Finding Meaning in Suffering

Buttrick, George A., *God, Pain, and Evil*
(a pastor tackles the "problem of pain")

Frankl, Viktor E., *Man's Search for Meaning*
(a Psychologist and Holocaust survivor discusses
the critical role a person's response to suffering
plays in their mental health)

Johnson, Daniel E., *When You Ask Why*
(a Christian look at suffering and loss)

Forgiveness

Morris, Debbie, with Gregg Lewis, *Forgiving the
Dead Man Walking* (the woman who survived
the rape and trauma depicted in the movie *Dead
Man Walking* shares her story of recovery and
forgiveness)

Stoop, David, PH.D., *Forgiving the Unforgivable*
(concise teaching and insights on forgiveness from
the Christian perspective)

Movies that Inform, Inspire, and Convey the Life Message

20th Century Fox. 2007. *Amazing Grace* (inspirational story of William Wilberforce and the abolition of the slave trade in Great Britain)

Lionsgate. 2006. *Bella* (adoption and caring for a neighbor in distress)

TAH.LLC film. 2010. *Blood Money* (abortion documentary from the pro-life perspective; www.bloodmoneyfilm.com)

Halmark Hall of Fame. 2009. *The Courageous Heart of Irena Sendler* (Warsaw ghetto rescuer of children during the Holocaust)

20th Century Fox. World Wide Pictures, Inc. 1975. *The Hiding Place* (story of the ten Boom family and their rescue efforts during the Holocaust)

20th Century Fox. 2008. *Horton Hears a Who!* (great pro-life allegory for the whole family)

Provident Films. 2011. *October Baby* (powerful pro-life film)

Websites

www.hdrc.org (Human Development Resource Council, Inc.)

www.unborn.com (human ultrasound images)

www.40daysforlife.com (prayer)

www.ramahinternational.org (abortion recovery)

www.menandabortion.info (abortion's impact on men)

www.abortionchangesyou.com (abortion healing)

www.standupgirl.com (pregnancy and abortion help)

www.hopeafterabortion.com (recovery/Project Rachel)

www.heartbeatinternational.org (pregnancy centers, maternity homes, and adoption services)

www.abort73.com (informative)

www.pregnantpause.org (informative)

www.issues4life.org (African Americans speak out on abortion/informative)

www.rainn.org (Rape, Abuse, and Incest National Network)

www.attwn.org (*and then there were none*: help and encouragement offered to employees working in the abortion industry)

www.saa-recovery.org (help for sexual addiction)

www.faithfulandtrue.com (Christian counselors provide help for men and women struggling with purity and sexual addictions)

www.pfi.org (Prison Fellowship International)

www.speakupforhope.org (help for families dealing with incarceration)

www.bethany.org (adoption services)

www.annaschoice.org (lead the *Who Am I* Bible study in your church)

Music

Chapman, Steven Curtis. *Speechless* (hear the song "Fingerprints of God")

James, Eddie. *Life* (hear the song "I Am" as quoted in chapter 40—lyrics used with permission; www.ejworship.org)

hushed

Women and Men Conceived after Rape: Living Lives and Making a Difference

Bomberger, Ryan. The Radiance Foundation
www.theradiancefoundation.org

Kiessling, Rebecca. Attorney and pro-life speaker
www.rebeccakiessling.com
www.hopeafterrapeconception.org

Martinez, Ray. Speaker, author, and former mayor
www.raymartinez.com

Stenzel, Pam. Author, speaker, and abstinence advocate
www.pamstenzel.com

Joel Patchen is the founder of Anna's Choice, LLC, a ministry that seeks to restore the dignity of life to the church and our culture. He is the author of four books, including *Love is for Eternity*, a daily devotional examining the biblical view of the sanctity of human life, and *Who Am I?*, a group Bible study designed to engage and equip the body of Christ for action in the arena of life issues. A native of Colorado, Joel loves to fly fish and spend time in the mountains. He has been blessed with a great wife and five beautiful children. The arrival of his premature daughter, Brooke, nearly three months before her due date, radically changed his life. After witnessing her living window to the womb, Joel has become a voice for the voiceless and an advocate for the sacredness of every human life.

To obtain other books by the author or to find out more about Anna's Choice, go to www.annaschoice.org. Joel is available for speaking engagements, conferences, and sanctity of life events. To inquire about an appearance, please contact Anna's Choice at joel@annaschoice.org.

also by Joel Patchen

What is the impact of a single life?

Letters to My Dad
Diary of a Preborn Daughter

JOEL PATCHEN

What will the impact of your life be?

Journey with Brooke Anna as she discovers her calling and the purpose for her life. Discover with Brooke the plans God has for each and every life—*the value of every created being.* Share with her the wonders of the womb and the joys of living. Experience how God's place of beginning (the sanctuary of protection we call the womb) is the foundation for everything we are and all we might become. Come with Brooke and discover *life!*

CPSIA information can be obtained
at www.ICGtesting.com
Printed in the USA
FSOW02n0014061115
12986FS

9 780981 887067